P A M E

ICE RIFT

ISBN: 1463570198
ISBN-13: 9781463570194

For Mum

Foreword

Ice Rift is entirely a novel of fiction and imagination, and although some real place names have been used to give the reader a realistic sense of geography, some details have been changed to suit the needs of the story.

ACKNOWLEDGEMENTS

As a layman interested in the science related to climate, I am once more indebted to Mark Lynas and Fred Pearce. Their clear and information-packed writing helping to make the vastly complex subject of climate systems accessible to the non-scientist.

My thanks, too, to friends, family and work colleagues, for all their support, encouragement and information. Particularly my daughter Sarah, who has worked with me on the MSS, giving invaluable advice on character, and many useful suggestions on editing. She has also proof read my final draft for which I am very grateful. And to my son-in-law who helped to organise my files ready for publication; his help is very much appreciated.

CHAPTER ONE

Humboldt Research Station
Greenland

"Sounds like they've arrived!"

Startled, Zoe Carter looked up from the deep frozen cylinder of ice on the bench in front of her. She had been working all morning carefully cutting the core into measured sections for later analysis. Fascinated already by what she could see with the naked eye, Zoe was eager to get these latest samples to the lab and co-ordinate the results with her previous research. She was particularly excited by one section which was thinly peppered with dust and debris, and where the ice was slightly more opaque than in the rest of the sample. Jolted out of her thoughts, she pulled her eyes away from where the hacksaw blade was chewing through the core, switched off the motor and spun round to see her colleague Amy James, framed in the doorway, whose smile was visible even from the depths of her parka hood.

They were early. Zoe hadn't expected her husband back until later that afternoon, but despite the interruption to her work, she felt relieved, as always, to know that he was back safe and sound. Two days ago he'd flown out to the drilling station to pick up their last consignment of ice core samples, taking advantage of a break in the weather. The forecast wasn't good for the next three or four days, so if he hadn't made it back by nightfall, the chances were that he could have been stuck there for the rest of the week. Zoe tried to flex her cold, stiff fingers, but the thick gloves restricted her movements, and she became aware that her legs and feet had become thick and clumsy with the cold while working in the ice store. She finished cutting through the last of the sample, laid it in its box and marked its code number on the end with a felt tip pen. She then keyed in some numbers into an electronic gun, fumbled to squeeze the trigger, whereupon it issued her a bright yellow ticket with a bar code on it, which she stuck across the cardboard flaps to seal it shut.

The noise of the plane was closer now, and Zoe, arriving where Amy was standing in the doorway, looked out just in time to see it land with a slight bounce on the nearby airstrip.

"Let's go get some coffee on," said Zoe, smelling it already, now that the thought had come into her head.

They walked over the packed snow path towards the living quarters, talking shop, but already feeling mentally distracted from their work. They'd been living at the Humboldt Research Station in Greenland for nearly three months now. Normally a brilliant place to work without all the distractions of modern life, Zoe had found that every deviation from the usual routine was now beginning to take on a huge significance. Like last week when she spotted a rare visiting sea bird. Having photographed it, she then spent the afternoon looking it up on the net, then detailing all this to everyone over dinner. After a ten minute monologue on the Arctic Skua, she pulled herself up, embarrassed that she'd bored everyone rigid, only to see that they were all rapt. No wonder small, isolated communities develop weird obsessions, she mused. After only three months they all needed some input.

When they approached the door to the living quarters, Amy said, a bit too casually, that she was going to wander over to the airstrip to check if any mail had arrived. Zoe smiled and nodded, knowing as well as she did that it was totally unnecessary, but that it would give Amy the opportunity to chat to the pilot for a few minutes.

"I'll give them a hand unloading the boxes, too," said Amy.

"OK. I'll get the coffee on. Don't be long!" said Zoe.

She watched the figure of her friend hurry across the snowfield to the waiting plane about a hundred meters away from the tiny cluster of huts. Although never exactly overweight, her round shape now looked about a stone lighter than when she first arrived at the base, despite all the extra rations they were consuming. Amy was delighted, and said she was going to ditch serious research on Arctic wildlife and make her fortune writing the Arctic Diet instead. Zoe wasn't so happy; slim to start with, she now felt too thin, and never had any energy, which made her feel the cold even more than usual. She wrapped up well all the time, and constantly monitored the state of her hands and feet, afraid of getting frostbitten. She'd seen how easy it could be to ignore the numbness of creeping cold, and to get caught out. The thought terrified her.

Against the intense blue of the polar sky, Zoe could just make out the familiar form of her husband climbing out of the plane, then straightening up as he stood on the runway. Oliver Carter, like Zoe, was a Geologist at the Isaac Newton College, London, where they were both specialists in the field of Paleo-ecology. They had been sponsored to research a project on the theory of Abrupt Climate Change, and so were in Greenland to collect ice core data and rock samples. Tall and broad-shouldered he was easily distinguished from the pilot, who had also jumped out of the aircraft and had gone round to the hold to help unload the cargo. Puzzled, she also thought that she had spotted a third figure, besides Amy, but from this distance, she couldn't be sure if it really was the case.

Pushing the door shut behind her, she felt the cheery warmth of the inside of the hut wrap around her as she peeled off her outdoor clothes and hung them over the back of a chair. She knew that Amy would put them away later when she did her own, and it had made her lazy. Anyway, she always made the hot drinks for her friend. Worked both ways, she reasoned.

While the coffee was brewing, Zoe reached everyone's mugs down from the cupboard and placed them onto the tray, then she cut some thick slices of chocolate fudge cake, making sure they were all the same size, and stacked those onto the tray too.

The door burst open.

"Hi Darling!" his presence filled the room at once. Still wearing his padded outdoor clothes he hugged her and gave her a kiss.

"Oliver!" she smiled. A bit shy herself, she loved his enthusiasm and uncomplicated warmth. "I'm so pleased you made it back before the weather closed in. Did you get the cores sorted out OK?"

"Yes, everything's fine. That's the last section – it's as deep as we can go. They've hit bedrock now."

"Fantastic. That's nearly two miles of ice sheet, all with its story to tell, just waiting for us to come along. Amy in yet?"

Just as she asked the question, she heard the outer door creak open, then Amy's voice, clearly chatting to someone. She looked towards her husband for an explanation.

"Hope you don't mind, Zo, but we've got a visitor. He's a photographer, compiling a book on Arctic Landscapes, I think he said. He'd been at the drilling station for a couple of days – asked if he could stay with us for a few days before heading back to the coast."

"Has he got the necessary permission?" said Zoe.

"Said that was all sorted. Don't suppose that would have been a problem, being a photographer – he won't be impinging on our remit, after all. Seems a nice guy, too. I think you'll like him."

Zoe didn't have time to reply before their visitor appeared at the door. He had a thin, quite drawn face which made it quite difficult to estimate his age. But that could have been the result of the harsh weather, and poor diet that beset all cold weather travellers. He had a straggly goatee-type beard which still had a few specks of frost clinging to it, now melting rapidly in the warm room.

"Lawrence Hewitt." He introduced himself flatly, holding out his hand to Zoe, not nervously, but without any warmth.

"Zoe Carter," she said in reply. "Pleased to meet you."

"Just been talking to Phil," Amy butted in, "and he said he was expecting the weather to close in by to-night. We're in for a rough couple of days apparently – gales, blizzards, the lot. Not very good for your pictures, Lawrence, I'm afraid," said Amy.

"Er no, I suppose not."

He seemed a bit uncomfortable with her breezy, un-reserved manner, which made him feel defensive, and, irrationally, that he was going to get their disapproval for not joining in.

"I'll try to get some atmospheric shots of the twilight – horizons – long shadows – and the buildings here," said Hewitt "if I get time. I guess the sun goes down pretty late here now. And maybe some shots of you guys at work – if that's OK....." he tailed off, hating the false heartiness that he had unwittingly put into his voice. He needn't have worried; no-one else was taking much notice. Zoe handed round the steaming mugs of coffee and the wedges of cake.

"Phil said we could expect some really heavy snow-fall," said Amy.

"Well we often do in spring," said Oliver. "These half-hearted winters usually have a sting in the tail."

"Said he was going to try to get back to Angmagssa-lik tonight." Amy attempted to look casual.

"Oh really," said Zoe. "How long for this time?"

"Not long. Just until the weather clears, then he's coming back this way to help Lawrence here get some aerial shots. Phil said we should all come too – the views will be amazing – he'll be flying right out over the sea ice." It was clear Amy wanted to go.

"Sounds like too good an opportunity to miss – what do you think Oliver?" said his wife.

"Yes, I agree, I'd love to go. After all, we won't be here for much longer."

"Neither will the sea-ice," said Hewitt.

For a while, no-one spoke. There was nothing to say, really. Everyone knew that the ice cap was melting at an ever-increasing rate, breaking apart at the edges; the smaller pieces melting more rapidly in the warm springs than ever a large ice sheet could do. And now what was left was so thin, the predictions were saying that once a certain tipping point was reached then the whole lot could be gone within a couple of seasons. Knowing it was one thing, but getting your head round it was another.

"Is that why you're photographing it?" Amy said, feeling that what she had just asked was a bit obvious. "Phil said you must be recording this landscape for posterity."

"Is there anything that bloody French-Canadian pilot doesn't have an opinion on at the moment?" said Oliver.

He'd intended only to tease her good naturedly, but suddenly aware that they were laughing at her, Amy flushed, then fell silent. Oliver, sorry that he'd embarrassed her, but now feeling awkward himself, flailed round for something to say. Hewitt looked uncomfortable, but said, matter-of-factly, and in answer to her original question,

"No, not really. I think the film-makers would make a better job of that than I ever could. I just love good photographs, and this landscape is visually stunning."

"All the more so for its transience perhaps," said Zoe.

"I think it's our own transience that we have difficulty in accepting," said Hewitt.

The others cast subtle glances at each other, startled by his reply. He'd cast a sombre mood into the room, but seemed unaware that what he had said was a tad deep for a first meeting. Never one for small talk as it made him feel self-conscious, he stuck to the subjects which genuinely interested him. He went on, "When we make our mark by building something, depicting something, or making something, we are not thinking only of the object, but of us in relation to it, or to a certain point in time."

"How do you mean?" said Zoe, intrigued. "I don't see how that relates to our transient stay on this planet."

"Well, in the sense that when we see something disappear from our surroundings, it makes us think of our own vulnerability, both as individuals, and as a species. When I take my pictures, I'm not only recording what's there, but my view of what's there – if you see what I mean. So at least I won't disappear without a trace."

"Wouldn't bank on it," Amy said under her breath, irritated. She thought of Phil with his breezy smile, regretting that he'd not been able to stay longer.

Zoe still looked puzzled, so Hewitt tried again to get his point across.

"Well, imagine a cave painting – like the Neolithic ones discovered in France – what do you think of when you see those images? It's not really the bison is it? You think of the man who painted it, and wonder what he was like."

"Or woman," said Amy.

"Interesting point," Hewitt said. "You see him, or her, as a cultural, social person. Perhaps he had a name, and a language, of sorts."

"I do that when I see an event recorded in the cores – to me it's not just a thin layer of frozen dust, but encoded information; and for anyone alive at the time, it would have been a cataclysmic volcanic eruption, which affected everything – their entire world," said Zoe, who then added "so, sometime in the future someone is going to look at your pictures, and imagine what you, and all the rest of us, were like."

"And they'll think how clever we all were for inventing digital photography," said Amy.

"More like, what the hell are those white lumps doing in the sea!" said Oliver.

Hewitt smiled thinly as he finished up his last piece of chocolate cake. Then the roar of the aeroplane engines in the distance, as the plane took off, brought everyone's thoughts back to Amy once more.

"Good of Phil to offer to take us out with you," Oliver said to Hewitt.

"He said we'd see some changes," said Hewitt.

"Really? That bad, eh?" said Zoe.

"Well, he'll know if anyone does, what's going on out there," said Amy staunchly.

"He sees the bigger picture, flying all over the area, whereas we only see our own patch.

"Should be interesting," said Oliver.

Hewitt took his luggage through to the room where he was to stay, and lifted the bulky holdall onto the utilitarian looking single bed. At least the mattress sagged a little under the weight, indicating that it might not be as uncomfortable as it had first looked. There was a thick quilt in a big roll at the foot of the bed and one pillow in its place at the head. He didn't know how he knew that it was Amy who had made the room ready, but he felt grateful that someone had. He felt dog tired. Despite weeks of travelling he hadn't got enough pictures that he was really happy with. He had to get some good material from this stay at the research station or he would be out of time, and back in London making excuses to his publisher. He unzipped the shoulder bag, still on the floor and took out his camera, a Lica with a Zeiss lens. He removed it from its case, its familiar shape cold in his hands. Sighing, and his head tight with fatigue, he forced himself to get to his feet, and to do some work before the weather closed them all down. He put on his bulky outdoor coat once more and pulled on his hat until he could feel it touch his eyebrows. He slung the camera over his shoulder and wandered outside the hut and over to the work areas. Pushing a door open tentatively, he peeped inside, hoping that he'd found the right place.

"Mind if I take some while you work?" said Hewitt.

Zoe looked up from her bench in the ice store, where she had resumed her work.

"No, of course not, Lawrence," she replied. The use of his name jolted him. He didn't feel ready to call her by her first name just yet. In fact he hardly ever used anyone's name in direct conversation, for some reason it always sounded forced when he did so. He walked around the room looking for a good angle to shoot from, but nothing seemed right. Zoe, a bit vain when it came to photographs, had become tense and self-conscious, and couldn't concentrate on her work anymore. Frustrated, Hewitt left her alone and went outside to capture the slanting light of the evening sun.

* * *

They were all eating together for once as they had a guest staying with them. Normally they would just get a ready meal out of the freezer and eat whenever it fitted in with their work, but tonight they thought it was worth making a special effort. Oliver had felt triumphant when he discovered four packs of the same meal whilst rummaging through the store. By now they were getting down to the stuff no-one had really wanted before, and it was mostly odds and ends that didn't go together. He could see that the pouches were all the same, but the writing was too small and frosted over for him to be able to read what they were, so he reached into his pocket for his glasses and rubbed off the frost from the packaging. Beef Madras. He could have punched the air – he thought they'd long gone. But then a moment of doubt clouded over his elation. He thought of putting them back, feeding their visitor on the disgusting fishcakes that were all crumbs, and having beef curry for himself four nights next week. No, Zoe would kill him. He found a large bag of rice that should do for four people and took it through to the kitchen where Zoe was waiting for him.

"You found the curries, then?" she said.

"You've been hiding them," he accused her. "You knew all along."

"I was saving them for a rainy day, or a snowy one in our case. Thought they might be a good morale booster, if we got closed down and all got cabin fever."

"You're a hard woman," he said. She grinned, pushing back her fair, shoulder-length hair.

"It was for your own good," she said.

Half an hour later they sat down at the specially scrubbed table, their plates of fragrant food steaming in front of them. They each had a piece of kitchen roll for a napkin, and an insulated metal mug in the wine glass place, now looking superfluous as they were all empty.

"I thought we'd asked your pilot friend to bring in another crate of beer," said Oliver.

"It wasn't his fault," said Amy glumly. "He had a lot of other things to remember. And you were there too."

Hewitt left the table without a word, and disappeared into his room. Zoe thought he'd sensed a row brewing and had taken flight, but a moment later he returned to the group carrying a large bottle of Scotch.

"This should do the trick," he said, working his way around the table and pouring a generous shot into everyone's waiting mug.

"Good man!" said Oliver, beaming and raising his mug towards Hewitt in tribute.

"Well done, Lawrence. You're a star," said Amy. Hewitt looked slightly flushed with his sudden popularity, so took a sip of his whisky to give himself something to focus on.

"Did you get any good shots?" said Oliver, starting in on the curry.

"No...don't know. Can't be sure till I get them up on my computer, and I can't be bothered with all that tonight. Funny thing though – I kept noticing this weird sort of smell while I was out there – I thought the air would be pristine up here."

"Maybe it was our waste tanks," said Zoe. "They must be getting pretty full by now."

"I wondered that," said Hewitt. "But I could still notice it even when I walked quite a way away. In fact, even at the drilling station we noticed it – some of the men were joking about it. They didn't seem to know what had caused it either."

"You know, I thought that the other day," said Amy suddenly remembering.

"I wondered if something had died, but then again, it's too cold for things to rot here, so it couldn't have been that either. I didn't notice it again so I just forgot about it till now."

"How odd!" said Zoe.

Hewitt looked at her and waited for her to say something else. The moment passed, so he pressed on with the conversation from another angle.

"So, your work here is studying the effects of climate change," he said.

"Actually, what we study is more the causes of climate change rather than the effects. We are paleo-ecologists..."

"Which means, exactly?" said Hewitt.

"Paleo is the Greek word for old," said Amy. "So they're really just a couple of old ecologists."

"Thanks Ames," said Zoe. "We're specialists in the field of abrupt climate change, and there's nowhere better to study the Earth's weather record than here in Greenland."

"Abrupt climate change. Is that a specialism or a theory?" said Hewitt.

"Oh, it's not just a theory," said Zoe, robustly. "We know from the ice records that changes to the climate when they did occur, were often very rapid. What we don't understand, is what made something happen, *when* it did."

"When you say rapid, do you mean relatively speaking, like thousands of years?"

"Oh, no. There is evidence of rapid coolings and warmings of eight degrees in a single decade. A warming could lead to a doubling of snow accumulation in three years, like at the end of the last Ice Age. And most of that doubling occurred in a single year."

"Our climate has been relatively stable over the last 11,000 years, in fact it is the only stable period in the last 110,000 years, enabling us to develop a civilisation," said Oliver.

"So you're saying that by understanding how these changes have happened, you hope to protect this brief warm interlude that suits us so well," said Hewitt.

"Exactly," said Zoe, through her last forkful of beef curry. "It seems that the norm, over the ages is rapid and quite dramatic change, with the cold times being more usual than the inter-glacials, or warm interludes. But weather systems are incredibly complex, and we don't fully understand what can drive the climate into such dramatic pulses of change. There have been about twenty abrupt alterations of climate in the last 110,000 years."

"And you've no idea why?" said Hewitt.

"It's got quite a lot to do with the ocean currents, but even with the huge amount of data that we now have, current computer models can't reproduce the effects of the sudden switches that occur – that's Amy's forte, she's working on a new climate model now," said Zoe. "We're trying to understand the process which drives these changes – if we knew that we could begin to estimate when they might occur. Pretty useful stuff when you consider how narrow our human comfort zone is."

"Yes," said Hewitt. "I suppose we're rather picky as a species when you come to think of it. I know I am anyway. I'm always complaining that I'm too hot or too cold."

"Well if we see another Ice Age coming, we'll let you know, so that you can up sticks and head for southern California," said Oliver.

"Sounds like a good excuse," said Hewitt. "Been there a couple of times. It's a fantastic climate."

They had started to settle into their own comfort zones brought about by the effects of a good meal and a shot or two of Hewitt's Scotch, and the talk ground to a halt. They left the table when the meal was finished, abandoning the empty plates where they were, but taking what remained of their drinks with them over to the easy chairs and sofa in the seating area. The conversation ebbed and flowed as the evening wore on.

"So apart from the fluctuations in the oceans' currents, what are the other culprits involved in this abrupt climate change scenario that you're working on?" said Hewitt, going over in his mind the conversation that they had had during dinner.

Zoe replied, "Well, the astronomical factors are extremely important, too, and might even be the ultimate cause of a climate flip. The Earth's orbit is elliptical, not round, as you probably know…" Hewitt nodded, so she continued, "Which means that sometimes the northern hemisphere is tilted towards the Sun in the summer months, when the Earth is at its closest point to the Sun, and sometimes when it's at its furthest away. Add to that the slight wobble in the Earth's rotation, which affects the degree of tilt in the Earth's axis, and you might just tip the delicate climatic balance and trigger an Ice Age."

"But surely that would be easy enough to verify," said Hewitt. "If you track back astronomical records and tie them in with the periods of glaciation."

Zoe was very patient.

"Of course. That's been done, and the figures do tie in – but that doesn't prove a cause and effect – and it's clearly not the whole story. We've a way to go yet."

Hewitt demurred to her answer, and, distracted, he became aware that between the talk in the rest of the room, every now and then there was a pause, as one or the other of them stopped to listen, and then glanced at the others to see if anyone else had noticed anything. Hewitt, now alert, had become aware of something too. It was like a deep vibration, more than an actual sound that seemed to disappear off the scale as soon as one strained to make it out. But as the sound of the wind began to build, gradually but persistently, it cancelled out anything that they might have thought they heard before.

"It was probably a bit of very distant thunder," said Oliver, astutely, speaking on behalf of all their speculation, "carried here by the storm winds we've been promised."

Nobody answered.

Then right on cue, they could hear the weather begin to close in as predicted. It started all at once with one big gust seeming to come out of nowhere and wrap itself around them. Any distant rumblings were now drowned out by the sound of the wind rushing past the corners of the hut they were in. At first a few sparse flakes of snow were tossed around in the turbulent air, gradually getting thicker as the gale gathered pace. The evening wore on and the rising wind groaned above the now rounded shapes of the nestling huts, piling up the snow against the exposed sides, till they, too, looked like soft drifts on the flat landscape.

For two days and nights, the blizzard was totally encasing. Only the dizzying diagonal lines of driving snow could be seen from the window, and to do any work, meant feeling one's way to the hut by hanging on to the ropes slung between the buildings. When they went out, they went together, the girls hardly able to stand alone against the wind, the snow on their goggles obscuring what little view they had. On the second night Zoe, restless, as though drained of energy by the constant whine of the gale, awoke with a start.

"It was the ice," she said out loud. Oliver woke.

"What?" he said thinly, his voice still full of sleep.

"It was the ice moving – that noise. We all heard it. It was never thunder. I've heard it when I've been on sea ice before, but never on land ice. You keep thinking that you hear something, but it's so tenuous that you convince yourself it's in your own head."

Oliver didn't answer. He didn't have to. He sat up, then turned and looked at her. He knew that she was right, as soon as she said it. Knowing what it meant, though, would have to wait until morning. It didn't sound like good news, that was for sure, but he was too tired to work on it now.

They both sank back into a deep slumber, the howl of the wind now no longer bothering them; instead it seemed to lull them dreamlessly to sleep, reaching its peak of intensity late in the grey night-time. By next morning it had stopped; blue sky breaking through the dense white layers of cloud, exposing the totally quiet, new landscape all around them.

Zoe opened her eyes, and it seemed that the strange half-recalled sound of the creaking land ice, was there in her thoughts already, waiting for her to wake up and to start thinking about it some more. She knew that something odd was happening out here, something that didn't quite fit the picture, and she was determined to find out what it was.

She heard the others stirring. Leaving Oliver to sleep a few minutes more, she fished around for her slippers and made her way to the kitchen.

CHAPTER TWO

Zoe, first up, shuffled into the kitchen and stared aimlessly at the snow covered window. She had eaten only a slice of toast for breakfast, and that was without any enthusiasm. She found it hard to say how she felt; listless and fidgety at the same time, and a longing for some fresh air. In her mind she couldn't get rid of the image of herself standing in an open field, the fresh, grassy air blowing energy into her lungs. And it wasn't even particularly warm in the huts. She drank her tea, and decided to take a couple of aspirins, in case she was going down with a cold. She really hoped not, or she might miss their trip over the ice fields tomorrow. Zoe had especially been looking forward to seeing the region from the air as on every other occasion that they'd flown with Becaud, the conditions had been cloudy. This was also an opportunity to see more remote areas, where commercial flights wouldn't normally go.

She heard someone else moving around. She hoped it was Oliver as she really couldn't be bothered with anyone else.

"God, I feel rough!" said Oliver, coming into the room with a glass of water, then sinking down beside her. He didn't look great. "Think we overdid Lawrence's Scotch last night. Feel a bit fragile, I have to say. You look bloody awful, too." He could say the sweetest things.

"Tea?"

"Yeah, please."

Zoe got up to make him some, which he drank in silence, closing his eyes between drinks, as though hoping to get a bit more sleep. There was no more sound from the other rooms. Maybe they'd gone back to bed.

Forcing herself to get showered and dressed, Zoe decided to make a start on the day. She got into her outdoor clothes, left the living quarters and walked over to the ice store to begin work on taking some more samples from the latest cores. This at least would give her something to do. And if it was only a hangover, then hopefully she would start to feel better soon. It was the obvious explanation – Oliver was probably right – but it wasn't as though she'd had that much to drink. The others had been a bit indulgent, having a few too many shots as the night grew late, but, not liking whisky that much, she hadn't kept up with them. Now, had it been red wine – well that would have been different.

Zoe had been absorbed in her work for an hour or so, when she realised all at once that she felt fine. Hungry, and her head feeling clear, she walked over to the corner where she kept the kettle and flicked the switch on. In the tin was a chocolate bar, a large slab of Dairy Milk. A few squares of that would go perfectly with the coffee. She sat down on the stool and leaned on the bench with her elbows, holding the hot mug in her cool hands, one by one breaking off the cold chunks, then clasping the mug again for warmth. She could hear the wind outside, which had steadily picked up since the still dawn. It had changed direction since the blizzard, and though not strong, it had seemed to freshen everywhere.

She had company. The door swung open and in walked Oliver, accompanied by Lawrence Hewitt.

"If it's any compensation, darling, Lawrence here felt as shit as the rest of us did – which I think is only fair, as it was all his fault." Hewitt seemed to be taking it in good part. He must be getting used to us, thought Zoe.

"I felt grim in the night," said Hewitt. "I got up to go to the bathroom, and I felt quite light-headed for a moment, it was very unpleasant, I can tell you."

The door creaked open again, admitting a third person to the room.

"Oh, so did I!" said Amy, who had joined the group and had begun to help herself to the chocolate. "I was lying in bed and suddenly I went all woozy. Must have been export strength or something, I don't normally react so badly."

Zoe sat, for a few moments lost in her thoughts, unaware that she was staring at her mug, till the ripples on the surface caught her attention. She started, then Amy said,

"Oh no, I feel dizzy again. Oh let me sit down, Zo! I think I'm feeling faint." The two men looked at one another, noticing something themselves.

"Look .Look at the ripples on my coffee," said Zoe urgently. "It's a tremor! This is what you must have felt last night – a slight quake – did you both notice it at the same time?"

"Well, I got up at about three-thirty, I think," said Hewitt.

"It was three-twenty-five – I remember looking at my alarm clock," said Amy.

This confirmed it in Zoe's mind as a seismic event; it would have stretched coincidence too far for them both to have had the same symptoms at the same time.

"I must get an email off to the guys back in London," said Oliver. "and see what the strength was."

"And where the epicentre was," Zoe said.

"Has this happened before?" Hewitt looked concerned.

"We've never experienced tremors before," said Oliver. "It's a first for me."

"Not the first hangover, though," said Amy.

The email came through from Isaac Newton College promptly, confirming that there had been a couple of minor tremors in their area, registering two-point-eight and three-point-one on the Richter Scale. The epicentre was, not surprisingly, on the south-eastern tip of Iceland, more noted for its instability and volcanic activity. Zoe was looking at the computer screen over her husband's shoulder, as he went back to the home page, when a news item caught her eye.

"This looks interesting," said Zoe to Oliver. "Solar storm about to hit Earth"

"Yeah, there was an item about it yesterday. Saw it when I was browsing during the blizzard. There's been a lot of sunspot activity lately. It seems that this flared up during the night, and it could be quite a severe one, so everyone's taking the usual precautions with their sensitive electrical equipment."

"What time is it due to hit?" said Zoe.

"In the early hours of tomorrow morning, by the look of it. We must remember to turn everything off – just in case."

"What's all this?" said Hewitt. He'd heard them talking about something hitting the Earth in the early hours, and had become alarmed. Oliver explained that a solar storm was heading their way, but the implications of this were more about any possible damage to computers or power supplies. All the major electricity producers would now be debating whether or not to shut down their transformers, or risk them overloading if the magnetic storm turned out to be particularly bad. Damage to systems on this scale would take months to repair, and the effects of being without power for long on a modern industrial economy would be catastrophic. No-one had worried about solar storms before the age of hi-tech equipment, although they were known about from as far back as the Victorian Age, but now they were something that no-one could afford to ignore.

"I can't say that I'd ever heard of them before," said Hewitt. Zoe decided to fill him in.

"We call them CME's or coronal mass ejections. They are solar flares which head our way. In the 1850's…"

"1859." Oliver had an impressive memory for facts. "September the first and second to be precise." Zoe carried on unfazed,

"A massive flare hit the Earth in record time, taking only a few hours to get here. It disrupted the telegraph system which is why we knew of its occurrence, giving the operators electric shocks and causing fires. Auroras were seen as far south as Mexico. It might be an idea to download any valuable pictures, and get some hard copies – just in case," said Zoe.

"Really? You think so? I'd never have thought of that. Glad you told me," he said, going back to his room to begin work on that straightaway.

The evening was ticking away comfortably, for the four now sitting in the living area of the hut. The curtainless square windows had gone from white to grey to charcoal, where they would stay for most of the night, now that spring was advancing, only dipping into blackness for an hour or two at most once they'd passed midnight. The cluttered walls were pannelled with tongue and groove unvarnished wood, which were lined with slatted shelves overflowing with books, papers and periodicals.

Zoe and Oliver's three children were smiling out from a photograph taken in their garden back home. Aged twelve, fourteen and seventeen, they were now staying with a best friend's parents, so that they could continue at their normal school without any interruptions. That was the only down side of travelling away so much. The children had coped really well – they were always round at their friend's house anyway – but Zoe found it hard not to be the one who heard the latest chatter, the funny remark in class which had had them all in hysterics, or who the latest hip band was.

She didn't even know if it was hip to say hip anymore. These things seemed to change hourly. Oliver, who'd been to boarding school, couldn't see the problem. Said it would make them independent. He was right, of course, it would. But she didn't want that at the expense of closeness.

The cast iron stove crackled and spat in the corner, its red glow, still showing through the smoky glass door. There was a threadbare, faded rug on the floor in front of the stove; a previous occupant's attempt at homeliness – a warm, dry oasis, in the middle of the glaring white coldness. No-one knew how the huge cascading spider plant had got there, the only bit of green for miles around on this deceptively named land. Spilling over the shelf, it was clearly thriving on its glut of Arctic daylight.

Amy put down the book that she had been reading, and got up stiffly out of her armchair, walking the few steps over to the stove where a pot of coffee was keeping hot on top of it. She poured herself a cup, then took a sip, pulling a face as she did so.

"Oh, I don't know about you guys, but I don't feel so good again."

"Come to think of it," said Zoe, "neither do I. How about you, Oliver – are you OK? We could all be going down with something."

"Actually I don't feel that great, I have to say."

At that moment Hewitt looked up from studying his photographs and said, "This is odd. I don't know what's happened here, but these pictures all seem to have got this very faint yellowish haze – can't be the filter – could be a bit of flare, I suppose, but unless I can edit it out I don't know if I'll be able to use these. It completely detracts from the image of the blue/white pristine landscape I was aiming for."

Amy put down her mug of coffee, without drinking any more, then flopped back on the sofa, feeling out of sorts, and not listening to him. She said, "I think I'll turn in if you guys don't mind. Maybe I can sleep this thing off whatever it is."

Zoe nodded sympathetically, thinking that it was the best thing to do. It had been a strange day. Earth tremors – a solar storm – and now they all seemed to be sickening for something, just when they'd got the flight with Phil all planned for tomorrow as well. It must have been Lawrence who they caught it from. They'd had no other contacts after all, and unlike popular mythology you don't get viruses from being cold; you catch them from other people. Zoe sighed. She was determined to go on the trip tomorrow, however bad she felt. Quite suddenly the isolation was getting too much. Thank goodness the work was nearly done. She needed to get home.

"Can I take a look at your pictures?" said Zoe, sud-denly, trying to be friendly in an attempt to banish the resentful thoughts which had welled up against Hewitt just now.

"Yes," he said, not looking particularly grateful for her interest. His off-hand manner could be very irritating at times. Trouble was, to him it wasn't off-hand. He'd just thought he'd answered the question. He handed them to her. Now she would have to look interested, she thought, wishing that she'd never bothered to ask to see them.

But when she did she was taken aback by the quality of his work. He'd shot Oliver looking as though he'd just been asked a question, which seemed to capture his whole personality in his reaction. She looked at that one a long time, wondering if she could ask him for a copy. His outside pictures were well composed and moody. The shot of their research station being taken from a considerable distance, the grey light from the approaching weather front, which brought their blizzard, forming a backdrop to the huddled huts. There was one tiny pinpoint of light coming from a window in their living quarters, emphasising the feeling of isolation, but suggesting a sense of purpose. She took in the effects for several long seconds before shuffling on to the next one. She opened her mouth to speak, but didn't know quite what to say. It was a picture of herself, sitting at the bench in the ice store, looking up at the stacks of catalogued tubes on the shelf just in front of her. She was back lit by the desk lamp and her breath hung in a motionless cloud in front of her. She had had no idea that he'd taken it. Normally she hated herself in photographs as she always looked awkward and self-conscious, but not in this one. Actually it doesn't seem like me, she thought. It's like looking at a stranger. The next four shots were landscapes, and sure enough there seemed to be a slight, faintly yellowish haze hovering just above ground level.

Oliver was unconcerned. "I'm sure that can be edited out – do some colour adjustments on the computer – they'll be fine. It's probably a cloud of Siberian pollution, from the chemical factories there – it wafts over here sometimes."

Hewitt looked tempted to say something, but bit his lip. These were meant to be professional quality pictures, not holiday snaps. But he decided not to make anything of it, as least this time.

The room settled again once more into its background quietness punctuated every now and then by the sound of a carefully turned page, the tap of a cup put back down on a table; a shuffle as someone moved position and tried to get comfortable on the utilitarian sofas. The stove continued its soft roar, the occasional snap of burning fuel pellets, not consciously heard, but soporific in effect, its living presence deeply comforting, and quite unlike the dead noise of an electronic hum. Zoe put down her book, and looked over towards her husband, still absorbed in a magazine.

"I think I might go outside for some air," she said.

"What?" said Oliver. "At this time?"

"I might feel better if I do. I'm a bit headachy."

"Well why don't you just turn in like Amy has done, it will take you forever to get kitted up to go out." Zoe felt discouraged by Oliver's attitude but decided to persevere anyway.

"Will you come with me?"

"No I bloody well won't!" Oliver said, still looking at his magazine.

Hewitt shifted a little in his seat, but didn't look up from his book.

"Oh, go on, I don't want to go out on my own."

"I don't want to go out at all – can't you just take aspirin, like a normal woman?"

"I already did. They didn't work. It's OK, you don't have to come. I just need some fresh air. I'll be getting ready." Zoe left the room. The exchange with her husband was without any ill-feeling on either side. Both even-tempered, and slow to take offence, they rarely argued, which was just as well as they had had to spend so much time together.

Zoe put on her outdoor clothes. Even for such a short time outside she had to put on the full kit, padded trousers, boots, fleece hat, gloves. Anorak. It was tempting to manage without the trousers and just put the coat on. But it was not worth the risk. Once outdoors, it was all too easy to get caught out in weather that could change extremely rapidly, and the more you got used to it the more you had to guard against overconfidence and complacency; you could be enveloped in a whiteout in minutes, totally unable to get any sense of perspective. What might seem like a distant bank of cloud could be only a couple of hundred metres away, turn your back, and the next moment, you can't see the person standing next to you. Buildings which were only a minute's stroll away, suddenly become unreachable, as your sense of direction goes, and to miss them could mean that you walk for miles, and never find them. Caught unawares in such a blizzard, without proper clothing, hypothermia will set in in about six or seven minutes.

Zoe stepped outside, slamming the hut's outer door behind her. The cold night air settled on her face immediately, stinging her eyes and nose. She breathed deeply, now wondering if it was such a great idea to be out in the cold, if she was in fact sickening for something. Anyway it would stupid to go straight back inside after spending so much time getting ready to go out. Oliver would never let her live it down, so she crumped along the snow path, past the ice store, and decided to do a circuit of the complex, before she went back inside. That strange smell that Amy and Hewitt had noticed earlier was again present in the still air, this time Zoe being aware of it too. Sulphurous and slightly sharp, it reminded her of something, but what, she couldn't quite say. She walked with quite a determined step, head bowed against the cold, until she was out past the work station, and at the furthest point past the complex that she could safely go alone. She paused and pushed her parka hood back a little so that she could see around her, banging her hands together and stamping her feet as she did so.

It was then that she saw the lights dance across the sky; a waving chiffon veil of colour and movement high above her, filling the sky with light and energy. She knew at once what it was; the Aurora Borealis, brought on by the arrival of the solar storm. A well-known but elusive phenomenon, this was the first time that she'd actually seen it in real life. It was breathtaking. The greens and blues streaked around the sky, the vertical folds then changing to red, purple and back to green again. Hanging like uplit cinema curtains the colours seemed to stretch into the infinity of space, playful but just a little threatening. Zoe stood there, lost in the moment, when she felt the familiar weight of Oliver's hand on her left shoulder. She didn't start; months of isolation having nullified her natural wariness of strangers.

"Thought you didn't want to come out here."

"Glad I made the effort now, though. This is fantastic!" He watched the prism-like colours ripple across the night sky, pausing then billowing in the solar wind. "I've never seen such a good show before – it's amazing."

"We must go and get Amy and Lawrence – we can't let them miss this."

"But Amy's in bed."

"She always wanted to see the Northern Lights – you know that. We can't tell her over breakfast what a fantastic show she just missed – she'd kill us. And as for Lawrence – well this is a brilliant photo opportunity for him. This could make up for all his blotchy pictures that he seems in such a strop about. Might cheer him up a bit."

"You haven't really taken to him have you, darling."

They trundled back to the living quarters, their heads all the time craning round to see the Aurora, bumping into one another as they didn't want to miss a minute of the show above them.

Amazingly Amy was out of the hut first, all traces of sleep banished in her excitement. It took Hewitt a bit longer as he had to sort out his camera equipment, and when he did appear he looked hassled and unusually clumsy. He was obviously afraid that by the time he got out there and ready to go, that it would all be over before he could get any good shots, but he needn't have worried. The show showed no sign of diminishing, even by the time they felt that they had all seen enough and were starting to get cold.

"Tell you what," said Zoe "I think that smell is stronger than ever. Surely it can't be the waste."

"You were saying that it reminded you of something," said Amy.

"The Underground," said Hewitt. "It reminds me of the Underground."

"You know you're right!" said Oliver. "Tottenham Court Road tube station. I'm right back there."

"Could it be anything to do with the solar storm?" said Hewitt. "All those excited ions." He'd been doing his research.

"Don't think so. Anyway we've smelling it for a few days, before the storm even left the surface of the Sun. I'm betting it's pollution," said Carter. "It's high time the Ruskies cleaned up their act."

The group fell quiet for a few minutes each lost in thought, and trying to come up with a plausible answer. Unless one has experienced it for oneself, it's difficult to imagine the quiet that falls around you when total silence fills your entire space, until you can only hear your own pulse ringing in your ears with white noise. Amy coughed, the sound jarring against the background of silence. Oliver suggested that they should be thinking of making their way back in, when they became aware, more or less at the same time of something; some noise that seemed to come from no particular direction. It was so low that it was practically off the scale, making them wonder if there actually was something to hear or was it just their imaginations filling in the void, caused by the lack of normal everyday sounds.

But there was definitely something, and it seemed to be getting closer, although the sound whatever it was still seemed to have no sense of place, and therefore seemed to be everywhere at once. Then a tight juddery vibration, like a train speeding past, went right through them, and disappeared into the distance, their respective gazes following it as though they had just seen something shoot by, right under their feet.

"Another bloody tremor!" said Oliver. "It's getting a bit lively out here tonight folks. I think we should go back inside."

Zoe put her arm around him, clearly not happy, as they trudged back towards the hut in silence. Once inside, Hewitt got Oliver on his own for a few seconds, and expressed his own concern. He was very agitated.

"What the fuck's going on, Oliver?"

"Nothing to get worked up about, Lawrence. Just been a bit of a crazy night that's all. Everything happening at once – but this Northern Light phenomenon is well known up here – nothing to worry about."

"Well OK, I accept that. But it's everything else. These tremors. That's not normal is it? You said so yourself. How do we know that they won't get any bigger?"

"To tell you the truth, we don't, but it's very unlikely. We're not in a place that normally gets much earthquake activity, but anywhere can get tremors. Remember we're not far from Iceland, which is very unstable geologically. What we're getting here are probably volcanic tremors caused by fissure eruptions in that area."

"And I'm supposed to be reassured by that am I? Now it's a volcano about to explode!"

"Poor Lawrence," said Zoe, hearing the last bit of the conversation. Feeling a little happier now that she was inside. He winced at her patronising tone, even though it was kindly meant. "Don't worry, a fissure eruption is not explosive – it's when large gashes or fissures open up allowing lava to flow out of them. It's happened before in Iceland many times. We're probably just feeling the ripples." She went on, "I did a paper on this years ago. There was a big eruption in the 1780's – I forget the exact year."

"1783," said Oliver, who, as usual had the facts to hand.

"Yes, thank you, darling. In that year massive fissures appeared, one twenty miles long, allowing huge tongues of lava to spread across the country, blocking valleys, filling up lakes, and causing flooding on a huge scale. Volcanic ash also covered vast areas of farmland. I believe it was by far the biggest lava flow ever recorded. About a fifth, or maybe as much as a third of the population died as a result, all in all – some of them from poisonous volcanic gasses which drifted over the land."

"And what was incredible," said Oliver catching Zoe's enthusiasm, and clearly enjoying having someone to talk to who hadn't heard all this before, "is that this toxic cloud actually came as far south as the UK killing many thousands of the unfortunate population there."

"Really," said Hewitt, clearly not as enthusiastic as he should have been.

"Somehow that doesn't make me feel a whole lot better." He paused for a moment, then added, "Anyway, how did they know, in those days, what it was?"

"Well, I don't suppose they did at the time," said Zoe, "but from the records of the day which reported a low lying, noxious smog hanging over the country, historians have been able to piece together what it must have been. Incredible, really."

"Sounds like what we've got, here. A low lying smelly cloud that's making everyone feel ill." Hewitt smiled, making an attempt at last to be sociable. But instead of smiling back Zoe and Oliver stared at him wordlessly.

"What? What have I said?" Hewitt looked from one to the other for an explanation.

"You know, I think he's right," said Zoe, staring at her husband. "Think about it! We all felt ill on and off for the last few days, but without any symptoms of infection. And whenever the breeze has picked up, we've all immediately felt a lot better...remember we all thought we'd got a hangover at one point, even though none of us had actually drunk that much. We've been casting around for explanations, but missing the obvious....."

"I wouldn't actually say a volcanic gas cloud was an obvious explanation," Oliver said. "There are simpler ones – after all, how many times have you woken up feeling ill and thought, 'Oh! It's that gas cloud again – there must be a volcano around here somewhere.'"

Zoe laughed, but persisted, "Well, OK....but as scientists, we shouldn't have settled for answers that didn't quite fit – we should have been a bit more thorough."

Hewitt suddenly realised that he'd been missing something, too.

"I've just thought of something else. It explains the yellow haze on my pictures. It really was out there – it's not my equipment or technique at all. I'm sure that we've found an explanation – but what does it mean? Could we all get gassed? After all, Zoe, you said there were many deaths when this has happened before."

"Well, yes. But it depends entirely on how dense the gas cloud is, and how toxic."

Oliver decided that he had better get on the internet and email the seismology centre in Reykjavik, both to tell them what they had experienced and to ask them for an advisory. He also got onto Isaac Newton College to keep them posted on the situation. Now the situation was beginning to sink in, Oliver was more worried about it than he liked to let on. If they were in fact in the midst of a cloud of toxic fumes it might not even be safe for them to spend the night here. Or they might have to re-think their plans for tomorrow, and leave Humboldt permanently when their plane arrived for them in the morning. That would be the worst – to have come so far and to be so near to finishing their project here – it would be a nightmare to have to leave now without all their research being quite in. Without all the data they might not be able to conclude their results and publish their paper. He knew also that Zoe would be thinking the exact same thing.

The advisory, when it did come back, was understandably vague and cautious. It confirmed that there had been a further tremor in their area, this time measuring three-point-four on the Richter Scale. There had also been some fissure eruptions in the area of Lakagigar, which had resulted in the release of a certain amount of poisonous fumes, two or three days previously, but these appeared to be dispersing rapidly. The advice was to stay indoors if there was evidence of gasses in their area, but that they shouldn't be strong enough to be a danger to health. If, however, they were still concerned, or the situation worsened they should make provisional plans to evacuate the station until the situation improved.

Oliver told the others what he had just found out, and they seemed reassured by the matter-of-fact tone of the reply and the information that there was no further gas on its way. They'd just have to be vigilant, in case it happened again. No-one wanted to leave in a panic, before the job was done. Even Hewitt, who could have left with the plane tomorrow, decided to stay until he had more work under his belt.

Feeling beyond sleep, but knowing that they had to get some rest before their busy day tomorrow, they each respectively slipped away to their rooms, and went back to their beds. But the dawn was already becoming well advanced, the pink early light beginning to give some perspective to the previously flat, two-dimensional landscape. Nevertheless they dipped into an unexpectedly deep sleep, until, way too soon, their alarms jangled them awake, and propelled them into the business of the new day.

CHAPTER THREE

Philippe Becaud was sitting in the cockpit of the Cessna Caravan 675, Turbo Prop aircraft; his old but reliable workhorse of a plane, which had become more than just a treasured possession; it was his work, a second home and his passion all in one beautifully engineered, aero-dynamic shape. An ex-mail plane, he had bought it six years ago with most of the inheritance that his father left him, accumulated from a working life manufacturing and selling packaging to supermarkets.

His father had been barely sixty when he died, before he'd had the chance to retire and enjoy the very comfortable amount of money that he'd made over the years, making Phil feel that he was almost obliged to enjoy the money on his Dad's behalf. He knew his father wouldn't have understood at all, seeing his carefully nurtured small fortune invested in an old plane that needed a huge amount spending on it to keep it airworthy, and could only depreciate in value as time wore on. So he'd told the old guy he was planning to set up an air freight business one day, which impressed him no end, but Becaud omitted to tell him that he was actually planning to buy a plane instead of hiring space on a regular run, like anyone else would do. Hell, he had to tell him something, or he might have left the money to the dog's home, or to his cousin, Brett, which would have been even worse.

He also justified his decision on the basis that he could see little future in the packaging business, which was where his Dad had always wanted him to be, as the environmental pressures to reuse and recycle, were starting to impact inevitably on sales. But really it was his passion for flying that made his decision for him. It was the only thing he had ever wanted to do, and now he'd found a way that he could make his living doing it. And after six years he found that he was making quite a good living after all. Maybe he had inherited more of his father's business brain than he had thought possible.

Now thirty-nine years old, Becaud had thick dark brown, almost black hair, which was just beginning to show the first small flecks of grey at the temples. He wore a leather flying jacket, and had a scarf thrown loosely around his neck. He could just stretch to five-ten if he stood up straight, but slim and keeping himself pretty fit, he felt OK about himself. His face was tanned with the harsh Arctic sun, making him look a little older than he actually was, the first slight lines around his eyes and mouth pointing up his natural expression, bringing out the character in his face. Not that he noticed or cared that much, and not being in the least interested in the fact that he would soon be forty, unlike all his friends who assumed he must be dreading it.

The morning was fine and clear, the blue sky strong in the thin Arctic air, reminding him to put on his dark glasses. His eyes and mouth held tense against the brightness, started to relax a little. As the noise of the warmed up engines rose steadily around him, filling the plane with a sense of suppressed energy and power, his hands tensed at the joystick, and his body melted into the fabric of the plane. He checked his instruments one last time, and calmly relayed to the control tower that he was ready to go. The familiar voice from his flight-follower in the control tower confirmed that he was good for take off, and wished him good luck and a safe journey.

The speeding land fell away from the aircraft as it rose firmly and steadily into the air, banking steeply as Becaud pulled round to the north, the sun momentarily flashing through the right-hand window onto the instrument panel in front of him. He checked his position once more and set a course for Humboldt. With this good weather and a slight tailwind, he estimated that he should be there in about an hour thirty-five. Normally he could reckon on an hour forty-five or fifty. The plane had seats for five passengers if you counted the one beside the pilot. It could take up to eight people, with all the seats in place, but he'd taken the back ones out to allow more room for freight. Soon he was hoping to upgrade to a newer model, even to a Super Caravan which could seat more people and carry more freight, plus it would have a longer range. Just lately he'd been turning down contracts, because of his limitations, which seemed stupid; and the rest of Dad's money was just sitting there doing nothing. He didn't need all that extra space today, though. Today he was travelling light. Hewitt had hired him to take him out over the sea ice where he could get some aerial shots to include in his latest book. They would need to try to find the broken edges of the ice if possible and if the weather permitted, as the really big icebergs set against a calm sea would be stunning, and make fantastic pictures.

It was when Becaud had been telling Hewitt how amazing it was out there that Oliver Carter said that he wished he could see it too, before they had to leave for England. Hewitt was only too happy to invite Oliver along, and so the trip was arranged.

Tilted back in his seat, as the Cessna climbed steadily. Becaud could see nothing but the inside of a blue sphere all around him. Not even another plane had made a vapour trail yet, making him feel like a pioneer, reaching out into an untouched landscape, giving him a sense of ownership of the day, and making him slightly resent the thought that soon, others would be sharing his province, and diluting his experience. The ascent was so smooth it was near perfect, and at ten thousand feet Becaud levelled out, bringing the white floor below him into view, and establishing a level horizon. The engines purred beautifully, and after one last check on his fuel he calculated how far he could risk going out over the sea ice before he would need to head for home. As he'd got just over five hours flying time in total he thought he could just about manage an hour out from Humboldt before he would need to head back, and that would be more than enough time for Hewitt to get some shots, and for the others to take in the scenery.

He smiled to himself, thinking how much Amy James would be looking forward to the trip. He was flattered, but didn't really want to raise her hopes, as he was happy as he was right now, and didn't want to go around changing things, so he flirted with her, knowing that it made her day, but trying to make it clear that it was only a bit of fun, and that he wasn't a reliable type. Well, not unreliable exactly; just liked his independence. He'd never really seen her as the well-travelled scientist and expert computer modeller that she was, but as someone who was nice, but essentially mumsy, and a bit dull.

He made excellent progress, and in no time at all was ready to plan his descent. He went through the familiar procedures, gradually losing height, until, after checking his position carefully on his instruments, he saw as a speck in the far distance the Humboldt Research Station. He banked round to get into the right direction for the airstrip. As often as he'd done this run he still took every landing as seriously as he had done the first. At only 800 metres it was pretty tight, and he didn't want to risk the skids if he went into the rough.

With a slight jolt he was down and the engines were braking. He radioed to base to let them know he'd landed safely at Humboldt, then jumped out onto the ice to greet the four waving figures hurrying over to the waiting plane.

"Hi, Phil!" Oliver shouted across the last ten metres as the group approached. He was slightly ahead, and was clearly impatient to get going. "Did you see the light show last night? We were all out here watching it. Spectacular, wasn't it?"

"Yeah. I saw it too. Absolutely amazing," Becaud said.

"And the tremor," said Amy, catching up. "Did you feel the tremors, too?"

"No I didn't – must have been airborne, I guess, or asleep, but I heard some of the guys talking about it back at the base." He sounded pretty cool about it, which made their enthusiasm seem a bit naïve. So somewhat self-consciously, they scrambled into the Cessna, trying to appear offhand about the trip. "I need you to tell me your weights, folks – you got much equipment there, Lawrence – tell me roughly – Amy, looks like you've lost another couple of pounds since you last flew…" He smiled at her with a slight wink in his eye as he wrote the weights down in his note pad, comparing what they told him now to his previous calculations. Amy smiled back at him, delighted at the compliment.

Oliver helped Zoe into her seat, then settled down beside her. She wriggled about and pulled at her bulky clothes until she got comfortable, trying now to look calm. She could feel her pulse racing despite herself as she was nervous of flying in a small aircraft. Hewitt climbed into the seat behind as he thought he could get a better view from there. He also used the seat next to him to keep his camera equipment handy. Amy, about to climb in next to him, then seeing that there was no room, thought that was typical of him, and was just about to say so when Becaud saw her predicament and called over to her.

"Hey Honey! I guess Lawrence is going to need both windows for his shots. You'd better come on up here, and be my co-pilot for today."

Amy grinned, and hurried on up to sit beside him before anyone had chance to make a different suggestion. Zoe and Oliver glanced at one another but didn't dare risk a smile, and instead stared hard out of the window. They all belted up, Zoe as tightly as she could.

Becaud taxied the plane around until it was right at the end of the airstrip. Revving hard he got the engines throbbing and gathered speed as quickly as he could. Now that he had the extra payload on board, he would need a few extra seconds to get to take off speed. He pulled back the joystick, and powered once more into the air, banking steeply to get onto the correct course. Oliver released Zoe's hand and leaned over to speak to her, raising his voice to be heard above the engine.

"You can open your eyes now, you silly bitch." Despite what he said, his tone was affectionate.

"I'm OK, I'm fine," said Zoe. The plane then levelled out a little creating the sensation that they were falling, like descending in a lift. She gasped involuntarily, and grabbed the seat in front, then seeing Oliver about to make another comment she reiterated

"No really, I'm fine." She put her hands on her lap, rubbing them together as they had become clammy with the tension, but now that they were airborne, she was able to relax more and begin to concentrate on the view. Oliver, noticing that the others had all put cans on to make conversation easier, picked his up and gestured to Zoe to do the same.

They were heading out over the Denmark Strait where the spring weather was already forcing the ice sheet to fragment around the edges and crack until great islands of ice broke off the main covering, drifting slowly into the warmer waters until at last they would disappear altogether as the season progressed. Towering, huge bergs dripped, crumbled and fell into the salty ocean, bit by bit, their blue-white translucency making them look fragile and insubstantial, which, of course they were, in the gentle spring air. Withering like plants in the wrong habitat, they could soon be facing extinction.

Seeing a particularly good field of icebergs Becaud dropped altitude so they could all get a better view, and so that Hewitt could get in close for some of his pictures. The old Cessna was the perfect plane for this type of work, having wings suspended above the window so as to give an uninterrupted view of the ground. The calm sea gave each berg a depth in its reflection, perfect for getting the right shot, adding some complexity to the light and symmetry to his compositions. Now very low and going in much too close for Zoe's comfort, they looked like huge white castles surrounded by their moats.

They flew out over the Denmark Strait as far as Becaud dared, before at last he was forced to tell them that he must turn back, and head for Humboldt whilst he still had half a tank of fuel left.

"Can't believe where that hour and twenty minutes has gone to," said Oliver. "It feels as though we've only just set off." The others all agreed.

"You mean an hour. We've been out for an hour – I've been timing it so that I'd have plenty of fuel for the return journey." Becaud pointed at the clock on the instrument panel.

"Well I make it an hour twenty with my watch," said Oliver.

Becaud looked at his watch, then sat up straight in his seat, desperately wanting Oliver to be wrong, but knowing already that he wasn't going to be. He tapped pointlessly at the clock in front of him.

"Shit! How could that have happened? It was reading OK when I left the base this morning."

"Will we be able to get back OK?" said Zoe, looking concerned.

"Oh yeah. We'll be OK for Humboldt – but I don't think I'll be going back to Angmagssalic tonight. I'll have to pick up some av gas from your stores."

"OK, no problem. But you said you'd got half a tank of fuel left. If that's true you might be alright anyway."

"That's true," said Becaud. "That's a good point. I thought it would have read a bit lower than that after an extra twenty minutes flying time, but the conditions are very calm, so I guess that has helped save fuel." Becaud said the words, but even as he said them he thought they sounded a little thin as an explanation.

After that, the flight continued in silence for a while. Hewitt hadn't said a word throughout, but was emitting a cloud of dissatisfaction from his seat at the back of the aircraft that Becaud was picking up on, making him feel defensive and irritable. Amy kept glancing at him as though she was going to say something, but seeing his expression, she thought better of it. Damn Hewitt. She thought. Trust him to spoil the trip. It was only a malfunction of one tiny instrument after all. They'd be fine. Why make a fuss? Hope his pictures are all over-exposed, she thought spitefully.

"Amy!......Amy!" Becaud was trying to get her attention, his mood lifting as he had spotted something that had engaged his attention. He was pointing over to her window as she was sitting on his right.

"Look down there – two o'clock – what do you make of that?"

Amy looked over towards where Becaud was pointing; searching the landscape carefully to see what had caught his attention. At first she could see nothing but the glaring white ice sheet, and didn't know, anyway what she was meant to be looking for. At a guess she thought that he'd spotted a polar bear, but she could still see nothing but an empty landscape. At two o'clock there was a thin jagged line running across the snow disappearing into the horizon, obviously a crevasse. It zig-zagged its way into the distance like a line graph, during an earthquake. She turned to him asking him if that was what he meant her to see.

"Of course, though I can see you're not impressed."

"Sorry," she said

"I'll go in lower, so that we can take a better look." He dropped altitude and banked round so that they had a better view of the crevasse. Gradually, as the plane lost altitude they could get a better impression of the size of the crack in the landscape.

"This is amazing. I must get this. I've never seen the like," said Hewitt, craning round and pressing his forehead against the cold window. He attached a zoom lens to his camera and started shooting from every angle. He then got the wide angle lens so that he could get a distance shot, and try to convey the scale of the thing.

"Can you get in any lower; it would be great to get in as close as possible?" Hewitt said without removing the camera from his eye. Becaud forgot his former irritation and replied without acrimony.

"I'll see what I can do," he said, swooping down low, making Zoe tense up with apprehension once more. But despite her nerves, she was as riveted as the rest of them at the incredible sight which lay below them. Now right overhead, they could see into the crevasse, the steep walls like cliffs whose base had disappeared into the shadows, it was so deep. So wide, there was room enough to fly in it, and Becaud took the Cessna down some more as if that was what he was intending to do.

"Don't you dare!" said Zoe. But she needn't have worried. Becaud knew that the turns were too steep for him to even try such a manoeuvre.

"I'm impressed now," said Amy. "I had no idea it was this huge. From up there I couldn't get the scale at all."

"How deep do you think it is?" said Zoe. "And how did we not see it on the way out? Surely we must have come this way if we're now doubling back?"

"I guess we just weren't quite near enough on the way out here. I only just caught sight of it in the distance, this time. As for the depth – gee – that can't be right – my altimeter is reading 9000ft! Say! What's going on here, for God's sake?"

Oliver leaned forward so that he could see for himself. "Isn't that barometric, based on our height above sea-level?"

"No, it's a radio altimeter, which calculates the time for a radar signal to bounce off the ground. Not standard on an old Cessna like this, it's a new toy I got while back in Canada last Fall. Look. If we fly back over the ice, we register about 500ft which I guess is about right. Becaud swooped away from the crevasse to demonstrate the point, then banked around once more till he was back over the void. He held the course steady so that he could get a good reading. Once again the altimeter read 9000ft, but then fluctuated wildly.

"The signal is probably hitting the sides of the crevasse. It must be almost impossible to measure its depth like this," said Oliver.

"But presumably, when we got the reading of 9000ft, that was when the signal hit the bottom. It seems incredible but that's what must have happened," said Zoe.

"Sounds like you've got another instrument malfunction," Hewitt said, tersely, not believing for a minute that a crack in the ice, however spectacular from the air, could be anything like that deep. Becaud swung round in his seat, and looked angrily at Hewitt, sitting there, detached, looking through the lens of his camera, and calmly trying out different filters, to see which would give him the best shot of the crevasse.

"And since when have you been the expert on crevasses, or my airplane, Lawrence?" Hewitt started slightly, uncomfortable at Becaud's tone, but nevertheless still believing that what he had just said was valid.

"I'm only saying what I think," said Hewitt. "There's no need to be so touchy."

Becaud bristled, and was about to say something else, when Zoe intervened, and said in a firm, calm voice, "Cool it, guys!"

In the silence that followed, Zoe stared hard out of the window whilst trying to sort out in her mind what was happening. Things weren't right, and she didn't like the way this trip was panning out. Maybe it was her natural nervousness about being in a small plane, but something was stirring a sense of unease within her and she couldn't quite work out why. Oliver seemed OK, and that was reassuring, but Becaud wasn't, and that concerned her as he was a very experienced pilot as well as a skilful one. Like all nervous flyers she had developed the habit of keeping one eye on the flight crew to see how they were reacting to what was going on around them, as long as they appeared calm she could assume that everything was OK, so unconsciously she'd been noting carefully Becaud's demeanour, and was now intently aware of his discomfort.

"Phil," she said, looking away from the window, and focusing instead on the back of his dark hair. He moved his head as if to say that he was listening, but didn't actually turn to face her. "You know, we could still be experiencing the CME – the coronal mass ejection –hurled out from the surface of the sun. Sometimes if we get a really big solar storm the bombardment can go on for days, but can fluctuate wildly. Your instruments might have been OK when you set off but if we are in the middle of huge wave of super charged particles hitting us right now, anything could happen. Your sat nav could be out if the satellite has been hit, and even your radio might be useless."

"My radio was fine when we left – you heard for yourself."

"Yes I know. But we thought the solar storm was over – now I think it might not be. There could be waves of sporadic activity that cause disruption, on and off, for weeks."

Becaud understood, and alarmed, he picked up the radio mic and called back to base. He got nothing but white noise, when he listened for the reply. He tried another two or three times but got nothing. He looked over his instrument panels, taking in their information, but now realising that he couldn't trust anything that they were telling him, if Zoe's theory were right, and at the moment that was looking more convincing every second. He noticed that the fuel tank was still measuring half full, when by now it should have dropped further, and the clock was still slow. He took out his mobile phone to compare the time on that, but the screen on that was blank too.

"Anyone got the right time?" he said, trying to be practical.

"Yes, I have," said Oliver. He looked at his wind up watch, and told Becaud that it was ten forty-two.

The pilot did some quick calculations, scratching on a piece of scrap paper, with a blunt pencil for a few minutes, then instantly making his mind up as to what they must do. He turned the plane right around until the sun was behind them and to the north, then explained to the waiting passengers what he had decided to do.

"I'm making for the nearest coast – anywhere will do – as at least that will be a landmark to guide us. If we continue inland and can't find anything to indicate where we are we could head for miles without anything to go on, and if the weather closed in we wouldn't stand a chance. I know this way I'm bound to hit the coast sooner or later, then if we head south, we will find a populated area to land in." He switched from the first fuel tank to the second, now rather than later as he could no longer rely on the gauge to tell him when to do so.

Nobody spoke. Nobody needed to. If anyone could fly them blind it was Phil Becaud. He seemed to have a feel for the landscape and an in-built sense of direction, which made him a natural aviator. Oliver hoped he was on form today. Strangely, Zoe didn't feel as nervous about being confronted with a real, potentially danger-ous situation, as she had done when at home she would endlessly envisage every worse case scenario, until she had got the whole thing out of proportion. Sitting there, staring out of the window, she just assumed that everything would turn out alright. The flying thing had always been weirdly irrational anyway, and had prob-ably stemmed from the time when she was a student, and an unfortunate incident had depressed and worried her, and had somehow got stuck on the loop of her consciousness instead of being dealt with and put away like it should have been. It had surfaced once more and she remembered it in vivid detail.

She'd obviously got a head for heights, as in her university days she'd been a keen climber. She had been a member of the Sheffield University Climbing Club and was out on Stanage Edge, a four mile long gritstone escarpment near Hathersage in the Derbyshire Peak District, on every available weekend. Her thoughts drifted back until she could feel the ropes in her hand once more and the hard rock pressing into the sole of her boot till her foot ached with the effort. She remembered the intense level of concentration, then the feeling of exhilaration relief and achievement that she always had as she hauled herself over the top of the Edge, the cliff behind her like a giant step; the open moorland sweeping out in front of her, on a new level. At these memories a familiar feeling started to creep into her consciousness, like a dark shadow.

One day, when she'd been about to start a familiar climb with a less experienced member of the club, it had all gone wrong. Her companion was a young man from the English department, Stuart Lightman, who was in training for an attempt on one of the faces in the French Alps. He was climbing with her to practise what he had learned on the indoor wall. They roped up, while she explained what he could expect on the climb. It was March. The wind was biting cold and some late snow lay on the Peaks, chilling the thin spring wind even more. It made them hurry to begin the climb, so that the exertion would warm them through. She set of confidently, making fast progress, and he did the same, eager to look competent in her eyes. But when Stuart was only about twenty feet off the ground he lost his footing on the worn crumbling rock face and he slithered down a few feet until she felt the rope tug slightly on her harness. She braced herself for the jolt that never came as the unsecured rope slid through her harness and then slipped down with him to the base of the cliff. Stuart hadn't fallen far, and with the base not being steep, he had managed to slow his fall by grabbing on to the rocks in front of him. He had a few cuts and bruises and a torn anorak, but other than that he was fine. Zoe hurried down to make sure that he was OK, shaking with adrenalin and the cold. She picked up the end of the rope. She looked at it and then at the young man, who looked back at her, saying nothing. How could she have been so careless? This was a basic error, and she knew it. There were no excuses, and she didn't try to invent any.

"I'm sorry," she said, feeling the uselessness of her words even as she spoke them. She secured the rope properly this time, and he checked it to make sure that it was OK. She didn't blame him. Once more they set off, this time making it to the top without any further incident. But Zoe felt clumsy and self-conscious all the time, never getting the feeling of total absorption that comes with a really satisfying climb. She felt like a traitor, letting down someone who had trusted her, and no amount of telling herself that there was no harm done, made the feeling go away. She kept on with the 'what if' scenario in her head until she was overwhelmed by a feeling of her own inadequacy. They could have been near the top, and Stuart would have been killed. She tried in vain to put the incident behind her, but she was a harsh critic of herself; more forgiving of other people. Increasingly it sapped her enjoyment of climbing until she missed more weekends than she attended. Then as the third year drew into its final term, she claimed a lack of time for anything but finals, and it was then that she stopped going altogether.

She stared out of the window, lost in thought, as they pressed on towards the coast. Oliver had dozed off beside her, and Amy was chatting to Becaud, inaudibly to her, as she had slipped the cans off to be more comfortable. Amy looked animated and from what she could read from the body language, Becaud looked relaxed in her company. Maybe they'd be OK, she thought, she'd seen less likely matches work.

Becaud sat forward in his seat and stretched to see if there was any detail yet on the far horizon.

"I think I can maybe just make out the coast – what do you think, Oliver?"

Oliver started awake, but had heard what the pilot had said. He agreed. He checked his watch again to confirm the timing was right, and after another quick calculation, Becaud banked round slightly and began to head south to where the coast would be more populated. The day was still fine and clear and when after a few more minutes they flew over the shore line they could make out a few dotted buildings and tiny settlements.

"Are you actually looking for a landing strip?" said Oliver beginning to feel impatient with the delay.

"If possible, yes of course. I want to get my plane – and you guys – down in one piece. The ice often looks smooth when it's not – we could get tipped over, and a lot of damage done. And I want somewhere big enough to have a supply of av gas. Or we could be here for some time."

"That might not be too bad," said Amy, flirtatiously, hoping he would catch her meaning.

"Well I have a business to run," said Becaud. Amy looked away sharply. He needn't have said that, but she could have kicked herself for saying too much.

He tried out the radio again, but still there was nothing but white noise. He began to drop altitude, and speed until they were coming in really low over the little coastal hamlets. They were all craning round now for any sign of somewhere that would make a suitable place to land. But it was like searching for a parking spot on main road. There was just nowhere that looked right. Oliver was scouring a map to see if he could work out where they actually were, but could get nothing to make him certain. Then there was a gap for about ten minutes when there were no buildings at all.

"We should have got down while we had the chance," said Hewitt, his anxiety mounting with every passing second.

"Well 20/20 hindsight is a wonderful thing," said Becaud.

"We'll be OK," Oliver said. "Look! What's that ahead, Phil. I think I see something."

"You're right!"

All eyes were now focused on the dark dots ahead of them that indicated that they were heading towards a settlement of some kind. Soon they could all see that there were quite a number of buildings and some boats clustered around a jetty, mostly fishing vessels but also a mail boat which indicated that this was probably a town which might have some supplies. Becaud tried over and over on his radio, but could still get no response. He circled round having decided to land here whatever, as it could be quite some time before they came across another place of this size. Then he saw what he had been looking for – a small plane on the ground a short distance away from the groups of houses. He swooped in low over the landing strip to indicate to anyone on the ground that he wanted to land, and to make sure that there was nothing on the strip already, then he powered up and round, once more gaining some height before attempting to line up the Cessna with the tiny runway. Zoe felt the clamminess return to the palms of her hands, and although she tried to be cool she could feel her heart pulsing away in her chest. She clocked Phil's body language. It was very natural, and he looked very much in control. This was all routine to him.

But her feeling of reassurance was short-lived. She felt a sudden jolt, that made her breath stick in her throat, and sent the adrenaline pulsing through her already nervous body. Becaud tried too late to switch from the second fuel tank back to the first. The second one had run dry on him, creating an air lock in the pipe, and had caused the engine to stall. The engines stuttered and choked for a few seconds as Becaud tried to restart them, but the silence, when it came, was total and unforgiving.

"Oh my God!" said Amy. "We're going to crash!"

"Just start the fucking engine! Keep trying!" said Hewitt.

Everyone was shouting at once, except for Zoe, who sat frozen in her seat.

"We'll be OK," said Oliver to Zoe, who didn't hear him.

"OK, folks," said Becaud in a warm steady voice. He spoke a little more quietly than normal so that they had to strain slightly to hear him. That was done deliberately to get everyone's attention. "Now if you all shut the hell up for a moment, I'll talk you through what I'm going to do." He paused a second, so that they could collect themselves, but only for a second. He mustn't let panic take hold again, or he might not be able to get them down.

"We're going to do an engine-out landing...."

"Like we've any choice," said Hewitt. Becaud was furious with him. He could destabilise the situation so easily with a remark like that. He could have punched him.

Instead he said very levelly.

"Now listen up, everyone.... I know this is scary, and it's not gonna be easy for you, but I've done this many times before – it's a well practised manoeuvre for all pilots. I'm going to tell you what we're going to do, then at least you'll have some idea what to expect." They were all now hanging on his every word. The silence had wrapped right around them. Zoe heard her seat creak as she changed her position. After that she was too afraid to move. Becaud continued.

"We're gliding now – that means we haven't the power to land – we'd be dropping down too quickly, so I have to go into a steep dive on the approach to get enough speed up to land safely. So make sure you're securely belted in. Brace yourselves when I give you the word...you OK with that? You all know what to do – just like you've been shown when we went through the emergency procedure."

Should've taken more notice. They all practised the landing position looking at each other to make sure they'd got it right. Becaud moved Amy slightly till he was happy that she'd got it right, then told the others to do like that.

Time appeared to crawl by as each suspended second expanded and seemed to hover, unmoving, but it was their rapid thoughts pelting through their minds that caused everything else to seem to slow down around them. Becaud banked the Cessna round so they were at right angles to the airstrip. He'd gained just enough height, after circling around before, to make the landing possible. He hoped. With the instruments out he was guessing anyway.

"Going into the dive now!" he said, taking them all by surprise. "Get into your positions and hold it there till I tell you move."

They pulled their belts a little tighter, and folded their arms over their heads as they'd been shown how to, never thinking in a million years that they would ever have to do this for real.

The nose dipped down, more steeply than they thought it would. Zoe felt that they were nearly vertical, the pressure popping in her ears, her stomach in a tight knot. *Love you* wouldn't come out. No need.

Phil Becaud gripped the controls firmly and fixed his gaze straight ahead. Each one of them became isolated in his or her own silent fall. Time became elastic as it merged with the space between themselves and possible safety. They let go, and let Becaud get them out of this.

The Cessna lurched over and for a moment Zoe thought that Becaud had lost control as he banked the plane round ninety degrees so that he was in line with the runway. As they pulled out of the dive, for a moment it felt like they were ascending again as the nose rose up until it was angled for the landing. All Zoe could think of was the space wedging itself between her and the ground, like an unwelcome presence. All she wanted now was to feel her feet on the floor, striding across the snow. Half a minute, a minute, seconds, she'd no idea of time; and she would get her wish. Her impatience was desperate. Becaud dropped the Cessna in lower. His concentration was absolute; he was totally at one with the plane as he gripped the joystick and made the final adjustments to his approach. This time there were no second chances.

"Five seconds!" No-one could remember who said that.

They touched down with a heavy bump that forced them against their seat belts, and jolted them harder than they had expected. They seemed to float for a moment before there was another hard jolt that tipped them to one side. Zoe thought that they were going to flip over, but it was one of the skids that had broken off forcing them to list to port.

"Shit!" said Becaud.

They skewed round on the one remaining skid, veering off the landing strip straight into a flimsy-looking lean-to shack that shattered into firewood under the impact. The Cessna slid on a few hundred metres further, off the smooth ice, then rattled and scraped into the scree and rocks that fringed the coast, before stopping dead. Silent and broken, the Cessna tipped forward onto its propeller, damaging it beyond repair. A trail of debris was left littered all behind it, and a deep rut had been cut into packed snow at the end of the runway.

"Is everyone OK?" Becaud said with concern. There was a pause while everyone took stock.

"I... think so," Zoe said on everyone's behalf. Oliver looked a sort of stony white.

A couple of guys came running over to the plane from a hut nearby.

"You OK? Is anyone hurt?" said one in English, with a slight American inflection.

"No, we're all OK," said Becaud, apologising for the damage they had caused.

"Nice flying, fella!" said the first man grinning. Didn't think you were going to make it out of that dive, though - you sure cut that a bit fine."

Zoe could tell by the look on Becaud's face that he knew it already. Saying nothing, he wound his loose scarf around his neck, before kicking the buckled, tilted door open with his foot, then jumping down onto the crunching grey scree that had finally brought his precious, now wrecked, aircraft to a halt. If it wasn't for the solar storm making them veer off course they would never have spotted the crevasse, which should have been the highlight of the trip. But now the day was a total disaster and his plane lay in ruins. He kicked a piece of the broken propeller in sheer frustration, and in some ways to show his relief.

"Hey, man," said the first man on the scene. "Cool it. You did good – and nobody's hurt – just remember that."

Becaud slapped the man on the shoulder in a gesture of camaraderie, and walked off towards the wooden buildings clustered in the distance, leaving the others to straggle shakily behind him. They were alive, and all in one piece, and, for the moment, that was all that mattered.

CHAPTER FOUR

London

London had been in chaos ever since the solar storm had hit, now nearly four weeks ago. It had been a mega, south polarity, coronal mass ejection event that had been particularly prolonged, lasting for eight days at its height but going on for much longer at a lower level after that. It had affected the entire northern hemisphere to some extent, but mainly the developed areas, especially the cities had been affected most of all. Goodness only knows what it would have been like if some of the transformers hadn't been switched off in time, protecting them so that they could be switched back on again once the danger had passed.

None of the power companies had wanted to risk losing revenue by shutting down supply, so they had dragged their feet; allowed to by an end-of-term government, wracked by internecine squabbles that had lost its sense of direction and purpose. In the end it was the Mayor of London who ordered a partial shut down of the power stations in a desperate attempt to save some of the transformers, and who salvaged the situation from becoming an utter disaster by rallying the leaders of all the other major cities in Britain to do the same. Now, a month on, power was sporadic, as the stations were not yet working at full capacity, but at least there was a supply.

The city streets seemed unusually quiet because so many cars had had their on-board computers damaged, and only priority vehicles were being repaired for the time being. Cycles weaved everywhere, now ridden with a new sense of freedom, and in some cases recklessness. Walkers and joggers vied for priority on the newly claimed roads, looking strangely undressed without their mp3's or ipods fixed to their ears.

There was scarcely a business of any size that hadn't been affected in some way by the storm. At first it had all been a novelty; candle-lit shops, writing letters by hand and posting them off, instead of sending an email. Time with the family instead of the telly; make your own fun, just like in the 1950's. But now the novelty was wearing thin. People were losing money, as the fabric of the lives they understood was becoming frayed. And as for evenings spent at home with bloody pointless board games. No wonder that the baby boomer generation had invented the sixties.

The real worry was the food supply. The British retail system, efficient, but pared to the bone, was now creaking at the seams, and failing to deliver to a population used to getting what it wanted any time of the day or night. But again London's Mayor had got the tone exactly right when the government had fallen into trap of trying to reassure people with unrealistic promises that things would soon be back to normal. The Mayor, Rosa Paine, told everyone that nothing was going to be normal again for months, even years, and that we'd just have to get used to it. She told it as it was – and so far, at least, the tactic was working, as well as anything was going to.

Zoe hurried along the Embankment, hoping to get to the shops and buy something for their evening meal before they ran out of everything worth having. The river glistened on her right, looking a silky brown-grey in the late afternoon sun. She had managed to finish work early for once and leave Isaac Newton College before the evening rush hour got properly under way. Having begun work at seven that morning, she was more than ready to set off for home by three. After their stint in the Greenland, she was finding it hard going to adjust to the city environment that was both utterly familiar and alien at the same time. Like the feel of the dry pavement, warm and dusty in the soft, late April air, feeling as though it were sticking to your feet, like it did when as a child you take your roller skates off and for a while all your body perception seem skewed. Where for months she had had got used to walking on packed slippery ice, or trudging through powdery snow, here she tripped along with minimal effort. Her feet felt unusually light in her new ballet-pump style slip-ons instead of the huge boots and thick woolly socks that had become her normal footwear over the last few weeks.

That was probably the reason why she was walking so fast, or maybe it was just the buzz of the city propelling her forward like it was doing to everyone else around her. But instead of giving her energy it was making her tired. And the crowds. They made her irritable. After being used to looking out and seeing a landscape empty to the horizon everyday, she was now being jostled and brushed by rude self-important strangers who clearly saw her only as another obstacle getting in their way.

Spring was doing its best to impose itself on the built environment, normally unresponsive to the seasonal changes that marked everywhere else. A few trees were covered in thick showy blossom, and the thin, cold wind that had been blowing for the last ten days had finally given way to a gentle southerly breeze that enabled one to feel the warmth of the sun as it broke through the clouds. A couple of streetwise starlings tugged apart a piece of discarded pizza, dropped on the pavement in front of her; thoroughly urbanised, they looked no more likely to go and forage for berries than she did. Although if Sainsbury's didn't have some in soon, that's exactly what she might end up doing, she thought.

Zoe was pleased that the paper that she was writing with Oliver was going well. With a bit of luck it should be out in October to coincide with the new academic year. Only then, when it had been picked over and pulled apart by their peers, could they begin to be sure that their latest research on the theories of abrupt climate change were good. The focus of their research had been to examine in detail the decade before a cycle of rapid change commenced. They had not expected to find, nor had they found, a link between a single event and the phenomenon of climate change, and so they had begun to look for a combination of factors, which could lead to a tipping point being reached.

What they had found was in the decade before a period of marked climate change, was a concentration of variables, such as the natural climate variations, which were cyclical in nature, the angle of the Earth to the Sun, the distance of the Earth to the Sun, volcanic dust in the atmosphere and so on. These factors were all known about and had been the subject of debate for some time. What Zoe was trying to understand was the difference between when these factors were absorbed by the system, and evened out, and when the tipping point was reached making the Earth's climate flip into a whole new ball game. Getting enough data to come up with a provable, repeatable formula would be the ultimate prize in their field, making prediction of a future major climate change a possibility. They were still some time from that, but at least now Zoe knew they were heading in the right direction.

Zoe's preferred method of trying to reach a useable method for predicting a radical change was to use a points system. Negative for any factors which could tip the climate into a colder phase, positive for factors which could trigger off a runaway greenhouse effect. Sounded simple enough, but in practice it was about as easy as trying to evaluate in marks out of ten each football player's contribution to a match, then to say with certainty whether they'll win the next one. She didn't know yet if it could be done. And the worst nightmare was that the climate could spiral out of control – if it ever were in control – before they got their answer. Human civilisation and advancement had flourished in this last ten thousand years of a benign climate, and it was too precious to have it all wither and die now like a garden overtaken by drought.

Drought. The word hung in her thoughts for a few transitional seconds while she became aware of her surroundings once more. The sky looked slightly threatening and she wondered if her current drought were about to end. Be alright for the moment. Didn't look too bad. But quite without warning, a few fat spots of rain fell onto the pavement in front of her, glinting and darkening, at first a long way apart, then clustering and overlapping, feeling cold on her arms and dampening her hair. She unconsciously hurried her pace as she hadn't got a jacket with her, assuming that if there was any rain today it would only be a light shower. But the clouds gathered and darkened rapidly, and after only a few minutes the sporadic droplets turned into a steady stream. The afternoon light became grey and thick and a rumble of thunder warned Zoe that this was not going to just be another April shower after all. Her hair now running with water and her damp feet sticking uncomfortably in her shoes, she began to jog, head down, along the street where she knew there was a café-deli just along on her left, that she often called into on the way home. However, before she got there she could hear the sound of raised voices, coming threateningly from down a side street, over on the right and just ahead of her. She sensed danger straight away, and felt her stomach tighten with apprehension, but was glad, at least that she was on this side of the road. Fights were getting more common now. The underlying tensions being brought about by shortages in the shops, together with a general feeling of disruption, was leading to an increased sense of lawlessness. Zoe tried to make herself inconspicuous and hurried on her way, but to her horror and in seconds the sounds of pelting feet were all around her, and angry, unnatural voices were right next to her. Two men had been caught up with by a group of youths and slightly older men, and looked as though they were going to get a beating. Then so close she could smell his fear, one of the cornered men then pulled a knife. Her head thumping, she became transfixed by the moment, stranded in the middle of the melee where everyone else had melted away. Unable to take her eyes off the bright cold blade, now thrust forward in a warning gesture, she stood there like a spectator, not thinking of her own safety. She didn't even feel the rain, or see the stranger draw alongside her in the deepening gloom. A hand gripped her arm and propelled her away from the group. She didn't even question what was happening, so overtaken had she become by the events around her. She walked an unknown number of paces, still feeling the grip on her arm. A door opened in front of her, and she was pushed inside the café, just in time and to safety as a huge crack of thunder echoed round the city street. Then the rain sheeted down, filling the gutters, and bouncing ankle-high off the pavements. The door closed behind her and she turned dripping and shaking into the shop, rubbing her face, with an equally wet hand.

"Lawrence!" Zoe said, unable to believe her eyes when she turned and recognised the man who had just rescued her. "What the hell are you doing here?"

He smiled thinly at the ingratitude. "I'll get you a cup of coffee. What would you like?"

She asked for her favourite coffee, a double-shot latte. Tall or regular. Tall. Really need the caffeine. He went over to the counter to order while she chose a good table and sat down. Zoe picked up a napkin and dabbed off the drips from the ends of her hair, then lightly wiped it over her arms and legs as she was beginning to feel cold. She kicked off her shoes to allow her feet to dry, but there was nothing she could do about the damp clothes that were clinging round her. Hewitt arrived at the table with a tray which he rested on the corner whilst placing the cups on the table. He'd bought a box of miniature cakes as well, four, in a cellophane wrapped cardboard tray.

"Help yourself," he said nodding towards them. He put the tray on the nearby rack then joined her at the table and sat down.

"Thanks, Lawrence, that's really very kind of you," she said, meaning it, and not just referring to the coffee. He nodded diffidently.

They were at a table next to the window. By now the rain was coming down in torrents and the café was beginning to fill up with soaked commuters all trying to get out of the storm. The street outside had become so dark that they could see their own reflections in the steamed up glass, now running with rainwater down the outside. With a bit of luck the deluge should have dispersed trouble out there on the street. A blue flickery light held the road in its grip for several seconds before a deep roll of thunder caused a few startled cries from some of the other customers, vibrating through the table, and causing the window to shake.

"It's right overhead," said Zoe.

"It'll soon pass over." Hewitt seemed remarkably unperturbed.

"I've always wanted to try a pack of these." Zoe reached for the tiny cakes.

"Go ahead," said Hewitt, but when Zoe tried to unwrap the fiddly packaging she found that her hands were shaking so much that she couldn't do it. Hewitt took the box from her hands and quickly tore off the cellophane putting the box down next to her coffee. She then picked up her latte and gripped it with two hands before bringing it to her lips. Despite her efforts to look calm she still couldn't hold the mug steadily and she managed to spill some on the table before finally getting a few sips down.

"You'll be alright in a minute," said Hewitt. It sounded more like an instruction than sympathy, but she appreciated it anyway. He took one of the cakes, and she did the same.

"I've just got back from a meeting with my publisher," said Hewitt. "So this is very fortunate, seeing you – I was actually wondering whether to contact you or Carter." The use of her husband's surname jarred, as it seemed inappropriately formal, and rather old-fashioned – typical Lawrence, she thought.

"Oh, and why's that?" said Zoe, puzzled.

"Was talking to this chap – a photographer – supplied military magazines – not classified information or anything – just had a book out too. He asked to look at some of my stuff after I told him I'd just got back from Greenland on a photo shoot, as that's where he was going next. I was a bit miffed that none of my aerial shots were used, by the way. My publisher said they didn't have enough impact. Anyway, I showed them to this chap, just to be sociable – Coulson he was called – and he just couldn't hide his surprise. Bombarded me with questions. Plenty of impact there I thought. But I couldn't work out why. As soon as I asked him some questions though, he clammed up. Said he was working on a government project, and wasn't at liberty to talk about it. Was at pains to tell me his work was general interest stuff, nothing sensitive, then goes all secretive about it. A bit odd, I thought."

"Sounds fascinating, I have to say, Lawrence, but I can't see quite what this has to do with either me or Oliver. Why did you think of contacting us?"

"It was when I showed him the pictures of the crevasse that his eyes nearly popped out of their sockets. I told him how massive it was and how high we were when I shot the pictures so he knew exactly what he was looking at. Being a professional himself, he took in at once what I was telling him, and could get the perspective. The photos weren't too bad, in my opinion, although I suppose if I'm honest, they didn't convey the scale of the thing as much as I had hoped they would. I had seen it, so I knew what I was looking at; to a casual observer, only having seen the photo, they wouldn't get that..... so I suppose they did lack impact in that way."

"But that wasn't the point was it? The photos, I mean. As a professional photographer, you'd think that would be what got his interest, the aesthetics, and quality of the picture, but you're saying that it was the actual feature that made him sit up and take notice."

"Exactly," said Hewitt. "That's my point exactly. He kept asking how big it was, whether we'd been able to get any idea of its length, but above all, *where* it was. He was very persistent about that, and became exasperated when I couldn't tell him. I told him that our instruments had failed and that we were flying blind, but he seemed to think that I was holding out on him."

"You said he was working for the government?"

"Yes. Became very cagey about that. But I can't work out what his problem was. It's a crevasse for God's sake – you get them in Greenland, and if he's that bothered about its position, he could look it up on satellite pictures of the region, I'd have thought."

"Yes, of course he could. Maybe he was just a nutter – not working for the government at all." Hewitt didn't know if she were being serious, so he didn't answer her remark. "But I'll see what Oliver makes of all this." Zoe took another sip of her coffee, calmer now that she had someone to talk to. She ate another cake, thinking the sugar rush might help, too, leaving the last one for Hewitt.

"I'd be grateful if you would," he said. "Not that I want to get involved, personally. I just think that someone ought to know, that whatever we found up there in the ice has generated a lot of interest in some quarters. And I don't know why."

"OK, I'll tell Oliver. See what he thinks."

The lightning was still catching Zoe's eye every few minutes, but the thunder was now rumbling away, passing gradually further into the distance. The rain had eased, too, now to a steady soft vertical shower.

"It's going over," said Hewitt. Finishing the last of his latte, leaving a lacy pattern on his glass mug.

"Then perhaps we'd better make a move," said Zoe. "I haven't bought anything for dinner yet. You know what it's like at the moment. Crazy, isn't it. Don't know when things are ever going to be normal again. Do you?"

"They're normal now," said Hewitt.

Zoe laughed. "I don't see how you work that one out, Lawrence – I'd hardly call this normal." She looked at him, closely to see if he'd been trying to make a joke that she hadn't got. But he looked deadly serious.

"I don't ever think things will go back to what used to be normal," said Hewitt.

"I think this is our new normal now. And this is probably the best we're going to get. So, I think we should all stop complaining, and start appreciating it."

Zoe stared at him, annoyed that he could be so depressing, but already half-believing that he could be right.

"Lawrence, you've just saved me from being killed in a gang fight – you're now supposed to be cheering me up!"

"Yes, sorry...I..."

"Oh, never mind...Look, here's my card...I'll tell Oliver what you said. Call us." Zoe paused to think for a moment. "Actually, why don't you come round for a meal one evening ... would you like that?"

"Well yes. That would be good. I'd love to. Are you sure that would be OK?"

Zoe picked up her bag, and nodded her approval. Hewitt on cue, stood up, and put on his jacket ready to leave. "How is Amy, by the way? Are you still in touch with her at all?"

"Oh yes. We're still good friends. She's fine. Actually, she'll be coming round on Friday night, all being well. Why don't you come too, if you're free then? We could have a reunion." Hewitt hesitated. "Well you don't have to say now – call us and confirm later. And thanks again Lawrence. Really. You were brilliant."

At that he actually flushed slightly, but said nothing. The rain had stopped. Zoe stepped out onto the wet pavement, still catching the reflections of the buildings on either side of the street, the water kicking up unavoidably onto her bare calves. The clouds thinned and parted allowing the sun to break through as quickly as it had been obscured only about three quarters of an hour earlier. Steam rose from the drying flagstones, hanging like dry ice a foot above the ground. She tried to call Oliver once more to let him know that she would be a little late home, but as usual she could get no signal. Now alone again, she could feel the events of the day pressing in on her once more, dragging her mood down. By the time she got home, Hewitt's concerns about Coulson had receded into a corner of her mind, so when she mentioned it to Oliver it was already with a tone of dismissal, and explanation.

"No doubt you'll hear the full story, on Friday if he shows," said Zoe.

"Can't wait," said Oliver, through a mouthful of chicken tikka lasagne. "What the hell is this?" he said staring at his plate with incredulity.

"I got it from Iceland," Zoe said, as if that explained it. She tried not to laugh, but felt her forehead knot and her eyes prickle with an attack of the giggles due to the look on her husband's face. She wheezed, "It was all they had left."

"Bloody tastes like it, too. My God!" he said, eating it anyway, with no lack of enthusiasm. "And I wouldn't tell Amy that Hewitt might be coming on Friday or she'll wimp out – and she promised to bring some fillet steak, remember."

"Wouldn't dream of it," said Zoe, collecting herself. "I've been saving a nice bottle of red to go with it, too. Wouldn't dream of letting that go to waste."

CHAPTER FIVE

Baffin Island, Canadian Arctic

The brown, varnished wooden boards of the Anchor Hotel creaked like a ship's deck when any guests pushed in through the heavy door and made their way to the reception desk. The desk was to one side of the entrance hall, next to a huge reclaimed anchor which was resting at an angle at the side of a carefully coiled circle of chain piled on the floor. The anchor had been carefully cleaned and painted by the current owner to make it suitable to keep in an indoor space, but even now the rust stains had started to show through the layers of white, which had never fully covered the blistered metal beneath. A faded sign above the desk, in large, once white, old-fashioned lettering, curved into a shallow arch, gave the name of the hotel, as if to confirm you were in the right place, if you had missed it on the way in. On the shelves, window bays and on the walls were maritime artefacts, compasses, barometers, old ship's logs, dutifully kept in flowing faded handwriting, now left open; all function lost in time, now only used as ornament. All around the walls were old-fashioned paintings of ships in every pose – stately at anchor, busy in port, or fighting a storm, all in heavy gilt ornate frames, mismatched in size and shape but brought together through their common sea-faring culture.

A middle aged, newly retired couple, now on their travels, heaved their cases up the bare stairs, holding tight onto the balustrade. Having just checked in, they were looking all around like newcomers do, and talking loudly about their forthcoming itinerary. Two athletic looking men in their twenties were on a canoeing holiday, hunched over a map on the desk next to reception, asking the owner about local conditions and nodding vigorously at whatever he was telling them. A guy on his own in the corner of the bar, his chair too close to a brown leaved neglected looking palm plant, was making a beer last until he had finished reading his newspaper. A bit grey, with a short beard, he looked absorbed and unselfconscious, as though he were used to being on his own. He had on dark blue, almost black cargoes and a light coloured shirt. Slung over the chair arm was a light grey micro fleece pullover with a zip at the neck, which he didn't need, sat close as he was to the glowing red stove.

It was getting pretty busy as far as things went round here at Frobisher Bay. Usually just a working town, and the only really populated part of Baffin Island, the hotel was mostly empty for a good part of the year, but now the spring weather had brought a handful of tourists, things were starting to look up a bit for the Anchor. The phone rang loudly round the reception area and the owner eagerly took down another reservation, for two days time. He called loudly to his wife out back, "Hey, honey, better get another room turned out for Thursday. Looks like we've got a rush on here."

"Maybe somebody's struck gold!" shouted the woman guest, almost halfway up the stairs and now resting with her case. The owner laughed good naturedly, saying nothing in reply, but clearly hoping that the somebody would be him.

The guy with the newspaper leaned over to take a drink of his beer, then sank back again in the comfortable leather chair, and turned over another page, ignoring the exchange that he had clearly just heard.

The door opened once more, and a man carrying a rather battered holdall, stepped inside, and walked confidently, not too quickly, over to the desk, putting his holdall down on the floor when he got there. His scarf fell away from his shoulder as dipped down, and with one hand he flicked it back over again with a well-rehearsed gesture. He reached into his pocket for his wallet as he straightened up and caught the eye of the proprietor, then gave him his name.

"Philippe Becaud," he said to the man. "Got a reservation for tonight."

"OK, er, Mr Bekko? Is that how you say it? Got you down right here for a single room. Can I just get you to sign here for me, sir? I'll take your bag for you if you like. Then I'll get my wife to show you to your room – she won't be long."

"No, don't put her to any trouble – I'm sure it will be fine."

"Did you have a good journey, Mr Becaud?"

"Yes, thank you, very good." He signed the form, then for the first time he looked around and took in his surroundings.

"Nice place."

"Yeah, thanks. We're real proud of it. Glad you like it – you er - said when you called you were meeting up with someone – your passenger to Angmagssalic – I believe," said the hotelier.

"Yes, that's right. We'll be setting off for Greenland early tomorrow morning, if the weather holds good. I'm assuming he's here already – said he would be. Could you tell him that I've arrived, if that's OK?"

"No need to Mr Becaud. He's right over there." He looked to where the other man was indicating. "See the guy sitting on his own in the bar over there? Well that's him."

Becaud thanked him and went straightaway over to introduce himself to his passenger. At the sound of the approaching footsteps he put down his newspaper, knowing at once who it was who was making a bee-line for him. He stood up, and offered his hand cordially. The pilot spoke first.

"Hi. Phil Becaud. I guess you must be Mr Coulson."

"Yes, that's me. Pleased to meet you, Phil. And you can call me Ray."

They both sat down and Becaud ordered two beers as he saw Coulson's glass was nearly empty.

"Are we OK for tomorrow?" said Coulson. "I really need to be on my way as soon as possible. I've been kicking my heels for two days here as it is, whilst trying to eke out my meagre budget. I'm really keen to make a start, if that's OK."

"Sure, we're fine for tomorrow. The weather is set fair, and I can refuel and get some supplies sorted out this afternoon. Sorry I couldn't come any earlier but I only got my new plane yesterday – a Cessner Super Caravan – you're my first client."

"No I'm not blaming you at all. I'm more than grateful you could fit me in at such short notice."

"It was lucky you called me. I've been back home in Canada getting fixed up with my new plane. So I was headed out in this direction to my place in Greenland, where my freight business is based. Couldn't have worked out better."

Becaud thought it wasn't a great idea to tell his passenger that the reason why he'd got his new plane was that he'd crashed the old one. Better save that one for later. He was in a buoyant mood. He was now in a position to expand his business, and could even cash in on the growing tourist trade, being able to accommodate larger parties of people. He had been thinking of advertising tours of the ice fields over the internet, and as he noted how well the Anchor was doing for visitors, he made up his mind to give it a go. He wondered whether Coulson was here for business or pleasure. Up to now his answers about what he was doing had been vague to say the least; Becaud didn't like to push him, believing that he would probably get more out of him in the long run if he didn't try too hard.

Coulson, if he were honest, was a little out of his depth. But he felt that he had been chosen to do something of importance and it had flattered his ego to comply. Approached because of his photographic skills and his association with the military, albeit rather tenuous, his response was enthusiastic and got him the task straightaway. The government didn't want anyone who was actually employed by the military or the Intelligence Services to be involved in this job in case it caused offence to a friendly foreign power. The presence of Ray Coulson, as a civilian photographer could be explained away much more easily than could military personnel if it ever came to that.

The brief seemed simple enough on paper – he was being asked to go into the icy interior of Greenland and try to discover the location of a large crevasse that reportedly been seen by Inuit hunters, but whose actual size and location couldn't be confirmed. At first it had created a buzz amongst the scientists in the region, but it was when these rumours began to get back to the universities and then the capitals of Europe that governments started to sit up and take notice. Having long been warned by environmentalists that the ice sheet covering the sea could calve and hasten the fragmentation of the ice cap, the implications of a huge split in the land ice was not at first appreciated by the various leaders until their advisors filled them in.

'It's easy, Prime Minister,' they would say – keep it homey – 'think of your gin and tonic. If your glass if full to the brim, and has some ice cubes in there floating away, when they melt your glass won't overflow as the liquid was already displaced. But fill your glass to the brim and then add your ice cubes – and G & T suddenly spills all over the place and spells Government in Trouble. If the land ice goes, we'll get flooding on an unimaginable scale – we're talking catastrophe for many of the big cities of Europe and Scandinavia.'

So Coulson had been asked to go into the interior of Greenland and see if he could locate the position of the rumoured crevasse, in order that scientific teams could be sent in to study its implications. Usually this wouldn't have been a problem as satellite observation would have provided everyone with the information that they needed. But the solar storm had changed everything. There was no trace of a large new crack in the ice on all the photographic records studied before the storm hit, and the storm had been so severe and had lasted for so long that the PolarStat satellite had sustained enormous damage and had been completely knocked out of commission. There were also the problems with the computer network and mobile phones. The result was that data, normally accurate, detailed and instant, was now non-existent. Information, the oxygen of modern society, was now suffocating under its own vulnerability. It was quite a culture shock to realise that in order to find out if these rumours were true that it was going to be necessary to physically send someone in to find out. And then they would have to post the information back or bring it back themselves. All this, of course was dependent on the weather holding out. If it closed in, no-one would be able to safely go into the interior. There was now no global positioning equipment or communications back-up if things were to go wrong and an expedition needed help. Under normal circumstances it would have been prudent to have delayed any expeditions until after new satellites were launched or the old ones could be repaired, but now that luxury wasn't available as time was pushing the need for information.

It was about mid afternoon by the time Becaud left Coulson down in the bar and closed the door of his hotel room behind him. He immediately cast an experienced eye around the furniture and décor of the place. It seemed OK. No, more than OK, it was good. The sheets and towels were fresh and clean and the furnishings, though plain, were fine. He hated the chintzy fussy rooms that he normally got when travelling, or the corporate hotel look that he got when he splashed out and paid a bit more for a better hotel. He unzipped his hold-all and pulled out a washbag which he placed on the shelf inside the shower cubicle, then rummaged around until he found his alarm clock, placing it carefully on the dark wooden, rattan fronted chest at the side of his bed, moving the lamp back as he did so to make a bit more room. The sheet and pillow cases were white and neatly pressed, the sand coloured, slightly patterned bedspread covered what looked like a generous number of blankets.

He then stepped over to the window and paused a while to take in the view. Not that there was much of one from this side of the hotel. He could see down onto the cubes and angles of the huddled, ramshackle buildings that made up the settlement of Frobisher. There was a tangle of aerials, telegraph wires, hoardings and stovepipe chimneys that gave the place a forgotten-about look more than a pioneering one. There'd be no goldrush here – this looked like a hard-work town based on fishing and the trade that came in and out of the little port. Becaud liked the place already. He thought that the roofscape would make a good black and white photograph, and he made up his mind to tell Coulson about the view from his room window, next time he saw him, which would probably be sometime during the evening.

He didn't know what to make of Coulson. Most of the people he knew led what he thought of as being rather transient lives out here on the margins of a habitable terrain. The teams of scientists and explorers, the hunters and fishermen, they were travellers who could never settle anywhere, and so were always passing through. And people like himself who had made travelling a living, unable to contemplate a life with a fixed routine and endless boundaries. Coulson came across as a man who liked his routine and might therefore find it difficult to adjust to the unpredictability of life out on the edge. Becaud made a mental note of his observations, imagining that Coulson was a man who could get irritable easily, if his plans were altered or delayed. Somehow a connection had been made, and an image of Hewitt popped into his mind. Must be something about photographers, he concluded inwardly.

The room was pleasantly warm, and pretty soon Becaud began to feel drowsy and certainly in no mood to go back outside and sort out the supplies. Instead he pulled out a book from his holdall, slumped heavily on the bed and started to read a few pages, before his early start caught up with him and his eyes gradually began to droop with the effort. He didn't fight it for long. Soon they were tight shut, and he was breathing heavily out of one corner of his mouth.

It was the noise of his book falling onto the floor, and the lamp crashing after it which started Becaud awake. Immediately filled with alarm, he was convinced that he had slept too long, and had missed out on getting the plane re-fuelled and the supplies bought, so it was with utter relief that when he grabbed hold of the little clock on his bedside table that he found that he had only been asleep for about twenty minutes. The clock was right on the edge of the table, and facing away from him, which he thought was strange, as he could have sworn that he left it in a more convenient position. He must have knocked the lamp somehow. It wasn't broken. He picked it up and put it back on the table. Becaud slumped back onto the pillow trying to shake off the deep sleep which was still clinging onto him, when he heard the sound of raised, excited voices in the vicinity of his window. The window was closed, so he couldn't hear what was being said, but the tone definitely told him that something was going on out there, perhaps an accident. He assumed it was something quite trivial, as he didn't know what passed for news in these parts, but then, just as he pulled himself up to a sitting position, he heard the sound of running footsteps in the corridor outside his room. His head now clear, he decided that he had to go and find out what was going on. He opened his door calmly, but started slightly when confronted with Coulson standing right outside and with his hand raised ready to knock on his door. His statuesque pose put them both off their guard and neither spoke for a second or two. The retired couple who had arrived earlier were pushing past Coulson, the woman grumbling at her husband to slow down as she couldn't keep up.

"We've got to get outside. They're evacuating the hotel, just to be on the safe side," said Coulson.

"Why? What's the problem?" said Becaud

"There's been an earthquake!" said the woman. "Didn't you feel it?" But she didn't wait for his reply. Instead she shuffled down the stairs, still in a panic about being left behind. He then looked at Coulson for an explanation.

"There's been a tremor – nothing much – but we've been told to leave the building in case there's any more." Becaud closed the door behind him and walked beside Coulson down the stairs and out through the open door to join the group of chattering guests now gathered outside the hotel.

"I was asleep. I guess that was what jolted my book and the lamp onto the floor and woke me up. Was it much?"

"No. It only lasted a few seconds. Didn't know what it was at the time. Just made me feel disoriented."

Becaud put his hands in his pockets and looked around at the scene, people joking nervously now that they knew they were OK.

"Might as well go down and pick up my stores, instead of hanging around here. Who knows what time they'll tell us to go back in. See you shortly."

He made a move to go but Coulson stepped after him saying he would go too if that was OK, and help him carry the stuff back. Becaud acquiesced. Wouldn't hurt to have an extra pair of hands. They walked the short distance to the store, passing groups of neighbours on every corner, the older residents confirming that they had never known anything like it before; the children all half hoping there'd be another one soon.

As they neared the store where they had a great view of the bay, with its clustered buildings and fishing boats that had been bobbing about gently in the slight spring swell, they became aware of a renewed level of activity down by the harbour, indicated by the sound of astonished voices. They looked over to where the noise was coming from and could see a group of men looking out to sea and pointing. One man had left the group and was running up the hill to the main part of town where the store was. Coulson was watching him, but Becaud was looking out to sea, wondering what had interested the group of fishermen. Not familiar with what it should look like, it took a moment for him to realise that the sea was behaving in an unusual way. The bay was full of standing waves, shuddering like a tank of water that has been struck on its side.

The grey waves were not particularly high but dense and agitated, the round incoming swell now trapped and splashing around angrily like the catch in a closing net. The smaller boats bobbed around quicker, while even the larger vessels lurched unpredictably, their rope masts tap-tapping incongruously as there was very little wind.

"Don't like the look of that," said Becaud screwing up his eyes to see better.

"What does it mean?" said Coulson. He was clearly worried. "Could it mean we could get a tidal wave?"

"No I don't think so. It's clearly to do with some sort of seismic activity – but if it were a tsunami the bay would be empty. No, but it could mean we're in for some more tremors. There were some quite recently in Greenland. Don't know if you heard about those. They were felt over at Humboldt, the research station I was supplying."

"Really? I never heard about those. Just how bad were they?"

"Not very. But you never know if we could be building up to something."

Coulson looked irritable. He clearly didn't want to hear that. By now everyone had got wind of what was happening down in the bay, and the owner of the store and all the other customers had come out to watch.

"Might as well go down to the harbour and get a closer look. What do you think, Ray? It's going to be some time before we get served here, that's for sure. Come on, let's go."

Reluctantly Coulson followed on behind Becaud who couldn't wait to be in the thick of things. Once down there at the Harbour they clumped noisily along the slatted wooden jetties getting as close as they could to the sea, but carefully going no nearer than the groups of seamen who were clustered all around fascinated by the phenomenon just as much as they were. The grey waves seemed to be vibrating, jelly like, pushing up and dropping, and going nowhere, and although they could of course only see the surface, the disturbance seemed to reach right down to the depths of the bay. One man, the skipper of a small packet, which was now dipping jerkily like a plastic duck in a bath tub, had served on a ship in the Far East and had seen the sea behave in this way before, but was exasperating his eager audience by not being able to remember whether it had happened before or after the accompanying earthquake.

While Becaud was engrossed in the old guy's telling of his story, Coulson slipped away from his side and began chatting to a middle aged man sitting alone in the doorway of what looked like a rundown shed, possibly a workroom or a store of some kind. The man was clearly Inuit, and Becaud wondered if that was what had drawn Coulson to go and talk to him. Perhaps he wanted some ethnic photographs. But five minutes later they were still deep in conversation, with no camera to be seen, and when he rejoined him, Coulson seemed just a tad too breezy.

Coulson took some pictures of the Harbour. Then, after about twenty minutes or so, they both decided that there was nothing more to see, and wandered back up to the store, then the Anchor, which by now had decided that it might as well let the guests back inside.

* * *

That night, Becaud pulled back the covers on the bed, then slid under the warm sandwich of sheets and blankets, pressing his face comfortably against the fresh smelling pillows. He was looking forward to a good night's sleep before another early start the next morning. He'd found a decent place to eat that evening, and he and Coulson had had a meal and a couple of beers, while they mulled over the day's events. Becaud thought it a little strange that he had made no mention whatsoever of his meeting with the Inuit man, even though he'd tried to steer the conversation round to it a couple of times.

And he was more disturbed than he thought he would be about the thought of more tremors occurring during the night. He wondered if something bigger might be building up, but he didn't really know enough about it to be sure if his fears were justified. He thought of the Carters, and Amy James. They'd be sure to know, he reasoned, and made up his mind to call them when he got back to base. He'd liked the little town well enough when he first arrived, but now there seemed to be a bad atmosphere about this place. A sense that something no good was hanging around the corner. He'd had an OK evening out with Ray Coulson, too, but there was something about the man that he couldn't warm to, that he just couldn't fathom.

Coulson, retired to his room quite buoyant after the strangely exciting events of the day had at least broken into the boredom and frustration that he'd been feeling whilst waiting for his flight out of Frobisher. He sat up in bed for almost half an hour studying his map of the area of Greenland where he now thought that the crevasse might be located. He pencilled in the locations where the Inuit man had told him the reported sightings were, brought back to Frobisher by the returning hunting parties. It didn't help him much. The sightings varied in their positions by so much as to be useless, little better than guesswork. The pencilled crosses on his map went in a snaking line from one coast to another, defying all credibility. His mood dulled as he realised that he hadn't really got what he wanted. So where some of the reports overlapped, he marked as the most likely sites, but without any great hopes that they were accurate – or even truthful. It occurred to him that he might have been told what he wanted to hear by the old guy, keen to get his hands on the twenty dollars that Coulson had offered him for information. He had been too eager, when he should have played it cool. But at least he'd got something to go on. Wished he'd been able to get more out of that photographer guy in London.

Growing tired, he folded the map and put it away carefully in the pocket of his jacket, hanging over the chair with the rest of his clothes. He clicked off his light and dozed off straightaway, unexpectedly sleeping soundly until the next morning, whilst Becaud, who normally had no trouble sleeping, drifted and fidgeted his way through a night of restless dreams that made no sense, and tired him mentally with their meaningless repetition. At about 3am he got up to go to the bathroom, then sat on the edge of the bed for a couple of minutes. He got himself a glass of water and took a couple of painkillers to help him sleep. Exhaustion eventually got the better of his anxiety and he drifted off, slipping into the dead silence of the town's empty streets, which seamlessly enveloped his consciousness, as it had done with every other silent household.

CHAPTER SIX

London

"Amy's late," said Zoe, feeling her previous calmness ebb away as the minutes ticked by. She was setting the table for dinner in the large open plan dining area of their Georgian London home. It sounded grander than it was. Bought in a very poor state of repair twenty years ago, before house prices doubled and re-doubled, Zoe and Oliver had been trying to modernise and repair it ever since, but had spent so much time travelling abroad for their work, had never really got on top of the project. Which had been a bit of a reprieve for the house, as things had turned out. The peeling, smoke-stained exterior still could boast its original sash windows and heavy front door, when most others in the street had succumbed to white plastic. Zoe had tried to feel superior to her neighbours about that, but couldn't in all honesty as she knew she would have done the same back in the eighties had she had the money. At least now the ground floor was all but done. The old cramped kitchen had been knocked through into the dining room; the breakfast room and an old pantry all combining to make a spacious area with a view into the garden framed by the original French windows. The kitchen units were light and modern set against white dairy tiles and glass splashbacks. The floor was black at Oliver's insistence as he hated anything that smacked of fake rusticity, or nostalgia for something that had never existed in the first place. It was a confident, quite masculine look, very much in keeping with the pared-down style of the early Georgian period. "This kitchen," he ranted to the astonished young salesman, "would have had a flitch of bacon, or some game hanging from the ceiling, and they'd have been lucky to have had a mat of hessian on the floor, not bunches of bloody dried flowers everywhere."

"But this is a period property, sir. I thought you wanted something that goes with it."

"Style goes anywhere," Oliver had said pompously.

And Zoe had to agree. She loved the comfortable simplicity of the room, that didn't tire you out with over-worked detail. She placed the cutlery all together on a folded napkin to the right of the charger plate and set the wine glasses at the top right-hand corner of each place mat, carefully wiping each glass on a cloth before she set it down. Being quite happy to eat out of foil trays when she was working in the field, she liked to give some time to make mealtimes more sociable when she was at home.

Amy should have been here by now, and Zoe was getting worried had that she might not make it at all. To make matters worse, Amy wouldn't be able to let them know if her mobile wasn't functioning. If! Zoe could hardly remember last time she had managed to make a call, and that broke up so much she might as well not have bothered. The best most people hoped for now was a network busy message – at least that indicated that there was someone, somewhere getting through. She was a bit concerned about Amy, travelling alone, too, especially after her own unpleasant brush with the street fight, last week. Oliver looked worried, too, although Zoe suspected he was more concerned about the failure of the steak to turn up, than he was about Amy's personal safety. Hewitt had already arrived just a little too early, but realising his mistake as soon as he saw they weren't ready, he wandered outside into the garden to enjoy the mild, spring evening and to read his newspaper out on the terrace.

Zoe rearranged the plates slightly to make sure they looked straight. She then put the salt and pepper in the middle of the table, followed by an opened bottle of decent Californian red nearer to where Oliver would be sitting so that he could preside over the wine pouring. He'd been saving this bottle of Fetzer until they had something special to go with it. And now Zoe thought that they'd probably be sitting down to peas, chips and mushrooms instead. Good thing she'd thought to make the sticky toffee puddings. At least no-one would leave her table hungry. It was difficult to know how long to wait before deciding to go ahead and start the meal, so she called out to her husband to ask his advice. Getting no answer, she walked over to the French windows and looked out into the soft evening light with its long shadows and deep contrasts.

A high stone wall formed a corner with the house wall, which created a courtyard area, its uneven stone flags and tangled planting holding the sun's warmth for as long as possible until the cool of the evening set in. A metal table and some chairs were set on what was the only piece of level paving. The large green umbrella remained furled around its pole as it was still only really comfortable sitting outside if one were actually in the sun. Zoe had often thought of restoring the old crumbling chimney set in the garden wall and now choked up with weeds. It would make a fantastic focal point for the courtyard, but Oliver said it was beyond repair. Originally built to keep tender plants protected from damaging early frosts, Zoe imagined the first owner of her house, sparing some precious coals or logs to set his chimney going when a late spring frost would threaten his carefully nurtured peach tree, or an exotic and tender specimen plant brought back from one of his travels. Of course, she'd made all this up; in fact she knew nothing about the original owner of the house, and all her good intentions to research the history of the property had come to nothing. But her theory was at least historically plausible, there being great competition at the time for a gentleman to provide exotic fruits and out of season vegetables for his table to impress his less green-fingered friends. Somehow, she felt she owed it to the garden, and its mythical former owner to tend it, but she never had the time to do it.

Zoe noticed that Oliver had gone out into the garden to join Hewitt, and the two of them were sitting, chatting affably as she walked over to speak to them. They looked round at her approach, already knowing what she was going to say.

"How long do you think we should wait, before we start?" said Zoe, clearly meaning that she thought they had waited long enough already.

"Start what exactly," said Oliver sarcastically. "If Amy doesn't show, we've got fuck-all to start."

Zoe sighed good humouredly, but already could feel disaster wafting over her attempt to host dinner. She wondered when to tell Oliver that the only peas she could get were tinned ones, as the freezers were all down at the local supermarket. Mischievously, she decided to let him find out in his own good time.

"Oh, I'd give it another half hour – what do you think Lawrence?" said Oliver.

"OK by me," said Hewitt, hardly able to do anything else but agree.

So Zoe went back inside the house and passed the time by sorting through their collection of CDs to play while they were having their meal. *Zero Seven* was always a good choice. Contemporary, but not intrusive, it would be good ambient music while everyone was talking. Looking back to when she bought it, she could still see the look of 'I'm not with her' on her son's face when she walked up to the counter at the Virgin Megastore and confidently asked for *After the Fall* by

Oh Seven. Well at least having teenagers keeps you up to date, she reasoned.

The three children had all gone out with friends for the evening. Tomorrow the house would be clamouring with their noise and activity. The hall would be full of their friends' kicked-off shoes and the kitchen would be like a coffee bar. It would bring the place alive again, just the way she liked it.

She looked along the rack, thumbing the plastic spines as she did so. What else? One album wouldn't be enough. Either *Portishead* or *Morcheeba* would be good, she thought. Lawrence probably wouldn't have heard of them anyway, and wouldn't like any of it. *Morcheeba*, definitely, but not *Portishead*. *Nightmares on Wax* would be better. Or both. For God's sake, choose. So she chose them all. Once they got talking they would probably be in for a long evening.

There was a ring on the doorbell. Zoe went to answer it and Amy bustled into the hallway carrying her precious package triumphantly.

"Sorry I'm a bit late, guys. Took me longer to cycle here than I thought. Must be a bit out of condition."

"Well at least you're here now," said Zoe, leading through from the hall into the kitchen. "We were getting a bit worried about you."

"You mean Oliver was worried about his dinner, more like," Amy said. Zoe didn't bother to contradict her.

"And, look at this! A jar of béarnaise from M&S. I thought I'd surprise you."

"Well, we've got a bit of a surprise for you too," said Zoe.

Amy looked at her trying in vain to guess what that could be. Then, right on cue, Oliver walked in, followed by Lawrence Hewitt.

It took a moment for Amy to recognise Hewitt, dressed now in a pair of well fitting jeans and a short-sleeved linen shirt. He looked strangely out of context, as though he'd got no right to be in anything but a bulky anorak, and fleecy hat. She noticed that he flushed slightly as he greeted her, making her suddenly aware that she must look very different to him, too.

"Lawrence! Hi…" said Amy, trailing off. She threw a puzzled look at Zoe and Oliver, who were smiling amiably and giving nothing away.

"Like your new top," said Zoe, stepping in before Amy could betray her disappointment at seeing their unexpected guest right there in front of her.

"Thanks," she said. "Got it yesterday. Do you think it's OK?"

"Yes. It's really nice," said Zoe.

Amy had lost quite a bit of weight whilst on the Arctic trip, and she'd been determined not to pile it all back on again this time, on her return. It suited her. So did the reddy-brown finely striped trousers she was wearing. They made her look taller, and more fashionable, Zoe noted.

"So how are you Lawrence? Did you manage to get your book published after all?" said Amy to Hewitt, now able to gather her thoughts.

"Well, I've got a compilation of pictures accepted by my publisher eventually, I'm pleased to say. But it's not out yet. Could be August. Not that that is a problem.

Right now, the way things are here in London, I don't think I'd be selling many copies anyway. People have other things on their minds at the moment. Might even be better to wait until autumn and catch the Christmas market."

"Talking of the situation here in London, Ames, you didn't know that Lawrence was a hero – I must tell you, as I know he won't mention it himself."

Amy looked intrigued, while Zoe told her friend of how Lawrence had intervened and saved her from the mob, which is what led to them all having dinner together this evening.

"Well, who would have believed it!" said Amy. Then she suddenly regretted saying it as it sounded so rude. Especially as Oliver laughed out loud, making it sound more than ever like a put-down. She knew she should have apologised, but she hesitated for a bit too long, and then the moment was gone.

Dinner was ready.

They sat down at the table eagerly, their appetites whetted by the good smells wafting over from the kitchen. Oliver carefully poured everyone's wine, in turn, making sure he didn't spill any by turning the bottle round as he filled the glasses. They each took a sip from their glasses, then began their meal.

"I've heard that power is about to be restored in three more districts of London by tonight, and that quite a few more who are only on for a few hours a day, will be back on permanently by next week," said Amy.

"About bloody time," said Oliver.

"Oh come on, Oliver, they're doing their best. This solar storm was phenomenal. No-one could have predicted that."

"They could. And did. Although not the exact timing, we knew it could happen sometime. The authorities should have been better prepared."

"These tremors are a bit of a worry, though, wouldn't you say." Hewitt took a sip of his wine, then went on. "I keep hearing reports that they are still happening, especially in the Greenland area, and there was one apparently on Baffin Island, according to Five Live Radio, only a few days ago. What do you think that's all about then?" It was Zoe who replied.

"Really? I must have missed that. Baffin Island. I bet we'd have felt that in Humboldt had we still been there, don't you think, Oliver? You know, sometimes, I've heard you do get increased seismic activity when there are times of increased solar events. We're not sure if there's a direct correlation, between the incidences or if it's more of a coincidence."

"I think coincidence is much over-rated as an explanation," said Oliver. "And as a phenomenon in itself things are rarely as coincidental as they seem."

"Oh, I agree!" said Zoe. "Perhaps I should have said, simultaneous events with a non-causal relationship."

"Perhaps not," said Oliver, getting her sarcasm. Zoe continued.

"There is often an underlying network of reasons or factors which make two unlikely events happening together, much more likely, whether we are talking about the physical world or the human social world."

"So, if I bump into an old friend who I haven't seen in twenty years since we were at school together, say at a football match, and I said that it was a remarkable coincidence, I take it you wouldn't agree," said Hewitt.

Zoe was warming to her theme. "Well, only in the sense that the two things don't have a causal relationship, and are therefore literally a 'co-incidence.' People often mistake coincidence for randomness, which then increases their sense of incredulity. But, take the underlying factors. You like football and so does he. And as friends you probably follow the same team – you come from the same town obviously as you were at school together. Also as you attending a specific event, the time factor is narrowed down to a couple of hours when you will be in the vicinity of your friend."

"But surely the odds would still be thousands to one against that I would actually bump into him."

"Yes absolutely. But then if you think of all the other attendees at all the other matches, who haven't bumped into a school friend in all the time they've been attending – well it's going to happen sometime. Looked at that way, instead of being a remote possibility that you will meet your friend on one occasion, when you go to football, it now seems statistically much more likely."

"Even very unlikely things happen all the time," said Amy. "After all it's fifty million to one against winning the National Lottery jackpot. Yet somebody wins it every week."

"Exactly…..and when you don't take all these enabling factors into account, it's tempting to see supernatural, superstitious or deterministic reasons why things
happen. Which, to me, is quite unnecessary."

"*It was meant to be*, is surely one of the most irritating phrases in the English language," said Oliver,
before anyone could annoy him by using it.

Zoe came back into the conversation now that
Oliver had made his point. "As you well know, I was
using the term coincidence to mean that there might
not be a causal relationship between the events that
we are witnessing at the moment. What you are talking about with the example of your football match, is
probability. A slightly different concept. But still relevant in the sense that people often bestow improbable events with a supernatural dimension, like fate,
or destiny, instead of thinking that it could have happened sometime anyway, and for perfectly ordinary
reasons. As soon as a pattern starts to arise we should
be looking for the underlying causes, but as scientists
we shouldn't be assuming them, or as is more likely in
this case, dismissing them."

"Take the Bermuda Triangle, for instance," said
Oliver. "As soon as it was discovered that it was an area
with an unusually large number of ships and aeroplanes
going missing, then there were people who jumped to
the conclusion that that they had to have been abducted
by aliens. Why aliens for God's sake? There was even a
whole new folklore invented around the loss and sub-
sequent return of Flight 19, which people were only to
quick to believe as the truth. Whereas explaining the

phenomenon as a statistical blip or because of bad weather in the area just isn't exiting enough."

"Well, those last two explanations didn't really work," said Hewitt. "Which is why a void was left by the scientists and rationalists of this world which could be filled with these fanciful explanations."

"That's true," Amy said. "Science doesn't always want to get involved with supernatural or weird stuff for the very good reason that it can end up feeding this nonsense rather than proving it doesn't exist. By engaging in debates with people who want to air their strange beliefs one can give them the oxygen of publicity."

"But sometimes that can be to science's detriment," Zoe said. "We have since discovered, due to the research into climate change, the phenomenon of methane clathrates."

Oliver and Amy nodded. Hewitt asked what the heck they were talking about.

"We have found that there are huge deposits of frozen methane locked into the sediment under the oceans, held there by the huge pressure and the cold temperatures down there. But occasionally the structure that holds them in place shatters – if the temperature rises for example – then the methane becomes gaseous once more and bubbles up to the surface of the ocean and into the atmosphere. This is important to climate scientists as it explains why, in pre-historic times there was a huge increase in methane levels that led to a mass extinction event."

"But what about the Bermuda Triangle?" Hewitt said.

"It seems that there are deposits of methane in the vicinity of the Triangle. If one of these lets go it fills the sea with gas bubbles, lowering the density of the water. Any ship caught in this would sink like a stone. No-one would stand a chance as lifeboats and people in life jackets would sink too. Horrible when you think about it," Zoe said.

"Doesn't explain the missing planes though, does it?" Hewitt said.

"Actually, it does. Any planes flying through a methane gas cloud would be in trouble. No need for aliens after all."

Hewitt laughed. "And it just goes to show that there was an anomaly there in Bermuda, after all, even though at first no-one could explain it."

"Absolutely. And it just goes to show that we scientists shouldn't be too dismissive."

"Like that massive fissure that we saw," said Hewitt.

He took the opportunity to turn the conversation in the direction that he wanted it to go. Oliver paused and took another mouthful of the fillet steak, he heard what Hewitt was saying but didn't take him up on it straightaway. He thought he'd better tread carefully, as this was the whole point of the evening, at least as far as Hewitt was concerned. Trouble was, he couldn't see why everyone was so interested in what he thought was a curiosity, but no more than that.

"Fantastic meal, by the way, Amy, said Oliver. "Don't know what you had to do to get this, but we owe you one." Amy nodded, gratified, but didn't rise to his innuendo. He then turned to address Hewitt. "I've been scouring the relevant websites at Isaac Newton for any updates, on but can't seem to see any mention of the fissure, not even blogs, although I didn't have time to check out all the sites."

"Your computers OK then?" said Hewitt.

"Mostly, but very slow. We shut down as soon as the solar storm hit. Trouble is we keep losing the power supply, like everyone else, so it tends to be only priority users who get on-line now."

"Could you get me some time, do you think?" said Amy, seizing her opportunity. "My office never gets priority."

Oliver knew he'd been cornered by Amy, and that he'd be accused of blatant favouritism by the rest of the department. But he knew that there was no way that he could say no, as he chewed through another mouthful of the delicious steak. He'd just have to take the flak.

Hewitt, clearly interested, steered the conversation once more back to the crevasse.

"Well, you know you not the only one interested in that crack in the ice. I expect Zoe's told you all about my encounter with a chap called Ray Coulson who I met by chance, shall we say, at the publisher's. What did you make of that?"

"I expect he saw a good photo-opportunity. Official government work sounds like a bit of a blag to me," said Oliver. "If it was all top secret, he wouldn't have mentioned it at all, would he?"

"What's all this?" said Amy, not knowing anything about it. "Who else is interested in our crevasse?" She had become suddenly alert, in contrast to Hewitt who looked rather crushed by Oliver's dismissal of his findings. After all it was that that had got him over for dinner. Hewitt had believed that Oliver would want to take up his findings and investigate further, but it seemed now that he'd scarcely given them a second thought.

He gave Amy only the briefest of explanations; now unwilling to sound enthusiastic about something that had got such a cool reception, and was beginning to feel a tad stupid for raising the issue in the first place. He didn't want to sound like some sort of conspiracy theorist, so he prepared to let the matter drop. But Amy persisted, until she was up to speed with the subject. And, like Hewitt, there was something about the story that made her suspicious.

"No, listen, you two, I think that Lawrence is onto something, here. That fissure that we saw was massive – very deep too. It isn't surprising that it's arousing interest, especially at the moment as it's difficult to get at the facts."

"And, of course, we don't know how big it actually is do we? It stretched for miles as far as we could see, but if we'd followed it, it could have gone on for miles longer – we just don't know," said Hewitt.

Oliver looked unimpressed, and was looking towards his wife, believing that she would be sharing his point of view. Quite often they unconsciously mirrored each other's body language, especially in a social situation; but instead she was staring hard at her plate, her forehead showing the tension of her concentration. She took a slow deliberate sip of her drink, then squeezed her bottom lip between her thumb and forefinger, still unaware that anyone had noticed her. The table had now gone quiet as the other two were finishing off their meal, carefully scraping up the last bit of béarnaise with a piece of the fillet, until Zoe spoke, tentatively, drawing in everyone's attention to what she had to say.

"You know, I think that Lawrence *is* onto something here....I'm not sure, what exactly at the moment. But what we saw out there has got somebody interested.... and I think we should be, too." Hewitt leaned forward in his seat, giving her his whole attention. Zoe continued. "Since we saw that crevasse, impressive as it was, we've all being playing it down. Saying that it couldn't be that deep; the instruments weren't working; it's maybe not uncommon in that part of the world; it might not have actually been any longer than the bit we saw, and so on. But now I'm thinking, hey, if we were to enter a period of abrupt climate change, then isn't this exactly the sort of extraordinary phenomenon that we should be keeping a look out for. Something on a bigger scale altogether than what we would normally see. Perhaps taken with many other factors it could be instrumental in either indicating, or even causing, the climate to convulse."

Oliver was staring at her incredulously. He could see where she was coming from, but he could also see her staring into the deep abyss of career suicide, if she started to make headline grabbing claims that catastrophic climate change could be imminent.

She rounded on him when he raised his objections to her.

"It's like saying that you don't believe in the truth of your subject!" she said with passion. "You can believe in the validity of the concept of Abrupt Climate Change, but only if it happens safely in the fantasy worlds of the distant past or the future. We know that we humans have the capacity to believe that utterly improbable events can happen if cloaked in the sort of otherness that a different point in time creates. But this is science. And if it could happen 150 million years ago, or 10 thousand years ago, it could happen next week."

"Shit," said Oliver, taking a large swallow of his wine, and emptying his glass. "That's told me."

Hewitt would have looked uncomfortable at one time but now knew them well enough to know that this was normal. Amy kept looking at Zoe.

"So what do you think this means?" said Amy.

"I think..." she replied. "Well, we all know that the sea ice is melting rapidly, and that land ice is thinning. But I think that this could, if we are right, mark some sort of a turning point, where something so big is occurring, then there will be no chance of the natural balance ever being able to reassert itself. Which is what we're all hoping for, let's face it. There are some climatologists who believe that the increased heat in the weather system will cause increased levels of precipitation. In the Arctic this would fall as snow, thereby building up the ice sheets again. This would increase the albedo effect, the amount of sunlight reflected back into space, which, in turn would lead to a cooling down, in that region. But if we lose a huge amount of land ice in one go, we would then get a stepped increase in the amount of heat soaked up by the Earth. The albedo effect would be very much reduced. We could even get an albedo flip...."

"A what?" said Hewitt."

"An albedo flip is when white ice becomes dark water – or land – or vice-versa. Suddenly the amount of sunlight reflected back into space becomes either very much increased or reduced. This could be the trigger mechanism needed to allow multiple dynamic feedbacks which could cause rapid climate change.

"But even a large crack in the ice sheet isn't going to make that much difference to the rate of its melting, surely," said Oliver. "In that area it's still 9000 ft thick."

"No – that's not how I see it," said Zoe. "We know that in certain circumstances that meltwater can seep down deep into the ice until you can get supercooled but still liquid water running between the ice sheet and the bedrock that it is resting on, lubricating the ice sheet so that it can shift en masse. What we've got here is an obvious weak spot, perhaps a line of debris on the surface, warming and melting the ice beneath it as it soaks up the warmth of the sun."

"But what would have made it crack open on that scale?" said Hewitt. "It seemed to appear from nowhere. It was just running all across the landscape like the San Andreas Fault. I got some great pictures of that, by the way, if anyone wants to see them."

Amy looked at Hewitt, who tailed off, aware that he had said something wrong, but not sure what. Conscious that they all experts in their fields and held a lot of common ground, not only in their work but in their attitudes and opinions, too, he felt like something of an outsider again, and very much the layman. Not that he disagreed with most of what they said; he just wasn't familiar with it. And they obviously weren't interested in seeing his pictures of the San Andreas Fault.

"My God! Why didn't we spot this before, Lawrence?" He started, noticeably.

"San Andreas. Don't you see? It's the tremors," said Amy, still looking at him. He immediately saw what she was trying to say, and with some relief he realised that he'd said nothing wrong, in fact, quite the opposite.

"The tremors have caused the ice to split open," said Zoe, immediately getting Amy's drift and articulating it. "There must have been a weak spot there, probably due to the irregular melting that we just talked about. The ground has shifted slightly leaving a chasm where the ice sheet has sheered off right down to the bedrock."

"But exactly how significant is that?" said Hewitt. "In a volcanic area won't quakes cause crevasses sometimes?"

"Well, yes, absolutely. But it's a bit surprising that what appear to be quite minor tremors could have caused such a massive fissure to have occurred. If only we had more information," said Zoe. "It's so frustrating to be stuck here, postulating, when what we need is some hard data."

"No wonder somebody sent this guy, Coulson up there to get some pictures. At least if somebody knows where, and how big this thing is, it gives you some parameters for investigation," said Oliver.

"We need to get back there," Zoe said.

"Impossible," said Oliver. "We've got months of work lined up from the last trip. If that's not completed we won't get backing for another one."

"I know darling, but we have to go. This could be so important. We need to think of a way. We must have more to go on than what we've got so far. Lawrence, is it possible for you to contact Coulson again somehow?"

"I don't see how. Anyway I would imagine he'll be there in Greenland by now. He said he was setting off as soon as possible. Not that he'd tell *me* anything anyway. Personally I thought he was a poor choice to send on a mission like that. Knew damn-all about intelligence gathering, if you ask me. And he doesn't know where to begin looking, for a start."

"Neither do we," said Zoe.

"Well I could make a better stab at it than he ever could," said Hewitt. I've got a good sense of direction and a photographic memory. If anybody could find that thing again, I think I could."

Because Hewitt said that in a neutral, matter of fact way, that was his normal, understated delivery, it didn't sound like a boast, and everyone took his claim at face value. But nevertheless it was an astonishing thing to say. Zoe's mind was now racing, trying to think of a way to sell this project to their sponsors. It would have to be that. There was no time to get anyone else on board. In her eyes it was the perfect follow-up to the work that they had been doing for the last three months, but with the added impetus that what they might discover could have major implications for the developed world. The best plan might be to say that they needed an extra month to complete their work, especially with the disruption that had met them on their return from Greenland, after the solar storm. Oliver agreed, but could still see too many obstacles for them to get the project off the ground within the timescale required. Amy, on the other hand, appeared suddenly radiant, and was already, mentally packing her bags.

"Lawrence, we need you on board," said Amy flatly.

"Well I don't know about that," he said. "I don't know how I could arrange it – it's all a bit sudden."

"Oh come on – be spontaneous for once. You're only waiting around here for your book to come out. And you said yourself you were the only one who could locate this thing. You have to come, or there's no point in the rest of us going is there?"

"We have to go darling," said Zoe to Oliver. I'm sure we can get this fixed. Maybe you could set up some meetings by the end of this week. We have to try. This is something big. I'm convinced of it. And I tell you what. I'll get in touch with Dorothy Redmires. If anyone can pull a few strings, she can."

"Good idea," said Oliver. "We'll need all the help we can get."

"It would mean me losing out on a lot of freelance work," said Hewitt, coming back to Amy's question.

"It would be so worth it," Amy said, persistently. "And I've just had another idea. I ought to contact Phil. If only I could get onto your computer." She looked at Oliver. "I could email him. We'll need a plane, obviously, and he will have the local knowledge to complement what Lawrence remembers. I'll also try to find out if he heard anything more about the cre-vasse since we left – you never know what he could have found out."

At this Hewitt's eyes darkened slightly, unnoticed by the group around the table. He was glad when Oliver chipped in. "Oh, this sounds like an excuse to go and see that bloody pilot again, if you ask me."

Amy flushed slightly, and was about to say something in reply, but Zoe stood up and began to clear the totally empty plates away.

"Ames? Could you help me get the puddings brought in? Sorry everyone you've been waiting ages. Darling, would you open another bottle, we seem to have emptied that one."

She stacked up the plates neatly and put the knives and forks on top before carrying the pile through to the kitchen area. The CD they had been listening to had finished. In the background the *Morcheeba* album had begun to play.

"Got any more *Zero Seven*," said Hewitt. "I liked their first album best."

Zoe looked at him for a few moments, taking him in with new eyes. She'd not expected him to say that.

Amy and Zoe passed around the steaming plates of light sponge, sticky with rich, sweet dates, and drizzled over with glossy toffee sauce. Everyone's glass was topped up and the table fell silent as everyone concentrated on enjoying their food. The recent shortages had made people appreciative of luxuries like this. Zoe flashed back to what Lawrence had said to her in the café, about them never getting back to normal. What if it were true that the good life was over; that environmental pressures were going to spoil the party; and that future generations could be in for a very hard time? She felt cold at the thought of it.

If there were major, and very serious events taking place in the Arctic region, they would need to get moving fast, in order to have any chance of understanding what was happening, and to attempt do something about it. And it was Lawrence's alertness that had drawn their attention to what might be happening up there, when they had all been guilty of sleepwalking. Perhaps they had all been to close to the situation to see what was unfolding in front of them; Hewitt had given them a new perspective – made them take a fresh look.

Now it was up to them to do something about it.

CHAPTER SEVEN

The Peak District, England

Zoe stepped onto the train just about to pull out of St Pancras station, lugging her case heavily behind her, and already wishing that she could have taken the car instead, as her bag slipped off her shoulder once more, jolting her arm and making her even more irritable. The train was already full and as she squeezed pointlessly further up into the crowded carriage, her case knocking against her ankles, she realised that there was absolutely no chance whatsoever of her finding a seat, this side of Leicester. Glancing around, she saw that everyone else who did this trip regularly already knew this as most of them were engrossed in a newspaper or a book, and weren't even looking for a spare seat. So she stood where she was and squashed up against the side of the aisle as best she could, tucking her case in as far as it would go. She wondered whether to try sitting on it, but as no-one else was doing that she decided not to, as it would be too embarrassing having to get up again if people stared at her, or she wasn't comfortable.

Zoe was heading up north to Sheffield on a hastily arranged trip to stay with Dorothy Redmires, her old tutor from university days. Dorothy knew everyone one needed to know in order to get things done. It was a desperate attempt to kick-start their stalled efforts to organise a return trip to Humboldt, which up to now had been met with either cool indifference or outright hostility. Funding for projects was always tight, and competition was always intense for any sponsorship. Oliver had got nowhere with his efforts, despite stressing the possible urgency and seriousness of the situation they had stumbled upon. It seemed that no-one would take on board the implications of what they discovered. He was reluctant to say too much at this stage about his worst fears, in case someone else took up their theories and got a rival expedition started before he did. Or worse; their ideas, still untested, could be rubbished by vested interests, until no serious sponsor would touch them.

So Zoe, wracking her brains for a solution, rang her former tutor and asked if she could come and stay for a few days. It seemed like an imposition to ring up out of the blue, but they'd stayed friends for a few years after she had graduated, and Zoe felt that it wasn't unreasonable to ask. She hadn't seen her in eighteen years but Dorothy, now in semi-retirement, said 'yes, of course,' with the sort of matter-of-fact, what's to discuss manner, as though she were arranging a tutorial, which made Zoe feel instantly that she'd done the right thing.

She was due to arrive in Sheffield at 11:38. What chance she had of being on time she had no idea, as disruption to services, though lessening, was still widespread. She had emailed Dorothy before leaving the house to tell her what time she would be getting in, as her phone probably still wouldn't work. She then planned to take a bus out to Castleton in the Peak District where Dorothy now lived, but instead got the blunt reply. "I'll be there at 12:30. You're bound to be late."

It would be strange, going back. She couldn't wait to see it again. Sheffield. Funny how when one sees a familiar place one hasn't visited in years, it isn't the changes that hit you; it's the sameness. When memory suddenly merges once more with reality the familiarity comes rushing back, only everything looks smaller than one remembered it. And more vivid.

But there would be bound to be changes too. Sheffield was a severely depressed area when she left, after finishing her degree. Now, at last, prosperity was breathing some life back into the city, she thought with genuine pleasure. She also hoped that the solar storm hadn't knocked back that hard-earned recovery too much. The economic changes that had convulsed the industrial north in the 80s were only just being recovered from. But that would be nothing compared to the ecological chaos that had hovered over her generation for the last thirty years or so, and now seemed to be about to engulf them in an icy wave of climatic upheaval. Or, perhaps, literally, in an icy wave.

Zoe wished that people would stop banging on about 'the planet,' as though it was something detached, out there and objectified, when what we need to be saving was ourselves from a return to subsistence living. Modern, comfortable conditions were the result of a complex interwoven society which could all too easily become unravelled if circumstances conspired, as the solar storm had demonstrated in such a timely way. Most people still thought of the current disruption as a problem with an end in sight, like a traffic jam that will all be clear in the morning. Zoe didn't. She could see it all slipping away and future generations seeing this as the point at which it all started to go wrong.

As she hoped, once they stopped at Leicester Station several people left the train, including a couple who had been sitting down quite close to where Zoe was leaning. Looking quickly around her to make sure that she didn't seem to be pushing in, she took the seat and pulled her case in after her as best she could. A youngish man in a business suit sat down beside her, and immediately opened up a laptop and started his days work without a sideways glance. They lurched forwards once more and in a few moments they had re-established the slow rhythm of the swaying carriages ticking over the rails as they gathered speed, its pulse quickening as the landscape rolled past.

Inside the carriage it was fairly quiet, except for the anonymous noises of a commuter train; the periodic rustle of a newspaper, the turning of a page, the soft tap-tapping of a keyboard. So when Zoe's mobile rang inside her handbag she started, but didn't realise that it was hers for a moment, until barely perceptibly, heads began to turn towards her. She fished in the bag and brought out her phone now loudly ringing around the carriage. She pressed the button when she saw that it was Oliver calling her, and held the phone to her ear. His voice was loud and clear. It was the first time there had been a proper connection in weeks, in fact, since the storm.

"Hi," she said self-consciously, knowing that everyone around her was listening.

Oliver got to the point straight away in case they lost the signal. He could not persuade anyone to give them any more funding, and had now run out of options. Zoe's visit to Dorothy Redmires was their last hope, as far as he could see, of getting anything organised. He wished her luck, and then quickly rang off. Zoe looked up and around at the other passengers to see nearly everyone pouring over their own phones to see if theirs was working again, texting and sending, now with a real hope of getting through. A few bleeps confirmed that this was in fact the case, and a rustle of excitement swept palpably through the carriage.

Irrationally Oliver's call made Zoe feel less hopeful about the outcome of her visit to Dorothy's than before. It suddenly seemed that she was wasting everyone's time; not feeling confident anymore that they were even on to something. She rehearsed in her mind the conversation she was going to have with Dorothy explaining about the ice crevasse, and she squirmed at the thought of being dismissed out of hand. Sharp and incisive, if her case sounded flawed or inconclusive Dorothy would straightaway have it in shreds. On the other hand, if she could convince her old tutor that their fears were well grounded, she could have no better ally.

* * *

Back at the university, Amy James walked into Oliver's staffroom, and found him sitting in his workspace which was not exactly an office, but still a separate area slightly removed from the other members of the department. The murmur of voices was punctuated every now and then with a too-loud remark and a replying laugh, the background filled in by the continuous tapping of the computer keyboards. At every other step there was the un-compelling waft of vending machine coffee, and a just eaten bag of crisps left behind an unpleasantly sweaty oniony smell. Its owner screwed up the empty packet and lobbed it across the staffroom, where it hit the rim of the waste paper basket, bounced off and fell onto the floor. Someone glared at him when he made no move to pick it up, but as this had no effect, she decided not to pursue it and got back to her notes.

No-one looked up as Amy pushed her way through the desks, that is, until she sat down in Oliver Carter's chair, after he stood up to make way for her. She immediately began to send an email to Phil Becaud. She typed quickly, knowing that she had no business being there, especially as this was not official university business, but they all knew at once what she was doing, and the looks that began to pass between them, soon were directed at her back. She ignored all of it, including the now audible remarks. Oliver muttered something about priority clearance that didn't fool anyone even for a nano-second, and gave rise to a cloud of indeterminate scorn, thickening the atmosphere. Oliver turned away, but could still hear someone say that the Head of Faculty was going to hear about this. Too bad. Oliver wasn't going to let the urgency of what was happening in Greenland get bogged down in office politics.

* * *

Phil Becaud woke up and pulled himself out of the wrinkled sheets, the light still hanging outside the window of his house in Angmagssalic, despite the blind being closed and the curtains drawn. It had felt like dawn forever, and too tired to get up and too restless to sleep properly, he was glad that at last the long night was over, and that it was a reasonable time to get up and put some coffee on. The long hours of daylight made it hard for him to get a good sleeping pattern together. He tried to be disciplined and go to bed at set times, but it never worked out in practice. He'd been brought up to think that when you were burning daylight you should be up and doing something useful, and that, to his dad, meant doing something profitable. It's amazing that however much one grows away from one's upbringing, and sometimes rightly so, in order that you can become your own person, some things stick. Last night Becaud poured over his new Cessna manuals until two o'clock in the morning unaware that it was anything like that late, as he'd catnapped the previous afternoon.

At five o'clock he woke to hear a familiar voice repeating his call sign on his radio.

"Mike-delta-tango – are you receiving me?" He rose out of bed and shuffled through to his kitchen where he sat down at the small table before picking up the hand set and acknowledged his caller. Reception was poor, leaving no room for conversation. It was his friend Joe Kristenssen telling him that he and his party had completed their mission and would be heading home at once. He double-checked the co-ordinates they'd given him the day before to make sure he'd got them down correctly – it seemed that they'd found the crevasse. They'd done it. But his congratulations went unheard as the signal faded out too soon. He went back to bed and dozed a little more.

The clock now read six-thirty. He walked barefoot into the kitchen feeling irritable, and pushed the kettle under the tap whilst flicking on the radio with his other hand. A familiar voice rattled out the news, but Becaud heard none of it till the weather report punctured his consciousness, when suddenly the words ceased to be background noise and took shape and meaning inside his head. Overcast, light winds, dry. Becaud clocked what he needed to know as he sat down at the kitchen table and put the pot of coffee down in front of him. He opened up his laptop and booted it up. It seemed strange, but the room always seemed empty, a bit dead, without it. Been living alone too long, maybe. He was just finishing off his first cup, and was thinking about putting on some bacon, when he opened up his emails and noticed that there was one from Amy James. Barely perceptibly, his eyes widened when he saw the name, as already a whole bunch of possibilities ran through his mind as to the likely contents.

He read it through.

Amyjames8@inc.co.org

Hi Phil.

Hope you are OK. Things are still pretty disrupted here in the UK, but getting back to normal slowly. How's the new plane? Not crash-landed it yet then? We are trying to organise a return trip to Angmagssalic if we can get the funding, as Zoe thinks that the crevasse you showed us is of more importance than we first realised. Oliver thinks so too. And guess what? We've met up again with, would you believe, Lawrence Hewitt, who would actually be coming with us, as part of our team. We need his expertise as a photographer – but he thinks he can locate the fissure again, because of his fantastic memory or something.

What do you think? Have you any further info on it? You must have heard something. Obviously we'll need you to fly us out there if we do return.

Will update you when we know more.

Amy.

He read it through again.

His immediate sense of relief, that the email's tone was bright and friendly, but nothing more, gave way to a slight feeling of disappointment, that she didn't seem to be missing him more, and his mood became if anything a touch more edgy. Out of sight, out of mind, he guessed, his nettled ego telling him that a few weeks ago his main attraction was that he was the only guy around. He dropped a couple of thick rashers into a frying pan, and poured himself another cup of coffee. And what's with this fucking crevasse, he ranted inwardly. Reports of were getting back to Angmagssalic increasingly from Inuit hunters who had seen it for themselves. And then there was Coulson. Becaud had used his contacts to set him up with a hunting party, led by Joe, who has taken him into the snowfields to see it for himself. Looked like he might have found it too, from what Joe had said over the radio, but even amongst local people no-one could agree on its location, some arguing that its position was hundreds of kilometres from where others had sighted it. It was obvious that there were lots of these cracks in the ice, especially at this time of year. Couldn't see what everyone was getting worked up about. The bacon smelt so good as it browned in the pan that Becaud decided to drop in a couple of eggs, too.

He'd reply to the email later. Right now he had to get dressed and deliver some mail to, and pick up some equipment from a party of Belgian scientists over at Humboldt, a large consignment that he would not have been able to take in one trip with his old plane. Still buoyed up by the novelty of flying the new plane, he couldn't wait to get started. His mood improved the more he thought about climbing into the cockpit of the Cessna. The weather was OK, and he had the added bonus of being able to fly up through the cloud and leave everyone else behind while he had his very own sunny morning. He always enjoyed the trip over to the Humboldt Station. He'd decided to stay over as there was a big consignment to load up and take over to the main airport at Nuuk.

In twenty minutes he was out of the house, his flying jacket flapping open. He dipped his head to drop a scarf casually around his neck, breathing in the sharp cold air, letting the door snap shut noisily behind him. And Becaud was still out twenty-four hours later, making it impossible for him to hear his phone which was desperately ringing over and over on the kitchen table next to his laptop, till finally it stopped and its echo died away to nothing. It had been Joe Kristenssen calling.

The empty house stayed silent until his return.

* * *

"It's very good of you to put me up at such short notice," said Zoe when they reached the door of Dorothy Redmires house in Castleton. The house was built of grey stone, its split stone roof looking mellow in the early summer sun. The wide, rather squat front door welcomed them in, as they struggled with the cases over the shallow, worn step. Zoe said how much she liked the house Dorothy made a dismissive reply, then pointed at the floor.

"Mind the rug, or you'll trip. Put the cases over there if you like, next to the hall table. We'll take them upstairs later. I expect you'd like some tea. Go and make yourself at home in the sitting room, while I go and make us a cup."

Zoe left the case and bag where Dorothy suggested, then went through to the sitting room and sank down on the sofa.

The inside of the house, after the stuffy journey, was comfortably cool and smelt pleasantly of fresh fabric and books. The décor was unfussy, but homely. The plants and objects sat easily in their allotted places without looking contrived. A sculpture on the side table drew Zoe over to take a closer look. It was a seated figure, about ten inches high, made out of bent lengths of copper tubing, now nicely covered with a chalky green patina. Its elongated L-shape was satisfying in its simplicity. Zoe was looking at it when Dorothy walked in with the tray.

"Got that in Crete from a local artist. Couldn't resist it. Don't know how I got it home. Looked like a semi-automatic weapon on the x-ray when my case went through."

Zoe laughed. "I really like it," she said walking over to the sofa and picking up the cup waiting for her. She drank her tea readily, so without prompting, Dorothy topped up her cup, and did the same with her own. Zoe felt at home immediately.

"So you'd been up in Greenland, gathering ice-core data for your research into abrupt climate change, when you saw this huge break in the ice."

"That's about it," said Zoe. Knowing that the grilling was about to begin.

"You must have spent months with all that drilling equipment so that could get down to the bedrock, and then it all opens up before you – you could have abseiled down and taken a few samples."

Zoe smiled and took another sip of tea. Dorothy continued, "What was different about this particular crevasse? Something has made you think that it was."

"Well I suppose it was the sheer scale of it. It reminded me of the computer simulations I've seen of the towering cliffs that marked the edge of the retreating ice sheet at the end of the last glacial. We'd never seen anything like it before. It stretched over to the horizon and seemed to go on forever. And the depth. It was sheer, straight down – at least we think it was if the altimeter was correct."

"Now let me get this straight. You talk about the vastness of this thing – but you only saw it to the horizon – four miles away – that's large but not unprecedented. And you don't know for sure how deep it was, as your instruments were malfunctioning; which is why you were there in the first place, and why you can't find the thing again."

Dorothy was cutting through her case like Zoe knew she would.

"But there seemed to be other things going on at the same time that, well, somehow all seemed strange – like the smell..."

"The smell!"

"We could smell something for a few days whilst we were at Humboldt. In fact we all started to feel ill. Then there were the tremors. We eventually put it down to a fissure eruption in Iceland giving off toxic gas. So the most likely explanation is that activity in the area triggered off this break in the ice."

"The tremors weren't very strong. Would they have caused such a huge chasm? Presuming it really is that big. Remember that at the moment you are extrapolating about its size from what you've seen. You don't know yet for sure."

"That's why we need to get back and get some hard data."

"That's all very well. But at the moment I don't see that you've got a clear hypothesis for you to work on. This feature is clearly very interesting, but you have got to know what you are looking for. Do you, for example think that this has any bearing on your study of abrupt climate change? If not, leave it to the geologists, who I'm sure can't wait to get up there and see it for themselves."

Zoe felt frustrated. This was so what she didn't want to hear. She decided to say what she really thought, even though Oliver had warned her not to say anything that could be damaging to her career, she at least felt free to talk in front of her old tutor.

"I think that this has not just a bearing on the theories of ACC. I actually think that we are witnessing the events that could bring about a drastic change. Sometimes it only takes a few years for the turning point to be reached. I think we've got one here. We are at a tipping point. Only I don't know which way we are tipping; into an ice age or a runaway greenhouse effect. But I think we are at that stage – right now."

Dorothy looked at her for several long minutes, while she turned over in her mind what she had just been presented with.

"I see," was all she said at last.

The really scary thing was that Dorothy hadn't blown her idea out of the water. It was almost as though she had wanted someone to tell her that it wasn't true and not to worry. But she didn't. Dorothy was taking her seriously, so now she had to follow through.

"Sometimes quite radical things happen in the climate as the result of a range of mostly cyclical factors, or sometimes one-off events. Like, for example in 542 AD there seemed to be some sort of cataclysmic event that caused atrocious weather and widespread disruption and hardship throughout the world. Scientific evidence tells us clearly that this was the case, even though we don't know for certain what caused it. It was probably what caused the so-called Dark Ages in this country. But it didn't cause a major change in direction of the inter-glacial. Only a blip. I'm not sure why I think that this crevasse is so important but I do. The trouble is, now that I'm telling you all this, it sounds unconvincing. No wonder we can't get any further funding."

She sighed, and put her empty cup back on its saucer. "I've done detailed analysis of the conditions surrounding ACC events for years. I've been trying to understand just what makes the climate flip, so that we could hope to predict it. I feel here that I'm seeing the pattern, but can't quite explain it yet – which is why I need more evidence. Even with that, it's like the guys who try to predict tornadoes, or earthquakes, it's never going to be easy, one hundred percent accurate, or even that much in advance. I'm worried now that I've actually tried to explain all this, that it all sounds a bit feeble."

"No, it doesn't sound feeble. You could just be 'Thin-Slicing'. Or, the other alternative is that you could be completely mistaken."

"What the hell is 'Thin-Slicing'?" said Zoe, ignoring the bit about her being mistaken.

"Oh I read it in a book about how we make decisions. Pop psychology, of course, and I don't mean that as a put down. Absolutely fascinating. Too much information can get in the way, apparently, of being able to make a good decision; makes us to and fro between all the different factors until we become paralysed with indecision, or talk ourselves out of what we know to be the right answer. It's not intuition, or anything woolly like that. What happens is that all the years of expertise can enable one to shortcut to the right answer, by condensing the relevant facts, and recognising these as a sort of signature. The trick seems to be to have the confidence to recognise the signature, and not to get misguided by information that eats at your decision. That's why I asked you first what you thought when you saw your crevasse. You saw an ice cliff in your mind, like the one that must have towered above Creswell Crags here in Derbyshire. That marked the end of the last glacial. So what you've seen leaves the signature that dramatic climate change is imminent. There was an early settlement there, you know, at Cresswell Crags."

Zoe shuffled uncomfortably, believing that Dorothy was about to wonder off the point.

"It's not enough, though, is it?" said Zoe. "What we think isn't enough to convince anyone."

"On the contrary, Zoe. I think you could be on to something. You clearly are aware that something is, well, different about this feature that you've discovered. And that in itself should be sounding warning bells, even if at this moment you can't explain what this difference is, or what the implications are. You have spent a great deal of time out there on your research trips, and you do know what is normal and could be viewed as a sort of control. We all know that the ice is retreating. That isn't the subject of debate anymore, so presumably you have factored that in."

"Yes of course, no-one doubts that anymore. But a slow melting of the ice caps could give us the chance to adapt to the new conditions, or even to try to ameliorate the effects of climate change. But if we are faced with a rapid and long term change, we might not be able to cope with its effects. Our way of life could be changed in a way that none of us would want."

"Exactly. And although the normal thing to do would be to set up a project to research your hypothesis, you don't feel that you can do that in this case. You say you can't get funding. Have you tried the environmental charities? I thought they'd have been interested in this one."

"I'm sure they would be. The trouble is, we just don't have the time to get anything fixed up. It could take months to organise, even if they were willing."

"Yes, I'm sure you're right," Dorothy said. "Yet it's absolutely essential that we do what we can to avoid environmental catastrophe at all costs. It's not about saving the planet – we are just an irritant on its surface – and it will keep on going with or without us. It's our way of life that's important. We need to preserve the hard-won freedoms of Western democracy, where civilised, Enlightenment values, have enabled the sciences and the arts to press forward, and where liberal social values have made life a kinder and more decent place for ordinary people to flourish. There are too many people around who would relish an opportunity to take power if society seemed to be breaking down. Too many self-serving interest groups who can't wait to re-establish a reactionary social code, where women's rights, gay rights, ethnic equality and so on, are sent back to the dark ages. Picking on minorities is such a cheap way to get cohesion in any elitist group, don't you think? They want to tell us all what to do, what to think and how to live our lives. And it's no way to improve the nation's morals. I think authoritarianism saps personal responsibility, and has caused untold private misery for those of us who don't fit in."

She stopped. Full of passion, she had lost none of her old spark.

"There should be more people like you, Dot," said Zoe. "You speak for what I might call the Uneasy Majority. People who are uneasy about what is happening to their society, but haven't got a voice because of their very nature in not having a big cause or an axe to grind. We seem to be swayed by people who can shout the loudest, not necessarily the ones who are right. I'm surprised you aren't out there campaigning for somebody."

"As you know, I've never been a joiner. I like my independence too much. You lose a bit of yourself when you become part of an organisation. Always seem to be run by busy-bodies who want to own people, I always think. Recruiting the like-minded can become an end in itself. Never been much of a one for the numbers game myself. It doesn't validate anything."

"How do you mean?" said Zoe.

"Well. Put it this way. Imagine that I believe the Earth to be round, and that I am the only one who believes that to be the case. Even if I live in a society where all the other five billion people believe that it is flat, then the Earth is still round. Evidence is far more crucial than popularity, when it comes to knowing things. That is the foundation for getting at the truth, and when, or if, new evidence comes along we must be prepared to be wrong and to move on."

Dorothy had spent her life teaching her students to think for themselves, and to look squarely at the evidence. Zoe felt that she now had a lot to live up to.

"OK. Well let's hope I'm wrong about this one anyway," said Zoe. "But all this doesn't actually get me any closer to going there. What I really need to ask you is can you help us get this project organised? I thought you might still have some influence..."

"Not any more. You see, there's nothing I can do for any of my old contacts in return nowadays.... no, there's nothing doing there." Zoe's face fell, but Dorothy continued brightly. "Anyway, we don't need them."

Zoe looked at Dorothy questioningly. What on earth did she mean?

"I'm going to sponsor you myself."

Zoe still looked at the older woman. She was totally wrong-footed, and didn't know what to say. Dorothy took advantage of Zoe's need to collect her thoughts to press on and tell her of her proposal, without any interruptions.

"I can do it through the magazine I edit, for women in science. We could feature your trip, photos, interviews the lot, then publish the paper when it's complete and ready for peer review. If what you say is true we could generate a lot of interest for the story on-line. We could do blogs, twitters and so on. If we really get a good response and you find that there is mileage in your theory we could even get a spin-off TV programme. At least for academic circles, and, you never know, we could even get it networked."

Zoe was reeling. She was being offered the funding she needed but it seemed that to get it she would have to agree to the publicity. Oliver's warning words were still sounding in her head, so she knew that she would have to speak to him first, before she agreed to anything.

"And I don't envy you descending down into that crevasse, from the sound of things you'll need all your old climbing skills just to get down there and take a look."

Zoe went cold. Suddenly she knew without any doubt that that was what she was going to have to do. Otherwise what was the point of going? Somehow she had avoided thinking of that aspect of the trip before.

"You'll be fine," said Dorothy, clearly not wanting to get bogged down in detail now that she could visualise a major and exciting project boosting the circulation of her magazine.

That night, Zoe lay in bed, looking at the unfamiliar shapes around her in the faint light that the thin, drawn curtains didn't quite shut out. The thick stone walls of the old house created an inner stillness and deep quiet that wrapped around the comfortable bed with its huge pillows and soft sheets. This would be so perfect in winter she thought. She was used to total quiet after three months in Humboldt, but that was a vast, open silence that stretched out further than one could see. This was altogether more personal, with the outside kept firmly beyond the boundaries of the house wall. The lack of distraction only made her thoughts ring round her head with greater clarity than usual, when she couldn't get off to sleep. Somehow during the course of the day she realised that it was understood that she'd agreed to be sponsored by Dorothy, and that they should be leaving in three weeks time if all went to plan. This Lawrence chap, whoever he was, would be perfect to photograph the expedition, and could video it as well, in case they needed the footage for a production, Dorothy enthused. And Zoe would have to do a video diary each day via webcam, to generate interest amongst the students. Zoe's chaotic thoughts ricocheted between seeing herself lying at the bottom of a crevasse or appearing on *Richard and Judy* plugging their spin-off programme. She longed for a routine morning in the lab, slicing up ice cores once more, but now this thing was set in motion, she knew that she would have to go along with it. Oliver had agreed. He just insisted that they made no extravagant claims that could be damaging to their reputations. The amazing thing for Zoe was her realisation that Dorothy respected *her* professional judgement. That, if nothing else made her feel that she had come of age.

Eventually, too tired to hold on to her conscious thoughts any longer, she drifted off, and slept undisturbed until the next morning.

CHAPTER EIGHT

Dorothy Redmires had already been on the phone for a full half hour when Zoe shuffled down the stairs and found her way into the kitchen. The sun was slanting through the window, lighting up a north facing corner of the room that would normally have been in shade throughout the winter months. The morning light, though mellow, was quite distinct from the evening sun that would later be creeping into this side of the house as the long days of midsummer were stretching out before them, only weeks away. It was fresh and full of expectation; waiting for the still unopened day to reveal its contents to them.

On the thick shelves which were set into the corner of the room was a row of well used cookery books, each with bits of paper sticking out from between the pages, and a selection of store catalogues kept randomly from various years and seasons. It wasn't over-tidy, but not cluttered either. The kitchen walls were painted a deep midnight blue, a confident and slightly more urban antidote to the bucolic look of the rest of the room.

Under the bottom shelf, on the work top, there was a stack of rustic serving bowls which had a folded pile of receipts and bills thrown in, together with a couple of paper clips, and some loose change; the minutiae of domestic life that Zoe had never thought of in relation to her old tutor before.

Zoe had rested so well in the deep, comfortable mattress which made her own back home seem mean and fidgety in comparison, that she was finding it hard to shake off the muffled sleepiness that hung around her head despite the pressing issues of the day which were waiting for her attention. Dorothy gestured to the pot of tea that was on the scrubbed wooden table in front of her, and silently, Zoe sat down, pulled a mug towards her and tipped in some milk, finishing off with the strong brown tea. She took a sip.

Dorothy finished her conversation and put down the phone.

"Morning, Dot. Slept like, I don't know, like when I was a child or something. What do they put in the air up here?"

Dorothy smiled.

"Whatever it is, I expect it's given you an appetite, too. Would you like some breakfast?"

"Please. Anything. I'm not fussy."

Dorothy got up from the table and went over to the fridge to get some things out for breakfast. She then went over to the cooker, taking her tea with her to drink as she fixed them both something to eat.

"I've been sorting things out, as you probably have already guessed. I've agreed a sum which should cover your basic expenses, with the co-owner of my magazine. Frankly, it's not much, so your budget will be tight, but it will have to do. Also I should be able to get you some climbing equipment on loan from a nearby outdoor centre in return for some free publicity. And maybe even some provisions. And I've stressed that we're on a very short time scale – that could be a problem – but the people at the outdoor centre are very good, and said they'd do what they could. You need to get an inventory together and let them know as soon as possible what you will need. The stuff that you will need to hire from them, they'll let you have free of charge, as long as you place an order with them for any other equipment you will need – and give them some photos for a promotional spot in the local paper."

Zoe nodded, knowing that she wasn't expected to say anything. Dorothy moved back to the table and put two plates of bacon and tomatoes down, followed by a rack of crisp, white toast, a dish of butter and a pot of marmalade for afterwards. She then remembered the salt and pepper pots from the cupboard, and got those before sitting down at the table to join Zoe.

"I'll make a fresh pot of coffee, soon, if you like," she said, getting started on the bacon. "I love a good breakfast. And I'll write you out a cheque when we've done here. Then it's up to you to organise the rest."

Zoe didn't know quite how it had happened, but it was all organised. Dorothy was animated with enthusiasm for the project, and was clearly not prepared to hear any negativity on the subject. They were going back to Greenland. Zoe's misgivings of the night before had given way, in the new mood of the morning, to a sense of, not really enthusiasm, more to one of urgency. She ate the cooked breakfast with the sort of appetite one normally associates with being on holiday. She then took a slice of the toast and spread it first with butter, then a thick layer of marmalade. Dorothy placed a cafetiere of delicious smelling coffee on the table, and helped herself to some of the toast. Zoe pulled out her phone from her bag, eager to tell Oliver that their trip was sorted. He'd be well impressed. Just wished she could see his face when she told him. She waited patiently while the dialling tone purred, plunging the coffee with her free hand, then pouring out a cup out for each of them.

"Thanks," said Dorothy as she rustled open her newspaper. Zoe got no answer from Oliver.

"Guess he must still be in the shower."

Dorothy took no notice, as she was engrossed in the paper.

"Oh, great!" she said smiling broadly. "Chesterfield won last night."

"Did they?" Zoe said.

"Two-one against Forest. It's so good to end the season on a high." Zoe nodded politely, not really understanding the significance of the result, then picked up the phone and tried Oliver again. She held the phone to her ear while Dorothy read out the match report, not caring in the slightest that Zoe wasn't really listening to her, but was staring vacantly at her coffee cup whilst waiting for him to answer.

As the tone purred in her ear, a strange thing happened. Her cup started to rattle slightly, as though a lorry was bumping past. But it was dead quiet, and they weren't that near the road. Then the ripples appeared. Rings of turbulence on the surface. Her mind raced back to when they were at Humboldt and the same thing had happened. She felt a bit light-headed too. This time she knew immediately what was happening.

"Dot! We're getting a tremor!"

The older woman looked over her newspaper, her mind still full of the injury-time winner that her team had inflicted on their old rivals, and not really hearing what she had said. Zoe looked around the room, trying to judge the quickest way out, but decided against it, instead shouting to her astonished tutor. "Quick! Get down. Under here!"

She pulled Dorothy out of her chair, and bundled her under the sturdy kitchen table, crouching down after her, hoping like crazy that this wasn't a false alarm.

"What the fuck are we doing under here?" said Dorothy, unfazed and looking around the room expectantly. "I didn't feel anything."

"I definitely felt a tremor, and I saw ripples in my coffee," said Zoe defensively.

"Oh, I must check mine," said Dorothy, ironically. She shuffled to the edge of the table so that she could reach up and get her cup and have the rest of it in peace.

She took a drink then put her cup down on the stone floor whilst watching it intensely. It was flat calm. "I've seen the Japanese do this," she said brightly. "They have to practise what to do in an earthquake." She then reached up and got the newspaper. "How long do you think we should stay...?"

Zoe was irritated. She could see that Dorothy was not taking this, or her, seriously. There was a loud crash on the kitchen floor. One of Dorothy's rustic bowls had shuffled to the edge of the work top and had smashed on the tiles.

"Oh no! I got that one from Santorini."

"How appropriate," said Zoe, sarcastically.

"I'll have to get up, I feel a bit dizzy, crouched down here."

"You're not dizzy. It's the ground that's moving. This is definitely a quake. Stay down."

Dorothy still appeared unconvinced. But a second later the rest of the ceramic bowls tumbled onto the floor, breaking, and scattering shards all over the two women. Then a loud rumble occurred. Far in the distance, or very deep in the earth. It was impossible to get its direction, so it seemed to be everywhere at once. All encompassing and deeply threatening. They couldn't tell whether it got louder or it just intensified, but they had the feeling that something was approaching fast. Zoe had been there before and knew that it would all be over in a second. She felt that she'd got the measure of it, when the unthinkable happened. The stone tiles on the kitchen floor started to show hairline cracks in the mortar joins. As they were crouched down on the floor she could see this quite distinctly and she pointed it out to Dorothy. The floor then rose up like a wave passing through and sank away again, the tiles broken, dust bursting up from the ground below.

Dorothy caught her head on the underside of the table so hard that she felt the shock pass through her whole body. She inadvertently shrieked in shock and pain as she held her head with her hands to shield herself from any further injury. The table tilted, tipping the contents all around them, the cups and plates breaking, glass scattering, tea and coffee spilling everywhere. Zoe, too, cried out, now terrified for their safety. Noises came from other parts of the house, where furniture was falling over and things were breaking. The house groaned and cracked under the stress. Zoe hoped the house was sturdy enough to withstand the pressures it was being subject to. The heavy stone roof and thick walls, though offering protection at the moment, would be lethal if they failed under the strain. A drawer fell out onto the floor, followed by a ringing metallic crash as a cupboard door swung open and a collection of stainless steel saucepans bounced down to land amongst the rest of the debris. The ceramic sink slipped out of its housing and hung down at an odd angle. On the wall a huge wide crack had appeared reaching right through, from the tiles behind the sink to the cornice, where it then changed direction, and ran diagonally across the ceiling, down the other wall and stopped at the door jamb. The two women clung together, wincing again when they heard a crash as the chimney pot hit the path outside the kitchen window; and still the floor zig-zagged underneath their hands and knees. A wide crack opened up under one of the table legs, and Zoe felt her own leg drop down, so that she lurched over onto her side. It was a weird sensation feeling the dry, gritty subsoil on her bare skin. Panic overwhelmed her as she thought, irrationally, that she was going to be swallowed up, even though, in fact, the gash was only about nine inches deep. The table tipped over, leaving them feeling dangerously exposed as dust shook down from the distressed ceiling.

"We have to go," said Zoe struggling to her feet, and pulling Dorothy behind her. They made for the door with the single purpose of getting out, not even looking round to see what the rest of the house was like. They crunched over the shards of broken ceramics and what seemed like thin triangles of glass, now strewn all over the kitchen floor. In contrast, everything looked completely normal in the hall except for a large lamp that had edged its way to the edge of the table it was set on. Dorothy stopped and automatically reached out to put it back when Zoe pushed her on towards the exit.

"There's no time for that – we have to get the door open – come on!"

Dorothy unlocked the front door and slid back the bolt. They both tugged at it. It had wedged as the door frame had buckled under the strain, but fortunately not by too much, the iron-hard oak at last proving its worth. They tugged again, the door squeaked, gave a little, and eventually they got it open. They then hurried away from the building, only looking around when they were safely away from its walls.

Dorothy stood there in the garden, a thin trickle of blood running down her temple, making a track in the powdery dirt that she was now covered in. She was shaking slightly.

Zoe was suddenly aware of background noise rising all around her like a radio suddenly being switched on at full volume. It was like a door being opened on her perceptions, her hearing, it seemed, previously only focussed on what was a danger to her, now blasted on once more. Afterwards, when she tried to recall the episode, she remembered that everything had appeared to happen in slow motion, and even the deep rumble, she felt as much as heard, as all her unnecessary senses had shut down, leaving her free to concentrate on essentials. They stood there, dazed for some moments, looking at one another. Zoe taking a deep breath as she tried to get it together, and think what to do next.

There were anxiety-ridden voices calling to each other in the distance, car and house alarms were blaring pointlessly. Already they could hear the sound of approaching sirens as the emergency services were being summoned by people who'd more presence of mind than they had.

"I never thought to call anyone," said Dorothy. "It just never entered my head."

"It's OK," said Zoe. "Neither did I."

"The house. There's so much damage. What are we going to do? Oh my God, look at that!" At the end of the garden there had opened up a huge crack, which had swallowed up part of the fence, and had left the old plum tree leaning at an angle of nearly forty-five degrees, its straggly roots, covered with clods of soil, half exposed to the air.

"I must phone Oliver," said Zoe, realising that if he heard about the quake before she could get through to him he would be worried. They would have been alerted to the tremor straightaway at Isaac Newton, and it was possible that someone from the department would have let Oliver know of it already. "It's all gone quiet now, I wonder if I could go back in and get my phone."

"It might not be safe," said Dorothy. "I'm sure your husband wouldn't want you to kill yourself trying to phone him when you've survived the earthquake unharmed."

She seemed to be getting back to her old matter-of-fact self. Zoe had to admit that she had a point, and was trying to think of what to do next when she saw Dorothy calmly walk back into the house, emerging a few minutes later with Zoe's handbag, her case from upstairs and her shoes which she had left in the hall. Zoe stared at her.

"You shouldn't have done that, Dorothy. You just told me not to go and get myself killed, and then you go and do something that could have put yourself in danger."

"Well, you have to get back to London today. Once I've called the emergency services and my insurance company, they'll probably seal this place off till a surveyor can inspect the damage. It could take weeks till this place is habitable – I won't be the only one, after all, whose house needs repairing. And you need to get this expedition organised. If this isn't a wake up call telling us that something big is going on, then I don't know what is. You need to find out what's happening. I can deal with this here. I'm just a bit wobbly at the moment. I only hope the damage is all superficial. I'd really hate to see this old place knocked down."

Dorothy appeared brisk, but Zoe could tell, that she was deeply worried. Her breath was slightly short, and her voice betrayed a faint tremulousness, despite her attempt to appear in control.

Zoe texted Oliver. *Slight tremor. Don't worry, I'm fine.* She didn't want to talk just yet or she'd get upset. She sent off the message, then turned to Dorothy.

"I can't just head out and leave you here, by yourself. Look at the state you're in."

"I won't be by myself. I have some good friends here and over in Sheffield if I need any help."

Zoe still wasn't convinced, as she stood there on the damp early morning grass, still wearing her dust covered pyjamas. Her bare feet felt cool and clammy, and she felt glad of the warming rays of the sun, gently helping her to resist the urge to shiver. A voice then called over to them, making them both turn towards the direction of the garden gate, to see who was there.

"My God. Look at your two!" said a middle-aged man walking up the path straight towards the two women. He was obviously local as he used the Derbyshire 'your two' for 'you two.' "You OK, duck?" he said with genuine concern to Dorothy, when he noticed the cut on her head. She nodded. "Hang on," he said, "I'll get you some help."

He hurried back down the path, now with a purpose, returning some ten minutes later followed into the garden by two young paramedics in their conspicuous green uniforms.

They sat Dorothy down on an old garden chair, and quickly but gently cleaned her cut, which by now was really painful, chatting easily as they did so. It needed a couple of stitches, and was very swollen and bruised. The man, who had introduced himself as Les, filled them in on what had happened all over the town. How he knew so much in such short a time was a marvel to Zoe, who questioned him closely about the situation. It seemed that most of the damage in the village was superficial, except for the George Hotel which had a bad crack down the gable wall. Some people had been hurt, he said, but he'd heard of no serious casualties, or loss of life. Zoe, getting impatient to make a move, asked him if he thought she would be able to get to Sheffield, to catch her train.

"I'm worried that the roads might be blocked or something. I was due to get a train back down to London today, and I'm just hoping that this hasn't messed things up just as they were getting back to normal. What do you think, Les?"

"You need to get to Sheffield station? No problem. I'll take you if you need a lift, like. I'll get t'car out."

"Really? But are you sure you don't mind? I'd be really grateful if you could, Les. You see I was expecting Dot, here to take me, but, I'm not certain that she ought to drive...."

"Don't worry about it, duck. Your friend can't drive like that. I'll take you – you go and get yoursen ready, while I fetch t'car round."

Without waiting to hear any more he marched down the path, glad to be doing something useful, and already talking to three more people who were gathering outside their gate to find out what news they could. It seemed that Dorothy's house was one of the worst hit in the village, and already neighbours were starting to congregate outside on the pavement to see if they could get more information. Then someone spotted the fallen tree, and two's and three's began to wander over the garden to have a look at it. The novelty of the situation had overridden the normal boundaries which existed, and defined people's behaviour. A couple of hours ago the same people who were tramping around the uprooted tree, pulling away at the fences, then looking at and feeling the walls of the house inspecting the damage, would never have dreamt of even walking up the path without being asked to do so. And Dorothy was OK about it. She rather liked the warmth and naturalness of their curiosity, and was now getting quite a crowd around her as she told and retold the way the kitchen floor had risen up in a wave, and almost swallowed them up in the process.

A patrol car pulled up outside the house, attracted by the small crowd hanging around there. The two officers got out of the car and made their way through the groups of people, blocking the pavement and spilling onto the road.

"This your house, love?" said one of the policemen to Dorothy, seeing that she was the centre of attention. "Better make sure no-one goes in there, till we're sure it's safe."

He looked around, knowingly at the group of blokes now earnestly discussing the fallen tree, sensing that they might be tempted to go inside and take a look for themselves. "No-one can go in there!" he said loudly. The officer was just about to get back to Dorothy to hear her account of events, when something caught his attention. Everyone froze, like a film on pause, as a noise from deep inside the house, more of a thud than a crack, could be heard as an old beam gave way under the stress. Dorothy looked round at the house. Everyone else looked at her. The group of men ran clear of the house in a split second.

The chimney stack melted into liquid rubble and disappeared through the roof of the old house, the broken split stones following in after it, leaving a gaping hole like a wound in the mellow roof; dust rising up like smoke from the hollow of a collapsed volcano. There were some shrieks and men's voices shouting. Dorothy glanced away, too shocked and distressed to stare like everyone else was now doing. The policemen took charge.

"Everyone, get back now!"

The women took care of Dorothy, and hustled her away. The men glanced shiftily at each other, not needing to say anything, knowing how close they'd come to being under tons of broken stone.

Zoe stood on the lawn, feeling mentally unable to keep up with events. Her heart was pounding with shock, and she was still standing there in her pyjamas. Her phone rang, its familiar tone starting to re-focus her mind as she fumbled with the buttons to answer it.

"You OK, darling?" said Oliver. He hadn't yet heard from Isaac Newton about the tremor, but had got her text and had noticed her missed call.

"Yes, fine," she said, unable to believe that she'd said something so bland and improbable, in answer to his question. She then explained to him what had happened, as briefly as she could, constantly afraid that the line would break up. She was determined to stay strong even though she could feel her face tighten up as she spoke. He didn't press her. He could tell by her voice that she was shaken up. Then almost as an after thought, she remembered that she hadn't told him that the expedition was all arranged and she'd got the funding sorted out. He listened hardly able to take it in.

"You mean it's all organised?"

"Yes."

"But how, so soon?"

"I can't explain now – my bare feet are all muddy, I'm standing here in my pyjamas, and the house is on the point of collapse..." Zoe heard her voice go tight as her eyes filled up and felt hot. The emotion hit her quite without warning. She wished Oliver was with her. Taking a slow breath, she continued.

"What am I going to do now?" said Zoe.

"I should get dressed if I were you, sweetheart. No wonder there's a crowd in the garden."

She took that as a compliment. It was just the right thing to say. He sounded reassuring and confident, although in truth was he was feeling overwhelming relief that she was safe. He so wished he was with her.

"But I feel awful leaving Dot like this."

"Not at all. She'll be OK. You have to leave, Zo. There's nothing you can do that her other friends and neighbours aren't doing already, by the sounds of things. And you need to get back as quickly as you can. There could have been other quakes in different parts of the country, and we must expect more after shocks anywhere over the next few days, which could disrupt travel. You mustn't wait until problems appear before you set off. If we've got the funding, we really must get moving. That's still OK, isn't it?

"Oh yes. Dorothy had already authorised payment, so that will still go ahead."

"There's something else as well, Zo. Can't explain properly on the phone – I'll fill you in when you get back – but we got an email back from Phil Becaud. Found something when he was flying over the ice sheet, not good news at all, I'm afraid."

Zoe wanted to press him for more detail, but she knew this wasn't the right time, and anyway, the connection was starting to break up, making a proper conversation impossible. She rounded off their call, trying to work out what on earth Oliver could mean by bad news. Feeling disturbed and frustrated that she had to wait before hearing the full tale, she now had to concentrate on the immediate business of getting herself organised. She knew both Oliver and Dorothy were right in insisting that she go back to London. There was nothing she could do by remaining here in Derbyshire. So, in a quiet part of the garden, she slipped into a pair of jeans and a tee-shirt, scraped a brush through her matted, dusty hair and forced her damp feet into the shoes that had been retrieved for her.

Dorothy was about to be taken to a neighbours house, where she could rest and be looked after, until she could make her own arrangements. Without fuss, she wished Zoe a safe journey home.

"Don't forget the video diary," Dorothy said.

Zoe promised that she would remember, and then stooped down, picked up her bag and slung it over her shoulder. Then she turned and hurried off to find Les so that she could begin the first leg of her journey back home.

* * *

Castleton wasn't the only place that had been hit by earthquake activity that morning. Reports were pouring into Isaac Newton College from all over the country of both felt and recorded earthquakes from as far afield as Dartmouth and Fort William. The main run seemed to be through the west coast of England and Scotland, through a spine of activity in the West Midlands, Lancashire, the Lakes and further north. The east of the country was not spared despite its history of being a quieter area, seismologically. Folkestone took a big hit comparatively speaking of four-point two, and Market Rasen broke its record five-point-five of February 2008, when it was the epicentre of a quake that was felt all over the UK, by reaching five-point-seven this time around.

The M5, east of Dudley, had to be closed to traffic when a crack, large enough to fit a tyre in, opened up. The crack snaked its way north for a seventeen mile stretch on the nearside lane before veering off to the east, less visible once it crossed fields and ditches, more obvious when it hit the built up suburbs on the approach to Dudley.

Ambleside in the Lake District was rocked for a few juddering seconds but suffered little in the way of damage to the sturdy stone properties in the area. However, it caused a landslide which fell into Windermere causing a wave to race across the water and flood some nearby houses.

In Widnes a lot of houses were damaged by the quakes. In one street every house was effected in some way, most with old fashioned chimney pots now lying smashed on the pavements, but some were more mortally wounded with cracks in the walls, and sagging roofs spilling slates onto the ground below. Two people were killed when a chimney stack fell through their roof and into their bedroom.

Oliver had felt nothing in his London home, or at least he had thought that at the time. But after Zoe had rung, he went back over in his mind exactly what he was doing when she said the tremor had hit Castleton. He remembered hearing a radiator rattle slightly while he was in the shower, and couldn't think at the time why it was doing that. Now he knew.

He could see the reports coming in on Breakfast TV and realised that Zoe's experience was not an isolated incident. Quakes in Britain were not that unusual, but normally they were slight and isolated incidents. More of a curiosity than anything else. This was different and he was impatient to get into work as quickly as he could to get the lowdown from Seismology. He tipped some cereal into a bowl and splashed on some milk whilst flicking the switch on the kettle. He needed some coffee before he could get out of the house. At the same time he collected some papers that he needed for today's seminars and stuffed them into his bag. He sat for a moment spooning the cereal into his mouth when the TV channel switched from the round-the- region split screen coverage and went over to Downing Street. There was a reporter standing in the road outside the Prime Minister's door, filling in whilst waiting for it to open, which it duly did. David Fellows walked in a deliberately relaxed way over to the guy with the mic and smiled a greeting. He waited for the first question, then ignored it like the seasoned politician he was, and proceeded to say what he had already decided to. The tremors were not as rare as we all thought in the UK and there was absolutely nothing to worry about. The emergency services were doing a fantastic job and no he wouldn't be cancelling his trip to the Middle East. There was a huddle of reporters behind a barrier calling out questions about whether this would affect the recent recovery after the disruption of the solar storm, but Fellows wouldn't get drawn in, instead he waved to them, muttered a thank you, and turned to go back inside Number Ten.

Odd. Thought Oliver. That seemed a lot of fuss over nothing. Why go to all that trouble just to tell people that there was nothing to worry about? He downed his coffee in a couple of gulps before grabbing his bag and jacket. He didn't bother to put the coat on in his haste to get out of the house and get to INC before the rush hour. Maybe Zoe was right to think that something big was happening, and happening fast.

Oliver would have to tell his Head of Faculty today that he would leaving for Greenland again soon.

Or maybe not.

Suddenly the thought came into his head that he might be better off not saying anything to anybody just yet. He became aware that this need for secrecy made him an outsider, outside the boundaries at least of what his university would find acceptable. It made him feel like a conspirator, even though he hadn't done anything yet, which went against his naturally open and straight-forward nature.

And that changed everything.

CHAPTER NINE

Angmagssalik, Greenland

When Ray Coulson had arrived in Angmagssalik a couple of days ago, he'd expected the place to be buzzing with rumours about the rift in the ice that he'd been sent to locate. How difficult can it be to find something that big, he reasoned, when after a few tentative enquiries he'd got nowhere. All the visitors to the area were tourists. When they learned he was a photographer they were eager to point him in the direction of the amazing landscapes they had just seen, but this was not what he wanted at all.

The small town of Angmagssalik was built right by the sea and was set on a deeply grooved promontory just south of the Arctic Circle on the east coast of Greenland. At one time it was only accessible by boat or helicopter. It was only since the arrival of Phil Becaud that the town had acquired its tiny airstrip. The houses sat on top of the snow fields like painted cubes, standing out with their rust, olive, brown and ochre cladding, relieving the blue-whiteness of the surrounding landscape. Their neat and clean shapes somehow didn't look at odds with their environment, but they did seem fragile and had an air of impermanence; even on this a fine, early summer's day. It would be easy to imagine the harshness of the winter gales hammering on these same roofs, until at first light there was nothing left to be seen of the town but a changed landscape of steep snow dunes, and deep curved hollows.

Unable to get a room at the only sizable hotel in the town, Coulson had booked a few nights in a nearby guest house which had been recommended by the hotel receptionist. She said it was called the Seagull, or whatever the Danish equivalent was, and when he'd looked as though he couldn't remember the name of it, she told him that it was the deep blue house on the corner. He thanked her gloomily. As he walked up the path of the only house around with dark blue cladding, he thought it had an unwelcoming air, shabby and peeling, and not his type of place at all. His sombre mood intensified. He knew this was a bad start to the trip. He really needed to be in the thick of things if he was going to get this project off the ground, and he needed to be based in the hotel where he could meet people and get to hear what was going on.

Ten minutes later and with the formalities over, Coulson had already decided to stay at the Seagull for only one night and to try the hotel again tomorrow. They might have a cancellation. But for now, here he was, sitting incongruously in a room with pine furniture, tacky ornaments and heavy, lacy curtains, feeling totally alone. He was being well paid for a mission that already had a sense of failure about it, and that made him feel both guilty and inadequate. He had so wanted this to work out. And to return home to a nice lump sum, waiting for him in a specially opened bank account. He had tried to talk to the elderly couple who ran the guest house. At least they might know something or have heard something that could have been useful, but to his annoyance neither of them spoke any English.

The following day he hired Phil Becaud to fly him out to the places on his map which he had pencilled in while still in Frobisher. At first he didn't let on to Phil what he was looking for or why, having grown weary of everyone in the tourist business telling him what they thought he wanted to hear. Basically that they'd heard of a field of crevasses, and that they were sure to be the thing he'd heard about. That was a mistake that had already cost him at least a day in fruitless enquiries. Anyone with more experience than Coulson would have seen Becaud as being the obvious first point of contact, and would have taken the trouble to find out that his main interest was a freight business that gave him access to local people. But because he'd been promoting his new idea of pleasure flights, Coulson took this to be his main line of business.

Becaud, however, was no fool. Straightaway he could see that Coulson was looking for something. He remembered the furtive conversation his passenger had had with the Inuit guy down by the harbour.

Coulson walked up to the Cessna. There was no sign of the pilot. He stamped his feet irritably and thrust his gloved hands deep into his pockets. He was freezing. He jumped when Becaud clapped him on the shoulder, appearing from nowhere and smiling amiably. He was wearing a thickly padded parka over his flying jacket. His scarf was wound tightly round his neck to keep out the penetrating chill. He opened the door and told Coulson to get in.

They'd been about an hour into the flight, when Coulson, weary of staring at the glaring whiteness rolling beneath them, looked again at his folded-back map, and said to Becaud, "Do you think we've time to head up this way?" pointing to a circle near the edge of his paper.

"Sure. But it might help if you told me what you hoping to find out there."

Coulson stumbled.

"I - well, I'd sort of heard a rumour that there was an interesting feature that had appeared in the ice, and I – um – just thought it would make for some great photographs." He thought his vagueness was an adequate answer, and turned again to look down at the landscape beneath them, but Becaud persisted, knowing that he'd hit on something.

"Oh, I've seen that crevasse, if that is what you mean," said Becaud dismissively, deliberately being mischievous. He wanted to know if he could get a reaction. Coulson turned his head quickly, saying nothing yet, but the sudden gesture had already given him away. Coulson knew it too, so he thought he might as well go with it now, and ask a few questions. Becaud was infuriating. OK it was understood that they'd had trouble with their instruments – it had been the same back home, but he couldn't believe that the pilot would have no idea where the crevasse might be. It seemed ridiculous.

"Have you heard of any reports from the locals which you think would be reliable?" said Coulson.

"I can ask around if you like. I'm sure somebody must have heard something. Tell you what. I'll ask Joe. Joe Kristenssen. He's part Inuit. Takes people on wilderness treks for the tourist board, as well as acting as a guide for serious expeditions. He's been out this way recently. I think he'd be our best bet. He'd know if anyone would."

"You said you'd seen it. You sure it was the one."

"Not a doubt, Ray. You'd know what I meant if you'd seen it yourself. It was awesome." Coulson turned in his seat, his body language urging Becaud to say more.

"I've seen lots of possibles – I ..." Coulson tailed off.

"Ray, believe me, if you see it you'll know it's the one. No mistake. All the other crevasses we've seen around here aren't even close."

Phil Becaud looked over at Coulson's map and after a few moments consideration decided that they could head out to the edge of the area he'd marked in. They wouldn't have the range to go over the whole patch, even with the greater capacity of the new Cessna.

"It can be hard to grasp the scale of this place," said Becaud. "You see Greenland on a map in isolation, and it's easy to think it's about the size of Britain. In fact it would cover all of Europe and Scandinavia, if you overlaid it. I think we could go and take a look at this region here," he pointed at the chart, "as you've heard reports of a sighting, but I wouldn't get my hopes up if I were you. If you want my advice, you'd be better off talking to Joe Kristenssen. At least then your search will be more directed, more focussed."

Coulson nodded. He had to agree. He stared hard out of the window for a few more minutes, willing something to come into view. He decided to be realistic and turned to Becaud who was waiting for him to speak.

"Let's call it a day, and head back," said Coulson.

The pilot nodded and pulled the Cessna round, banking steeply.

"I'll call Joe, for you," said Becaud.

* * *

The meeting with Joe Kristenssen took place the next day, in the bar of the Angmagssalik Hotel. Ray Coulson bought three beers, and took them over to the table where Becaud was waiting with Kristenssen. He looked very young, Joe. He had jet black, longish hair, bright eyes and a high colour, not yet the lined brown skin that the older Inuit men had developed. He wore some coloured beads around his neck which looked like the ones kids wore for fashion back home. They could have been traditional, like some sort of ethnic thing; or maybe he was just into boarding. Coulson was uneasy, believing that he needed someone older and more experienced for a job like this. Joe drank some beer, then outlined the plan he'd already come up with to Coulson.

"I've got two other guys to come along," he said, Coulson gradually realising that all the arrangements had been made without him. "They're sound. Lots of experience. And one of them has a good idea where this rift is. Says he's talked to people who've seen it. Going to spend the rest of the day getting the trip provisioned if you're up for it. The weather's good, and the forecast is good for the next week or two. We set off first thing tomorrow morning, if you're OK with that?" He took another drink of his beer and waited patiently for Coulson to reply.

Coulson didn't know whether to believe that they knew where the crevasse was, but he wasn't in a position to doubt them openly. He looked at Becaud to see if he could gauge his opinion. The pilot saw the glance and put his drink down, tapping the glass on the polished wooden table as if for emphasis, before he spoke.

"These guys want to find this thing as much as you do Ray. They know there's something out there, but the sightings are all over the place. Some many hundreds of miles away from others – but these are reliable guys. You can trust them." He paused, as if to let the point sink in. "And they know this country – they know if something's not quite right. They're getting reports of seismic activity from all over the country, and the auroras have never been so active – almost continuous in the most northerly regions. A lot of the old timers connect the two; the light show and the quakes. Don't know if there's a link there, but hell, there's something going on. And I would say these guys are worried."

Their silence only confirmed Becaud's assessment of their mood. Coulson knew anyway that he had no choice but to go with their plans as he had no other ideas or leads of his own.

"Tomorrow morning, then," said Coulson. "Can we be ready so soon?"

"We have to be," said Joe. "Things are getting difficult. I hear that no foreign nationals will be allowed into the interior soon unless they have an acceptable reason to be there. Unless we find the crevasse soon, we're not going to be allowed anywhere near it. And you'd better have a good excuse to be here, just in case."

"I'm a photographer, officially," said Coulson. "But I'm reporting back to the MoD on what I discover here...."

"I really didn't want to know that," said Joe.

"Shit!" said Becaud. "I didn't know anything about that....sorry guys..."

Joe nodded. "It's OK," he said, tucking his hair behind his ear. "Forget it."

He wasn't interested in the politics. He could see his world crumbling beneath him, and his way of life going with it. That was what mattered to Joe. This crevasse was of a different order to what had gone before. He could sense it. Like a harbinger of what lay ahead, it signified a broken land that couldn't take the strain any more. And if he could do something to help, he would. He could sense, too, that it had created panic amongst those politicians whose role it was to do too little, too late, and for whom time had now run out.

Joe emptied his glass, and looked first at Becaud, then at Coulson. "Tomorrow morning, then. We meet outside here at six. You OK with that?"

Coulson agreed. They shook hands, as they rose from the table. As they left the hotel the door closed softly behind them.

CHAPTER TEN

Greenland

Next morning, Ray Coulson stood in his bulky outdoor gear, just outside the main hotel in Angmagssalic, where he'd agreed to meet Joe Kristenssen and the other two guides. The fully laden snowmobiles were waiting there already, but as yet he couldn't see the others, who must have gone into the hotel building for something. He'd had a good breakfast back at his guest house, but was glad to get away from the awkward domesticity of his accommodation. He would have preferred the anonymity of the hotel, but they still had no vacancies. He was pleased to be setting off at last for the vastly empty, icy interior.

Last night, he'd felt utterly depressed by the enormity of the task ahead of him, with the prospect of failure getting more insistent all the while. He might not find anything. But this morning, his mood was much more bullish. He knew with Joe's help he could give this mission his best shot. *His best shot*. That phrase kept reverberating around his thoughts. Crack or no crack in the ice, he could use this trip to get some of the best photographic shots in his life. Could kick start his career, which hadn't been going too well lately, and make him some money at last. Together with the money for this job, things could be looking up. He'd never had a break like this before and he was determined to make the most of it, whatever.

He'd never been on a snow-mobile before, either, so he was hoping that he'd be OK on such a long trek. Coulson told Joe that he'd ridden a quad bike several times before. "You'll be OK," was his reply.

"You seem in pretty good shape," said Joe, coming alongside the older man noiselessly, surprising him slightly. He'd been examining the handlebars of the snowmobile in order to familiarise himself with the controls before they set off. Joe Kristenssen stood about two inches taller than Coulson, but was lean and slight looking, even in his thick arctic clothing.

It was overcast, giving the early light a flat grey feel, the still air holding their breath in clouds around them.

"Yeah. I like to think I am," said Coulson. He sounded diffident, but actually, he was thinking to himself that he might have much more stamina for a long journey than the others, as he was thickset and had always been quite strong.

"How about the cold? How do you think you'll cope? You got all the gear on we told you about?"

"Oh, I'll be OK. Yes I've done exactly per instructions."

"OK. We'll be going a lot further and faster than we would for the tourists – but you're not one of these explorer guys who've training for months in a freezer back home. You must tell us when you need to stop and rest. And if you start to get cold we have to take action straightaway – don't struggle on or you could end up with frostbite."

Coulson agreed, and, thanking Joe for his advice, climbed onto the snowmobile, now eager to get started, as he noticed the other two guides had now arrived and were getting onto their machines.

"Hi," said Coulson to them. They nodded courteously. Joe intervened and introduced them properly. He gestured to the first of the men.

"This is Kouvageegai, and this is Iqniq. Ray Coulson, guys." They both smiled, but didn't attempt any conversation.

Coulson then asked Joe a couple of questions about how the vehicle handled, and how far they expected to go by the end of the day. Two hundred kilometres sounded a lot to Coulson, but he knew they would have to make good progress over fast terrain, to make up for the days when the ground was much slower. They had radios, to maintain contact with base and to call Phil Becaud if they needed a supply drop, but that was unlikely as they'd got plenty of provisions with them. There was still no SatNav or GPS, so navigation was going be by old fashioned maps and compasses. The lack of high-tech back up gave the expedition a slightly nostalgic quality, mixed with a feeling of authenticity that was very satisfying to Coulson and even quite exciting for Joe Kristenssen and his two colleagues. Should've gone for the huskies, too, he thought.

They started up the engines, the sound jarring against the silence of the early- morning town, making Coulson feel uncomfortable that they would be waking everyone up. Joe had no such scruples and revved loudly to get his machine warmed up quickly. He shouted to Coulson to do the same, and asked once more if he was OK. They took a minute to settle comfortably in their seats, when they were interrupted by someone calling to them from the hotel doorway.

"Good Luck guys!" It was the now familiar figure of Phil Becaud looking cool and dapper in his loose scarf and dark glasses, giving them a wave and a big grin to send them off in style. "Watch out for crevasses!" he said, and turned to head off back to his airstrip. The two Inuit guys waved, Joe hurled back some abuse, and revved a bit louder, signalling for Coulson to tuck in behind him and let the other two go behind. He couldn't explain why, but Ray Coulson felt quite moved by Becaud's gesture, of coming out here to see them off. It's something that never happens when you live alone.

That first day was tough. Tougher than Coulson had thought it would be. It was hard work riding a snowmobile; quite demanding, physically, but it was also hard mentally to concentrate on keeping to the smoothest terrain. Must have been a lot harder for Joe out in front, even with his experience, Coulson thought. The weather stayed overcast, which was quite a relief, as being out in the glaring arctic light was very tiring on the eyes, even with goggles on. But still the whiteness was relentless. It would be weird seeing grass again in a landscape, mused Coulson. In his imagination he pictured the countryside back home. It was thickly textured and very dark green, even a bit gloomy. Despite its harshness, this pristine blue-white world with its clean lines and thin dry air had a sort of hollow minimalism about it that was getting to be addictive.

They pressed on. The vibration from the snowmobile's engine juddering through his arms and making Coulson's back and shoulders ache with the effort of staying in control. If he'd thought that the morning was long, then now the time seemed endless. He needed a drink, but didn't really know if he was hungry or not as he hadn't had chance to think about it. But now he had thought about it, the appeal of a rest break with something to eat and drink seemed overwhelming, as they hadn't stopped since midday, and then only briefly. Joe had told him not to struggle on, but he seemed to have little choice as there was no way of getting his attention. The fact that Joe hadn't asked him if he was ready to stop again indicated to Coulson that it was still far too early to waste time by breaking their journey once more. Keep going. Maybe another twenty minutes and Joe would need a break, too. Didn't think he could manage another half hour at this pace, but in the end it was another hour and forty minutes till Joe turned in his seat and waved to get the party's attention. He indicated towards some dots on the horizon to let everyone know that that was where they were headed.

The dots turned out to be a weather station, not routinely manned, but visited occasionally by groups of scientists checking to see if all the instruments were functioning correctly. The accommodation consisted of a single hut, sitting squat in the snowy landscape, its thick walls looking utterly dependable against the penetrating cold all around it, the low roof looking as though it had got used to hunkering down and so had kept its pose all year. The meteorological instruments were housed in an oblong wooden structure with louvered access doors on the front. There was a wind gauge on top, whirring gently round, and a store nearby, with supplies of emergency rations, a large pile of wood for fuel, bottles of butane gas for cooking and lighting, and a row of cans of petrol. Joe had made plans to use some of the petrol to make their own supply go a little further. In return he had brought some boxes of dried meals, which he piled up in the corner on the wooden pallets stacked there to keep the boxes off the floor, and brought in a new power-pack to keep the digital thermometer going, as the old one was about to give out.

Joe emerged from the store to join Ray Coulson and the other two men, stiffly walking about trying to regain the use of their legs. The Inuit guys talked together quietly, Coulson not even trying to join in as he was too tired to be bothered with small talk. And he didn't feel that they wanted to be intruded upon.

"You OK Ray?" said Joe

"Yeah, I'm OK." Coulson nodded. Joe noticed that he looked at bit drawn.

"I'll fix us a brew," said Joe, his manner concerned but unfussy. "I guess we could all do with a hot drink. Sorry if the pace was a bit tough today. I thought it was better to press on to this station rather than make camp earlier. We don't have the bother of getting the tents out, and we'll all rest better here tonight, than we would have done under canvas. We can sit in front of a good fire, too, when we get the stove going."

Coulson agreed. Joe went inside the hut and straightaway found the kettle and the two-ringed butane gas stove. He packed some snow into the kettle, lit the burner, then set the kettle on top of the ring while he went to find the packs of tea and coffee and the insulated tin mugs from his pannier on the snowmobile. The other two guys had stowed their machines away under a sloping roof next to the hut, and had then gone back for Coulson's. Should have done that himself, but they seemed to know that he was struggling, and didn't mind helping him out. Thought that he hadn't done too badly for a rookie.

Joe lit the fire in the stove, the wood and firelighters carefully laid ready by the last person to stay here. Joe liked that. It made him feel part of a community, even if it was in effect by proxy as he'd never met the people who'd stayed here. Often isolated, he had become deeply self-reliant, but it drew you out of your own limits, to be part of the wider network of shared values and responsibility for others. Never a religious man, he'd not seen the need for anything organised or supernatural. He had around him, what Phil Becaud called a quiet sense of self. Something that Becaud himself had only ever experienced when he was flying alone at night.

Joe watched as the firelighters took hold, their white flames reflecting on his face, as he waited for the logs to catch. They smoked as they were so cold, but stubbornly refused to burn, so Joe picked up an old newspaper and held it in front of the opening of the stove to allow the fire to draw. After a few minutes it worked and the logs began to glow red, fresh flames roaring in the chimney, sending the first bit of comforting heat into the room. He put the newspaper down on the bare floor and reluctantly pulled himself away from the tiny pool of warmth pouring from the stove, to go over to the now boiling kettle. Joe made three large mugs of strong coffee and one of tea, nodding to his two friends that their drinks were ready. They had just come through the door. They saw the fire starting to pick up and grinned appreciatively. He picked up one of the mugs and took it over to the bunk where Coulson was resting. As he got closer Joe could see that the older man had fallen asleep, his mouth slightly open, he was breathing noisily, his head nodding awkwardly to one side. Joe was loath to wake him up but thought that he needed a drink and something to eat more than he needed to sleep.

"Here's your drink, Ray," said Joe quietly

"Ah!" Coulson jumped awake. Thanks. Sorry, must have dropped off..."

"That's OK."

He took a drink of the tea. It was painfully sweet and he couldn't help a slight grimace.

"That's bloody awful!"

"Sorry, Ray. We all take sugar out here. You'll need it for the calories. You'll soon get used to it."

Coulson wasn't so sure, but by the end of the cup he had to admit that he felt a lot better. The room was now reasonably warm, and they were all able to take off their big coats, and padded over-trousers. Joe removed his hat and tucked his flattened hair behind his ear before unwrapping an untidy-looking parcel that he had retrieved from his pack.

"Make the most of this, guys. It's the only fresh food for miles around. After tonight it's either dehydrated, or it's not dead yet."

Coulson perked up, impatient to know what they were going to have. On the small, rickety table the paper was pressed open to reveal a string of fat, dark sausages sitting in a foil tray. Looking like that a week ago, he would have thrown them out; but tonight they looked just perfect. He could taste them already. Joe placed some potatoes in the red glowing wood embers, and said they would eat in about an hour. Coulson acquiesced but didn't know how he was going to wait that long. Then he remembered that he'd got some chocolate in his pack. He handed it round to be sociable, but really he could have eaten it all himself. The effect of the cold was draining, and this was summer. God knows how people trek through a winter out here.

It was getting late, but it was difficult to gauge any sense of time. The sun hung low, just above the horizon, as it would do all night as they were now just inside the Arctic Circle. The light reminded Coulson of a late winter afternoon in England, but instead of the long shadows presaging the onset of a crisp cold darkness, they just hung there meaninglessly, as though the world had somehow forgotten to go round.

The hour passed at last and the food was ready. It was handed round to each of the men in turn by Joe. Tasted fantastic; hot and savoury. Some cans of lager were cracked open, ice cold and gassy, straight from the can to wash the food down. Nobody spoke during the meal, but afterwards as they opened another can of lager each, the conversation rose and bursts of laughter periodically sounded around the hut. The exertions of the day were beginning to take their toll, even on Joe, who up till now had still looked animated. The lulls in the conversation were becoming longer, and Coulson used one of the gaps to suggest they turn in. He didn't want to sound like a lightweight but he had to be realistic. Luckily they all readily agreed, and retreated to their respective bunks, without complaint. Joe closed the shutter on the only window, so when Coulson lay down the only light that he could see in the room was the glow from the dying fire in the stove. The bunk was rock hard, but so much better than the tent would have been. Joe had been right to press on.

He sank into a black sleep, which would have lasted all night, but he woke after muddled dreams of a deep and penetrating noise eventually disturbed him. He leaned up on one arm. The noise seemed to have been there for a long time but he had no way of judging how long. He strained to listen but now he was alert he could hear nothing. He wondered if he had dreamed it. He dozed off again, but woke with a start, when he felt a sudden sense of being pushed up, then stopping with a jolt, like when you have a falling dream, only the other way round. Tense all over, he listened to see if there was any reaction from the others. There was no other sound but their steady breathing. Gradually Coulson let go his pose and sank down again into the mattress, convinced that over-tiredness had made him restless. He turned over and fell asleep once more, only waking to the sound of Joe putting the kettle on the gas burner ready for breakfast.

Coulson realised to his shame that the others must have been up for at least half an hour, probably more, as the stove was cleaned out and laid ready for the next occupant. The hut, sparse anyway was left bare of any traces of their visit, save for the three rucksacks that were piled in front of the door. Joe carefully poured the now boiling water into the insulated pint mugs and dropped some coffee into each of them in turn. He then spooned in two heaps of dried milk followed by the same of sugar. After the coffee had infused he put another two sugars in each, knowing that they had another demanding day ahead and wanting everyone to get off to a good start. They ate a dehydrated breakfast, straight from the foil pouches that they came in, the dried food tasting of nothing after the sweet coffee.

"Did you sleep well?" said Joe to Coulson.

"Yeah, OK, thanks. Some strange noise woke me up, though. Don't suppose anyone else heard it - you all seemed to be asleep."

"Guess it was the ice moving – makes strange noises sometimes," said Joe.

"Yes, I guess so. There was something really weird, though. Don't even know if I dreamed it. Felt as though I was rising up – I was lifted up – like on a ship in a

183

rough sea. Did you guys feel anything?" Nobody had. And nobody looked interested. Coulson, sensing that he wasn't being taken seriously, decided not to pursue it.

They finished their coffee, Coulson making the most of every last drop, before wiping out their mugs and stowing them away in their packs. Joe hurried them out, banging the door of the hut firmly shut behind him, all the while talking to one of the guides about the route that they would be taking that day. Coulson wasn't close enough to hear what they were saying but the tone of the voices indicated to him that there was some disagreement about which direction they should be taking. He went over to his snowmobile and climbed onto the machine, feeling that as he could make no useful contribution to the exchange, then he might as well keep out of it.

Eventually Joe walked over to him and explained what the trouble was all about. Both the Inuit guides, Kouvageegai and Iqniq, had heard reported sightings of a new and massive crevasse, but the positions that they had for these sightings was many hundreds of miles apart. Each insisted that their report was reliable, so Joe had no choice but to side with one of them, thereby offending the other. Sensibly he'd chosen the nearest sighting as there were no other factors to go on, but this didn't appease the other guy, who said there was no use taking short cuts if there was nothing at the end of it. Joe told Iqniq that he would just have to accept it, but he wasn't happy. Dissent didn't make for good expeditions, and it was still early in the trip for things to start falling apart.

Still angry, the younger of the guides, Iqniq, revved up his engine hard, and without waiting for Joe to go first, he sped off ahead leaving the others to try to catch him up. They set off as quickly as they could, but had to go at Coulson's pace which meant that the first snow-mobile got further and further ahead. Joe was furious. You don't mess about out here. When they caught up with him, Joe would tell Iqniq either to get over it or go back home.

Coulson, noticing something odd, tried to pick up the pace a little and he pulled level with Joe who was carefully watching the terrain just in front of him.

"He's gone, Joe!" he shouted, pointing at the horizon. "He's just disappeared. One minute there, the next nothing."

"Shit! Where the hell's he gone?"

Joe scanned the white space in front of him, desperately trying to make out where the man could have gone. Anger, in a second, turning to concern, knowing how quickly things out here can go wrong. Then suddenly, only a few metres ahead, a figure leapt up out of nowhere, his bright blue anorak standing out against the white all around him. His arms were spread far apart and he was waving and shouting for them to stop. They braked hard, but still his shouts became more desperate, until Coulson thought that heard the word turn, and immediately realised what he had to do. He screamed to Joe and the other guide to veer right, while he pulled round hard left as tight as he could go. He stopped the machine in a drift of soft snow, now at right angles to a steep drop just ahead of him. He wouldn't have had time to stop. If he hadn't swerved he would have been at the bottom of a twenty-five metre sheer vertical drop, totally invisible until you were virtually upon it.

The argument was now wiped away from everyone's mind. Joe climbed off his snowmobile calmly, and stood over the edge of the ice cliff looking down. It wasn't a crevasse; it was as though the landscape had simply sheered at that point, the flat plain continuing into the distance twenty-five metres lower than it had been before. The guide's snowmobile lay on its side on a ledge that had saved him from the drop. If he'd been travelling a few metres to the right or left, he would have been killed. No doubt about it.

"I need a hand with the snowmobile," he said to Joe. Joe looked him levelly in the eye. The other man looked back openly, but without staring, which would have been aggressive, then he looked down, as though to admit he had been foolish. When he glanced back up, Joe was still facing him. Joe blinked before dropping his gaze. The gesture said thank you. He'd saved their lives. They both understood, and needed to say no more.

"OK," said Joe. "We'll haul you out, then get going."

"How come the land has just dropped like this?" said the other Inuit. "This shouldn't happen."

"It hasn't," said Coulson. Everyone turned to stare at him. They were supposed to be the experts in this terrain. What did he know? But he had earned their respect just now. His quick thinking and reactions had saved them all.

"What do you mean?" said Joe, intrigued.

"The shelf we're standing on now has risen up – we're on a plateau – the land we see ahead of us is what's normal. That's what I felt last night. And all that noise when the ice sheets were straining. I felt the ice sheet push up. It happened in seconds."

The two guides were deeply uneasy; strange things had been going on for some weeks now, which were getting harder to explain away. The massive solar storm; the quakes, and the crevasse they were searching for. Something so huge, it seemed that the land ice was beginning to disintegrate. And no-one knew what the consequences of that might be. Joe looked calm but seemed to be worried himself. He'd not felt anything the previous night, but immediately he thought that Coulson was right. He wondered how big an area had been elevated. He knew something bad was going on deep underneath the ice, something on a scale they'd not seen before. The once familiar landscape now looked like a stranger to him, which made him feel uneasy. He banged his hands together in a gesture of exasperation, then addressed Coulson, as his thoughts were focusing on the need to get going and not waste any more time here. Joe took control of the situation.

"Ray, we need a rope to get the snowmobile off the ledge – can you go down with the other two and get the snowmobile upright if you can, then get the rope attached. I'll tie the rope to my machine, then we'll pull her up. OK?"

Without replying, he made his way over the edge of the drop and lowered himself carefully onto the ledge.

Kouvageegai and Iqniq did the same, and between them they soon had the snowmobile upright and the spilled luggage stuffed back inside the panniers. They attached the rope with awkward gloved hands, then pulled the knot tight. Joe, at the top of the ledge, eased his snowmobile forwards until the rope became taut and then strained with the effort. Gradually the second vehicle started to move then with a sudden jerk the machine leapt forwards, revving loudly and creating a fountain of loose snow behind it as it powered up the slope to the plateau above. They unhooked the rope and stowed it away carefully.

"Now, we've just got to find our way off this plateau so that we can continue heading north west," said Coulson.

They had no choice but to follow the rim round until they could find a way down, which they did eventually a good fifteen kilometres away. They'd used up most of the morning by the time they were down on the level again and heading were they wanted to go. They pressed on for longer than they had intended. It was mid afternoon by the time they eventually stopped for a rest break.

And by that time they were so weary and achingly hungry that they never noticed the soft, dull yellow haze forming like a jaundiced sunset on the horizon, arcing from edge to edge under the pale sky. It spread like a creeping flood over the flatness of the land, lying thickly in the windless air as the poisonous fumes escaped from a distant fissure in the earth's crust.

It had been very late by the time they had made camp. Joe was pleased that they had made up the distance, by pushing themselves to keep going for the extra two hours, but now he was worried that maybe he'd pushed everyone too far. Erecting the tents had been too much for Coulson, who could hardly stand and was clumsily making mistakes while setting up the camp. And one of the Inuit guides had retreated to his sleeping bag without eating anything at all, saying he'd try something later. Hoped to goodness he wasn't ill, Joe thought. They really couldn't cope with a passenger, and would have no choice but to abort the expedition and return to Angmagssalic.

The next morning, after a deep, black sleep that left him not knowing for some minutes where he had woken, Joe sat up in his sleeping bag only to feel a tight band grasp the top of his head and a pain shoot across his eyes as he looked towards the light. He closed his eyes again instinctively, and cradled his head in his hands, tucking his limp hair behind his ears as he did so. He was afraid that he could be ill, their worst nightmare now they were so far away from base, especially as Kouvageegai had seemed to be sickening, too. When Coulson awoke, Joe looked at him for signs of illness, wanting to get the whole picture before he admitted to anyone that he was afraid that they'd picked up a virus. At best this could mean the trip would have to be abandoned; at worst it could put all their lives in danger, if they were very ill and couldn't look after each other. Coulson appeared grey and drawn, but didn't seem to have a temperature and drank his strong sweet tea without complaint. Joe took two painkillers, and ate what breakfast he could manage. The two guides were more of a cause for concern. Kouvageegai could only manage to drink some hot water for his breakfast, while Iqniq was clearly having some problems breathing. He kept taking deep awkward breaths which only made his dry cough worse and his chest sore. Neither complained; and Joe knew that they were both thinking the same as he was. Admitting that they were ill would mean having to confront the issue and make some difficult decisions, and they were all hoping to avoid that possibility for as long as possible.

Working like robots, they broke camp and set off once more heading to the north-west. It was still early, and Joe had already decided to take the day at a more realistic pace and include more rest breaks, at least until they all felt better. They drove hard and made good distance for the next two hours, over smooth terrain. Joe's head thumped with the noise of the engine, and it was with huge relief that he slowed to a halt and turned off the noisy machine. When the others did the same the silence was like balm washing over him. He drank it in for several seconds before mustering the energy to speak to his companions. His head still felt tight, and he felt his arms and down his back grow hot and uncomfortable under his layers of thick, padded clothing. This was not good, he thought. If he was running a temperature, he would have to tell the others.

Coulson was the first to make a move by pulling a can out of one of the panniers and stuffing it with snow to make a brew. He paused while he was doing that and looked at the snow in his gloved hand with interest. There were two things that were strange about it. One

was its colour. It was slightly dull – dirty, yellow looking not the blue-white translucent colour it normally
was. And it was soft, like the wet snow you used to
get in the UK in spring. A lump of ice on the ground in
front of him had partly lost its whiteness and was going
clear, like a melting ice lolly. He picked it up. It was
wet and slippery on the outside. He, too, like Joe, was
beginning to feel uncomfortably warm, and he pulled
off his hat and gloves, and unzipped his anorak while
he set the little stove going. Joe noticed that with alarm.

"Hey! Don't do that Ray. You'll get cold. You could
be running a temperature – I feel I'm burning up, too.
But you must say warm."

"You never said," stated Kouvageegai, accusingly.
He still hadn't eaten for twenty-four hours, and looked
haggard and weak.

"I didn't want to worry anyone. I thought I could
soon shake it off. Sorry. I thought I'd wait and see."

Kouvageegai looked angry but didn't say anything.
After all, he'd been doing the same, pretty much, hoping he'd feel better soon, too. Iqniq wasn't listening. His
chest rattled under his laboured breathing, the air sharp
and aggravating, making him wheeze with the effort.
He couldn't find the energy to speak.

Coulson was about to do his coat up again, as Joe
had told him, deferring to the younger man's experience, but he hesitated before doing so. He felt hot, but
he knew he hadn't got a fever; he didn't feel great, but
he knew what it felt like to have flu, and he didn't feel
like that. Also, he was suddenly aware that his hands
didn't feel cold, even with his gloves off. He touched

his neck with his left hand. His fingers were still warm. He stretched out his arm, pulling the thick sleeve of his anorak back to reveal his wristwatch underneath. He pressed a button on the side of the watch and a digital display lit up in red figures the ambient temperature. It read twenty-two degrees Celsius.

Coulson showed it to the others without comment. They looked at each other not knowing what to say. One by one they peeled off their thick outer clothing and the hats that were now becoming bothersome and sat down on their packs of luggage, feeling like they'd got dressed for the wrong party. OK, it was summer, but not like any Arctic summer that they'd known before. This was weird.

Joe sipped the hot, sweet, tea that Coulson had made for them. He though it might be easier to drink than their usual coffee. They munched on the chocolate that he handed round, deep in thought. Joe noticed that the tea tasted odd, a bit sulphurous, but he was too concerned about the record breaking temperature to comment on it. He bit off another piece of the chocolate to take the taste of the tea off.

And still no-one noticed faint yellow haze that hung just above the ground.

"I must radio Phil," said Joe at last. "Tell him about the temperature that we've just measured. He can pass it on to the guys who run the little weather station. I'd like to see what they make of it."

"Do you think it's widespread, or just a local phenomenon?" said Coulson.

"I've no idea," said Joe.

"I can't get my head round this," Coulson said. He'd peeled off another fleece and was down to his shirtsleeves. "Is this freak weather part of the pattern of global warming we're seeing all around here, or is this something else, something on top of that? Maybe it's to do with all this seismic activity – that and the solar storm. I'm beginning to think that it's all connected. We have to go on and find out if this crevasse really exists, and if it's as big as they say. Even if we are ill, we can't turn back now, Joe."

Joe agreed, but was worried about Iqniq.

Coulson took some pictures on film, as he couldn't be sure that the digital ones would be safe. They all now sat in their shirtsleeves drinking tea and smiling for the camera, except for Iqniq who looked distant and slumped as he sat.

"You OK to press on?" Joe said to Iqniq, when he could talk to him without the others hearing.

"We have to," he said, his voice hoarse with the effort of breathing hard all the time. "It's not far now. We should find it tomorrow. The crevasse. Then I need to get back as quick as we can."

Joe took him at his word, but still wasn't one hundred percent sure that they should continue. He saw Coulson looking at him impatiently, and decided that they must go on with the trip. He dosed the Inuit guide up with as much medication as he dared give him and just hoped for the best. Iqniq was a tough cookie, and had been through a lot worse than this.

* * *

By the next morning the chill air had returned to its normal level, clinging around the camp, like a dead weight. There was no wind, no sound, and no movement, the thick, dull cloud keeping the day as grey as the night had been. None of the men wanted to stir so early, but hauled themselves out of their sleeping bags, pulled on by the thought that today would be the day that they could find the crevasse, and then make for home. Their heads were as thick as the worst hangover could be, and breakfast was eaten in silence, save for the sporadic wheezing, spluttering, involuntary cough that came from Iqniq. He looked terrible. His eyes were too bright, and his face was flushed. Joe gave him his medication for the day and told him that he'd be OK soon. Iqniq took it wishing that he could believe him. Joe took a couple of painkillers for his throbbing headache, and noticed that Coulson and Kouvageegai did the same. The sooner they were out of here the better, he thought. This had been a bad trip from the start, and all he could think about now was getting a result and getting home. He hadn't told Coulson yet, but he'd made up his mind that this was going to be the last day of searching, no matter whether they found anything or not. If the crevasse wasn't here then someone else would have to search for it – they were not well enough to go on, and would only be risking their lives needlessly.

But they were not ill, as they all assumed they were. They were slowly being poisoned by the toxic gasses in the creeping yellow cloud that was closing in on them. Leeching from the fissure eruption that had opened up hundreds of miles away in Iceland, wherever it became

concentrated in still cold air, its effects could be insidi-
ous and deadly. No-one had yet seen it let alone realised
the danger it posed; at Humboldt it had been mistaken
for the similar-looking Eastern European pollution.
Joe just needed just one more day of searching to complete their mission and get Coulson and the others back
home.

Meanwhile, the cloud was getting thicker.

CHAPTER ELEVEN

London

Lawrence Hewitt's flat already had the dead, too tidy look of a place that was going to be unoccupied for a while, anytime soon. His bags were zipped up and padlocked, and ready to be tagged with the bright airline luggage labels that he was waiting to get from Zoe. He'd left it to the Carters to book the tickets to Nuuk, which made sense, but was irritating him now that he was ready to go and he still didn't know the exact date and time. He'd washed and dried the single mug and plate that he had used for his last meal there, and put them away in the cupboard, even wiping out the stainless steal sink till it was dry and shiny, keeping the place in a permanent state of readiness for his departure. He didn't really know why he was so fastidious before he left the flat to go somewhere, when most of the time it looked a mess. Not dirty. He wasn't that bad, just unkempt.

He'd lived alone too long to be bothered about what his surroundings looked like. He travelled frequently for his work and spent as much time out of the flat as he could. It was just a place to stay. The rented furniture was clean and modern, even quite tasteful, with a couple of light-coloured fabric sofas set at right angles to each other on an oak floor. But there was little, if anything of him in the room. No personal photographs, in fact no photographs at all, which was a little surprising as he must have had so many that would have been worth display. There were no plants either, to bring life and vibrancy into the room. It was a place that lacked energy. If Hewitt socialised it was mainly to go for a drink or a meal with his colleagues. He'd never invited anyone round to his home since he moved in five years ago, and, as far as he was concerned, could see no reason to do anything different. And yet something stirred in him since his visit to the Carters' home.

It was funny how he'd hit it off with Oliver Carter. Normally his colleagues were just people to talk to about a mutually interesting subject. Someone to go out with to pass an evening. But right from when they first bumped into each other at Angmagssalic and he'd hitched a lift to Humboldt, Oliver had always looked pleased to see him, and had brought a warmth and cheeriness into his life that Hewitt hadn't experienced for years.

It had been a long time since anyone had been pleased to see him.

Not since Ben died in a car accident eight years ago. After that, he and his wife had each retreated to their own private despair and had been unable to help one another. All he remembered now of those early days was a blur of pain, acrimony and the utter pointlessness of the everyday humdrum life that still went on around him. And in that reality which he'd sunk into, he'd hardly noticed when his wife grew ever more distant and then one day was no longer there.

He put all his energy into his work, which for a time distracted him and numbed the pain. But then it got to be a habit, a mindset. Work became the only thing he could safely think about without going back there, to the black times. So he stuck with it, living this pared-down existence that got him through.

Hewitt found his thoughts often returning to his evening at Zoe and Oliver's, and not just because of the crevasse, his reason for going there in the first place. It had the atmosphere of a family house that hit him as soon as he walked through the door and saw the collection of coats and trainers, bags and sports equipment in the hall, that reflected all the different ages and interests of the Carters' three children. It gave the place a dimension one never gets in a house occupied by a couple, or a person living alone. It had a light and energy about it that twanged something deep inside him. Only it didn't threaten to knock him back down to the black space. Instead there was the germ of a feeling that he might want to be part of something again; that it was OK to think that without letting out a cataract of emotion, a wave of regret and loss which used to threaten to overwhelm him.

Hewitt had walked through rooms full of loud banter and laughter as Matt, Emily and Jack got ready to go out, where music thumped away upstairs and out-fits were checked over before they went. Everywhere seemed full of noise and movement. Even after the front door slammed shut to shouts of *see you later,* and *don't be too late back,* the house didn't seem empty. The garden room curtains billowed out like sails in the breeze, bringing in with them the sweet warm air of the spring evening, and some twittering birdsong. A couple of cats, the Carters' children's pets, rubbed lazily around his legs as he walked out into the courtyard with his newspaper. The image of comfortable domesticity was complete, and Hewitt realised how much he'd missed it.

When he'd pictured his own flat in comparison. The coldness and negativity reminded him uneasily of what he had become. But it was his comfort zone, and he wasn't going to be able to prise himself out of there too easily.

Hewitt checked his watch. Time was getting on. He thought Zoe would have rung by now and let him know something. He had arranged to give Amy James a lift to the airport, and he had to admit he was looking forward to seeing her again.

He looked out of the window of his flat and noticed with annoyance that a red truck was still parked opposite his drive making it difficult to back out if he needed to. Somebody must be having some work done over the road, he thought as it had been there several times this week. He hoped it wouldn't be blocking his way when he was due to set off. It would just be bloody typical. He reached up for the cord at the side of the window and tilted the blind so no-one could see that he was looking, but the movement caught the attention of the man sitting there in the truck. Hewitt pulled back feeling self-conscious, then a few seconds later he heard an engine start up and a vehicle pulled away. He guessed it was the truck but didn't like to look again.

He had just decided to flick the switch on the kettle and make himself some coffee when the phone rang, jarring on the silence in the living room. Hewitt covered the ground from the kitchen in five or six quick strides and picked up the handset, pressing the answer button with his thumb.

It was Zoe Carter.

CHAPTER TWELVE

Greenland

By late morning the last-mile energy that had kept the four going, when all they wanted to do was stop and rest, had begun to ebb away. Each break now had less and less effect as the point of the expedition seemed to be no more attainable than when Coulson was flying around in the Cessna trying to spot the crevasse from the air. Iqniq however, was adamant that they were going to find it soon. He'd better be right. But Coulson could see them all heading back empty handed, and could already hear his excuses forming when he would have to radio back to his contact in London. What the hell was he doing here, anyway? Despite this, he had so wanted this mission to be a success.

The terrain here was slow, too. Large ripples made the ice difficult to drive over and hauling the machines over stacks of ice boulders was exhausting the men. And then the patches that looked level were soon found to be ice hollows filled with recently fallen soft snow, which sank under the weight of the snowmobiles. Joe could feel morale was at rock bottom and was aware of the dangers that this could bring. The biggest threat to them now was not the cold, but poor judgement. He could feel it creeping up on him even now. Whereas yesterday he had made a clear plan to go no further than they could reach today, now he was wondering whether to go on for just one more day. He was tantalised by the thought that they might turn back only to find later that the crevasse was only just over the horizon. He also knew that they could press on till they were too ill to get back home safely. He felt torn, but Iqniq was still confident that his reported sighting of the crevasse was correct.

"Two hours will do it," he said, breathing carefully, so that he didn't start coughing again.

Joe hoped he was right.

Two of the longest hours that Coulson could ever remember passed by before the men stopped for another break. Joe went straight to the supplies to dig out some food, while Coulson automatically got out the metal can and began to press snow into it, lighting the butane gas stove without speaking. He started slightly at the sharp tap on his shoulder, as he wondered if he'd done something wrong. Iqniq was standing over him, urging him to put the can down and walk with him to the top of a ridge, nearby. Kuvageegai was already at the top, looking out over to the horizon through a pair of binoculars. Coulson wearily climbed up beside him, and took the binoculars offered by Kuvageegai. He looked across the ridged and buckled landscape to see what they had discovered. He could make out nothing of interest even though he swept back and forth from the foreground to the horizon. Coulson looked from behind the glasses and readjusted his vision before he spoke.

"I don't see anything. What exactly is it that I'm supposed to be looking at?"

Iqniq smiled at his impatience, and pointed to a blue-grey shadow in the middle distance which zig-zagged its way over the horizon on their far left. Coulson spotted it, and now that he had a bearing he raised the glasses once more to his eyes, re-focussing the lenses as he homed in on the area that he was searching for. Suddenly the soft grey shadow became a sharp edge, and he could see immediately what was right there in front of him. It was the crevasse. Had to be.

"Joe! Joe. It's there! We've found it. It's right over there. Quick! Come and take a look."

Joe dropped what he was doing and ran up the slope to the top of the ridge, where he grabbed the binoculars and cast round to see the crevasse for himself. It took him a minute to find it through the powerful glasses, but when he did he gave a whoop of delight that made the two Inuit guys grin with unashamed told-you-so pleasure.

Filled with an energy that must have been buoyed up by their excitement, Coulson and Joe spilled back down the ridge, where they slapped each others backs in delight, turning and shouting at Kuvageegai and Iqniq to hurry up and join them. The two guides trudged steadily back to where the snowmobiles were parked and gratefully took the tea that Coulson offered them. Iqniq gulped and had another coughing fit when he realised that there was a shot of celebratory brandy in the warm, sweet brew, then laughed appreciatively before taking a long second swallow. The effect of the alcohol eased his tight painful airways making him feel better than he had done in days. Coulson then took out his camera, and got some shots of the crevasse from the top of the ridge while Joe got onto the radio to give the news to Becaud back in Angmagssalik that they were no more than an hour away from the crevasse. He gave his position as best he could without his GPS. And said that he'd be in touch again when they actually got there.

"Do you actually need to go there?" said Becaud, while writing down their co-ordinates. "Why don't you just head back now and save yourself a few hours, especially as Iqniq doesn't sound too good."

It was good advice, and Joe's persistent nauseous headache tempted him to heed it, but Iqniq wouldn't hear of it. Now he was so close, he had to see it for himself, and, he reasoned, they had to make sure that it was really the one, by seeing how big it actually was. Coulson agreed. To come this far only to get it wrong would be a disaster. They had to go on; and he had to get his pictures.

They each ate a couple of tough, chewy chunks of salami, and drained their mugs, before climbing once more onto the snowmobiles and continuing their journey, only this time knowing that they were on the last lap. They raced on now, bouncing over the ripples at speed and ploughing through the most recent falls, pushing fountains of soft snow into the air behind them as headed towards the crevasse.

They made great progress, but keeping up that speed was proving to be very tiring, so an hour into the journey Joe waved the group down to indicate that he was stopping. They all pulled level, then stopped their engines, once again the silence flooding over them as they took their hands off the handlebars and slumped back into their seats. Only it wasn't quite as silent as they thought it should be. Joe was the first to speak. There seemed to be something in the background, like white noise instead of the hollow nothingness that they had become accustomed to.

"Is that in my head, or can you guys hear it, too?"

"What the hell is it?" said Coulson, looking around. "It sounds like a waterfall."

"Yeah, right," said Joe, with good humoured sarcasm. "A waterfall out here. I think it must be a mirage." He pushed back his hood and tucked his lank hair behind his ear.

"Can you have an audible mirage?" said Coulson.

"I don't know." Joe thought about it.

"I can smell water," said Kuvageegai flatly.

Joe looked at him, and so did the others. He wasn't joking. He swung off his snowmobile, and like Joe, pushed his hood away so that he could hear better. He got his bearings then started to walk in the direction that he thought the noise was coming from. Tentatively the others followed him, as he walked quickly on. After about fifty metres it was definitely getting louder. Kuvageegai was making his was up some gently rising ground and was some way above them when he stopped abruptly, then stepped back two or three paces waving to the others to stay well back. Joe, Coulson and Iqniq, continued to walk towards him but only very slowly. As they edged to his side, and could see what he had seen the shock passed through them all at the same time.

"Oh my God! What the fuck is that?" Coulson reeled.

A river of meltwater was rushing through a deep groove in the ice, foaming and splashing at the white river banks, full of violent agitation and noise, incongruous in what should have been a silent, frozen world. The water was bouncing off the fragile banks, snaking through the white terrain before disappearing down a hole, hurtling at a speed that was making the ground shake beneath their feet. The hole, known as a moulin, reached right down to the bedrock two kilometres below the surface. The men, of course, had no way of knowing how far the water was penetrating into the ice, but the sound it made as it swirled and fell into the moulin, by the thousands of litres every second, appeared to come from the dark, untouched depths of the ice sheet. Joe gasped. He'd heard of these things, but he'd never seen anything like it before. Coulson was gripped by a feeling at the pit of his stomach, as his mind played over and over an image of him disappearing down into the abyss, swept along by the cold power of the water to his death. Unconsciously he drew back a few steps further from the edge. Taut with fear, he muttered something about going back to fetch his camera, but still he remained there, unable to take his eyes off the scene before him.

Eventually, as they stood on, the spray began to settle around them like an icy fog, chilling them through. When they felt their wet cold hair clinging round their heads, they knew it was time to move or risk getting seriously cold. Joe pulled on first his hat, then his hood noticing the others copying his example through his peripheral vision. But there was something slightly odd about Iqniq's body language that made him turn and look at his friend directly. Normally he was a reticent man, having a calm acceptance of whatever came his way, but Joe could see that Iqniq's face was wet, and not with spray. Deeply touched by his distress, Joe moved towards him and tried to touch his arm with his gloved hand, but Iqniq moved away, turning his head down and to the side, then shook his head.

"We are the last generation," was all he said. Joe backed off, unoffended as he could see that his friend needed some space.

None of them had had any idea that the ice was going so quickly. Nothing gets rid of ice and snow quicker than liquid water; and there it was gouging out a river before their eyes crashing down deep into the ice sheet. It was forcing its way through fissures and hollows creating ever more channels as it did so. Its power fracturing the ice, which in turn would let more meltwater in from the surface. The dynamic seemed unstoppable; they were witnessing catastrophe on an epic scale. No wonder Iqniq was weeping. Joe's head was reeling. Suddenly he recoiled from his own reaction only minutes before of elation that they found the crevasse. It was as though in the heat of the moment they had forgotten why they were here. The existence of the crevasse could spell disaster for the ecosystems of this land, and the repercussions of that could be felt all over the northern hemisphere. They were possibly on the brink of an episode of abrupt climate change, and were here to look for the first real signs that it could be happening. But now he had seen the look on Iqniq's face. That look had said that they were too late; they'd gone past the point of no return. The tipping point. And Joe was overwhelmed by a feeling of total despair.

Coulson got his pictures, whilst once more Joe got onto the radio and told Becaud what they'd seen. Becaud listened to the report in glum silence. He was no scientist, but he didn't need to be, to know that what he was hearing was not good. There were just too many pieces of the jigsaw fitting together now that were all part of the same depressing picture. Like the news items he'd heard about from Antarctica when, in 2002, the break up of the Larsen B Ice Shelf had been reported. It was catastrophic and totally unexpected by the teams of scientists who were studying it. A piece of floating ice, larger than Luxembourg, the Larsen B, which had been attached to the southern tip of the Antarctic Peninsula for thousands of years, suddenly shattered into pieces like a smashed pane of glass.

In the space of three days.

The thinning of the ice shelf had been happening since the sixties, and pools of melting water appeared regularly on its surface, putting the shelf under strain. Cracks appeared and bits broke off during the nineties, but in the record warm temperatures of 2002, water filled ponds and crevasses, its greater density, in effect, creating thousands of wedges exerting mechanical pressures from deep inside the shelf. So at the beginning of March the entire structure gave way, breaking the shelf into thousands of iceburgs that then floated away into the Southern Ocean. Becaud had pricked up and noticed this report when scientists said, at the time, that this was probably also happening in Greenland. But he'd heard no more about it since, and he'd put it to the back of his mind. Until now. He didn't know if the land ice would be subject to the same pressures that an iceberg had been, but he didn't like the sound of it, and he, like Joe, was deeply concerned. He thanked Joe for keeping him informed and signed off.

After a break for some sleep, Joe and Coulson agreed that they wouldn't stop again until they reached the crevasse. They could now see it plainly without the help of binoculars, a great jagged gash parting the ice sheet from one side to the far horizon, where it disappeared over the curve of the Earth, no-one knew how far. But the scale was deceptive, and it still took longer for them to reach it than they thought. From a distance it looked to be about ten to twenty-five metres wide, but as they edged closer they could see that their estimates had been way short of the mark. They parked their snowmobiles a good fifty metres away from the edge of the crevasse and gingerly walked the last stretch, four abreast, and each of them looking only straight ahead. It felt like walking to the edge of the last Ice Age, looking down and seeing the exposed Earth's surface for the first time in 10,000 years. The pale Arctic sun was high enough in the sky to light the white-walled valley to its base, where, from the grey shale, and banked up moraines, there occasionally rose something that looked like smoke or steam. The other cliff wall must have been the length of two football pitches away, its white wall glaring back at them, so sheer, it could have been man made.

"My God! It's on the scale of the Grand Canyon!" said Coulson, his voice hoarse with emotion.

"It's awesome," Joe said. "Absolutely fucking awesome."

They stood and stared for some minutes, trying to take in what was before them. Coulson crept as close to the edge as he dared so that he could look down, but, skyscraper-high, the view from the top was terrifying. His stomach churned with adrenalin and his head spun as his eyes followed the long drop down.

"I'll get the camera," he said glad to be moving away from the edge.

"I'll get the co-ordinates worked out," said Joe, secretly feeling the same.

Joe sat side-saddle on his snowmobile with a map in front of him and his compass resting on the paper, engrossed in his calculations while Coulson clicked away on his camera getting the evidence he needed to send back to his unofficial MoD contact. When they were ready with the information, Joe picked up the radio and tried once more to call Phil Becaud in Angmagssalik. After a few minutes trying, Joe looked back at Coulson and shook his head. Coulson could hear the radio hissing blankly, frustrating their attempts to get their discovery back to the people waiting for news.

The solar storm was still spraying the Earth's upper atmosphere with interfering particles, making radio contact sporadic and unreliable even after all this time. Joe waited a few minutes, then tried again.

"It's no good. I can't get a signal. Mike-delta-tango, mike-delta-tango, do you read me?" He turned to Coulson who was watching anxiously. "Mike-delta-tango – are you receiving me?"

"Echo-alpha-romeo. Receiving you. Over," came back the crackly faint voice of Becaud at last. Joe at once became alert and hunched over the radio, speaking slowly and deliberately and desperately hoping that the signal would last while he got the co-ordinates out.

"Great work, Joe," Becaud said when he'd carefully written down all that Joe had told him, while keeping one eye on the two thick rashers of bacon that were cooking on the stove beside him. But Joe never heard that last bit. The radio fizzed again with interference, and this time he could not re-establish the link with Angmagssalic. Joe switched off the set and said to Coulson.

"You finished with the pictures, Ray?"

"Yeah. I've shot off a couple of reels. I think I've got what I need."

"Great. Then let's head out of here. For all his brave face, I don't like the look of Iqniq. And my head still feels as though I've got it in a vice."

Coulson nodded.

"You, too? I've been taking painkillers for days. They just don't seem to be having any effect."

"It's like you can't breathe out here. I can't figure it out."

They took one last, long look at the ice canyon. Where the sun caught the wall head on, it was a total flat white, hard to look at for long without one's eyes going shadowy. But just below them they could see the crystalline wall was glistening with dewy meltwater, which was running down it before re-freezing at it reached the colder air trapped in the valley. A lump of ice broke off the fractured wall quite close to them, and tumbled endlessly down to the bedrock, skimming the sides at it went, landing with no sound, far below them. A huge vent of steam rose up from the bottom, and surged high into the air, forming a cloud and then thinning to nothing in the cold air. A common enough sight in Iceland, it was un-nerving to see such a thing here. In one or two places further along from where they were standing, they could make out thin, glistening stripes on the walls of the crevasse where streams of running water were tricking down and wearing away at the vertical sides, than disappearing into a fuzz of spray as the liquid water fell into the sheer drop. It seemed like the whole place was on the cusp of change. Coulson thought how it reminded him of spring back home, and how welcome a dripping thaw seemed after a long cold winter. Suddenly, it felt hard to fight back the feelings of optimism, and new beginnings, trying to remember that the repercussions of the effects of a rapid thaw here, could create problems on a scale not known in historical times. Joe's urgent voice brought him back from his thoughts.

"Hey, come on, Ray. We'd better get going." He looked around to see that the others had started to pack away their stuff, so he strode over to the group and began to do the same with his camera equipment. In ten minutes they were ready to leave the crevasse and head back. They revved up the engines of their snowmobiles, and after one more long backward look they powered off, to begin their return journey.

* * *

Eager to get back as quickly as they could, at first they made excellent progress, bouncing and skimming over the ice field. Ignoring the normal night and day routine, they took short regular breaks, sleeping for four hours at a time, and making use of the endless daylight to speed them on their way. Then, about twenty-four hours into their journey, they were slowing down to pull in for a chance to stretch out and catch up with some sleep, when Joe noticed a golden, yellow glow hanging low over the horizon. It was up lit by the early day sun. He pointed it out to the others, who thought it was strange, too, but deeply weary and focussed on getting something to eat to try to ward off the creeping exhaustion, they didn't see the haze gradually get closer to them.

It began to thicken and bank up higher in the sky, a dirty yellowish fog, rolling forward looking like a dust cloud looming over the desert. Cloud was forming and coming in from the east, too, eventually catching up with the gassy haze. The dull grey of the heavy, low cloud took much of the colour out of the landscape as it obscured the sun and turned the feeble daylight into dusk once more.

Joe emerged from his tent to take a look around before trying to get a couple of hours sleep. The others were already in their sleeping bags, resting soundly. The ongoing nausea which they'd all been feeling was beginning to get the better of him. He needed some air. His gaze was pulled over to the eastern horizon where he noticed the gathering clouds. They would have to watch that, he thought. It would almost certainly bring an end to the still, calm weather that they had experienced up until now on this expedition. It could even bring some heavy wet snow, which he hated far more than the dry cold powdery stuff that fell in the winter months. But in the gloom he failed to notice the now brown-yellow wall of fog that hung below the cloud and was merging in with it whilst creeping across the snowfield. It was difficult to get the perspective and he'd thought it was further away than it in fact was.

It was now very close, and moving in steadily.

As the gas cloud grew nearer the first really thick wisps began to swirl around the camp. Joe unwittingly was breathing in the fumes that were making him feel drowsy, and so he remained unaware of the danger as he sat on a pack near his snowmobile reading his map for the next leg of the journey. As he studied the lines on the map they started to look blurry, and at first he thought that he was just sleepy and needed to get his head down like the others had done. He grew angry at himself for missing so much of his chance to rest and hoped that it wouldn't affect his ability to cope with the next leg of the trip. He stood up quickly and was met with a thudding band of pain around his head as he did so, forcing him to sway as he tried to walk back to his tent to lie down.

Suddenly he knew that something was wrong. The air smelt putrid, and as he looked around to where he had thought there was just some incoming weather, he could now see the bank of poisonous volcanic fumes, blowing around in the rising wind. Soon it would be smothering the camp. He hurried as best he could to the sleeping men in the tents to warn them of the encroaching danger, but calling and shaking them could not, at first, arouse any of them from their drugged sleep. Then Coulson dragged himself out of his stupor and tried to focus on what Joe was telling him.

"We've got to get out now! We're being gassed. There are fumes everywhere. Get everyone up. Leave the equipment. We've just got to run for it. Come on! Get going!"

Coulson got out of his sleeping bag, only to find that his legs wouldn't move. It was like a bad dream. He shook the two Inuit guides with more and more impatience, and called at them to wake up and get ready to leave, as Joe had done with no success. He shook Iqniq again and called his name another couple of times, but he could get no response either from him or Kuvageegai. With rising frustration, he couldn't think of what else he could do to get them out in time. Already he could smell the pungent fumes seeping into the tent, and in desperation he shook Iqniq once more.

Then he froze as the realisation hit him.

He backed off and let his hand rest by his side. It was no use. Kuvageegai and Iqniq were both dead already. He tried once more to move and help himself, but could not get out of the tent. He gave up trying and slumped onto the floor, his head diving into a pool of blackness. He slipped into unconsciousness.

Out on the snow near his snowmobile, lay Joe too. He had in his hand his cell phone. He'd tried to call Becaud in desperation to airlift them out, now that they were deserting camp with no equipment or supplies. The call rang unanswered around Becaud's empty kitchen, too late. The door had just slammed shut behind him as he zipped up his flying jacket and tucked in his scarf on his way to the Cessna. He was still going over Amy James email in his head, and heard nothing of that last, desperate call for help. The phone stopped ringing eventually, leaving a tangible, hanging silence where the insistent ringing had cut uselessly through the air.

Joe, like the others, had been overcome by the toxic smog before he had chance to make it onto his machine.

* * *

Two days later, the sound of a small, approaching Cessna aircraft broke into the deathly quietness that now hung over the stricken camp site. Over the course of those two days the rising breeze had steadily turned into a persistent wind, bouncing around the stranded snowmobiles and supplies now left lying around like debris on the snow.

The tents flapped and billowed in the wind, no-one now hearing the occasional crack of fabric as the tents worked their way loose from their tethers. The cloud of noxious fumes had now gone without trace, the cleansing wind having done its job, but just too late to save the four men from its choking effects. The water in the tin kettle, once boiled, had now re-frozen. The map that Joe had been studying only a couple of days before, blew along the snow aimlessly, torn and dirty from scuffing the ground.

Flying low, to come in as close as he dared, Becaud swooped around and made a return pass, dipping the portside wing so the pilot could take a better look at the tiny cluster of tents that he'd spotted with misplaced relief some moments before. He saw the snowmobiles and the trailers of supplies, and identified them immediately as being part of Joe's expedition.

After trying to raise Joe on the radio for two days without success he had decided to see for himself if they were all OK and maybe drop them fresh supplies if that was what was needed. He wasn't unduly worried about them as he knew that communications were still unreliable, but thought he'd better check them out to be on the safe side. He craned round in the cockpit to try to get a better look at what was down there and knowing that they must have heard his engine by now, he was expecting to see some figures waving at him as he swooped past. He was preparing to go in as low as he could so that he could acknowledge their greeting. But there were no waving figures, and Becaud had begun to wonder if there was something wrong down there.

He jumped inwardly when he saw the slumped form of Joe on the snow below him. He knew it was Joe straightaway because of the orange anorak which showed up so starkly, against the white background of the snow field. He then saw the yellow of Coulson's coat, halfway out of the first tent. God! What the hell's happened out here! There was also no sign of the Inuit guides. They could have gone for help - but no, their snowmobiles were still standing there. Becaud ran cold with shock. He couldn't land. He couldn't help them. He knew that they were already beyond help. He turned the Cessna around and set a course for Angmagssalic. Then he picked up his mike and radioed back to his flight-follower in a strained, tight voice.

"This is mike-delta-tango, mike delta tango are you receiving me – over." The rescue services were alerted and would begin their work as soon as they heard what had happened.

Becaud swallowed the catch in his voice and flew, stunned and feeling completely gutted, back to Angmagssalik.

CHAPTER THIRTEEN

"Lawrence? It's Zoe." She paused a moment, gripping the receiver tightly. "Coulson's dead."

"What!" he said, although he'd heard her perfectly first time.

"We heard today from Phil Becaud. Oliver got an email this morning. The rest of the party, too, it seems."

"No! That's terrible. I can't believe it." He took a moment trying to take in what Zoe had just told him. He had in his mind an image of their meeting at the publisher's. He hardly knew the guy, but the news of his death really shook him. He tried to rally his thoughts. "What caused it, does anyone know?"

"They don't know yet, it's too soon to say. Phil's devastated. One of them was a good friend of his. The bodies have been recovered, but the autopsies haven't been completed yet."

"This is all we need," said Hewitt. "This could jeopardise our whole trip. Unless it turns out to be a genuine accident, there could be repercussions. I think we should try to bring the whole thing forward a few days. Try to get into the interior before the results of the autopsies become known. You don't think it could be foul play do you?"

"Foul play! If it is I'm not sure that we should be going at all. I don't think so. I don't know. Oliver thinks the most likely explanation could be polar bears, but I don't know. They would all have been armed – and there were four of them."

Inwardly, Hewitt winced at that as an explanation, and really hoped that that was not the case, but said nothing. He never came across well.

Zoe was struck by Hewitt's apparent lack of concern for Coulson; after all he was the only one of them who had actually met him. But she had to agree with him on the timings of the expedition. It was now imperative that they move as quickly as possible. She continued.

"Can you be ready to go in forty-eight hours, Lawrence?"

"I could go tomorrow," he said. "In fact I'm ready now."

"No. That's too soon." There was a slight laugh in her voice which made Hewitt feel over-prepared and a tad stupid for admitting it. "The first available flight isn't until the day after. I'll get Oliver to confirm the bookings, then I'll let you know what we're doing."

She rang off.

Her instinct had told her that she was onto something and now she knew her feelings were justified. She didn't think Coulson and his guides had been killed deliberately. That would have been taking conspiracy theories too far. And she didn't buy the stuff about polar bears either. Two of the expedition were Inuit hunters after all. No. This had to be something to do with the weird pattern of events that was happening up there. Maybe other crevasses were opening up, cutting off their route home. Hopefully the results of the autopsies would be through before they themselves set off into the interior.

She'd seen that massive fracture in the ice sheet with her own eyes, so its existence was not in doubt. Becaud was due to fax her the co-ordinates of Coulson's sighting later today, so that she could plot its path on the map, giving her some idea of how long it was. That data was crucial. Once she knew that it would give some indication of whether they had discovered an interesting local phenomenon, or something on a continental scale. What nagged at her were the small pixels of information that were hovering in her mind, but still, frustratingly, she couldn't see the bigger picture.

If there is one thing the human brain is supremely good at, thought Zoe, it is our capacity for pattern recognition. It's a highly necessary tool for any animal that relies on advanced social skills for its survival and progress. That same ability makes it possible to recognise an individual human face from many thousands of other similar ones in a crowd, but it is also what makes us see patterns where none exist in purely random natural phenomena, the most common example being of a face in cloud formations. These images are known as simulacra; we see them everywhere, often in vivid detail, and once the pattern takes shape in our minds it then becomes impossible to see the object in any other way. It is also true of other kinds of incoming data, up to a point, which we can see as part of our pattern of experience. An expert in any given field sometimes knows in an instant that something isn't right – but then has to begin the process of working out why. The point then, is to know the difference between cause and effect, and things which co-exist but have no causal relationship. The difference between scholarship and surmise. We see information as part of a pattern of theories or models which shape our existing world view. Some of that information bolsters what we already know and expect to hear, but sometimes things don't quite fit the pattern, and when that happens, either, we assume the data is faulty, or if it turns out to be unassailably true, then we get to change the theoretical models and have a paradigm shift. In Zoe's case it wasn't the academic theory of Abrupt Climate Change that was at fault, or the quality of the incoming data. In this case it was just the feeling that amongst all the stuff that had been happening in Greenland there was something that didn't quite fit – something that was not as it should be – and it had flicked on the red warning light inside her head.

It was the tremors that were key. Had to be.

The one that they'd experienced at Humboldt, she now knew was part of a pattern of disturbance that had been felt in many parts of Greenland. She had collected reports of tremors from the internet now that gradually people were getting back on line, and Oliver had been collating seismographic data that was connected to the Greenland area, spreading down through northern Europe and Scandinavia. The quake she had been caught up in, in the Peak District had spread from the Highlands of Scotland down through the midlands – all low levels stuff – but the frequency and unusual location of these disturbances were all pointing to something happening, that was over and above their normal range of expectation.

Looking at the history of climate change, Zoe understood that sometimes small factors affecting the planet could in some cases cancel each other out, but in others could amplify the effects. Like, for example, with the methane cycle. During periods of cooling like at the onset of the last Ice Ages, this was a time of great aridity, which in turn probably helped to dry out the wetlands which gave off methane, thus adding to the cooling effect.

But that isn't always the case. At times in history it's been the other way round, causing negative rather than positive feedback .It seems that it is at the heart of this matrix of hugely complex modifiers and amplifiers of the Earth's natural systems that the triggers for climate change exist.

Man-made carbon emissions are only a small part of the total picture, but could just be the amplifier that tips the balance and sends the planet into a warming phase that would destroy the comfort zone that man needs in order to thrive.

New and complex factors have to be taken into account by climate modellers all the time. The North Atlantic Oscillation, second only to El Nino as a climate cycle, is a variation in relative air pressure that affects the strength of the winds over the northern continents. During a strong, or positive, cycle, the strong winds pick up warm moist air from the oceans and heat the land. In a negative phase the land in these regions cools accordingly. Over the last thirty or so years the North Atlantic Oscillation has been in a positive phase, which would explain some of the warming trends in terms of natural cycles. But man-made greenhouse gasses, it seems alter the energy distribution within the stratosphere, which in turn drives the jet streams that circle the Arctic every winter. So the effects of the Oscillation are amplified by the greenhouse effect, an example of positive feedback.

But how did this fit in with the tremors? Were the ice sheets collapsing at a much greater rate than anyone had dared to believe before - their movement and instability triggering off seismic events in the Earth's crust? Or had a volcanic event caused a rupture in the ice sheet to occur, thereby sending shock waves through the surrounding areas.

Basically Zoe was convinced that the crevasse and the quakes were interconnected, but quite how was what she had to find out. Which was the cause and which was the effect? She had a hunch that it was the former. She thought that the ice sheet had sheered at a weak spot – perhaps meltwater had seeped in deep inside the ice cracking it apart along a fault line maybe.

Then liquid water pours down to the bottom of the crevasse lubricating the ice sheet by lifting it from its anchorage to the bedrock below.

This was the nightmare scenario. Unstable land ice, breaking off from its 20 million-years-old moorings and sliding into the sea causing a tidal wave like a newly launched liner as it hit the water. Or by rapid melting land ice could cause sea levels to rise maybe at the rate of twenty metres in 400 years, which is exactly what happened 14,500 years ago at the end of one of the last major glaciations.

These events are not just theoretical possibilities.

They have happened before and they could happen again.

Zoe feared that they could be witness to an unstoppable process, where their best hope might be that they could buy some time. Or maybe they could stall the process if they understood it better. Zoe knew that it was imperative that they find out what they could as soon as possible.

No-one else seemed to realise the urgency of the situation. She was convinced that Coulson's tragic expedition to locate the crevasse was both tentative and ill judged. The MoD with the connivance of the government wanted to look as though it was doing more than it was; staging an enquiry, which in reality was a holding operation. Instead of showing clear leadership and taking responsible action, they'd used Coulson on a time-wasting fact-finding mission. Poor sod. He'd only been chosen for his low profile and, she thought cynically, for his expendability. If he'd come back with clear evidence of the break up of the Greenland ice sheet the government wouldn't have known what to do with it anyway. Or him.

That thought brought her up with a start. She hoped Hewitt wasn't right about there being a possibility of foul play. That frightened her.

Zoe called Oliver and told him to book the first available flights to Nuuk. "Lawrence is ready. We need to make a move." She spoke briefly into the telephone, looking around the hall as she did so. She saw the pictures of their children on the table, forever smiling through their frames, and she felt a twinge of guilt that she would be leaving them again so soon.

"You OK, hon?" he said, picking up on the slight pause.

"Yes I'm alright," she said. She knew he'd tell her they'd be fine. But in a sense that was worried her. They'd got used to her being away, and she almost wanted it to matter more.

"I'll call as soon as I get the flight times confirmed. See you tonight." He hung up and she put the receiver back in its cradle.

Zoe climbed the stairs and opened the door to the walk-in cupboard on the landing that served as a dumping ground for all their expedition stuff. She'd only just packed it all away. She pulled her bags out from the back of the cupboard and threw them on the bed in her room, first unzipping them then propping them open. Zoe packed with the well rehearsed absorption of someone who knew exactly what she could and could not live without.

She folded the thermal long-sleeved tees in half and placed them in the bottom of her rucksack, followed by four waffle-textured thin fleece tops, pushing them carefully into the corners to get them as flat as possible. The thick winter weight fleeces went in next. She then rolled up two pairs of thick fleece lined trousers, and put those on top, together with some base layer merino leggings. In the spaces around the tight rolls, she stuffed several pairs of socks, some thin for lining, others thick and woolly. Then came the hats gloves and seven pairs of briefs. No, eight. She was always running out. She checked out the medical kit, methodically. The suture needles, together with the silk sutures were there, and so were the sterile hypodermics, the pressure pads, and some re-hydration sachets. She noticed with irritation that she needed some more of the everyday stuff – aspirin, antiseptic cream, and some glue. Probably wouldn't need it as it's summer, but cuts don't heal in sub-zero temperatures and holding the tissue together with glue till you get back to base is often the only way to keep out infection. Lastly she folded up her bulky anorak and pushed it down till she could get the flap over and fasten it securely. In her holdall she packed some lighter clothing for wearing at base, two micro fibre towels, one large and one small, and a few essentials like toiletries. Her one permitted luxury was a bar of very expensive soap. Zoe liked to think of herself as womanly without being girly, and when out in the field she sometimes needed a reminder of her feminine identity. It might seem frivolous, but it was worth every penny.

They would not be staying at Humboldt this time. They were going to rent a house in Angmagssalic to be near to Phil Becaud. Phil had suggested it and Oliver had agreed instantly that it was the best plan. The hold-all, now packed to capacity, stretched and bulged with all the bulk of planning for a trip to the Arctic. She thought enviously of how easy it would be to have a rucksack lightly packed with a few rolled up tee-shirts and to be heading for the tropics, before picking up her laptop and sliding it neatly into the pocket down the side of her bag. She was done. If she'd forgotten any-thing now, she would have to do without it.

* * *

Forty-eight hours later, across town at his flat in north London, Hewitt lifted the tailgate of his silver, ten year old Golf and pushed his bags inside, leaving enough space for two more cases at the side. He was relieved to be setting off at last after two days hang-ing around his flat kicking his heels, and being able to focus on nothing else but the trip. His sense of urgency increased as the media chatter was beginning to pick up on rumours that a new crack had been discovered by scientists in the Arctic. At the moment the reporting was merely curious, even benign, along the lines of it being continued evidence of climate change. The reports were as yet unconfirmed and it could be that the story might not pick up any momentum. For the time being. Experts who were already familiar with the rumours, had heard the news gravely, and were deeply worried by its implications. All it would take would be a savvy science correspondent to root out those fears and start searching for some facts and the word cataclysm would start being bandied about. Then there'd be no chance for a maverick expedition like theirs to go ahead. Any official response would have to be controlled, measured and very played down.

He slammed the tailgate shut, then, keys in hand, he got into the car and turned on the ignition. He tweaked the rear view mirror somewhat needlessly, mainly to get a quick look at his hair before checking the road behind and swinging out into the flow of traffic. He was setting off to pick up Amy James from her house, as she needed a lift to the airport, and had readily accepted his offer to call round for her.

The evening was warm and fine with just a few bands of high cirrus cloud streaked across the pale sky. Great weather for flying, he thought, and was already looking forward to his in-flight scotch. But then he imagined Coulson doing the self same thing as he was setting off only a couple of weeks ago, and it made his mood more sombre. He arrived at Amy's place in good time, to find her already waiting in the hall of her house, the door open, with the luggage all ready to go.

"Thanks, Lawrence. I do appreciate this. It's just too much hassle to try to get a taxi, at the moment." He noticed that she looked a bit down, despite her attempt to be sociable. The news of Coulson's death had cast a shadow over all of them, and they knew that the loss of the other guides must have left the tiny community in Angmagssalic reeling.

"Oh, that's OK," he said, lifting her bags into the space he had left for them. They fitted just right, but this time he closed the door more carefully, squashing the bags slightly as he pushed it shut.

"You OK?" he said.

"No, not really," she said. He didn't press her on her answer, as he knew exactly what she meant.

"Let's go," he said, and putting his foot down hard on the accelerator, they set off to join the Carters at the airport.

* * *

Unnoticed by either Hewitt, or Amy, a man in a red Toyota covered pickup that was badly rusting along the sills and round the seams of the tailgate, was parked opposite her house, and had been there for at least the last hour. It wasn't the first time that he'd been parked up in that road during the last two days, either, but sitting there, ticking off imaginary jobs on a dog-eared clipboard, he'd attracted no attention, and Amy wouldn't have registered that there was anything unusual in his presence even if she had noticed him there. Without turning he saw Hewitt and Amy drive off in the Golf, through his wing mirror, and methodically he looked at his wristwatch to make a note of the time. He then switched on the engine, and in one smooth movement he was following them at a discreet distance to try to find out where they were headed. They were obviously going away for some time as they had luggage with them. The traffic was too dense for him to keep right

behind them and he lost them at the next big rounda-
bout for a while. But he persevered, and after about
fifteen more minutes he thought he recognised the Golf
in the distance. They were now on a dual carriageway
so he sped up the outside lane until he was almost level,
when they took the next exit marked with the aeroplane symbol that he'd been expecting. He drove on,
not needing to follow them further. He'd got Hewitt's
name from his publisher, then found out where he lived
by following him home. He'd got Amy's name from
the electoral roll, and now that he'd got Hewitt's regis-
tration number, too. Should be able to get some more
details now by hacking into the relevant data bases.
More difficult, but not impossible. He wondered if they
were having an affair, but he didn't think so, from their
body language, and from the fact that Hewitt hadn't
been staying at the house. He'd got a couple of other
names on his list; academics who worked at Isaac Newton College, but he didn't yet know where they lived.
That was his next job. He stopped off at the next garage
for some fuel in case he couldn't find one with any petrol later. He never liked to get lower than half a tank.
While he was there he bought a sausage sandwich from
the hot cabinet and a coffee to go. The sandwich was
reduced in price as it was late in the day, and he hoped
it would still OK to eat. Back in the pickup, he opened
the lid of his laptop, and checked out the flight depar-
tures from Heathrow. There was a flight to Reykjavik in
about two hours. That would be about right, allowing
for check in time. Then they would get a small plane to
Nuuk, the Capital of Greenland.

He snapped the lid of the laptop shut and slid it onto the passenger seat. Not a bad day's work, he thought as he peeled off the wrapper and polished off the sandwich while it was still hot.

CHAPTER FOURTEEN

Greenland

"I've been trying to piece together as much as I can about the crevasse from everything we have got so far, and, at the moment as you can see, there are still a lot of discrepancies." Becaud drew a circle with his finger the size of a dinner plate on the large-scale map that was laid out across the dark brown dining table. The overhead light was on, creating a patch of glare in the middle of the map, making it difficult to see the detail there, but it was too dull a day to manage without it. His finger jabbed at the centre of the imaginary circle and all eyes were focussed on where he was pointing. "This area is where we were. I'm convinced of that." He arced his hand around once more. "If you calculate the time we were flying before we headed for the coast – look – here's where we landed – we had to be somewhere in this vicinity." He then took out a highlighter pen and drew a transparent yellow circle on the crisp new paper.

Zoe winced inwardly at this act of vandalism. She liked to keep new things neat, but felt somewhat prim next to Becaud's ease and boldness.

This was the first time that they'd been to his house, and he seemed strangely out of context. She'd hardly ever seen him without his scarf and dark glasses. He continued in his slight Canadian accent.

"But Joe's co-ordinates are way over here."

He pointed again, this time to a specific point on the map, and left his finger there as if for emphasis. Oliver and Hewitt leaned over the table to get a better look at where Becaud was pointing. Zoe was doing a mental calculation of how far away the two positions were, to work out what the margins for error were, and whether there was any possibility of them both being right. She was under no doubt that Joe had found the crevasse, but she was cautious about his figures as they'd had to calculate their position without any technological backup. Then the thought suddenly struck her. What if the solar storm had affected the accuracy of their compasses? Coulson and the others could have lost their lives for nothing. The thought crept in that they could be about to do the same. A great hollow opened up inside her, ready for fears and doubts to rush in, and gain a foothold in her consciousness. She closed it up again quickly by asking a question.

"Phil, you said the two Inuit guides disagreed about the sightings of the crevasse. It caused a bust-up or something. But they'd heard reports from hunters that they believed were reliable. Just out of interest – where was the other sighting – the one that Joe didn't head for? Did he ever tell you?"

"Well he didn't bother to tell me the co-ordinates of that one, no. But as you can guess, there's been a lot of talk about the tragedy in town, and everyone reckons that the place that Iqniq wanted to head for was to the north-west of where they eventually found the crevasse. Probably a couple of hundred kilometres away. Would have been out of their range anyway, I guess."

Zoe leaned over and put her finger on the map where the crevasse was marked then followed a line to the north-west for an estimated two hundred kilometres. The distances involved now looked vast. Especially when they looked to where they thought their original sighting might be.

"So where do you think we should head for?" said Oliver.

"The obvious place is where Joe found the rift." Becaud was puzzled that anyone needed to ask. "We've at least got the co-ordinates for that."

"If they're right," said Zoe. She hadn't meant to say that to Becaud, but felt she had no choice.

"What do mean, if they're right? Joe knew what he was doing." He sounded short, but Zoe pressed on. She had to.

"We might have to allow some leeway for inaccuracy even with his conventional instruments, Phil. I'm sure he did his best, but...."

"What the hell are you trying to tell me? That he was wasting his fucking time out there? That this information he lost his life over isn't worth anything?"

He banged his fist on the table, making the map crackle as he did so. He opened his mouth to speak but stopped, knowing it wasn't them who'd asked Joe to go out there in the first place, and it wasn't their fault that he'd not come back. Zoe bit her lip, and looked away. Becaud blew hard to regain his equilibrium. Amy James said,

"I think we need some coffee. I'll go and make us some."

She slipped away to the kitchen. After a couple of minutes Hewitt was the first to break the tension.

"I think that we should try to retrace our path when we flew out there the last time." Becaud looked at him in silence. "I was looking at the landscape constantly as we went. I've got a good memory for things like that. I'll be able to recognise any landmarks on the way." Hewitt was only trying to help, but he could have picked a better time to say what he did.

Becaud looked at him with incredulity. Who the hell does this guy think he is? Now he claims to be an expert navigator.

"OK, as we came into land at Angmagssalic, how many houses were clustered round the landing strip to your left?" said Becaud, cynically.

"Five. And what looked like a derelict fishing boat next to the yellow one."

Becaud was astounded. Smart ass, he thought. But said nothing. He was mentally reckoning up whether there were in fact five houses just there, and had to admit he was not dead certain himself now that he thought about it.

Zoe whispered to her husband *that was a bit tactless,* imperceptibly glancing towards a smug-looking Lawrence Hewitt, but Oliver looked amused, and didn't see why Lawrence should have to apologise for being right. *Those two will never get on,* he grinned and winked at Zoe. She couldn't see what he found so entertaining.

Zoe was still pouring over the map, trying to work out why there were still so many discrepancies in their data when she thought by now they would have been able to home in on a site.

"It's obvious," said Amy, walking back in the room with the coffee. "There's not just one crevasse. There are at least three of three, all massive, and there could be many more if only we knew where to look."

"Of course," said Hewitt. "We should have thought of that before."

"That's not good news," Oliver said. "It might mean the break up of the ice sheet is more extensive than we thought."

"The break up of the ice sheet?" said Becaud. "Sounds a bit heavy. Are you guys serious?" He looked around at the faces staring back at him and saw the anxiety in their eyes.

"I'm afraid so. When it came to global warming, we were always told as scientists that our imaginations were running away with us, when we tried to warn people of what could be happening. Now, though, I think it is reality that's running away with us, and leaving our imaginings looking a bit tame. We try to envisage a worse case scenario, and when we find the evidence, it's nearly always even worse than we thought." Oliver took a drink of his coffee.

"Hang on a minute, guys." An idea had clicked in Zoe's head. "Amy, think about it. What's even more obvious than the conclusion that there is more than one crack in the ice?" They all waited for her reply.

"That all these different sightings and reports are of one and the same mega-fracture of the ice sheet." She bent over the map once more, only this time picking up Becaud's highlighter pen. She drew a zig-zag line starting at their sighting from the plane up through Joe's position and then over to where the Inuit hunters had insisted that they had seen it, too. "Amy, can you get me a contour map of Greenland, I've got a hunch that it could give us a clue as to what is going on here."

Amy opened up her laptop while the others waited impatiently for the image to appear. She focussed in on the area that they had highlighted on the map then got a 3-D image of Greenland with cut-away images of the ice with the contours of the land marked out below. She turned and tilted the image till she got an aerial view of the landscape then entered in the co-ordinates of the sightings of the crevasse. The contour lines seen from above marked the height of the ice sheet as it increased in thickness towards the middle of the continent. The sightings followed the 2,500 metre contour in a north-westerly direction perfectly. This was no random effect. Amy drew on the screen a jagged line joining up the marked sites to emphasise the point. She highlighted the contour line, then tilted the image back to get the elevation. Along the contour line was a join in the ice sheet, probably marking the edge of a previous interglacial. A weak spot in the ice sheet.

"Wow, look at that!" said Amy. "You could be right, Zo. We're definitely onto something here. Now this is interesting."

Zoe replied, "Yes. Look at that. It matches more or less exactly, in this area anyway. I wonder if it follows the contour right round or veers off to the south-west and across to the other coast. Phil, if you have any more reports of any sightings – even if they're only rumours, could you let Amy know. She could plot them on the map and just see if any of them sit on our line here. I bet you they do."

She was firing on all cylinders now.

"We have to get out there. This looks like we've found an ice canyon that would dwarf the Grand Canyon in scale. Goodness knows what could have caused it, or what its consequences could be."

"Hold on, we haven't actually found anything yet." Oliver was trying to keep up.

"I know...so we've got to act fast." Zoe was looking to her husband for support. "And get confirmation that it's out there. This is what I think we should do. We need to try to pick up the contour line as close to the coast as we can, and then follow it inland to try to establish where the crevasse first opens up, and how deep it is as that point." She darted a look at Becaud who was studying the maps on the computer screen. "Do you agree with that, Phil?"

He did.

"We then need to follow it – the crevasse – that is, and see just how far it goes on for," said Oliver.

"I'll calculate a route and work out how far we can go. If I can arrange fuel stops on the way we can aim to go a lot further if we need to. I'll get on to that now," said Becaud.

"We really needed Coulson's data after all, in order to get the bigger picture. We might never have twigged otherwise. It looks as though Joe's co-ordinates were spot on if our theories are verified. He did a good job," said Oliver.

Becaud nodded appreciatively, then went over to his desk to gather together his charts for the trip before adding,

"We ought to set off tomorrow by seven a.m. Is everyone OK with that?"

They all agreed, and taking that as their cue to go, they finished their drinks and began to get their stuff together. Amy turned off the computer and Hewitt collected the cups together and took them back into Becaud's kitchen. Someone fetched the coats and handed them around. Any trip outside needed hats and gloves even if one wasn't going far; it wasn't worth the risk of getting complacent. They were ready, and, shouting out their goodbyes to Becaud, eventually stepped out into the cold glare to walk the short distance to the house they had rented for their stay.

The next day, muffled in thick four season clothing against the chill early morning air, the Carters, Amy James and Lawrence Hewitt trudged across the snowy landing strip to where Becaud was waiting for them with the engines of the Cessna Super Caravan already warmed up and ready to go. The sky had streaks of thin white cloud stretching out in a fan just above the horizon, diffusing the sunlight to a milky glow that cast faint shadows of their figures far behind them. The throbbing plane, larger and newer than Becaud's previous one, still looked small and fragile to Zoe who had been OK about the trip until she saw it standing there on the runway, waiting for her to climb inside. Her stomach tightened and her heart rate quickened despite her thinking that she had overcome her fear after the traumas of her last flight.

"You'll be OK," Oliver nodded to her encouragingly.

Hewitt helped Amy into the plane, then sat down beside her. Zoe settled into her seat and pulled on her seat belt this time sitting to the right of Oliver to balance up their weight as Amy was on Hewitt's left. Becaud gave the flight details and expected time of return to his flight-follower on the radio that was now working loud and clear. Everyone in the cabin reached for their headphones and slipped them on without having to be prompted.

"Everything functioning this time, Phil?" said Oliver.

"No problems." Becaud looked confident. "The solar storm now seems to be over at last."

They were moving. Zoe tensed her hands into tight fists inside her mittens. The engines revved hard and they were committed to go for take off. The ground sloped away and as it got smaller, became a picture through their window. She could look at it now. She let out a breath and sat back. She'd be OK.

They flew on for about one hour and twenty minutes pretty confident that they were following the same route that they'd been on before. Hewitt's claim to have a remarkable memory proved to be no idle boast either. He sat riveted to the landscape below them, each time he noticed a familiar feature giving the pilot the route confirmation he so desperately needed. They must be drawing near to their original sighting of the crevasse Zoe thought, but then Hewitt said,

"I don't remember anything here. Suddenly nothing looks familiar."

"OK, Lawrence, we'll turn north and head back – there's certainly no point in heading out further – we're up to our time limit of the previous journey."

Becaud banked the Cessna around steeply, almost retracing their path except that they were now further north. The pilot had a hunch that they were in the vicinity of the crevasse. Trouble was, they hadn't got that much flying time to search, and if he was wrong they might all have to go back empty-handed.

"Why don't we just head straight for Joe's co-ordinates, and forget about trying to find where it begins," said Amy, trying to be helpful but creating a situation where everyone would have their own opinion, and Becaud would have to adjudicate.

"No, not yet. If possible we need to find out where it starts so that we can discover how long it is. That could be crucial in estimating its importance," said Zoe.

"But we can do that anyway – if we head to the one definite sighting, we can then fly along it in either direction and get its dimensions – seems obvious to me," said Hewitt, backing up Amy.

Zoe still wasn't sure that that was a realistic option as it would mean a lot of doubling back even when they'd found it. Becaud was just about to come in and explain that he'd give it bit longer before setting a course for the known sighting when Hewitt butted in with an exclamation.

"Hey! We are on the right track! That feature down there, look, there's a field of crevasses. You can see them really clearly with the sun at such a low angle. I got a shot of that last time. I just know it's the same one!"

The landscape didn't look familiar to Becaud, but he deferred to Hewitt's greater sense of conviction. They all looked out of the windows of the Cessna now with urgency. Zoe had some powerful field glasses, which she hadn't used up till now as she had preferred to have a wider field of vision, but now she used them to scan for any sign of the fissure. She scanned intently; several times thinking that she'd got something. But then, at last. She got it. She knew straight away without a trace of doubt. There it was. A thin line appeared on the starboard side of the Cessna cutting a corner off the view from the right hand side over to the horizon where it disappeared into infinity. She took a deep breath and paused for a moment, the thrill of the discovery totally hers for a few seconds.

"I've got it," Zoe said. Her voice was quiet and firm, while a rustle went round the cabin. Oliver put his face close to hers so that he could follow her gaze and see for himself. She moved the binoculars with an effort from where they were pressing close to her cheekbones and slid them over to Oliver, so that he could take a look.

"You see it yet, Phil?" said Oliver.

"Er, I'm not sure...yeah, wait a minute. I think I do, now."

He readjusted the plane's course a little to starboard so they were headed straight for the rift. As they got closer the hard black line became thicker where the deep shadow picked out its shape from the white snowfields around it. Somehow it looked unnatural, even in a world where the unexpected was becoming the norm. The landscape beneath them would have sent shock waves of disbelief through any experienced Arctic traveller, who hadn't seen the area in a decade, or maybe two at most. They flew over a huge melt lake, maybe a thousand metres across, glinting blue-green in the building sun, the water suddenly making the seemingly immovable ice look fragile. They looked down in amazement as the soft grey shadow of the plane was replaced by their reflection as they passed overhead, then back to shadow again. The Greenland ice sheet once a permanent stabilising factor in the Earth's climate, like the rain forests of the Amazon, now seemed extremely tenuous and vulnerable. Everywhere they looked they could see evidence of change. In the distance was the glint of another meltwater lake, its contents slowly seeping down into the gaps and fissures in the ice cup beneath it. The shrinking coastal glaciers were revealing patches of naked, stony river bed as they eased their way seawards, and to a close observer, they were moving at a rate that made their momentum visible to the naked eye. It seemed that the once hard edges of the ice sheet were beginning to fray, as the climatic processes that they were all trying to understand were becoming inexorably unravelled.

The engines of the Cessna buzzed in a constant drone now that all conversation had ground to a halt and a sense of purpose settled around the cabin as every individual once more became focussed on the task ahead. A sense of the importance of what they were trying to do welled up before them as their immediate aim of drying to discover the whereabouts of the crevasse had now been achieved.

The once distant line in the ice thickened gradually from a delicate pencil line to a thick scrawl from a marker pen. Now they were closer they could see that as a feature it had some depth and irregularity. To the east it was definitely getting wider, to the west it disappeared before it reached the horizon. They had found its limit, on this end at least. From the air the crevasse looked about twenty-thirty metres wide at this point, and its shape was too irregular to get a reliable depth reading, even with Becaud's prized gadget, his radio altimeter. They swooped down low over it banking to port to line up with it, then Becaud worked out their position and did a quick calculation to get a ball-park figure of where the crevasse probably originated. They followed its path as it widened and deepened. Becaud took some more depth readings.

"One thousand nine hundred metres," he said, without elaboration.

"Then we could be down to bedrock," said Zoe. "It's not like a crevasse. It's like the ice sheet is broken, more like a fracture line."

They all had to agree; it was like nothing they'd ever seen before, its edges were sheer and clean, emphasising its newness, glinting blue-white against the blackest of shadows where the sun couldn't penetrate.

The pilot suddenly asked a question.

"What's an Ice Blink?" said Becaud, voicing to them all his private train of thought, and taking them all a bit by surprise.

"I think it's a mariner's term," said Hewitt. "It's to do with the colour of the sky - whether it reflects ice or land, the sky appears to be a different colour so they know what lies ahead."

"Fancy you knowing that," said Amy. "Why? Why did you ask that, Phil?"

"It was something Joe said when he radioed me to tell me that they'd found the crevasse – or whatever you want to call it now. He said we had a two mile Ice-blink. I didn't know what the hell he was talking about – thought he'd got snow-blindness or something. But it was a phrase that I couldn't get out of my mind afterwards, and I kept wondering what he meant."

"You're right about the sea-faring term Lawrence, but it also means something else out here," said Oliver. Zoe turned her head to listen to him. He was a store of information. "It's a Danish name for the great ice-cliffs of Greenland, an Ice-blink. And Joe had stood at the top of one, two miles high – or two miles deep, depending on which way you look at it. I'm sure that's what he was meaning."

"Gee, I never knew that," said Becaud. "But I think it's a great name for it – sounds more dramatic than a crevasse. Well here it is folks. We've found it at last. It's the two-mile-high Ice-Blink. Shall we go down and take a proper look?"

"Can we land here, Phil?" Zoe said, surprised. She'd been desperate to get in close and begin the process of gathering some hard data at last, but hadn't any real expectation that they would be able to do that on this trip. "It would be fantastic if we could, and get the whole process moving at last."

"Sure," Becaud said, coolly. "We haven't come this far just to leave empty-handed, have we? I'll keep my eyes peeled for a good place to land. "

And so he did. Zoe, relieved, after all their plans and speculation, to feel that she was getting her teeth into this project. She nudged Oliver and smiled at him. He made no remark, but she could tell by the animated look in his eyes that he was as excited as she was, at the thought of being down there, and seeing the Rift for real.

CHAPTER FIFTEEN

Greenland

Zoe looked awkwardly out of the aircraft window at a pall of smoke or steam – she couldn't tell which – that poured out of the gash in the ice sheet at its widest point so far. She knew at once that this was what she had been looking for, though up to now she had not said a thing to the others about her hunch, even to Oliver. She'd have to get on to Dorothy Redmires as soon as they got back to base.

"Can we land anywhere around here?" Zoe said to Becaud.

"Maybe. I'll go in low and take a look."

As Becaud scoured the ground for a big enough piece of level ground to get the plane down, Zoe got a better look at the dense ashy cloud, coming, she could see now from a deep hole in the side of the ice cliff that was acting like a chimney.

251

"Get as close to this as you can, Phil, I really need to take a look down there if I can."

"OK, I'll see what I can do." He circled round a couple more times, so that Zoe could get a good take on the rising cloud. He got in as close as he dared, as even tough the cloud was not that big, he didn't want to risk deposits of ash clogging up the engines. He then found a place that was level enough to land the plane, but only just. He banked around, lining up the aircraft with the area he'd spotted that had the longest stretch of smooth ice, then began the final descent with an ease that made the touchdown seem effortless. The Cessna was brought to a halt some little way off from the crevasse. Becaud cut the engines and the silence rushed in as though filling a vacuum. They pulled on their hats, gloves then outer gloves and gathered together their equipment, checking that they'd got everything they needed, talking only of the job in hand.

Zoe and Oliver were the first to arrive at the edge of the precipice, cool and business-like. Amy and Hewitt trailed along after them, Hewitt videoing the scene as he walked, Amy struggling with equipment that was heavier than she thought when she agreed to carry it. Zoe was making notes on the ambient temperature as they neared the crevasse, but could detect no change in the readings. Unbelievably to them Becaud had said he would stay in the plane, and twisting round in his seat to get more room, he shook open his newspaper and settled down to pass the time in comfort and relative warmth.

"If you want to know what the headlines are," said Oliver as he got ready to jump out of the cabin. "just take a look over there." He nodded towards the huge rift, significantly.

"I'll let you guys take care of all that," said Becaud taking out his pen to do the sudoku. "I'm OK right here, taking a rest."

"But surely you're curious to see it, after all the hype," said Amy.

"I have just seen it. I've just flown over it," said Becaud, still slumped in his seat, and clearly not changing his mind about moving. They left him to it, still surprised at his off-hand attitude, but more concerned with seeing it for themselves and getting some data together.

As they approached the precipice they slowed their already slow walking pace as though in awe of what lay before their eyes. The jagged line on map-like landscape had become a feature of planetary proportions, telling of events that might have happened in the comfort zone of the distant past, but unimaginable for such cataclysms to come back and disturb the present. The edge grew closer, and Oliver raised his arm to indicate to the others that it was time to stop. Zoe took the ropes from her shoulder and some pegs out of her pack, and together with Amy they hammered the pegs into the ice – three – to be on the safe side. Amy secured the ropes very firmly and Oliver tugged hard on them to make sure that they were secure. Amy and Zoe then harnessed the ropes around their bodies, checking each other in silence before, as one, lying down on the ice and crawling the last few paces to the very edge of the cliff.

Hewitt set up the webcam that would send pictures back to the students waiting with Dorothy Redmires for their first contact. He got a fantastic view of the crevasse, then turned it on.

Mindful that the edge could be undercut, Zoe had no idea whether there was two kilometres of packed snow beneath her thumping chest, or a couple of feet of fragile overhang, waiting to crumble into the void. She felt the ropes which were pulled tight around her torso and pressed on, occasionally looking at Amy to see if she was OK.

Another few seconds and they were both peering over the edge. She had imagined that it would be like looking from the top of a skyscraper, but instead it was like looking out of a plane window the drop was so vast. The sides were sheer and almost perfectly vertical from where they were, like something out of a film set; they were so smooth that they looked as though they had been computer-generated. Further along, the sides of the ice cliff were more rugged and stepped where the ice had broken away less evenly, and looking through her powerful field-glasses, she could see how the gap narrowed at the bottom and disappeared into deep black shadow. To the left she could see the gently rising cloud of smoke, signalling a presence, like a giant's campfire. She focussed in on it, but inevitably the drifting smoke at the base of the column obscured its origin.

"Pass me the camera, Lawrence – I'll start to lower it down. Let's see what we've got down there."

Zoe began to lower Hewitt's remote camera down into the gorge, bit by bit, feeding it through gradually so as not to damage it against the side of the crevasse.

It was taking some considerable time. Hewitt, in exasperation said at last.

"Just let it go. We'll be here forever at this rate. Feed it through as quick as you can Amy."

Amy? Lawrence never used anyone's name. Zoe and Oliver exchanged glances.

"It's an old camera I've used on diving expeditions, built to withstand pressure. It's as tough as old boots." Pity you didn't mention that before, thought Zoe, through gritted teeth, and lowered the camera down faster as Amy now fed her more cable, letting it virtually free-fall.

"No point in smashing it, though, Lawrence, is there?" said Oliver. "We won't get any data that way." Zoe appreciated that.

Amy stepped in. "Lawrence, can you take control of the cable here, while I start with the temperatures and air analysis data. Oliver was watching the monitor of the digital camera as it made its way down into the crevasse, the giddying images going by too fast for the eye to register, as it spun and tumbled its way towards the bottom. The cable then stopped and tightened as it ran out, leaving the camera hanging there, slowly turning but still some way from the bottom.

"Damn!" said Oliver, despite knowing all the while they were unlikely to have enough wire to reach the base of the crevasse.

They huddled around the monitor and waited for the camera to stop swinging enough for them to make out a recognisable image. Hewitt was able to tilt the camera slightly but the mechanism was clumsy and it took him quite a few attempts to get it right. At last it was pointed at forty-five degrees so that they could see the bottom of the crevasse, albeit some distance away. He zoomed in, paused, and then zoomed in again, on the highest magnification that he could get. The field of vision was very narrow now, but they could definitely see bedrock. There could be no doubt about it now; the ice sheet had split open right down to its base. They could where see the first sprinkling of ancient snow had touched the cold, dry rock some thousands of years ago, and where it had remained, compacted under thousands of kilos of pressure per square centimetre, ever since.

Slowly, they panned the camera around, but looking into shadow, they could make nothing out in that direction, and so pulled back again. They tilted the camera again, but this time at a less steep angle so they could see more into the distance where the smoke appeared to be coming from. Zoe strained forwards over the monitor to get a better look at the fuzzy image in front of her.

"Can you bring this into focus for me, right here, Lawrence? I think this is what we need to be looking at." Hewitt did his best to get a really good image, but it was too far away to be really clear.

Zoe squinted intently at the screen, and after a few minutes beckoned to Amy to take a look at what she'd seen. Amy moved from the edge of the assembled group and pushed in next to Zoe to get a closer viewpoint.

"It's no good. I'll get these images computer-enhanced when we get back to base," said Amy.

"There's definitely volcanic activity going on down there, though. We can be certain of that. But we need to know how much, and we need to know more detail – like whether it's mostly ash and smoke, or if there's lava flowing."

"Whatever it is, it's starting to smell pretty bad. Can you all smell it too?" said Hewitt.

"Yes, now that you mention it, I suppose I can," said Oliver, taking in a deep breath to confirm his first impression. "It's just like that sulphury smell we experienced at Humboldt."

"Only stronger," said Amy, suddenly getting a blast as the foul, gassy air drifted over them all at once.

"Oh my God, that's terrible!" Amy said pulling a face in disgust.

"Zo, better pull the camera back up," said Oliver, deciding for all of them. "We can't work till this has blown over."

He and Hewitt started to wind the cable as Zoe fed it through to them. She was still tethered to the ice as she was working, like Amy nearest to the edge, but now she was standing upright to make bringing up the camera quicker and easier.

As the fumes intensified Zoe began to feel nauseous, and she hurried as much as she could to retrieve the camera so that they could get away and into some fresh air. It came over the top of the ledge with a bump. Zoe bent over to pick it up and hand it over to the two men reeling in the cable, but as she did so she had the weirdly unsettling sensation that her hands felt too large to hold the camera which now felt tiny and out of proportion.

She was having an Alice in Wonderland moment, as her perceptions had been skewed by the effects of the fumes. She could hear ringing in her ears, so she turned to her husband to tell him that she didn't feel well, only to see him sagging down towards the ice. Beside him, Hewitt had done the same and was already slumped over the cable reel. Amy was trying to crawl away, but could go no further as the ropes held her back. Zoe held her breath in an attempt to stay conscious but could not do it for more than a few seconds without gasping in some more of the toxic air. She tried to untie herself from the tethers but could not make her hands work, which was fortunate in the circumstances, as just before she passed out she staggered unknowingly towards the edge of the precipice. The rope tightened and pulled her down onto the ice as everything went dark around her.

Becaud looked up from his sudoku lazily. He'd got one more line to go, and it would all fit neatly into place. Or at least he hoped so. If it didn't, it could all be wrong and he would have to go through it all again. He pencilled in some numbers in the margin of the newspaper, then one by one he began to cross them out as he fitted them into their squares. Then he noticed his mistake. The number eight couldn't be right as it appeared later in the line. Goddam! He could have sworn he'd cracked it this time. Now he would have to go through it all again. He tapped the pencil on the newspaper impatiently, and looked up towards Zoe and the group out there on the ice. They all appeared to be lying down again this time. He went back to his puzzle and began the process of working his way through the lines and squares to see where he had made his mistake. Three or four minutes went by and he couldn't see where he had gone wrong. Suddenly he lost patience with it and tossed the paper over onto the other seat, picking up his binoculars to take a closer look at the scientists as they worked.

They were still lying down.

He put the binoculars down, and wondered whether to give the sudoku one last try, but couldn't get back into it. Something wasn't right. He'd been glancing up at the group every now and again for the last hour. They'd been animated and busy-looking although a little too far away for him to make out what they were actually doing. But in the last five minutes no-one had moved at all. He took up the binoculars again, and stared hard at the group to detect any sign of movement, but instead he could just see this tableau of shapes in unfamiliar poses.

Hurriedly Becaud forced his arms into the sleeves of his padded coat. He wound his scarf around his neck and pulled on his gloves before jumping down onto the ice. He walked at a fast pace, cupping his hands around his mouth as he rushed on.

"Hey! You guys OK?"

He called as loudly as he could, and he could hear his voice travel over the ice, but got nothing in reply. He started to run towards his friends as by now he was definitely concerned, and was getting an image playing through his mind of Joe and the others lying on the snowfield. It wasn't far, but by the time he reached Amy the nearest figure to him, he was panting heavily, the cold air catching in his throat. He bent down to her. She was still breathing. Clumsy with hurrying, he untied the rope that had thwarted her attempt to escape, and lifted her into a sitting position. He then hauled her over his shoulder and stood up walking heavily back to the plane. He set her down under the wing unable to lift her unaided into the cabin, and also aware that he must hurry to get the others back as soon as possible. He went back for Zoe. She was dangerously near the edge of the cliff, one foot swinging over the void. Becaud felt his stomach lurch to see her so close to the precipice. He grabbed her coat and pulled her back, leaning over her to grab her leg and move it back to safety. He was kneeling down, and as he did so he caught a glimpse of the drop below them only inches away from where they were perched. He gasped in sheer disbelief at the scale of the drop, and he felt his legs dissolve with shock. He felt vulnerable in a way that he had never done in an aeroplane, and unnerved, he felt like digging his fingers into the ice and not daring to move. Get a grip. Don't look over the edge, just keep looking at Zoe. Get her away from danger, and take her back to the plane as quickly as possible. He couldn't figure out what was wrong with them, but knew it must have something to do with what had overcome Joe.

The gas cloud had already virtually dissipated. It had disappeared as quickly as it had come so Becaud didn't smell anything unusual. But as he didn't know what had caused the problem in the first place, he began to worry for his own safety. He thought that he if he lost consciousness they would all perish out there on the ice, so his only concern was to get everyone back to the plane as quickly as possible, and head out of there while he could still fly it. He untied Zoe from her tether and carried her with heavy, thudding steps back to the Cessna. He took a quick look at Amy, and shook her to see if there was any response, but she still remained dead to the world.

The distance back to the other two seemed twice as far now as Becaud was becoming exhausted with the effort. And he knew that the worst was yet to come as both Oliver and Hewitt were heavier than the girls, especially Oliver. He reached the two men at last not knowing how he was going to get them back to the plane, but knowing that he had to do it, however hard it was. Without hesitating he positioned Hewitt over his shoulder and tried to lift him up. He strained and made another effort but just could not get to his feet with the weight. He was wondering whether to try dragging him across the ice using the ropes, when he heard a noise somewhere between a sigh and a groan coming from Oliver as he lay there on the ground. He let Hewitt go and rushed over to Oliver to see if he was OK.

When he got there he could see that Oliver's eyes were open, but seemed, as yet, unseeing. Becaud shook him, and said to him in an urgent voice.

"Hey! Come on buddy. Wake up. Come on. You can do it. Oliver! Come on now!"

Oliver's eyes suddenly came into focus, and he looked around quickly.

"Where's Zo?"

"She's OK. She's back at the plane. We have to get back there too. And Lawrence. I can't lift him. You'll have to help me. Do you think you can do that?"

"I'll try," said Oliver without conviction. Becaud lifted Hewitt to his feet, and Oliver got on the other side of him. Between them they stumbled and staggered back to the Cessna, Oliver like a drunk, still wobbly on his legs.

When they got there, the girls were starting to come to.

Somehow they got each other into the plane, while Becaud retrieved their equipment from the cliff top and dragged it all the way back. He felt utterly exhausted, but found the energy to jump into the cockpit and start up the engines without delay. He taxied round to a good position for take off, and hurried through his pre-flight checks before opening up the throttle, feeling the plane begin to move, then gather speed. In a moment they were airborne. His tension and anxiety started to drop away like the ground beneath him. Now safe, he was mulling over just how close they had all come to disaster, his silent passengers no doubt going through the same thoughts now that they were recovering from their ordeal.

"My head feels like the worst hangover, it aches like you wouldn't believe," said Zoe rubbing her forehead with her fingers.

Amy looked green as she lay slumped in her seat, leaning on Hewitt's shoulder, who dozed unaware of her. Oliver wasn't too bad, but was more concerned about his wife who still looked white-faced. Luckily,

Oliver had not been aware of how close she had been to the cliff edge when she lost consciousness. Becaud thought it better not to tell him. Or her.

"Don't worry, I'll soon have you guys home," said Becaud. He glanced at his discarded newspaper still lying on the floor of the plane where he'd thrown it. It occurred to him that if he'd gone out with them instead of wrestling with his puzzle, they'd all have been dead by now. "I'll radio on ahead to get the doctor ready to get you checked out as soon as we land....."

"No don't do that," said Zoe, suddenly concerned. "Especially after what happened with Ray Coulson. They might not let us back out here, and after what we have found today, we have to come back. No matter what."

"OK." Becaud shrugged. He levelled the plane out and set a course back to Angmagssalik. He told his flight-follower what time they were expecting to land, and he heard the words *yes we're all fine* drift round his head for some moments after he said them, as untruths often do. Zoe was right, he had to admit. They wouldn't be allowed back here if anyone in authority knew how dangerous and unpredictable conditions were near the crevasse. And she was also right to say they had to go back. He knew this landscape like the back of his hand, and he had seen nothing to prepare him for the scale of the ice fracture that they had just witnessed, now once more receding into the distance and becoming a thin black line on the map spread out beneath them. He didn't know what the hell was happening to this place, and, just maybe, these guys could do something about it before it was too late. Or at least warn people what was about to befall them. Whatever. He had to back them now.

"Thanks for not saying anything, Phil."

"That's OK Zoe. Just as long as no one else goes and dies on me," he said, trying to make light of the situation with a shot of black humour. But there was a catch in his voice, and no-one tried to say anything else for the rest of the trip back to base.

* * *

It was just as well that Becaud had decided not to say anything about the gas cloud and the effects it had had on his party.

He switched on is TV and sat down to eat his dinner in front of it. There had been some demonstrations in the capital by green activists which had turned ugly when protesters had refused to disperse when told to by the police. Normally well tolerated, green protesters were always seen as benign by the local government, sticking up for the integrity of their country, against the exploitative nature of the rest of the world. Seeing themselves primarily as victims of other peoples wastefulness and pollution, environmentalists were always portrayed as being responsible and reasonable pressure groups.

But not any more, it seemed.

The government defended its heavy-handed reaction to the green demos by saying they had been infiltrated by outside agitators who had another, more sinister political agenda. There were also a growing number of people in the country who had started to say the unsayable; that global warming was actually a good thing and that it was going to benefit Greenland in many ways. For one thing, as the ice cap retreated the country would have more usable land for agriculture, and would have easier access to its own natural resources. The benefits to local people could be immense, it was being argued, and local politicians who embraced this philosophy were being elected in on a tide of populism and self-interest. Understandably so by people whose life was a struggle and could see boom-times ahead. The middle-east's day is over, they said. Now it's our turn. They might have a point if climate change were to be gradual, giving ecosystems time to adapt to the new conditions, but unfortunately, that was never going to be the case.

And just as environmentalists in the sixties and seventies spotted the phenomenon of global warming and campaigned of its dangers long before it was accepted by even the scientific establishment, once more there were one or two who were ahead of the game and had smelt danger. Like Zoe Carter, they were beginning to think that the tremors meant that something wasn't right, and were starting to say so. News travels a lot faster today than it did in the hippy age, when *Silent Spring* planted its seeds of doubt that resources were not limitless, and the *Ecologist* spoke only to its self-chosen handful of readers. Blogs and twitters now mean that any individual can address the world, and rumours were gaining ground that the Greenland ice sheet was becoming unstable.

Phil Becaud had seen all this on the evening news bulletin, and was tired of the same footage rolling around his screen on a loop. He unhooked his padded outdoor coat from the back of the door, slipped on his scarf and walked over to the Angmagssalic Hotel for a beer.

He sat at the bar and was joined by a couple of guys he knew from the airstrip. They talked shop for a while, and Becaud learned that restrictions were being put into place soon for foreigners coming into the country. He tried to glean as much information as he could without sounding too keen or giving too much away. He knew that Zoe and the gang would be leaving Greenland soon for London, but would need to get back again in the near future. He made light of the situation and ordered another round of beers. Said he hoped it wouldn't affect his tourist business too much.

"Everyone's wondering if your scientific buddies will be allowed back in if they leave soon," said the first guy, drinking his beer gratefully, and obviously fishing for information.

"Oh I think they'll be staying put," Becaud lied in a moment of inspiration. He knew the man was one who couldn't keep his mouth shut. Now red-faced and changing the subject to American football, he'd be spreading that information all around the local community by tomorrow, doing Becaud's job for him. That would take the pressure off the Carters. And the spotlight off him.

Especially as he'd just hatched a plan to get them out of country without anyone knowing about it, and, more importantly, back in.

CHAPTER SIXTEEN

London
Isaac Newton College

One by one, Zoe went to each window in her work-space at the university and closed each venetian blind in turn to blot out the intensity of the hot, bright summer day. Only as the last blind was tilted shut did it make any real difference to the feel of the room, though. The hanging dust motes disappeared from view as the harsh bleaching rays of the sun gave way to the even yellow of the fluorescent tubes, creating an interior space disconnected from the world outside. Still not sat-isfied, she reached through the last of the blinds and banged the window shut to deaden the noise of some over-exuberant undergraduates calling and laughing on the walkway below. In the centre of the room the desks had already been pushed together to make a large con-ference table, and some chairs were set round on three sides of it, so when seated, everyone would get a good view. Except for one. On the forth side of the table, a chair, obviously Zoe's, stood out on its own.

The computers were humming and chattering away like an audience waiting for the concert to begin. Phil Becaud stood with his hands in his pockets facing the closed blind. He was peeking through the gap in the side where the slats didn't quite touch the wall, down at the bustle going on below and trying not to look as bored as he felt with the delay in Zoe starting her talk. This all seemed a bit dramatic and contrived to him anyway. If she'd got something on her mind why the hell didn't she just say so? This was his first visit to London and he was impatient to get out into the city and take a look around instead of being stuck in some college classroom, but Zoe had insisted that he was part of the team and should be there, so he complied, hoping to get some sightseeing in later. He rested his sunglasses on his shirt front, feeling a bit naked without his scarf, the day being too hot even for his silk one.

Amy was busy getting the computers ready to demonstrate the models that they had prepared after collating their new data. Lawrence Hewitt was absently listening to his voice-mail and email messages on his phone, in an attempt to catch up with his life after his spell away in Angmagssalic. Zoe looked at her watch and noted that it was almost exactly ten o'clock. There was an air of quiet absorption in the room that was almost soothing. She suspected that it wouldn't be lasting for much longer, and she smiled to herself now that her little surprise was about to be revealed to them all.

"OK," she said.

And without any further prompting everyone in the room made ready to take their seats around the table. Zoe put her bag on the seat next to Amy's, which made everyone stare questioningly at the chair sitting in grand isolation across from them.

At ten o'clock sharp the door burst open and in strode Dorothy Redmires, with a presence and purpose which immediately filled the room. She called out Zoe's name and wished everyone good morning. She had a strong, no-nonsense voice that was clearly used to being heard first time, shattering their silent composure and allowing the hubbub from outside to once more enter briefly into their space and taking all but one of the assembled group unawares. She let her large bag tumble from her shoulder and fall noisily onto the table. The door behind her slammed shut. With a hard push adding to its own momentum, it made the blinds billow in the draught. Without even sitting down, she rummaged inside the bag for her glasses and a pen, before sliding out her laptop and booting it up ready for later. Dorothy was totally prepared and in command of the room, which Zoe thought had now taken on the atmosphere of an incident room rather than a seminar or meeting.

Dorothy then marched over to where Amy had been focussed on the computer screen in front of her. She leaned on Amy's desk taking her weight on both arms while she tried to take in and assess what she was seeing. Without any attempt at introduction or small talk, she began.

"Right, then, let's have a look at these pictures. Did you get them enhanced, Zoe?"

Zoe looked towards Amy James, who replied, "Yes, they are much better now. Much more detailed, and we've brightened up the ones in the shadows, but I still don't know what they mean. They're still confusing."

Dorothy peered at the images, unaware that everyone else in the room was looking at her.

"Can we get this one up onto the big screen?" said Dorothy, settling on a particular shot which interested her. Amy put it onto the smartboard so that could all look at it at once, and the detail seen on a big scale. Dorothy gestured at one area with an open hand.

"Can we go in on this?"

Amy brought the image up close.

"That's the most I can do," she said.

"OK. Now see this area here. This appears to be lava, and here, where the shadow has become impenetrable, it looks like the base of the cliff has been eaten away by the hot lava, creating snow caves. And look at this. These two pictures taken, what, half an hour apart." She flicked between one and the other. "You can see that the edge of the dark area has moved, indicating that there is an active lava flow going on down there. Here, you can just make out a step where the bedrock has sheered in a classic faultline pattern. And, of course, there were the noxious gasses that nearly got the better of you all. There can be no doubt that there is volcanic activity, and seismic activity occurring there. The questions are: how much, which came first, the earthquake or the volcano, and are we now getting after shocks, which would mean that the main event is over, or are we getting precursors to some major cataclysm yet to come?"

She paused for a long moment while everyone took in what she had just said, suddenly aware that they seemed wooden and unprepared in her volatile presence.

"I'm Dorothy Redmires, by the way."

Not that she had needed to say so. They all knew who she was by now. She sat down.

"I hear you lost your house to one of these precursors," said Hewitt, matter-of-factly, but with some sympathy.

Dorothy looked over at him for the first time, and seemed to take him in in one go. She was good at first impressions, and she liked his directness.

"Well, not lost exactly. It will be repairable, so they tell me. But uninhabitable for the near future, I have to say."

"Gee, I'm sorry to hear that, ma'am," said Becaud.

"Thank you. And I can guess by your accent that you must be the Indiana Jones of this outfit, the intrepid aviator."

Zoe flushed to hear her description of Becaud now used publicly and to his face, but he seemed quite pleased to be thought of in that way, and he laughed.

"Some journey, getting back to the UK, too, I hear. Hopping from Iceland, the Faeroes, Scotland then London."

"Well, travel in and out of Greenland was disrupted because of a baggage-handlers' dispute, and we'd no idea how long it was going to last. We couldn't afford to wait around so Phil said he'd fly us back hereto the UK in stages," said Zoe. "He was brilliant."

"Baggage-handlers', my ass!" said Dorothy.

Zoe looked at her tutor for a moment trying to work out what she was saying. Then she stared at her incredulously. Dorothy never said anything unless she meant it.

"What do you mean?"

"I mean that the clamp-down has already begun. And if it wasn't for Mr Jones here, you wouldn't be able to get back into the country at all. He'll be allowed in as he's a resident and has a business there. You'll probably have to sneak back in without telling anyone you're going. Risky but necessary. I've already heard of my scientist friends who can't get out there, to Greenland. But, course, Phil knows all this…" She'd got him sussed.

Zoe looked at Becaud, who shrugged, and pursed his lips in a gesture of amicable culpability.

"You knew all along?" said Zoe. He didn't reply. She then looked over at Oliver, who appeared grave.

"You were taking one hell of a chance, Phil. You could lose everything if you're found out. Getting us back over there could get you into serious trouble."

"I can get you back there, don't worry. No-one in Angmagssalic will ask too many questions. They'll just assume you've been out in the field for a few days. And they are worried about what is happening to their country. They feel that you are following up where Joe left off, and they'll back you for that reason alone, out of respect for him."

"But you could lose your licence, Phil. If you can't fly, what would you do? And if things are as bad as we think they are, you will not be treated leniently – the authorities are already getting nervy."

Becaud took the point and his demeanour became less jaunty, but he persisted. "We could lose a lot more than my licence if the ice sheet goes."

Everyone in the room looked from side to side, trying to gauge a response or get an answer. The unthinkable was taking shape in the minds of all those present, at the same time. The enormity of what could be happening to the polar ice sheet was growing as the realisation settled in that what was occurring to it was on a scale not witnessed in historical times. Zoe, who had been worried about there being a catastrophic event about to unfold, now felt sick with fear that her theory might be right, and had become a here and now reality.

"What exactly are we talking about, here?" said Hewitt, breaking the silence.

"Rapid meltdown?" He'd warmed to Dorothy immediately, with her lack of small-talk, he'd recognised something of himself in her demeanour. She didn't answer.

Zoe, Amy and Oliver all nodded slightly.

"Flooding, an albedo flip, all amplifiers which could lead to a runaway greenhouse effect......" said Zoe.

"No!" said Dorothy, interrupting and making them all start slightly. "It's worse than that. Don't you see?"

They all stared at her, trying to second guess what she meant. She turned to her own laptop, and got her own programme to appear on the smartboard. She got a 3D image of Iceland and Greenland to demonstrate the range of volcanic activity now affecting the area.

"This volcanic activity has triggered off earthquakes and tremors all over this region, and, as we know, quite far down into northern Europe. And here," she said pointing to the area where the crevasse was, "the sudden movement of the rock below the surface had fractured the ice completely, leaving this huge gash which roughly follows the contour line originating somewhere between Scoresby Sound and Angmagssalik. It goes south, then north, then south again just skimming the Arctic Circle, but whereas the contour line then curves round into the interior, it seems from your reconnaissance and the other reports that have been coming in, that the crevasse heads out in the direction of the west coast to a place with the intriguing name of Disko, or perhaps a bit further north to Umanak. We don't yet know if we have one unimaginably big rift, cutting across the whole of the country of Greenland or if it's a chain of cracks following this line, but even if that is the case, its not much comfort as we still have a weak spot in the ice, from one coast to the other." Dorothy demonstrated this with the graphics. "Also, the problems with water undermining the ice are well known to all of us monitoring the situation out there. But now we have this other factor, with the potential to make the whole scenario a hundred times worse."

Becaud was alarmed and looked around the room to gauge what effect these words had on the others. Amy shook her head slightly at Hewitt, who was looking her way, not yet understanding what Dorothy Redmires meant. Oliver didn't move a muscle. Zoe gripped her pen uncomfortably, not knowing but not liking where this conversation was going. Dorothy got up a model on the screen with a cutaway view of the ice sheet which demonstrated how veins of water were branching through the ice, pooling across the bedrock and, in some cases, lifting the ice from its surface, making it unstable. She pointed to the base of the ice sheet. Suddenly, in one moment, Zoe knew what Dorothy was going to say next.

Lava.

It had to be. If water was rapidly damaging the ice sheet, then just think what lava could do. It was tunnelling its way through any cracks and fissures in the snow, its heat relentlessly boring out new ones, the steam honeycombing through the snow faster than any meltwater could go. The massiveness of the ice could cope with a small incursion of lava flow, and had probably done so many times in the past. But if this activity was on the scale it appeared to be then the damage would be catastrophic, especially as there were so many other factors already putting the northern ice cap under strain. Of all the other factors, this was an amplifier, an example of positive feedback, which could push the whole system over its tipping point.

"It seems to me," said Dorothy still sounding quite detached, as though she were discussing an event from the Younger Dryas period to a class of first year undergraduates, "that what we have here is a weak spot along this contour line where an earthquake has caused this split in the ice, probably also helped by the combined effects of meltwater lakes and moulins all along this path. As one of my students reminded me when looking at this projected path of the crevasse, it follows roughly the line of equilibrium, where, below that line, summer melting is faster than can be made up for by winter accumulations of snow. As it is, this line has already migrated northwards. The Greenland ice sheet has been showing signs of melting since 1979. Just think back to that year.1979. It seems a long time ago that we thought The New Seekers were cool – or maybe not," she added, smiling.

She thought for a fleeting second of going off on one of her famous tangents, but resisted the temptation and resumed her look of concentration. "But for those of us who were into the Stranglers, that year suddenly doesn't sound all that far away, does it? And yet the landscape of parts of Greenland has been transformed in that short time." Zoe smiled. Dorothy had always been a great lecturer. "But the most rapid melting has been taking place over the last decade, very much endorsing the concept of rapid climate change; in fact the more we know about climate it seems that all climate change has been rapid. It is in fact the norm. Anyway, above this equilibrium line, the ice sheet is more stable. Incredible as it seems, this whole chunk of ice below that line is at risk of thinning more rapidly than over the rest of the continent. But now," she tapped the board to emphasise the point. "Now, the worst case scenario is that the whole lot could break off and slide into the sea, as it has already been fractured. It is being lifted and lubricated by the cushion of lava currently seeping underneath it. If that happens, we are not talking meltdown, we are talking tsunami." She stopped and waited for the response.

"Fuck me!" said Oliver, interrupting the rapt attention that had been gripping them all.

The resonance of what Dorothy had just said was still bouncing round the room and being slowly absorbed by all those present. Stunned couldn't describe how they all felt as they tried to take in the reality of what she had just said.

"Are we talking like...? Boxing Day?" said Hewitt, trying to get a handle on the perspective involved.

"No," she said, quietly. The bleakness of that statement had more effect than if she had tried to describe what she thought might be possible. For a brief flicker, Hewitt thought that she was being reassuring. She wasn't.

"I'll have to get some of my research students to do the maths," she said. "And I'll let you know what they say."

"So what can we do?" said Zoe. Her voice had a slight shake to it that Oliver recognised. She was not about to break down, she was buzzing on all wires, trying to think the problem through. "There must be something we can do to stop this.

Oliver? We have to do something. We can't just sit back and let this happen to our world, to our lives."

Oliver looked desperately at her. He couldn't think of anything to say.

"I'll do anything I can to help," said Becaud. "I just need you science guys to think of something."

The meeting had come to a natural pause and chairs scraped as people left their seats and moved about the room. Amy still sat at her screen looking closely at the footage they had taken, hoping for inspiration. Becaud got up and went over to her, leaning close and peering at the screen to see what he could make out. He expected her to lean ever-so-slightly towards him and then make eye contact, like she always did, before she spoke, but there was nothing, not even an unconscious response. When he looked over the room he could see Hewitt deep in conversation with Dorothy. Amy then seemed focussed on them although she couldn't have made out what they were saying. Hewitt nodded several times during the conversation, and when it was over he glanced up and caught Amy's eye. His eyes smiled almost imperceptibly, but Amy noticed and flushed slightly at the attention. The penny dropped with Becaud. It was obvious that Lawrence fancied her, and a little stab of jealousy nudged at him. Amy's attention was now fixed on Hewitt, and not him. Becaud had flirted with her, and taken her attraction to him for granted, but he'd not appreciated how genuinely nice she was before now. Surely she couldn't see anything in that miserable old loser. But he was out in the cold and he'd only got himself to blame.

Oliver broke his chain of thought and brought him back to the matter in hand with a jolt.

"When do we have to get back to Greenland, Phil? We are somewhat dependent on you for any of our plans to be carried out. I don't suppose we can be out of the country long before there's a risk of not getting back at all."

"Well, I'd say maybe three days, could push it to five, I guess. But the longer we leave it, the more complicated any explanations will have to be. A week might be too long, and could scupper our plans altogether."

"What plans?" said Hewitt, dryly. "We haven't got any bloody plans. And what the hell are we supposed to do to prevent half a continental ice shelf from breaking off and slipping into the sea. Prop it up? Or hope that Superman flies by?"

Dorothy chuckled, and Oliver was saved from trying to answer Hewitt's question by his phone which buzzed insistently in his pocket. He took the call, much to the irritation of everyone else in the room who'd agreed to a no-interruptions think tank session.

"I'm sorry," Oliver said when he'd finished the call. "There's news from seismology. There's been renewed activity this morning. It's a wonder we didn't feel anything here. A large tremor in the Midlands, and a lot of damage in south-east London and Kent. We are talking roads closed and properties collapsing. Quite serious stuff. Reports are coming in from all over Scandinavia of minor tremors – the epicentre is to the south west of Iceland, roughly equidistant between the UK and Greenland."

"On the faultline?" said Zoe.

"Sounds like it," said Dorothy. She noticed Hewitt had retreated to his seat and was looking resigned to being ignored. She continued, "Be that as it may, Lawrence has raised a valid point. We have amassed a great deal of data, and we now have our theory of what that data could mean, but that still leaves the question of what are we going to do about it? Is there, in fact, anything that we can do?"

"We have to warn people," said Amy. If nothing else, we can do that."

"We have to do more than that," said Zoe. "We have to try to save the towns and cities and the structures in society that supports our rights and freedoms. I don't want all that washed back to the Dark Ages, not if we can help it."

"We could all go hungry. It was bad enough in London when the power went down after the solar storm," said Hewitt. "We've no back up in this country. No structures in place to keep things going if centralised services break down."

"We have to divert the lava flow," said Zoe.

At first she didn't think anyone had heard her as there was no reaction to her statement, so she went up to the smartboard and pointed to the map there of Iceland and Greenland. She ran the 3D image of where they thought the lava flow was emanating, seeping up through a fissure in the bedrock under Greenland, leeching its way through tunnels and gullies under the ice, now visible where the quake had ruptured the ice sheet and formed the crevasse.

"If we can divert the lava flow out here," she pointed to the east Greenland coast.

"The lava under the vulnerable ice sheet will cool and solidify, and we could get some stability back into the system. If the lava continues to flow as its present rate the undermining of the ice sheet could mean a major collapse of all this ice south of our rift in three to five years, tops."

"With any large calving events causing tsunamis on a vast scale," said Dorothy.

"And if we had an explosive eruption – maybe due to ice collapsing into the magma and creating a steam build up – then it could go anytime."

"In one terrible day and a night," said Hewitt with his usual deadpan delivery.

"Quite," said Dorothy.

"The Atlantis Rift! That's it. That's what we should call our crevasse, as its not really a crevasse at all now is it?" said Becaud, picking up on Hewitt's phrase.

Oliver groaned. "And get every bloody whacko and conspiracy theorist all worked up over it. Can you imagine?"

"Well I think it's a great name," Becaud said. "It'll get us noticed. People will have to listen to us then."

"No reputable scientist would speak to me again." Oliver sat back in his chair and looked up at the ceiling.

"We are on the edge, career-wise, here as it is," said Zoe. "I don't really want to jump into the recycle bin yet, if I can help it."

"Science needs its mavericks and pioneers, as well as its dull conformists," said Dorothy provocatively.

"Oh, and if we step into the lunatic fringe, then what's the difference between us and any other idiot with a pet theory, an axe to grind, or a myth to perpetuate."

Oliver's voice was scathing. He hadn't spent years as an academic to throw it all away now.

"Evidence," said Dorothy. "Impartial evidence, good scholarship, rational argument, and an ability to be prepared to be wrong and move on, is what distinguishes us from the bigots and sensationalists who have a vested interest in obfuscation. Atlantis is an excellent example of this." She was now warming to her theme.

"Say *Atlantis* to most people and you get mixed up ideas of lost worlds, lost cities (confused with the lost cities of the Incas, which is totally different) and lost civilisations, combined with aliens, a super race who got too clever by half and blew themselves up, meteorites, volcanoes and a dozen different possible locations, to boot. But if you look at the basics of the legend i.e. that a largish volcanic island in the Atlantic was destroyed by a huge eruption, and that the flowerings of an early civilisation, perhaps like the Egyptians or Sumerians, or Aztecs perhaps, was disrupted, well it doesn't seem too unlikely, and certainly not impossible. Once you cut away the nonsense, it doesn't seem so weird after all. Atlantis might have been a real historical event that got elaborated upon and exaggerated because it made such a good story. It is well known that the Greek philosopher Plato reported the Atlantis event, too."

"But, of course, that still doesn't mean that it happened, does it?" said Zoe.

"Absolutely," said Dorothy. "We should only believe that Atlantis once existed if we find empirical evidence that it did. If we haven't got that crucial evidential back up, then we're basically making it up, and it remains just a myth. Or if we discover a seed of truth wrapped up in a good story then we have a legend. We must not dismiss the idea of the mythic, however. We must always remember that before we had scientific explanations for natural phenomena, things were understood through mythology; it was early culture's way of dealing with things. At least it shows imagination and a wish to make sense of the world. The problem is when people hang on to these allegories as fact, when in a modern society we should know better." She paused for a moment while a thought occurred to her. "After all they thought that Troy was just a myth until Schliemann went out to Hissarlik in Mesopotamia and dug it up. That doesn't mean that I think Paris and Helen were real people, though. We must be careful not to throw out what might be a nugget of truth, just because it has been contaminated by fantasy."

"Well that might be alright for an academic discussion, but I wouldn't like the tabloids to get hold of it. They'd be bound to twist it round," said Oliver.

"For God's sake, guys! We are contemplating some kind of mega-disaster here, by the sound of it, and you're discussing Greek mythology," said Becaud, his voice rising in frustration. "Don't you think we need to get some sort of sense of urgency around here?"

"Of course, Phil. Sorry. You shouldn't have got me started," said Dorothy.

The group regained its focus in the face of Becaud's outburst, and looked towards Zoe who had been the only one so far to come up with an idea of what to do.

"I think it's like lancing a boil," said Zoe, once more getting to her feet and tapping on the smartboard for emphasis. "The pressure must be building up under the ice sheet or we wouldn't be getting lava being pushed up through it. I don't know if we can do anything to be honest, it's a long shot, but I think what we need to try to do is relieve the pressure by creating an exit for the build-up of lava, so it can drain away from the ice sheet. That way we can stem the flow that is causing the rapid melting, and avoid a worse-case scenario of a major eruption, which could shatter the ice sheet and cause massive tsunamis heading straight for Scandinavia and northern Europe."

"And how, exactly, are we going to do that." Hewitt looked unimpressed.

There followed a long silence.

"Well by 'we', I didn't mean us, here, to go and do it personally. I just meant that someone would have to do it. I – don't know really..." said Zoe.

"We have to let someone in authority know what we have found out and then let the experts deal with it. A job on this scale would be a military matter, surely," said Oliver.

"But who do we let know?" said Zoe. "Who can we trust to take us seriously?"

"If we go official, you won't be allowed back into Greenland," Becaud thrust his hands in his pockets, then continued. "That might not matter if they take up action for us. The problem is, if they don't take you seriously the matter will be out of your hands, and it might then be more difficult for me to fly you back there to do anything yourselves."

"I've got contacts," said Amy James.

Everyone turned and looked at her, and she reddened slightly.

"My cousin. He's a top government advisor. Works in the PM's office, helps write speeches, works on policy detail. Knows everyone, spends weekends at Chequers, that kind of thing."

"I didn't know that," said Oliver, staring at her with new eyes.

"How did you think I got you your fillet steak, when the shortages were at their worst during the solar storm? People like that never go short of anything."

Oliver retorted, "Well, to be honest Ames, my first thought wasn't that you were well in with the Government elite. It wasn't exactly an obvious conclusion to draw, was it?"

Oliver was beginning to sound testy, but Amy knew him too well to be bothered by his tone.

Dorothy, looking thoughtful, said to Amy, "The only problem is, that he may be your cousin, but for anyone in a trusted position like that, their first loyalty will be to the PM, not to us. I'm not sure if he could help us. You might even end up putting him in a really difficult situation."

"I don't see that we have much choice in the matter, if you ask me," said Hewitt.

"We know that someone was gravely concerned about what was happening in Greenland, as the MoD used Ray Coulson in a semi-official role to get some intelligence. Why don't you see if your cousin can find out who this contact was, and we'll go from there?"

"I suppose so," said Dorothy.

"I'll do what I can," said Amy. "I'll call him, and arrange to meet him in person. He'll help us if he can. I'm sure of it."

The others weren't so sure, but felt that the situation was getting too big for them to handle on their own. The trouble was, after the solar storm, no-one seemed to have any confidence in officialdom anymore. In the face of a major challenge they had floundered around not knowing what to do. With a few exceptions they had all looked so ordinary, so like you and me that people had begun to realise that they could think things out just as well for themselves. The tick-box culture of little empire builders and money-makers had been tested, and had been found wanting. But what could they do by themselves? They were only six in number and were running out of time to avoid a major catastrophe. Amy's cousin might be able to help. He at least had contacts and experience of how things worked at the top level. If they were going to be able to do anything at all, they needed to get him on board. They needed to act fast.

CHAPTER SEVENTEEN

As Amy and Zoe stood on the hot, breezy Embankment, taking their leave of a tall, slim, still quite young man with thinning fair hair, they failed to notice the seated figure only metres away from where they had been sitting, straining to hear what had passed between them. Amy had set up this meeting with Marcus James, her cousin, who, remarkably had found time to see her straightaway, despite his packed diary.

Their voices only raised when they were swapping family pleasantries, there were long periods of hushed intense conversation that he couldn't even get snippets of, much to his intense irritation. He walked close by on one occasion, but the noise of the traffic increased at just the wrong time for him to get anything at all, and he didn't dare risk getting up again and drawing attention to himself. Out of the corner of his eye he saw the three of them stand up eventually, and with a light handshake and a brush of the cheek the meeting suddenly concluded. The man stayed seated and watched Marcus James as he walked briskly back towards Westminster. The two women looked at each other in a neutral sort of way that made him think that they had been politely stonewalled. They hadn't got anywhere on the issue of finding out Coulson's contact, and his manner of sincere concern for their worries, only left them feeling that he knew more than he was letting on, and was meeting them only to find out how much they had got hold of. Amy, quick to cotton on to this, told Marcus nothing else that he couldn't have got from the newspapers, but the desire for a meeting had aroused his suspicions, especially by mentioning the MoD contact, and she knew at once that he would be sidling up to the PM as soon as he could arrange it, to tell him what he knew.

The man wondered for a minute whether to follow Amy's cousin over to Westminster to see if that was, in fact, where he was heading, but thought against it. He would be more likely to get noticed for behaving suspiciously in the vicinity of the Houses of Parliament, and he knew for sure that that was where the fair haired man was going.

He folded up his newspaper, willing the two women to make a move. His mouth felt dry and his heart-rate had risen slightly now that he had decided it was time to go in. That decision, once made, expanded to fill every part of his brain, blocking out all other thoughts, reasons and emotions. He'd run out of patience, and now wanted to take hold of the situation. All he'd found out so far were some names and addresses, and nothing else of any real value; he was wasting his time going on like this; he needed to take some action.

At last the two friends started to walk back long the Embankment, chatting intently as they did so. The man got up from his seat and followed them closely, pushing through the lunchtime crowds which made it hard for him to keep then clearly in view. Eventually they arrived at the multi-storey where they had left Zoe's car. His vehicle was there, too, where he'd followed them in. He looked round for any CCTV, but couldn't see anything pointed his way.

Zoe and Amy had agreed to give Lawrence Hewitt a lift out of town, and he said he would wait on the pavement outside the car park, which would be easier than trying to find her car, amongst all the others. Had Hewitt been on time, he would have seen a figure furtively focussed on the two women as they made their way over the footbridge and towards the stairwell. He was gripping his folded newspaper and casting around only with his eyes so as not to appear suspicious by obviously moving his head around. Zoe took off her dark glasses to see the number of their floor more easily, while Amy rummaged in her bag to get the ticket out to pay at the machine just to the left of the doorway. The coins dropped and clinked down into the machine.

"Don't forget the ticket Ames. We'll need it to get out at the barrier."

So Amy picked up the ticket and obligingly kept it in her hand, so that she could hand it to Zoe on their way out.

The pungent smell of stained concrete greeted them as they made their way up the first flight of stairs. The shade should have been welcome after the hot city sun, but the yellow florescent light was just depressing. From the bottom of the stairs they vaguely heard some more coins fall one after the other into the pay point, then the door beneath them squeaked open and banged shut again, echoing as it did so. They found their storey and leaned against the double doors leading to the car park landing, then let them swing shut behind them. Zoe walked along the row of cars, now gradually growing again in number as the repairs to their electrical systems were getting done, until she found her own tucked in behind a scruffy, red Toyota pickup, which, she remembered, wasn't there when she parked. Probably driven by some high-flying executive, she mused when she saw the rust, whilst waiting for his Merc to be repaired.

Zoe sat down in the driver's seat and waited for Amy to get in beside her. Distracted while she was fiddling about with the CD player, she saw a figure walk towards the pickup out of the corner of her eye. She thought nothing of it until he dropped his newspaper, but made no attempt to pick it up. Something not quite right there. She tensed a little but didn't know why. The man then went around the back of the pickup and disappeared from view for a few seconds, and as Amy opened the rear door to put her bag and jacket on the back seat, he suddenly approached their car, too close. Before Zoe could process what was happening there was a scuffle. He roughly pushed Amy inside, then sat down heavily beside her. He locked her door as she tried furiously to open it, and stifling her cries for help when she refused to shut up. Zoe froze with terror, not daring to think where this could end. Her heart was thumping so loudly in her chest that she thought everyone else could see it. She thought of running for help, but didn't want to leave her friend. *Oh God just take the money and fuck off.* Why had she not noticed him before? He spoke in a hoarse, abrupt voice and was breathing rapidly as he rapped out his demands.

"I just want some answers. All I've had up to now is bullshit, and I don't want any more. I need some facts. There's some weird stuff going on at the moment and I want to know what you lot had to do with it."

Zoe now felt even more terrified. He sounded like a paranoid schizophrenic. She didn't know what to say in case she made him worse. If he didn't get the answers he wanted he could get even more violent. He was extremely agitated, and had started to sweat profusely. She was trying to frame some sort of an answer that would not provoke him into harming them, when he stunned them further by barking at them, "You are Amy James, and your name's Carter." He jabbed his finger in Zoe's direction which went through her like a jolt of electricity. "I know where you both live, and I want some answers, now."

He was shouting. Amy and Zoe were astounded to hear their names. Not a mugger, a stalker. Must be someone from the university. Zoe had never felt the presence of danger so acutely. She felt a wave of rising panic, and thought pitifully of her children. Amy had gone so pale she looked as though she could pass out.

Now the attack on them seemed personal and intrusive in a way that made her feel violated. Her anger rose as she felt like a total victim.

Desperately trying to think of a way out, Amy's mind raced through every scenario, her thought processes flashing past in the face of danger. But then the penny dropped. This was no mugger or stalker. They were under surveillance, she thought, and this creep had been sent to frighten them - and she had just made a whole lot of trouble for her cousin by getting him involved. She wanted to warn Marcus, but wondered if further contact might only make things worse for him.

"I want to know who you are working for, and what is going on in Greenland." The man gripped Amy's wrists, and she answered incoherently about the university and a research project.

"You're hurting me. Let go! We've done nothing wrong. Just let us go! We don't know anything." But he'd no intention of letting anyone go till he'd got what he wanted.

Just then, Zoe saw a figure that she thought was Hewitt open the swing doors at the top of the stairwell and look around. He'd obviously got fed up with waiting for them and had come to see if he could find them. She was willing him to walk their way. He took a few steps along the row of cars, then hesitated as though he was going to turn back as he couldn't see them anywhere. Zoe knew this was their only hope, so with a last-chance recklessness, she bolted out of the car and began calling and waving at an astonished Hewitt. At first he thought they were mucking about and didn't hurry his pace, but then he realised that something was badly wrong, when he saw the distress on Zoe's face. The man let Amy go and got out of the car. He was trying to scramble into the red Toyota when Hewitt caught up with them. He grabbed at the man's shoulder, gripped a lump of his clothing and forced him to turn around. Hewitt felt his fist tighten in anticipation of a struggle and was about to confront the attacker, but as they came face to face, he stopped short and gasped in shock.

"Coulson!"

The man started as he heard his name. Too late, now, his reaction had given him away.

Explanations were running through Hewitt's mind yet none of them made any sense. The two women stared to see a figure inhabiting a name that had become well known to them. How had he got back? He was supposed to be dead. But there was something not quite right about this guy's appearance, that Hewitt couldn't place. Maybe he'd died his hair, or lost a few pounds. He obviously didn't want to be recognised. Hewitt's mind was racing through the scenario of him being lost on the expedition, now wondering if were all some cock and bull story to cover the whole thing up.

"Everyone thinks that you're dead," said Hewitt. "So how the hell did you get back here? And why? Why tell everyone a story like that?"

"No, that wasn't me." Now realising that he'd given himself away needlessly, as Hewitt thought that he was Ray, he let it all spill out. "I'm Terry Coulson, Ray's younger brother. Did you know Ray?"

Hewitt felt a glimmer of normality creep back into his mind at the news that this wasn't, in fact the Coulson that he had known. Seeing what he thought had been Ray's face there right there in front of him again had shaken him very badly. But he answered matter-of-factly,

"I only met him once. We shared the same publisher." Hewitt wisely decided to play down his involvement.

"He was sent out on some mission, and he never came back."

"I know," said Hewitt. "I'm sorry." Coulson studied Hewitt's face, trying to work out how much he knew.

"They told us that he'd died of hypothermia."

"Did they?"

"Well, I'm trying to find out the truth. He was an experienced traveller, and he was well equipped and had excellent guides. I just don't believe it. You, all of you, were out there, in Greenland. I've been piecing things together, and I think you know something. What's been going on out there?"

"Well you're right to say it wasn't hypothermia. But it was a tragic accident. He was overcome by poisonous fumes. I'm sorry."

"He was gassed, you mean?"

"In effect, yes," said Hewitt.

"So, that's why there's a cover-up. An experiment that went wrong. And were you lot involved?"

"No. It wasn't an experiment either," said Zoe. "It was naturally occurring, due to volcanic activity. It nearly did for us, too."

Coulson looked as though he was starting to believe them. He looked down at the ground and blew hard to regain his composure. Zoe felt that they now had the upper hand and so confronted him about his earlier behaviour. Hewitt, now fully informed of what had occurred a few minutes before was incensed by what he had done. He grabbed Coulson by his shirt, and shook him angrily.

"You stupid bloody idiot! What did you think you were doing, scaring two women half to death."

"I—I don't know. I'm sorry. I guess I just lost it. I don't know. I'm really sorry..." He looked towards the two women, but couldn't yet meet their gaze. They were still deeply shaken, and weren't ready to say it was OK. It bloody well never would be OK. "I just wanted to do something for Ray...."

The awkwardness rendered them all immobile, until, at last Zoe spoke.

"Did you talk to your brother, while he was on this mission, Terry?" It was strange, but by using his name, he seemed more human, and less of a threat, which made Zoe feel more in control.

"Yes. He called whenever he could. Video clips, voice messages, photos. I've studied the photos, but since his death I can't bring myself to look at videos or play the messages. But I know he was very worried about what he found out there. It was bad news and I guessed that he'd paid the price for being the messenger. Why the MoD wanted him involved, God only knows. I'm the ex-soldier; I thought I might have been more use to them."

"He did his best," said Hewitt.

"He had a lot to live up to," said Amy, hitting the nail very firmly on the head.

Coulson took her remark on board, and blew out through pursed lips, as the implications of her words reverberated around his head. Maybe Ray had bitten off more than he could chew because he wanted to prove himself.

"An ex-soldier, did you say?" said Zoe. Coulson nodded.

"Captain. In the Commandoes. Retired a couple of years ago."

Hewitt suddenly thought that grabbing the man and shaking him hadn't been such a great idea.

"We could maybe use that data," said Amy. "The stuff that your brother sent to you. We're very short on time, and we need as much to go on as possible, before we...." Amy tailed off suddenly remembering that she shouldn't be telling anyone that they were heading back to Greenland.

"You going somewhere, then?" said Terry, immediately picking up on what she had said.

"Mayb,." she said, unsure of how much she ought to admit, now that she had aroused his suspicion.

"You've got nothing booked. I hacked into the airline's computers."

Zoe, Amy and Hewitt all stared in disbelief at what he just said. Both Hewitt and Amy realised at the same time that the red pick-up reminded them of the one they had seen outside their homes just before their last trip to Greenland, but hadn't thought anything of it at the time. A rush of apprehension, even fear passed through Zoe's mind, at her realisation that he'd had them under surveillance and had the means and the know-how to spy on them. She felt that she was sinking deep into a world that she didn't understand and couldn't control. Her instinct was to get out of this situation before it swallowed them all up, but she knew that that wasn't an option now that they knew what danger the crevasse posed to them all. Too late now. They had to press on no matter what. He knew they'd got nothing booked. So how could they get back to the Arctic with Becaud, now? This might complicate everything. She didn't know where Terry Coulson's loyalties lay, therefore she didn't know what she could say to him. She needed to talk to Dorothy Redmires. She'd know what to do. In the meantime, she didn't want to let Coulson out of their sight, till she was sure she knew what he was about.

"We are all meeting up again at a pub just round the corner from the Isaac Newton College, tonight, at about 7:30," said Zoe.

"Would that be the King's Head?" said Coulson.

"Yes, actually it is," said Zoe, wondering if he spied them going into there, too.

"Why don't you come along, and bring all Ray's stuff with you."

He nodded, and said he'd be there, and then, before anyone had time to say anything else he slipped into the Toyota, pulling the door shut with a soft, awkward bang. He started up the engine and without a look back, he shot off down the concrete ramp, and out of sight.

"Let's hope he can be of some use to us, or he could screw everything up," said Zoe.

"We need him on board," said Hewitt. "He's got the background and the skills we need if we're to get anything done when we get out there. Look at us! What good are we?"

"Well we've found out about this thing in the first place, and I've got climbing skills, and...."

"OK, I don't need a CV," said Hewitt. He could be harsh, sometimes, thought Zoe, feeling foolish at her naïve, let's-make-the-best-of-it tone that she had just adopted. But he could have been a bit more sympathetic after what she had just been through. He made it hard to feel grateful to him at times, and this was the second time he'd helped her out of a dangerous situation.

"He'd be more use with us than against us, that's for sure," said Zoe. Amy shrugged, unable to disagree with what they were saying. "What do you think Ames?"

"I think he's got poor judgement, if you ask me," she said, still physically feeling the push in her back that could have ended very differently. She still looked very pale and tremulous, and her eyes gave away that she was close to tears. "There was no need for what he did just now, it was way over the top. But, you're right. We need him, so we don't have a lot of choice. And, we don't know how much information Ray managed to send back to the MoD, do we? For all we know they could have their own scheme in place by now."

Basically Amy was protesting that she really didn't want to have to see this guy again, whilst working through the fact that she would have to. Zoe gave her a hug and gently ushered Amy into the car. Lawrence Hewitt got into the back seat beside her. He sat quietly knowing that she needed some space. Zoe rummaged through her bag until she felt the familiar shape of her mobile as she fished it out and then pressed one of the presets.

"Dorothy?" Zoe was on the phone to her former tutor, as soon as they drove out of the car park. "I think we've boobed making contact with Amy's cousin. I'm afraid you were right about where his loyalties might lie. It seems that political ambition is a lot thicker than blood, when it comes down to it."

"How much did you tell him?"

"Not that much. We tried to emphasise the academic side of it. But when we mentioned Ray Coulson's contact at the MoD, he became very guarded. Tried to draw us out. I asked him to try to fix it for us to go back there, as the main reason why we needed his help, and he just said he would see what he could do. Then he just scurried off to find someone to tell, I just know it. Sorry."

"Never mind. It's done, now. Anyway I think the shit is going to hit the fan soon enough…"

"How come?" said Zoe.

"The blogs have become very popular. Got quite a following, your last adventure. All sorts of students, not just the science ones. My magazine is becoming quite a cult…"

"What's happened, Dot…I just know I'm not going to like this, am I?"

"Phil Becaud did a pod-cast for us. Stole the show, I have to say. Was absolutely brilliant, but when someone asked him if we had a name for this crack in the ice, as they were wondering whether to start a competition he let it slip that we'd thought of a great name already, and the phrase 'Atlantis Rift' is now on so many lips that you'd think we were the new Arctic Monkeys."

Zoe felt her academic reputation sagging.

"I can hear the comments from the staffroom old guard from here," said Zoe.

"Fuck 'em," said Dorothy. "The only emotion they've got between them is envy."

"It's OK for you. You are virtually retired. I have to work with these people."

"Whatever. But now this is out, people are beginning to ask questions. So we have to move quickly. Can you be ready to fly out to Angmagssalic by the day after tomorrow?" Zoe agreed that they would have to. She was acutely aware that she hadn't mentioned that they'd just been attacked. It seemed ridiculous not to say anything, but Zoe couldn't face it, over the phone. If she said anything now she was afraid she might cry.

"Tonight, Dot, we're going for a drink at the King's Head, with – some friends. Can you be there? Great. We'll see you at 7:30." Zoe clicked off.

The Atlantis Rift. They would have to go along with it now. To do anything else would make them look squirming. She could hear the interviews now in her head. She would have to do what all apologists do when faced with a genuinely challenging question, a comfortable laugh, followed by the *well, we don't take ourselves too seriously, you know,* line. Look confident and amused, then they don't go for you.

She just hoped their Rift, whatever it was now called, didn't end up being the cause of another cataclysm on that scale, or that our own civilisation didn't end up becoming nothing more than someone else's mythology in the future.

CHAPTER EIGHTEEN

Whitehall

Marcus James stood by the Georgian panes of the office window, his hands in his pockets, looking down onto the courtyard below as the late afternoon activity was drawing the day's business to a conclusion. This was the place to be; the centre of it all, and everyone was doing their bit to look part of it. There were no bored looks or aimless journeys here. The tiny faces below were driven, purposeful, and armed with all the tactics of personal ambition. He could see himself in every face that scurried past, and felt a sense of belonging to a world that he loved every part of. His rise to his present position of a trusted advisor and speechwriter to the PM, from working on policy detail, had seemed somehow inevitable, given his natural talent to sus out a situation and turn a phrase. A Classics graduate from Oxford, he had the necessary authority of a heavyweight intellectual, but with a charm and ease of manner that made his populist approach believable. Perhaps his greatest asset was his ability to smooth people over, so that up to now he'd made no real enemies. Tall and blond, his good looks appealed in almost equal measure to both sexes, and he used that connection, often unconsciously, to draw people around to his way of thinking, and to get them to give him their support.

The mellowing summer sun was beginning to slant through the oblong panes, lighting up the dull corner of the office where he been sitting earlier while waiting to see the PM's Deputy, Ron Bowman. The dust motes hung on the diagonal rays, hardly moving on the still internal air in the sombre room, cool and comfortable in a way that air conditioning could never replicate. The plastic and paper smell of most modern offices was absent here, and he tried to remember the compelling smell of pipe tobacco, which would, at one time, have hung about this room, the blue-grey curls mingling with the furnishings, until one smelt very like the other.

A tastelessly ornate clock ticked quietly on the mantelpiece, reminding Marcus that he had been waiting for just a fraction too long, causing a feeling of slight irritation to pass through his mind. He knew, too, that the secretary would be aware of precisely how long he had been kept waiting and would be judging his place in the pecking order accordingly. She had perhaps even been told how long to keep him there.

He sat down in the armchair, the soft leather creaking slightly as he did so.

There was a faint bleep from the console on the desk, making the secretary look up towards him after she had acknowledged the signal, and with a warm smile, she told him to go on through.

"Thank you," he said, pushing himself out of his seat with both hands on the chair arms, then walking confidently towards the connecting door. He closed the door behind him and held out his hand to the waiting Deputy PM, who clasped it not quite firmly enough.

"Marc!" he used his diminutive, which Marcus preferred in general as it made him seem less the toff in public life, but somehow in Ron Bowman's mouth it sounded too matey and lacked sincerity. "You know my PPS, Harrington, don't you?"

They nodded, and Marcus James took the seat he was offered, on the other side of the desk. He began without further prompting as he felt the other man waiting for him to speak. He got straight to the point.

"I know we've all been asked to play down the rumours coming back from the Arctic, but I really feel, Sir, that things are getting, well, a little pressing." Marcus chose his words carefully.

"Oh, we're monitoring the situation all the time, Marc. And keeping the PM fully informed while he is away. He is a busy man who has more urgent things on his plate, at the moment, like the latest stock market fall, amongst other things. We, of course take these green issues very seriously, but, they are, after all, more long-term issues. Once these blessed tremors have died down people will forget all about the environment for a while. We're only just recovering from the solar storm – that nearly did for our creaking infrastructure, I can tell you. Right now what we need is a time of calm for the recovery to settle everyone down."

He pushed aside the papers he had been glancing at while talking, his half-attention emphasising that he more important things to do. He still didn't look up, but scarcely perceptibly his body language began to change. Marcus suddenly felt defensive. He tried hard to stay relaxed.

"I'm pleased you came to talk to me, first, Marc" He said, pausing to let the meaning of his words sink in.

"So, perhaps you'd like to tell me a bit more about what you know?"

He leaned forward, demanding an answer, rather than asking a question, his somewhat aggressive tone taking the younger man totally by surprise. In a second Marcus James knew that he should have waited until the PM got back, and insisted on speaking to him personally. He now felt that was looking at a usurper, who was trying to get a political advantage while the main man was away. And now he himself looked like a conspirator. What was more, now that he was here, he had to give the DPM something, or risk looking as though he was holding something back.

Somehow, dobbing in his cousin Amy, suddenly didn't seem like such a great idea.

He had thought that telling the DPM what his cousin had found in Greenland, would have proved his soundness as an advisor. Indeed, not saying anything about the crevasse would have been regarded as gross disloyalty had he been found out. But now he could see how the land was lying. The PM was in a very weak position after the debacle of the solar storm. He was perceived as dithering and ill-informed by the electorate, who were now sensing a change in the air. Ron Bowman had spotted his chance to seem competent, strong, and up-to-speed, as he could feel another crisis on the way and had started to gather people around him. Marcus' mind raced through the possibilities. If the future PM was sitting before him he would do well to keep in with him, or risk damaging his career. But he was not a back-stabber. It would be wise, he decided, to try to hedge his bets and say as little as possible without coming across as a time-waster.

While keeping his well-practised composure, he said coolly,

"The scientists working out there in the field are getting increasingly concerned at the rate of melting that they are encountering out there, and are warning us of the heightened risks of flooding, especially if a large break-off occurs, which it seems is now a real possibility. But research has been difficult – the solar storm has meant that hard data is still difficult to get hold of – we need to get our experts back out there, sir."

He thought that sounded general enough, but still convincing. But the DPM wasn't wearing it.

"Yes, yes, we know all this – I can get all this from the newspapers – I thought you'd got something of interest for me, I really hoped that you'd got something new. Is the ice cracking up or isn't it – I can't afford to look like a scaremonger." He glanced at his desk calendar to give him something to focus on, then went for the jugular. "You're related to one of these scientists, aren't you, Marc?"

How the hell did he know that?

"Yes, that's right."

"Been meeting pretty regularly, too, I gather."

"I've seen her once or twice, lately, that's true. Nothing strange about that. I let her have some supplies when things were running short."

"And today? What about your meeting today? The shops all appear to be quite well stocked when I last looked."

And when would that be? Like you do any shopping. Marcus James seethed.

"She came to see me to ask about easing the restrictions on travel – all the scientists are having trouble getting permission to go back to Greenland, apparently."

"Well, that's not our problem – it's not up to us, if they want to be difficult." The DPM said.

They were getting nowhere.

Bowman sat at his chair tapping his papers with his glasses, irritably. He'd been hoping to get more information from this interview. He'd heard the rumours about the ice cracking up, but had no idea whether that would impact on Britain, or whether they were talking long-term, maybe in the next 30-50 years for the sea-levels to rise. Politicians think in time-bites, where the legendary week is a long time, and elections mark the boundaries between one era and another, not millions of years. The PM had been wounded by his poor response to the solar storm, and the Deputy saw his moment approaching. Marcus suddenly saw his own back-tracking during his interview with the DPM reflected in the way Amy James had approached him, looking as though she had something urgent to tell him, and then going on about travel plans. She knew more than she was letting on, but didn't really trust him, that much was clear. And now the DPM was thinking exactly the same about him. What to do.

There was a buzz from the desk console, and the secretary from the ante-room said that it was time for the DPM to go to the Commons.

"I'm a bit disappointed, I must say Marcus. I like to know where people's loyalties lie." Bowman stood up, ready to leave, his action underlining his point. He liked to have the last word. It was a shot across the bows. Marcus smiled warmly and looked unruffled,

"Well you know where you stand with me, sir. I'm right behind the PM. Whether he's abroad, or right here in front of me."

He got a look back that said 'smart ass' and the door closed behind Bowman as he departed for the Commons, leaving Marcus alone with the PPS, for a moment while he made ready to go. He took a couple of steps towards the door, but before he got there Harrington said, "Excuse me, just a moment, Mr James. If you could spare me a few minutes, I just wanted to show you this." Surprised, and a little wary, Marcus walked back to the desk, where Harrington had just got up a website on the lap-top. "My son showed me this, the other night. He's a student – they're all riveted by it, apparently. The daily blogs have got everyone talking – there's even a web-cam pointed at the so-called crevasse. Look."

Marcus looked at the website with growing interest. The crack in the ice did look pretty big. And the graphics were illustrating that it could be continent-wide. There was a guy with dark glasses and an open-weave scarf saying that he had discovered this major geological feature they had dubbed 'The Atlantis Rift,' while flying over the area in his Cessna Super Caravan. Marcus clocked its name immediately. The Atlantis Rift. He felt sure it would make the papers now there was a handle on the theories and speculation. He could already see a brief taking shape in his mind to give to the PM. He could see a press conference only days away if this got out. He would have to try to put a call through to the PM straightaway, even though he was in the Middle East, or they would look as though they were trailing incompetently behind the media.

Then he saw the undeniable figure of Amy James on the screen.

She was explaining the link between the crevasse and the seismic activity that had been experienced in the UK and the rest of Europe. She'd been there. She'd seen it with her own eyes, and she was clearly more worried about it than she had so far let on to him, at least. Hence her contact with him. Her only way of getting back to the Arctic and taking any action was to stay the maverick, to stay away from official control, but she was torn between that and needing to warn everyone of the potential consequences. That, Marcus James concluded was why she had dipped her toe in the water by contacting him. And had decided to go her own way after he had been less than helpful. Harrington looked glum.

"Have you shown this to the DPM?" said Marcus.

"Oh yes, sir. But he thinks it's unreliable. Says you can't make government policy on a bunch of under-graduates arsing about. I think he thinks it's a bit like Facebook."

"But what do you think, Harrington?"

"I'm worried, Mr James. Very worried. Environ-mental issues always seem so worthy, but a bit abstract, if you know what I mean. I've been talking to my son about all this, and he thinks it's the real stuff on that web-cast. The DPM was worried that it might all be a hoax. The problem is that both he and the PM, and everyone else is seeing the threat as a political one – it's how we think here, after all. They can't really grasp that they might be dealing with an actual physical threat, something on an unprecedented scale."

"A clear and present danger."

"Exactly."

"I keep thinking of my elderly mother who lives in a bungalow on the coast. It's almost embarrassing to say this – but if the ice sheet breaks off in a big enough chunk, the first she will know of it will be the view of a hundred foot wall of water heading her way, while we're sitting here playing musical chairs, gossiping about who will get the top job, unable to take anything outside of Westminster seriously. We have a duty to serve the public, after all."

Harrington stopped, already feeling that he had said too much, but Marcus was very much taken by what he had just heard, and felt a little chastened to think that his motive for coming here today had really been to cover his own back. In an effort to make amends, he thought he would at least make an attempt to help Amy out, and to see if he could get her the information she had really been after, Coulson's contact.

"Harrington....." He looked warmly at the other man, and his expression showed that he was genuinely concerned. "I think that you get to know more about what goes on in this place than I ever will. It seems that someone over in the MoD sent an – envoy – to Greenland – some sort of fact-finding mission, I suppose. Maybe he had something interesting to say. I wonder if he sent anything useful back here – some intelligence for us to go on. Maybe if I knew the right person to talk to over at Defence, we could be better placed to push for something to get done. A name, or a phone number perhaps?"

Harrington understood immediately what was being asked of him, but he was already ahead of the game.

"I wouldn't go there, Marc," he said, the use of his first name giving the older man some authority as well as expressing some genuine concern. "I don't know all the details myself, but I heard that whoever it was – well – didn't come back – and now nobody wants to know about it. Not really a good idea to admit how much you know. No-one wants a scandal if there's to be an election sooner rather than later."

Harrington was clearly troubled and he hesitated for a couple of seconds before writing a name and number down on a piece of paper, which was then left lying there on his desk.

Marcus James thought for a long moment before answering.

"OK," was all he could think of to say, until at last he collected his thoughts, and made a move to go.

He tentatively reached out to pick up the piece of paper. Harrington looked away sharply, so Marcus folded it up and stuffed it quickly into his top pocket. He thanked Harrington – and meant it. He then wished him a good evening before making for the exit and leaving the office, closing the door behind him. He should have got straight on the phone to the PM, but instead he called Amy James, deliberately not using the secure phone, and told her to stop poking about, and to forget about going back to Greenland. He hoped that might buy her some time. With the phone tucked under her chin, she reassured her cousin that he had no need to worry on that account. She thanked him all the same, and said that she was sure they'd get their clearance all in good time, while with her free hands she was busy packing up her rucksack, ready for whenever Phil Becaud would send them the word that they were good to go.

* * *

In a hotel room in Dubai, the British Prime Minister had just turned in after a gruelling eighteen-hour day, backing trade agreements with the various ministers and businessmen who had all worked so hard to close their deals and had been counting on him for his support. He'd done all that had been asked of him, but now, exhausted beyond sleep, he had finally shut the door on all of them. He sat slumped on the side of the bed, wearing only his boxer shorts, his arms on his legs, his hands hanging limply between his thighs. His head was down. He had eaten too much pretentious corporate food, and could have murdered a beer, but didn't dare ask for one in case it caused somebody or other offence. Rules were not so strict for foreign nationals as they were for local people, but in his position, he didn't dare risk doing the wrong thing, or all the goodwill that he just garnered could be wiped out in one go. He sighed heavily. More than anything, he wished he was home. Not Westminster, where he knew that they were all plotting against him now that he was away. He meant his own home, with his own bed, his own chair, and his family around him. There'd be an election soon, anyway, and the Deputy Prime Minister was going to have to settle for being leader of the Opposition.

Serve the scheming bastard right.

He'd been catching up with the latest on the website that Dorothy Redmires had set-up. He'd been following it avidly, ever since his wife had tipped him off about it, and in his mind he called the mismatched group of scientists, photographers, and adventurers featured in it 'the gang'. He knew that they'd discovered the horrifying truth about the Arctic climate - and that they – the gang – would be assuming that he could do something about it. He smiled a flat, unhappy smile. He really wished he could forget about politics and get something actually done. But he had do deal with reality, and take responsibility for any decisions that had to be made. It was all very well thinking that people had to be warned that an iceberg might break off into the sea – what then? Where do you put 10-15 million people with no homes, no jobs, no money, and no food? After all he owned a tiny cottage by the sea himself, for God's sake and he'd no idea whether to sell it or not. He knew, too, that they'd be staying there next month if Caroline had anything to do with it. And if it all turned out to be a false alarm the country and the economy would be in ruins after so much disruption. For a moment, he thought cynically, there had never been a better time to lose an election, and to hand the poisoned chalice over to the Opposition.

He'd gone into politics genuinely thinking that he could make a difference. Full of energy, drive and ambition, he still couldn't believe it when he, David, had been made Prime Minister. He'd wanted it so much. He had been buoyed up by the thought of having the power to do what needed to be done. Deep down all he'd wanted to do was to leave the place a little better than he'd found it. Now at the end of his tenure, and it was the end, he had no doubt of that anymore, all he felt was a sense of failure and shame. With the crystal clear perception of hindsight all he could see as he looked across the twinkling nightscape of Dubai through his hotel window, was what he hadn't done when he had the chance. He hadn't insisted that the country's wealth during all those good years had been used to modernise and renew the UK's infrastructure. Instead he'd allowed the banks, the corporate giants, the utility companies, the financial institutions to grow fat and top heavy on the work of minimum-wagers and long-hours drones. They had been dazzled by the myths of wealth-creation; like the one where entrepreneurs should be as unhindered as possible to make money, and then that wealth can trickle down through society, showering everyone with its benefits. A more apt metaphor would be that of a sponge, where the wealthy have used their power to soak up the prosperity that ordinary people could have better spent on their own families.

The utility companies should never have been allowed to profiteer; instead they should have been investing in renewables, and alternative, secure energy supplies. We should have been preparing for the future and we haven't. The solar storm shouldn't really have caused that many problems, but it did. It proved how fragile as a society we are, and now we could be facing something many times worse. Too late now, David reflected. The economy was in downturn and the money was gone.

He felt dog-tired, but the tight band around his head wouldn't allow him to relax into sleep.

His phone rang, its familiar tone filling the room with at least the promise of some human contact. He wanted it to be Caroline. He pressed the button automatically.

"Hello."

He waited for her usual 'Hi Darling.' but instead got a man's voice apologising for calling so late. Marc James! This had better be important. The Prime Minister listened patiently while Marcus filled him in on the situation back home.

"Thank you, Marc. No, it was OK to call, no, really. You did the right thing. But, you see, it hardly matters now. There's not a lot we can do, looking at it from a practical point of view. I can't order a coastal evacuation – there are just too many people to put anywhere, and the whole situation is still too speculative. And we can't keep the lid on the Atlantis Rift story now...." Marcus was stunned that the PM already knew its name. "It can only be a matter of days now before the papers hit us with their doomsday headlines. And then we're finished, as a Government, totally finished."

Marc James didn't answer.

He didn't need to.

CHAPTER NINETEEN

There was no doubt now that Terry Coulson was a member of the gang, after what he'd just done.

They needed him, too. The girls didn't even try to oppose his inclusion, despite their unpleasant introduction to his way of doing things. They just hoped that he'd grow on them, now that he was on their side.

His red Toyota pickup looked more out of place in London than it did only a week ago, as the streets filled up once more with modern vehicles which were now getting repaired. He'd pulled the tarpaulin cover tightly over the back of the truck and roped it neatly to avoid any unwanted attention, then got out of the city as quickly as he could. He'd wondered whether to wear his uniform after his visit to the Bulford Army camp at Salisbury, just in case he was stopped, but decided against it, opting instead for outdoorsy civvies. He was tall and broad-shouldered, too, which helped to make him look every bit the landowner. If necessary he could say he was running a course in army games for off-duty City types, and that he was only carrying blanks and thunder-flashes. The trick was to look confident, and he'd always been able to do that. Then people don't look too closely. Terry was glad to be leaving London. He'd got the call from Oliver Carter, and within the hour he was locking up his front door and swinging his bags into the passenger seat of the pick-up.

His cargo did not consist of blanks, though. In fact, he was carrying enough live explosive to take out the centre of a small town. It had been pretty easy at the army camp, too, once he'd talked his way into using an army vehicle for an hour or so. It would have been harder trying to get hold of a single piece of explosive, or a gun. But collecting a small truckload of equipment seemed more legit. Terry had talked convincingly to the other guy about Afghanistan, as he'd done a tour of duty there. Missed the lads a bit sometimes. Knew that what he had done today would separate him from them for ever. Could mean prison. Best not to think about that too much. Told himself he was still fighting for his country, in his own way, and for Ray.

He left London behind without incident and was heading out now for the West Country, through Wiltshire. He would soon be in Somerset, where Oliver had told him they would all meet up. Security had been getting tighter in London, so immediately after their meeting at the King's Head, Phil Becaud had decided not to risk them leaving from London but to fly the Cessna to a smaller airfield where their departure would be less likely attract attention. The one Becaud had chosen seemed to be right out in the sticks. That suited Terry just fine.

He looked at the map until he found the airfield. It was at a place called Westonzoyland, and he made a mental note that he would have to leave the M5 at Junction 23. It felt like he was on operations again, and when he thought of it like that, everything seemed normal for a while, till reality caught up with him once more. He tried not to think of it too much or the cold panic would set in. He was acting alone, with no leadership structure and without the camaraderie of his fellow soldiers. Also he lacked the legitimacy that the army had given to his previous actions. He checked himself. If he thought like that and was stopped he would give himself away. He must concentrate on the story of his army games business. Make himself believe it for a while. Then everyone else would.

The first grey light of dawn had just spilled over the horizon when Terry Coulson drove through the last few bends of the narrow Somerset lanes which led up to the airfield at Westonzoyland. Up until then all he'd been able to see was farmland. It was still too dark to make out the runway, and the view was obscured by the thick hedgerows anyway. There should be a sign somewhere, he thought, straining around to see better. But then he saw the fuzzy but unmistakable outline of the Cessna standing there by the bunker-like buildings at the end of the runway. The figures of Zoe and Oliver Carter were talking together while they were waiting for him to show. The air was only slightly cool even at this time of the morning; it was going to be hot later and they wanted to get the plane loaded up before the sun got any stronger, and before they attracted any attention. Dorothy Redmires, standing at the metal five bar gate, opened it on seeing Terry's headlights draw closer to her, and pointed him in the right direction. He turned off his lights as it was just getting light enough to see without them, then pulled up sharply next to the plane and jumped out of the driver's seat.

"You got the stuff?" said Oliver.

"Yeah. No problem."

"You made good time," said Zoe.

"I needed to," said Terry. "We need to get moving as soon as we can."

A farm vehicle drove past the gate, noisily bumping along as the driver hurried to begin his long day's work. Instinctively, they all froze, but Terry noticed out of the corner of his eye that the passing farmer stared a little too deliberately ahead. Looked like they were used to minding their own business out here.

* * *

Terry Coulson had been on board since he joined them at their table at the King's Head, and sat down to the pint that Hewitt put on the mat in front of him.

"I feel I've just taken the King's Shilling," he said after pulling a long draught of beer, and looking first at Hewitt, then at the others. Amy James was next to Zoe and Oliver, opposite Hewitt and Dorothy Redmires.

"Don't worry, he's too tight for that!" said Oliver, trying to put him at his ease.

Zoe had told him straightaway that they needed someone with them who could handle explosives, as they'd come up with a plan that they thought would release the pressure of the eruption and allow the lava flow to escape into the sea. Terry had stared at the faces around him, stunned by what they were expecting him to do. Blasting out some samples rock for research purposes, he could have understood, but this was just crazy.

"Are you guys for real?" he said, not knowing whether this was some kind of joke. But he was met by a ring of solemn stares, patiently waiting for his answer. To buy some time he got out his phone with the video clips and voice recordings that his brother Ray had sent to him, and he handed them over to Zoe for her to look at. She took them and immediately began to study them intently.

The flat screen TV on the pub wall had the latest news on the tremors that were still rocking the country. This time Scotland and the Shetlands had the worst of it, and reports were coming in from France.

"They are getting worse – more frequent, and stronger. Something's building. This is not just going to go away," said Dorothy, looking at Terry.

And somehow, by the end of the evening he had agreed to get the explosives and all the gear, and to go with them back to Greenland.

* * *

He lifted the first of the boxes down from the back of the pickup, handing them first to Oliver, then Zoe and Amy between them, through Hewitt and finally to Becaud who carefully weighed the cargo and loaded it as he knew how it should go. They each had one rucksack or holdall, which were wedged among the boxes for extra stability. They were a good hour, loading the plane, even though no-one paused for a moment until it was done. The light now brought some colour into the landscape, and the warmth was pleasant and fresh as only an English summer morning can be. It was Phil Becaud who broke the spell by speaking,

"OK folks. I guess that's it."

It was time to go. Hurriedly Dorothy poured out some cups of hot tea from a flask, fussing and making sure that everyone knew what to do. Secretly Becaud was glad she wasn't coming along, as he couldn't really warm to her. He couldn't work out why he felt that way, but he'd never seen anyone do a sodoku so quickly, and he found everything about her more irritating after that. He jumped into the plane's familiar seat and started the engines to warm them up while he did the cockpit checks. Having finished the deliciously welcome drinks they tipped out the cups onto the grass and handed them back to Dorothy who put them in the Toyota. They were relaxed, and off-guard, the atmosphere becoming more like a picnic.

It was all going too well.

Then when they heard the sound of more than one vehicle speed along the road, the tyres crunching as they rolled over the gravel that had collected at the side of the little used lane, they came to with a burst of panic that brought them straight back to what they were doing and why. First they saw a couple of car roofs above the hedgerow, in the distance. They were police patrol cars. Then the first car swung into the airfield by some other gate, followed by a second which stopped in the nearer gateway, blocking off any potential escape. Terry's mind was racing. Did the pickup look suspicious, or did it fit in around here? He tried not to look at, or think about the Cessna, now bulging with its illicit cargo, or it would make him look shifty. Dorothy went into action seamlessly.

"Go!" she said. Right now! You have to go!"

Zoe and Amy were in the plane, hardly before Dorothy had finished speaking, yelling at Oliver to move, as he looked as though he was he didn't want to run. Hewitt pushed past him, while Terry sprang into the co-pilot's seat. Becaud was already rolling, racing through the last of his checks. The police, seeing some activity, started to head towards the plane, fast. Zoe was shouting at Becaud.

"You can't go without him, Phil!" She was beside herself with fear.

Becaud knew that they had a window to go of a few more seconds, otherwise the patrol car would be pulling up right in his path. They'd never get out of that one, not with their cargo. If they were charged with being eco-terrorists they would never see the light of day again

Oliver was still on the runway. He hesitated when he should have jumped aboard the plane, he hated running away, thinking it would be better to sort things out now. Dorothy knew that the police wouldn't believe a word of anything that Oliver was thinking of telling them.

"Get in that plane – move, you idiot!" she said. "They are not waiting, go!"

As the patrol cars got closer, the plane picked up some speed just as Oliver made up his mind to go for it. He ran to catch up at full pelt, and only got in because Zoe held the door open for him while three straining pairs of hands helped to pull him inside. The door closed safely, he put on his belt, and sat there breathless, and shaken. The engines roared. They sped along the bumpy airstrip. They were airborne. Zoe burst into tears. And nobody bothered to tell Oliver what a fucking prat he was as he knew it already.

The Cessna roared into the summer sky and was over the treetops by the time the policemen had jumped from their vehicle. Doors left open, they jogged uselessly towards where the plane had just left. Then they looked at Dorothy and walked slowly and deliberately in her direction.

"Good morning," she said, cheerfully. She smiled and looked as though this was her normal way to start the morning, and waved at the plane as it became a small speck in the sky. They owed their escape to Dorothy's powers of persuasion. The police had been alerted to the activity on the airstrip, presumably by the farmer in the tractor who went by earlier. There had been problems with contraband in the area, usually illegally imported cigarettes, but sometimes drugs.

But Dorothy had been able to prove to the officers that she was a respected academic, and to persuade them that the flight was a field trip for an archaeology project. Yes, but why the rush to leave, they asked. Dorothy blagged as only a seasoned lecturer knew how. They were taking pictures for some new archaeological project near Stonehenge, she said. Needed the early light to get the relief effect, otherwise you don't really see anything. She'd gone to all that trouble and considerable expense to get a plane sorted out and they can't even get their asses out of bed, she grumbled on. They were cynical, but had to admit that she didn't look like a drug runner, more of a County type. When they accepted her offer of a cup of tea from her one remaining flask, and sat down on the back flap of the pickup to drink it, she breathed a huge sigh of relief. It might not go any further. If they been in any way suspicious, the Cessna would have been met by security when they tried to land in Scotland, and the plane searched. She felt hot when she thought about it, so adeptly, she steered the conversation away from the plane and told them all about her poor house in Derbyshire. They were sympathetic, and nodded at her now and then in between drinks of tea. Then the policemen left her abruptly when they had another, more urgent call come in. They knew what they had been looking for here, and none of what they saw fitted in with an illegal drop off. Off the hook and slightly tremulous with adrenaline, Dorothy slammed shut the badly aligned door of the old Toyota, now adopted by her and seen as her prize for all her efforts.

Feeling that her role of the getaway driver was now wearing a bit thin, her sense of incredulity at what she had become a part of, was still clinging to her uncomfortably. It was time to go, before there were any more complications. Sighing a huge gasp and blow of relief, she turned over the Toyota's engine and eased the vehicle forward. Dorothy then bumped over the field to the gate, and sped down the road which led eventually out to the motorway. She headed up north, and straight for home as quickly as the battered old pickup would take her.

Meanwhile the Cessna made for a quiet landing strip in the west of Scotland to refuel, then on to the Faeroes, Iceland and finally Greenland, re-tracing its stepping- stone path back to Angmagssalik. When they got there they were utterly exhausted.

They were back. They couldn't believe how they'd done it, but there they were, pushing open the door of their rented house in Angmagssalic, with utter relief that only lasted until they crashed out on the beds unable even to eat, shower or unpack anything first. Zoe only remembered feeling the soft pillow give under her cheek before she slept for twelve solid hours

Phil Becaud was now doing the video diary, and he got straight back to it as soon as he had recovered from his epic flight. He was great at it, they all had to admit. But somehow on his latest webcast he managed to forget to mention that he'd taken a detour to London, and that he'd now arrived back with a planeload of illegally acquired explosives. That could wait. If their plan was a success, he'd tell 'em all about it in good time.

CHAPTER TWENTY

Greenland

When they flew over the Atlantis Rift again, it was amazing to see that it had visibly widened, so much so, in places, that Becaud could fly the Cessna down into the valley that had been created. It was not like that all along its length. In some areas the ice sheet was intact, holding together as though it has been stuck; in others there was the menace of a deep slit, the darkness sucking in shadows, that would fall a long, long way down, until at last, as the walls moved apart, the gap grew so wide the light penetrated and brought daylight once more to the forgotten bedrock below. The widest part of the Rift was concentrated on the area where Becaud had first pointed it out to Amy James just a few weeks ago. Here was the centre of the volcanic activity. The ground steamed and boiled in between the two ice cliffs the Rift had created, undermining their bases and ever widening the gap between them. And Dorothy was in danger of being proved right.

The Atlantis Rift was sitting on top of a huge fissure eruption, and the enormous amounts of lava that were oozing out of the Earth's broken crust was worming its way though the caverns, voids and tunnels that existed at the bottom of the ice sheet. It was not the slow, steady, drip, drip of ice in the sun; it was like pouring boiling water over a bucket of ice cubes. They were gone in an instant. The Rift was the open and visible wound in the ice that could be seen, but it was underneath that was the most disturbing. The hot lava was spreading thinly but penetrating over a vast area under the ice, turning the bottom of the sheet into liquid water which was lifting the ice from its anchorage on the bedrock, making it unstable, and sliding it slowly towards the sea. The rate of crumbling around the already fragile southern coasts of Greenland was already increasing, and like pennies building up on an amusement arcade cliff-hanger machine, the pressure was building but would let go all at once, when the tipping point had been reached. And if there were to be a calving event, then it would be bound to cause problems with flooding somewhere, as the ripples it created became waves on someone else's shore. Zoe's worst nightmare, that the ice sheet was becoming unstable, was now becoming increasingly the most likely possibility, and not the one-in-a-million event she hoped for.

The eruption, far from slowing down, was increasing in its intensity all the time. The fissure itself was now over forty-five kilometres long and could actually be seen at the bottom of the Atlantis Rift. It was spewing out lava relentlessly, and even where the lava had begun to congeal, its heat was sufficient to melt the ice around for tens of metres, creating lakes and mini rivers, steaming and dripping in the summer temperatures. Steam rose above dense banks of fog, giving the landscape an ethereal, other planetary feel, that was both beautiful and threatening at the same time. In places the ice sheet looked intact where the Rift was actually filled to the brim with vaporous clouds of pure white. Some areas would be stained with yellow, like an ugly chemical spill on the pristine landscape. Becaud gave those places a wide berth. He didn't intend to get caught out a second time.

Back in Angmagssalik, Zoe had got Amy to incorporate all their available data into the computer model which Oliver had had sent from the seismology department at Isaac's; and it wasn't looking good. Even if the eruption shut down straightaway, the long-term effects could still be devastating, with huge lumps of ice breaking off into the sea, accelerating climate change and causing smaller but no less deadly tidal waves. The heat from the solidifying lava would continue to be an amplifier of climatic variables which could prove to be the last straw for the straining ice sheet.

That was the good news. Over and over again the model showed the collapse of a massive layer of destabilised ice, falling into the central area of the fissure eruption, the caldera, and causing an explosion of such magnitude as the steam hit the pressurised magma layer that the ice sheet fractured over a vast area, and already loosed from its moorings, it would slide unstoppably into the sea. Europe, Scandinavia and parts of North America would be engulfed in the ensuing tidal waves of unimaginable proportions. Zoe looked at the model for a long time before she spoke, an unimaginable sadness spread over her face.

"We'd be finished, babe," said Zoe to Oliver.

"I know," he said quietly, and took her hand. "I know."

* * *

"We've got Ray's contact," said Oliver to Terry Coulson.

Oliver felt his heart thump as he said it. Lawrence Hewitt looked up from his book but said nothing.

"Amy's just got an email from Marcus James – I don't know how the hell he did it, but this could be useful to us, what do you think?" Oliver waited for Coulson to answer. He was still uncomfortable on hearing his brother mentioned.

"It could be. Let me see." Coulson looked at the printout and made a note of the name. "So he has decided to help us after all. This means someone out there is worried. Very worried indeed. Anyway, it would help us at least if we knew which way the wind was blowing. Is our government planning any action of its own, or is it still trying to smooth things over and pretend there's nothing happening out here?" Coulson sounded cynical. He folded over the paper and placed into his pocket.

Zoe and Amy wandered back into the room and flopped down onto the sofa, where Hewitt was already ensconced. They were all back at Phil Becaud's house, which had been turned into an operations base for the duration. Zoe picked up the remote and flicked on the TV in the corner. She then got into the menu and scrolled down till she got Sky News, and sat back to watch. The headlines were rolling across the screen in a loop. Some journalists had sniffed out the rumours of the ice fissure from reading the blogs on Dorothy Redmires website, and the story now seemed to be gathering pace. The women both sat up and looked at the reports intently. Oliver looked grave. He knew they'd got no time to waste.

"Zoe, I think you should contact Dorothy, and get her to call this guy. If he sent Ray out there in the first place, my guess is that he is more clued up than most on the implications of what's happening out here. And he might have some plans of his own in hand."

She agreed, and went at once to call Dorothy.

Terry Coulson sat down in the armchair. He took out the piece of paper and unfolded it slowly, looking vacantly at the name on the sheet in front of him. He seemed withdrawn and depressed as the thoughts of his brother crowded in on his mind once more. He ran his hand over his bowed head in a gesture of frustration that was bordering on anger. Oliver watched him uneasily, wondering if Amy's opinion that Coulson had poor judgement, might be right; and that he would need to be watched carefully.

When Zoe came back into the room, she too, took in the slumped figure of Coulson. She looked up and her eyes met her husband's; she knew he was thinking the same thing, and without having to speak, they both agreed to keep an eye on him. Then she spoke, firstly to Oliver.

"I've emailed Dorothy. She's going to get back to me. Hopefully by this afternoon." She then addressed Coulson.

"Hey, Terry!" He glanced up on hearing his name called out. "I'm going to make some coffee for the gang – you can give me a hand, I'm putting you in charge of rations. If you go and commandeer the coffee cake, dole it out, one large slice per person, that would be great. I think we all need a morale-booster – OK?"

Terry Coulson jumped up. He was used to responding to orders, and didn't feel threatened by Zoe, good-tempered as she was. And he was glad to have a job to do. He felt that things had thawed out between him and Zoe, after Oliver had taken him to one side, and told him what he thought about the car park incident. You threaten my wife again and I'll break your fucking arm, was the gist of it. Which made Coulson smile somewhat as he was the commando. He didn't smile too much though, as Oliver Carter was tall and broad-shouldered and at least matched him in physique. And he'd got guts. He respected him for that. So Coulson apologised, and it had seemed to put the matter to rest. It was different with Amy though. She avoided him; he could feel it. And she never allowed herself to be alone with him. Couldn't blame her really.

Zoe went into the kitchen with Terry. She boiled the kettle and spooned six heaped scoops of fresh aromatic coffee into the pot. Then two more, as an after thought.

Next she lined up the six mugs and found a bag of sugar in the cupboard, which she put on the counter ready. Becaud had nipped out, but would be bound to appear when coffee was made. Right on cue the front door banged and Becaud strode in throwing his jacket and scarf over the back of a kitchen chair.

"Hi guys," he said brightly. "I see I'm just in time." Zoe grinned.

"Do you take sugar, Terry?" said Zoe.

"Yeah, I do in fresh coffee – it's a bit strong for me. Funny. Ray never used to take sugar – but he told me he'd started to since being out here. Needed the calories, he said. Told me that just after they stayed overnight at a shelter on the first night of his trip. That was where he felt as though the whole Earth's crust had lifted up by several feet as he slept – well it woke him up. Then just after that they found a sort of drop."

"What sort of a drop?"

"It must have been almost twenty-five metres. Only they worked out that it wasn't a drop at all. They were on a plateau of ice that had been pushed up. It took them nearly a day to get round it – it curved round for miles. If that hadn't held them up, I don't suppose they would have been caught out in the gas cloud. I often think of that."

Zoe nodded sympathetically. This was the first time he'd opened up to her, and she was keen to encourage him.

Coulson carefully cut the cake into six neat even-sized pieces and put it on the tray with a pile of plates. He seemed very calm and dextrous when he became absorbed in the job he was doing, and Zoe had a mental image of his fingers twisting a delicate wire around a terminal as he carefully laid an explosive. She was thinking of what he had just said.

"Do you know the name of the shelter where they stayed? Was it a hunting lodge or something?"

"It was a weather station, I think."

Zoe shouted to the others that the coffee was ready and one by one they trickled onto the kitchen, and made straight for the·cake. Her eyes by now were alight with excitement.

"Phil, what's the name of that weather station – the one that Joe would have stopped off at, on his first night of the trip?"

"Oh, that would be Bear Camp, I guess. Why? We won't be heading that way. We'll be flying the first leg anyway and heading further east than that."

"No, no. It's not that. It's something Terry has just told me, about what Ray experienced when he was at Bear Camp. From what he has just told me, I think we have just found the caldera!"

"What! What do you mean?" said Oliver who stopped chewing even though he had a mouthful of cake.

"Are you serious, Zoe?" said Amy.

"Absolutely. Look." She marched through into the room where the map was permanently spread over the large dining table. She made a pencil cross on Bear Camp, then asked Becaud where he thought the doomed expedition would have got to by the time they reached the ledge. Amy helped by going through Ray Coulson's video diary till they got to the bit where he warned the others about the drop. She took note of the time, and from that Becaud was roughly able to estimate how far they were away from Bear Camp.

"Without the benefit of GPS, this is only a best guess, a ball-park figure. I reckon that they were about here when they found the edge of the drop." He drew a line where he thought it should be. "They then said they curved around in this direction for several hours before they found a place to cross down from the plateau." He marked a huge quadrant on the map.

"So if we continue this curve round until it makes a full circle, then we have the position of the caldera! It's here. Has to be!"

"Hold on!" said Amy. "You could be right, but we have to have more to go on than that."

"Unfortunately we don't have the time to verify this at the moment. But it fits the picture – and it makes it all the more imperative that we make our move."

Zoe was now buzzing with energy, and was trying to drive the others along with her. Oliver looked alarmed as the reality was sinking in that they were going to try to blow a hole in the side of the caldera to release the building pressure and avoid a catastrophic explosion. Actually doing it. With no authorisation, and no guarantee that they were right. If they were wrong.....He felt sick at the thought.

Zoe pressed on.

"The Atlantis Rift meets the caldera here, where, it seems, the Rift skims past the rim at a tangent. They, Ray, Joe and the others, couldn't have made the connection as they were miles away from the point of intersection, and would have had to cross the ice for some considerable time before they met up with the Rift. This, at the moment, is where we see the most activity from the fissure eruption. Lava is being forced under the ice sheet and weakening it all the time. We need to release the pressure on the east side, the side nearest the coast, so that the lava can run down the channel created by the Rift on this side, and into the sea. That should, in theory channel the eruption, and as more lava exits the volcano on this side it will reduce the flow, everywhere else. That will at least slow down the pace of destruction, until the eruption runs its course and stops of its own accord."

"This isn't going to be so easy, especially as we don't have much time," said Terry, studying the map. "I think your theory is good, but unless I can get more info it's going to be difficult to know where exactly to blast our way in."

Zoe appeared frustrated, but she knew that he was right. The trouble was, this was not really her field. What she needed at this point was a specialist vulcanologist to advise her. But then again, even the world's greatest authority wouldn't be much use to them without data, and there was clearly no time to arrange a proper study. They'd got here what appeared to be a sub-glacial eruption, and if there was one thing about sub-glacial eruptions that she remembered from her university days was that they melted ice at a phenomenal rate. Something like one unit volume of magma can melt ten units of ice. Zoe explained this as best she could to the line of chewing faces in front of her, then waited for them to say something. *Come on, guys! You've got to get back to me on this one.* She was urging them inwardly to help her out.

The long silence that had descended onto the group was broken only by Amy's phone, buzzing in her pocket. She answered tentatively, not recognising the number on the display, but then at once became absorbed in the call. She walked into another room so that she could give it her full attention, without feeling that everyone else was listening to her responses. Two minutes later, she rejoined them all, dropping the phone into her pocket as she entered the room.

She looked shaken, and clearly didn't know how to tell them that Marcus James, her cousin, had been arrested.

"He's being held in military custody. The call was from someone, a woman, called Hazel. Do you think that is a code word? I don't like this," she said.

The shock ran around the room, as each in turn felt both guilty and responsible for this in equal measure. And they were trying to work out what this could mean for them. Terry Coulson felt his pulse quicken with anxiety. He had the feeling that things were closing in on him. Now the only way out was to make this operation work.

Otherwise it was prison for sure.

"We can't just think of ourselves. Whatever the repercussions," said Zoe. "What's happening to the ice sheet could mean that abrupt climate change happens in a season. In a single season! Think about it. This is what we have to face if we fail, here."

"It's beginning to dawn on people back home that we have a real threat here, and not just a possible one. That's why the powers that be are getting twitchy," said Hewitt.

Coulson turned away, glumly. He wished he was fighting a war that he could understand.

"I'll get onto Dorothy," said Zoe. But that didn't help this time. After trying her number all day, Zoe gave up, leaving Hewitt to get on her website and see if there were any clues as to her whereabouts there. It was not good news. On the blogs it said that she'd been seen leaving the building with two men in an unmarked car, and had not been contactable since. Amy bit the bullet.

"I'm going to call the contact that Marcus gave me. He's obviously behind all this, and is probably trying to reel us in."

"And tell him what?" said Hewitt.

"Well, I don't know," said Amy. But I just don't feel that we go ahead with the situation as it stands."

"We have to go ahead, whatever," said Zoe. But I agree, you should try to contact this person, whoever he is."

"And what if he tells us not to do anything or they'll prosecute Marcus and Dorothy," said Oliver. "They are obviously holding them for a reason."

"Then we're fucked," said Hewitt.

Tempers were getting frayed, and their voices grew louder. The truth was that none of them knew what to do.

"We can't just leave them to their fate," said Amy.

"Why not?" said Hewitt. He was not afraid to disagree with her, even if it risked making him unpopular.

He never pandered to anyone. "We are all involved in this for one purpose, and that is to avoid a natural catastrophe occurring. They know that too. Yes, even Marcus James, or he wouldn't have stuck his neck out, and which is why they all agreed to become part of this thing in the first place. So we have to go ahead. Zoe's right. Otherwise they are in a hell of a lot of trouble for nothing."

"Thank you!" said Zoe.

Amy looked crushed, and was going to say something else, when Becaud butted in by saying that she was only trying to do the right thing. She ignored his gesture of support, which hurt him. He turned away and wished that all these guys would get out of his house. He was sick of the whole business. Deep down he knew that he'd only got so involved with this project because he'd wanted to stay close to Amy. But she just didn't seem to notice him anymore.

Then Amy's phone buzzed again. She looked at the others.

"Well answer the bloody thing then," said Oliver.

At least the call saved them from having to decide whether or not to ring the guy at the MoD. It was Frank Gilmore, himself.

This time Amy didn't leave the room. Her hand shook slightly as she strained to take in everything that was being said to her.

"We're on a secure line, so you can tell me exactly what's going on up there. What the hell do you think you guys are doing? And this had better be good, or I'll have your cousin on assisting terrorism charges."

Amy swallowed back her fear, and answered calmly,

"Have you got Dorothy?" She nearly said 'as well' but saved herself just in time.

"You mean that Redmires woman?"

He sighed heavily, still reeling from his interview with her. When asked to wait in his ante-room until he was ready to see her, she rattled open the door, kicking the base of it where it stuck, pouring into his office and filling it with her outrage at being held there against her will. She loathed officialdom at the best of times and meeting it face to face gave her a full opportunity to vent her spleen on the man seated in front of her.

"You!" she said, "Ought to get out and see what's happening out there!" She pointed angrily at his window. "We are contemplating disaster. The country's being rocked by earthquakes..."

"Oh, I'd hardly say that, Mrs Redmires..." he began, we've had a few tremors it's true, but its nothing to worry about. No need to panic." He was trying to sound smooth and in control but clearly he'd said the wrong thing, and she pounced on him at once, making him sound weak and out of touch. Her eyes flashed as she rounded on him.

"How can you say that? Don't you read the papers? My house is in ruins! And the tremors are getting worse by the day. Five point eight was the last one, and if you don't already know, each point on the Richter scale is an exponential jump. Another few degrees and we could be facing major damage. Especially if one hits a populated area."

She jabbed the air between them with her finger, and wouldn't release him from her stare. "And while you politicians mess about, we, at least are trying to do something about it...."

"About what, exactly, madam? We knew that things weren't looking good up in the Arctic, when these rumours of a giant crevasse were starting to filter back. I'm doing my best, here, in the face of the hiatus created by a worn-out end-of-term Government and an Opposition scenting power, and who can think of nothing else but who's going to get what job if they win. Which is why I sent the unfortunate Mr Coulson on a low-key fact-finding mission. The truth is that nobody wants to face facts; most people are in denial as to how bad things are in Greenland, I know that. But before I could get people to face facts, I had to have some. Now I find that your little expedition seems to have found plenty, but as you are acting on your own, without any official authorisation or sanction, how do I know you're not terrorists, exploiting a volatile situation for your own ends?"

Dorothy sat down. She took in people very quickly, reading every nuance of facial expression unconsciously, whatever they said to the contrary.

She sensed an ally, despite what he said.

"Mr Gilmore. You know as well as I do that we are not terrorists. But what we have discovered has meant that either we do something now, or it will bee too late. It's as simple as that."

He sat back, waiting for her to elaborate. Secretly he knew that something had to be done to reverse or slow down the rate of change in the Arctic; he was well ahead of the game, and already understood that a natural disaster could destabilise the country; but he hadn't figured out why this maverick little band of scientists had snuck into Greenland illegally, with an ex-commando who was an expert in explosives. For all he knew they could be eco-activists who were just using the situation to get publicity for their cause. He pursed up his lips, then relaxed his face while he waited to be impressed, which didn't happen very often.

"Mr Gilmore. What we found was this. The tremors and the Atlantis Rift were linked – they had to be. At first we thought that the huge strains put upon the ice sheet as it melted, cracked and moved were causing the movement in the Earth's crust deep below. After all the ice is two miles thick in the centre if Greenland. That exerts monumental downward pressure on the Earth's crust, which is bound to be affected if there is any lessening or movement of that pressure."

"Yes, but I didn't think there was a faultline there in Greenland. I thought the nearest one was in Iceland."

"It is. But sometimes there are old faultlines from millennia ago that can give and weaken if the pressures are great enough – a bit like old scar tissue. It's never quite as strong as the skin around it. There's liquid water everywhere. You know – people who haven't been back there since the late seventies can't believe what they're seeing. Anyway, we thought that this fissure in the ice sheet was causing the tremors, but now we think it's the other way round. An old, previously dormant volcano has been roused from its very deep slumber and....."

"A volcano, you say?"

"Yes. We get fissure eruptions in Iceland, where lava flows, but we didn't know about this one."

"A volcano!"

"I'm afraid so."

"And it's erupting?"

"Yes."

Frank Gilmore put his elbows on his desk, and rubbed his face hard with both hands. He didn't speak for several seconds, then he looked at Dorothy and said, "So what the fuck do we do now?"

We. He said 'we.' Now she knew he was on their side. Even though *he* didn't, yet. She went straight to the point while he was still reeling from what she had just said.

"We blow a hole in it. Like lancing a boil, it might relieve the pressure enough to avoid a major eruption. We are afraid that the melting water might cause the fragile ice to crash into the caldera where the ensuing steam would cause an explosive eruption which could shatter the ice sheet, sliding any break-offs into the sea. We are going to get some ice breaking off anyway due to the damage that has already been done. What we are trying to do is to stop a continent-wide iceberg sheering and plunging into the sea. If that happens it would mean massive tsunamis. And I mean massive."

His astonished eyes bored into hers as though he were trying to dig out the truth of what she was saying. He wanted her to be wrong, but the longer he stared the more he was convinced that she was utterly sincere. And she wasn't given to exaggeration. As a reputable academic, he also suspected that she could be right. But the remedy sounded off the wall to him.

"Have you taken leave of your senses?" he said when he could find the words to speak. "Blow a hole in it? You could cause a catastrophe all of your own! What if your hare-brained plan doesn't work? What then?"

"Then we'll all look pretty stupid, won't we? Which I think might be preferable to being engulfed in a tidal wave that could kill hundreds of thousands, if not millions of us – although I'll probably be alright in the Peak District, I wouldn't hold out much hope for you."

"And how do I know that you are not some sort of green warriors, pulling some sort of highly risky stunt to get the world to listen to you?" he said. She spoke tersely.

"I've always tried to act with integrity in my professional life, well, in fact in all aspects of my life. I've not always succeeded, but I've done my best. However, I'll say this. I am deeply sceptical of Great Causes, whether they be social, political, religious or even environmental in origin, and I'll tell you why. Once people start to believe that their cause is great enough to suspend normal moral perameters, and act in its name, then I think that we are into power trips, ego-trips, and elitism; where one group believes that they know better and can therefore ride roughshod over everyone else's rights. I'm not into that, believe me. I'm not acting for a Cause; I'm simply trying to use my expertise to do something practical to avoid a lot of needless deaths and suffering."

He sighed again, "And this is what you plan to do? Blow a hole in it?"

"Absolutely. We have to do something. Lava is seeping under the ice sheet destabilising it much more quickly than even the meltwater has been doing. Even if there is no eruption, that factor alone could still cause massive calving events to occur, with the same risk of tidal waves, only smaller ones. If we release some of the pressure, now, and slow the whole process down, it will at least buy us some time. If the ice sheet suffers major damage anyway, it could trigger off an unstoppable greenhouse reaction that could have planet-wide repercussions. What we want to do is a holding operation. There is still much more to do if we are to avoid climate meltdown in the near future. But if we don't act now, this could be the one factor, the last straw, that sends us over the tipping point with no way back. This could be pivotal for our whole future; it's as bad as that."

"Do you think it will work?" Gilmore looked shaken.

"I don't know," said Dorothy. Her honesty in that answer impressed him more than any sales pitch could have done. He felt himself wanting to help. He wanted to say something, but felt that it was too soon to be seen to be going over to her way of thinking. Also she could be quite wrong. The normal procedures would mean setting up a scientific working party, and seeing what they would advise. But that would take time, and would mean getting others on board.

He gestured to his secretary, Hazel Briggs, that the interview was over. She was a slim, well groomed woman in her mid fifties, whose thick black hair draped over her shoulders as she got up. Hazel walked over to the door and opened it to show Dorothy Redmires out. Hazel caught Dorothy's eye for a split second, and she registered the gesture, returning it with the most imperceptible of nods. The two minders outside jumped up when the door creaked, and they both looked at Gilmore for instructions.

"We're keeping you for now, Mrs Redmires. I need time to think."

Dorothy looked at him as though she couldn't believe her ears.

"On what grounds? I need to get back to my work."

"And get straight on to your friends in the Arctic, no doubt."

"Of course I will!" she said, exasperated that he needed to point that out. "We can't afford any more delays."

"And I don't want you giving them the go ahead. Not yet. There's too much at stake."

"As if I didn't know that already."

"I need more time."

"And I'm held prisoner in the meantime, am I? Like Marcus James?" He winced at that. How did she know that they'd got James?"

"Hah! I thought so!" So that's how she knew. He'd just let her know. Must be slipping.

"I might need to see you again. I can't afford to let you go just yet. And I can't prove to anyone else that you're not up to no good. I could be carpeted if I let you go now."

"Jobsworth!" she said unkindly, as she was guided out of Gilmore's office by the two men waiting patiently for her to acquiesce. She shrugged off their touch, and walked between them out of the room, feeling a lot more satisfied with the way the interview had gone than Gilmore did.

"Hazel, have you got that contact number for Amy James?"

She had, but spent a moment or two longer looking for it than she need have done.

She gave him the number. It looked like her mobile. That was OK. He wanted to speak to her direct. Things must be bad for them to have taken things into their own hands. He wondered already if the situation was beyond their control. He thought of his daughter, and her small children. He loved nothing better than listening to their young, quiet voices when they were telling him some-thing that mattered to them. He could hear them now. Their high voices full of cadence and surprise. But he couldn't imagine a tsunami, or a world where you didn't know how to get your next dinner. That's what mattered to him. These were the monsters that lurked in the dark, the fear of them gnawing at him till he couldn't rest. He felt strangely nostalgic for a future that he'd always had in his mind and was gradually working towards, but now could have gone. His vision of retirement, extended holidays and family occasions was so cruelly dependent on a world that that might not be here for much longer. Snatched away by a dystopic nightmare of hardship and loss. His image of what should have been had been taken away, totally without his permission; his teleological journey through life, was slowly becoming unravelled. He called Amy's number.

Her phone was ringing, and the switchboard handed him over. He didn't know which was worse. The break-off of the ice sheet the entire width of the continent of Greenland, or the explosive eruption; not much in it really. Or another interview with Redmires.

At last Amy answered. She laid it on the line, and stressed that theirs could only be a holding operation at best, if they were realistic. But they had to try to avert the catastrophic eruption at all costs, or nothing else would matter anyway. Secondly they would be diverting the lava away from the ice sheet till the eruption subsided naturally. Their explosion would be comparatively small, so shouldn't trigger anything else off, it would just relieve the pressure.

They hoped.

They hadn't a hope in hell of making this scheme work, Gilmore told her flatly. Three scientists, a photographer, an ex-commando and a bloody cargo pilot? And this mad old harridan who I've put under house arrest for the duration. *On what grounds?*

"On the grounds that she scares the shit out of me," said Gilmore, and rang off.

* * *

Two men in uniform opened the door of the dingy office where Marcus James had been sitting waiting for a little over an hour and three quarters. Marcus braced himself, but for a while neither of them spoke.

He had been in turmoil since his arrest. He had no idea of whether anyone could or would help him since this miserable building had become his world. The walls were a sort of dull, intense yellow made more sickly by the fluorescent light that never went off. There was no window in the room and it and smelt of old nylon carpet. There were patches all over the walls where shelves had hung previously, and rectangular shapes remained on the paintwork where posters or notices had been taken down and rammed into a bin which stood abandoned in the corner. Apart from that, the room was bare and purposeless in a way that was utterly depressing. As James sat there, he had gone through, in his mind, what he was going to say when the questions started, as he knew they would, and then had changed his mind a dozen times. He was disoriented, bored and uncomfortable. He needed a drink, and the toilet, and he wondered how long he would sit here until he was driven to call out to someone and ask for those things. He hadn't eaten since the previous day, but he was definitely not hungry. He'd been held for two days now. Definitely two nights. This was the third one coming up. He thought he was being held at a military installation or hospital of some kind; he couldn't work out exactly where, with no access to night or day, and no watch or phone. He felt that another twenty-four hours here and he would lose the timescale altogether. No-one would tell him why he was there, or when he could go. He'd been treated pretty well, but was losing the world that he understood, which, of course, was why he'd been put there. And now he'd been brought to this office, where he feared that the ugly yellow walls could about to become the backdrop to his unravelling. He imagined there being a light shone in his eyes, or a blow to the elbow. He had to keep it together. That was the only thing that mattered now. Marcus closed his eyes in order to gain some reprieve from his surroundings, but the dingy, jaundiced shadows had coated the inside of his eyelids, recreating the shell of the room inside his imagination as he sat there. The enforced confinement had been emptying his head of all his normal busy pre-occupations, allowing random thoughts and memories to nudge their way back to the forefront of his con-sciousness, to torment him with their wakened exist-ence, adding to his feeling of helplessness.

Becca should never have dumped him in that way. He felt full of self-pity. Just when he thought things were going so well, and they'd really got it together. He'd even thought that she might be The One. Kids, pensions, the lot. He thought she felt the same way, too. But when her firm offered her a job in Switzerland, she took it without even consulting him. Seemed sur-prised that he expected to be part of the decision mak-ing process. Expected him to be happy for her. So hard to be last, when you thought you were first in someone else's life. He'd not seen that one coming. Funny what memories come pressing in on you when all the normal distractions are taken away. Believed that was all in the past. The same thought kept coming back like a sharp bone that had stuck in his throat, and wedged itself there. Wouldn't have done that to her, he kept thinking on a loop.

When the door had opened his heart thumped. He was struck by fear.

One of the uniformed men in the brightly lit door-frame eventually addressed him.

"You can go, Mr James," said the taller one, in a business-like voice, bringing him back to the world of social contact.

Marcus James looked at him for a second while he climbed out of the mire of clinging emotions and tried to regain his equilibrium. He'd seriously thought that he might be tortured.

"Thank you for your assistance, but we don't need to keep you here any more. You can leave right away. Sorry for any inconvenience." It was said without any nuance of human contact or warmth, a bit like a tannoy message that you hear in the departure lounge, when your flight has just been cancelled. Marcus James hid his rising feelings of anger and indignation, still feeling that he was in no position to annoy anyone right now, especially someone who had just told him that he could go.

A wave of relief washed away his rising tide of anxiety and hard memories, as he murmured his gratitude, and then immediately regretted his subservient tone. He left at once, and made straight for the fresh air of the busy street. It took him a while to work out where he was. He needed to get home, but could not stomach the confines of the inside of a cab just now. He walked all the way back to his house, and had never enjoyed the feeling of pavement under his feet so much in all his life.

CHAPTER TWENTY ONE

The Heatwave

June, that year, had been the hottest month ever recorded in the UK, busting the average values right out of the record books. Even so, the Tuesday after the summer solstice was something else. On the previous evening's news the weather people were getting feverish about the next day's predicted temperature. It was mainly the influence of some incredibly warm nights that had shot through the averages for that time of year. The clear, blue skies typical of a high pressure, had not brought about the cloudless, chilly nights that often accompanied the hot days of high summer. And now the temperatures were set to go up into another gear. The Monday night news bulletin featured the heatwave as its headline story, as the Met Office were predicting the possibility of the highest temperature ever recorded in Britain, and so both amateurs and professionals alike were eagerly checking their thermometers, setting them up in places where they would record an accurate air temperature. They watched as the thin needles of silver grow longer with every hour, effortlessly passing each notch on the gauge with confident ease.

Only those with air conditioning got any sleep on that Monday night, when the mercury didn't dip below twenty-six degrees in the towns, and twenty-four degrees in the countryside, and it was, of course, much hotter than that indoors. Thick-walled cottages, normally cool and shady, and a gentle refuge against the glare and wearing heat of high summer, now held stagnant hot air within their rooms. Rooms which seemed solid with the totally permeating warmth of night were giving off yet more stored heat into spaces that were already saturated with it.

But that was nothing compared to the modern concrete and glass blocks of houses and flats in the cities, which were roasting like greenhouses, till the inhabitants wilted under the pressure.

The elderly and the very young suffered the most, with heatstroke claiming more victims as each day wore on without a sign of a break in the weather.

Instructions were given to shade the sunny side of the house, and open the windows on the shady part, if the position of one's house made this possible, and to keep curtains drawn all day, opening up at night to cool the place down. White sheets draped over the outside of large, heat-trapping glass, appeared like tokens of surrender all over the city streets, and only the people with air conditioning, who kept cool behind their smug, closed up houses, carried on as normal.

For everyone else, despite all these precautions, the city streets bounced the heat back through the wide open windows, filling the cramped rooms like a presence.

The only way to cope with the heat was to go with it and embrace it like the warmth of a blanket. To fight it only led to endless frustration and pointless squabbles. At the weekends the young, the affluent and the cool sat outside most of the night at the pavement cafes and bars, now doing land-office business in cold drinks and ices. But in more deprived areas, the streets crackled with the effects of cheap beer and over-heated attitude, making them dangerous places for the unwary.

That first Tuesday morning after the summer solstice dawned pink and grey. When at last the sun broke over the early horizon it brought back some shape and definition to the landscape, out of the blackness. There was not a trace of wind or freshness in the air. Lazily, the first bird of the morning chorus put out a tentative chirrup that sounded like a phone ringing, and waited for another of its kind to reply. A seagull at last answered with a long call that died into silence. Then the whistling and chattering slowly gained momentum and signalled the start of the new day.

Across the country, stretching out from London to the west, then down in a diagonal to the south, a long beaded strip of glinting metal pearled along the motorways as people everywhere took an impromptu day off work and decided to head for some fun and respite by the coast. By 4 a.m. the road down to Brighton was full to capacity with cars, everyone in them mistakenly thinking that they were going to be the first to get away.

Progress was slow, but steady, and by mid-morning thousands of people were crowding onto every available beach and seafront in the country. It was like the early days after the war, when whole towns decamped to their nearest resort. Then people would sit wedged together side by side for two weeks while their factory was shut down. Their workmates and neighbours would be just by, gossiping, as they'd always done, only this time over flapping wind-breaks instead of garden fences.

The thronged beaches had begun to look like shanty towns. Families and groups of friends, once they'd marked out their precious bit of territory, realised that the only thing that now mattered was getting some shade. The lucky, or well-prepared ones had their umbrellas with them and were hammering them into the sand, the soft clunk of wooden mallets drifting over washing sound of the waves. Everyone else made do, with rugs, tarps, hastily bought rush mats and anything else they could get their hands on to make their stay more comfortable. No-one went without a hat, and even the most foolhardy had stopped sunbathing by 11 o'clock, when the still cold sea filled up with jumping, shouting bodies, bobbing about in the foaming waves. The sea felt delicious in its coolness, as the soothing water slipped around hot skin, causing goosebumps on limbs that had grown used to the unrelenting heat.

The freedom of a day at the seaside tasted all the sweeter for the ones who had sneaked a day out of the office, justifying their absence by reasoning that they couldn't have done any work in this heat anyway. The only topic of conversation was the heatwave, and for some reason, once the temperature reached above thirty-two Celcius, people reverted to Fahrenheit and began to refer to 'it' being in the nineties, as though the bigger number values added weight to their suffering.

The thermometer climbed until it topped 100.9 degrees, at midday at Saunton Sands in Devon, topping the previous record of 100.6 recorded at Gravesend, Kent in 2003. By one o'clock it had nudged an unbelievable 101 degrees in Cheltenham.

Excitement was turning to nervousness as people were being warned to stay indoors. On the city streets of London the temperature was nudging 103 degrees by the middle of the afternoon. Everywhere was eerily quiet for a weekday. Railway lines buckled, and cars overheated. No-one ventured out without a bottle of water in their hand.

All along the packed Devon and Cornish coasts the holiday mood continued. Bathers walked heavily, as they pulled themselves out of the sea, dripping salty water on their fellow refugees, as they made their way back to their encampments for a heat drugged siesta. Late lunches and a few cans of cold beer soon meant that, after the exertions of swimming and surfing, heads went down on piles of rolled up tee-shirts, and deep motionless sleeps made up for the restless nights that most of them had had for the last couple of weeks. Children, red-faced and caked in powdery sand, gave up their tap-tapping on the bases of plastic buckets, and curled up to sleep alongside their comatose parents. Only the teenagers refused to let go; smoking cigarettes and exhaling blue clouds of couldn't care-less-defiance, while plugged into their music machines and doggedly wearing their prized tribal gear, no matter what the weather threw at them.

On the sea front a row of pretty cottages slumbered out the afternoon, the inhabitants picking at late, lazy lunches washed down with ice cold glasses of white wine.

"We'll have dinner on the boat tonight," said one man. "We'll sail out into the bay and get some air."

Everyone agreed it was a great idea. They were a party of VIP's down from London. Gleeful that no-one had recognised them, they were in holiday mood. Even the two security guys tucked into the shadows had slipped off their jackets and allowed themselves to stretch out. They'd packed enough heat for one day.

By late afternoon, many of the locals who normally kept away from the beaches during the season, were leaving their shops and offices. They too were heading for a dip in the water before returning home for the evening. The sea was now warm enough to be inviting, but still wonderfully refreshing, after a day at work in the stifling heat. Slippy salt water ran over tired arms and backs, lifting and crashing in a way that was both soothing and invigorating at the same time. The ringing punch and smack of a football as it was knocked to and fro drifted round the bay accompanied by loud shouts and laughter as the young guns started showing off to the girls kicking about in the shallows.

Then, quite suddenly, it all went wrong.

One young man, around twentyish chased after the ball as it bobbed around in the swirling water near the shore. It settled on the wet sand as the wave retreated, so he bent to pick it up, then looked around to see where his friends were so he could throw it back to them. But when he spotted them, they were standing only knee-high in the water, where only minutes before they had been up to their necks. They looked a bit foolish as they stood there, and some of the girls giggled. The man ran out to join his friends, but by the time he got there, the sea had drained from around their ankles and had left them standing on firm wet sand. All around the bay it was the same. Surfers lay on their boards on the sea bed, and watched with incredulity as the water retreated further away until it was virtually out of sight. Like a ripple running round the bay it grabbed the attention of the still only half-awake trippers, who nudged each other, sat up and pointed at the beach in amazement.

A man was sitting, perched on a tiny wooden boat, where he had been working on a long-intentioned repair, and was now absorbed in his task. He slowly and patiently scraped at a patch of rotten wood, filling in the gaps that he had made with a paste that was going off almost before he could press it into the cracks. He smoothed off the joints with his thumb to get a good finish that he could paint over, maybe tomorrow, or even tonight the way the filler was drying. A streak of sweat trickled down from his temple and dripped onto his chest. He picked up his chisel and began scrape once more at a patch of soft wood, until he, too, became aware that something was happening around him. He started, his eyes wide with disbelief. He had a deep tan, with wisps of fairish sun-bleached hair showing underneath his broad-brimmed hat. He seemed to be local, and wore cropped, calf length, beach-comber shorts and a white shirt, which was half unbuttoned. He cupped his hands over his eyes to shade them from the glare as he stared at the emptying bay.

He wondered if he was the only one who knew what was happening.

He jumped from his fishing boat which had lying resting on one side on the beach, and ran barefoot, over the scalding sand towards the life guard post, a sort of tree-house structure overlooking the whole beach. He talked and gestured frantically to the lifeguards for a few seconds, one of whom then grabbed his microphone and shouted to the astonished crowds to clear the beach. For a few dumb seconds no-one moved. Thoughts crowded in one after the other. Had they heard right? Was anyone else going? Was it a drill?

Someone said tsunami.

Fuck off! Don't be stupid! I'm not going anywhere just yet. I'm not leaving all my stuff. What the bloody hell's going on! I'll look stupid if I run and no-one else does. People hesitated. They looked out to sea, then again at one another, and the loudspeaker warnings got lost in the rising hubbub. Most of the people on the beach were unfamiliar with what was normal for the tides in the area, and so felt in no position to judge if something wasn't quite right. Then someone, sensing danger, grabbed her two children by the arms and ran, their small legs scuffing the ground as she tried to make haste over the soft sand, like running in a nightmare. She left everything, even her handbag, and didn't look round. Someone else said we'd better get going too. Then the siren started. The lifeguard couldn't make himself heard quickly enough to warn all the people, so he'd sounded it. Its mournful note reached down to the ex-swimmers who were still far out in the bay. They were walking about, or standing hands on hips, drying off in the hot sun. On hearing the siren many of them started to walk back to the beach, but too slowly, too carelessly. The man from the boat stood, helpless. It was agony to watch them, and not make them see.

The lifeguard could be seen talking urgently into his radio as he contacted the Coastguard base for information.

Then a girl screamed.

The distant horizon, which had sparkled all day in the hot blue light, had suddenly changed. The perspective had all gone wrong. It now looked to be higher and closer than it had before, and was topped with a line of white foam. There was a series of angry, bright flickers as lightning danced along the wave's crest, and within the space of a single second everyone on the beach knew with absolute certainty what was coming towards them.

As the siren wailed on, families pushed and panicked to stay together and run at the same time. Umbrellas, windbreaks, all the beach paraphernalia was trampled in the melee and the clutter held everyone up. In their desperation to get away, the slow got knocked over, and those who stooped to help them stayed down as the crowd poured over them. There had been many thousands of people on the beach that day.

Only a few hundred got to safety.

The tsunami was about four metres high by the time it bore down on the wide beaches of the Devon and Cornwall coasts. As soon as it appeared on the horizon, and began looming down on those in its path, it was accompanied by a terrible, deep rumble. High sharp cracks of thunder, and the flickering blue light of the electrical discharges running along its brow, signalled its menacing approach. It sped inshore like a cavalry charge. It gained the beachhead before the running, desperate holiday-makers had time to get away from it. The silver-grey cliff of water running them down, and overwhelming them and their bedraggled possessions. When it hit the shallow sea wall with its worn stone steps and polished railings, it burst upwards into the air, crashing down onto the ones who'd made it to the road, then followed through with water, and yet more water, which continued to force its way through the tiny streets, till it petered out many hundreds of metres inland. Unlike a normal wave which has only one crest so that the water level rises and falls back again, a tsunami wave is the front of a raised plateau of water that keeps on coming, making escape all the more difficult. Some were carried by the wave to higher ground and survived. Most other survivors had crammed in the upstairs floors of the houses as the seawater swirled dangerously around them. The ones on the lower floors weren't so lucky. Those clinging to the gathering debris in the streets were pulled inside windows by guilt-ridden arms desperate to help, but already it was too late for some, and the sickening, sobering sight of floating bodies, became more common with every passing second.

After some minutes; it was impossible to gauge the time, the water began to recede, especially on the outskirts of the village where the ground rose steadily away from the coast and into the rounded green and straw coloured hills of the Devon countryside. Dazed survivors picked themselves up and looked around to see what they do to help. Others screamed for their missing families and friends, already knowing that their lives had just been washed away with the inundation, shaking with a cold that no sunlight could ever penetrate. Strangers risked their lives to help others. Strangers who, ten minutes ago, wouldn't have offered one another a can of coke. Now intimate in their fear and suffering, people who had never met before, clinging together like lovers, their mutual need forcing out all normal boundaries.

All along the western coasts it was the same story, from the islands and coasts of Scotland, Blackpool and Morecambe, Ireland, right through to the tip of the West Country of England. The giant wave rolled over the land through the wide open, flat beaches of the Somerset coast, reaching inland as far as the eye could see, spoiling in an afternoon what had been gently tended for the last 10,000 years of human settlement. The hard bulwark of the granite cliffs of the Cornish coast took the full force of the inrushing tide, the wave bursting like a water bomb as it hit the unyielding rock, flinging itself high into the air and breaking over the hard-bitten land, out-storming even the most violent tempest that had washed over it before. The tiny creeks and coves packed tight with stone houses, shops, pubs, cafes and narrow roads that led down steeply to the sea, where miniature beaches provided the only inlet to land a small boat. They were hit the worst. Often having no warning of the onrushing tsunami until the glinting wall of water appeared at the entrance to the coves, the people there had no chance to escape before the sea filled their entire world, and took away everything they had.

Back on the beach in Devon, the water was slowly beginning to ebb away, revealing the devastation it had caused by its incursion into human territory. Holiday paraphernalia floated uselessly around, so carefully chosen and used only minutes before, in a different world. The beach itself was still under water, troubled and dangerous with swirling currents to those already picking their way back to see what they could find of their ruptured lives. Great wet dunes of sand and shingle were piled up over where the sea wall had been, one massive hill of sand banking up to gutter height in the main street, now strewn with dense mats of seaweed, and tangled branches, as well as the wrecked mess of floating cars, tables, chairs, broken hoardings, an ice cream fridge, still with its contents intact, and all manner of broken things, bobbing and swirling in the brown and white foam.

The row of pretty cottages were as good as gone, now with their front walls caved in and their shattered roofs hanging down and creaking under the strain; the sea washing around the lower storeys, ready to finish them off. There was no trace of the VIP party, who were so looking forward to an evening out on the bay, in the Prime Minister's boat. He'd brought his family and a few friends down to his seaside cottage for a last break before election campaigning really got under way, any time now.

Caroline had urged him not to sell up, ostensibly because it sent out the wrong message to the public, although in reality, it was because she had loved the place so much. Their cottage was tiny, but compared to the polished grandeur of their London lives, its scrubbed-down simplicity gave them a place where they could be people again and not a title or a role. It was the only house that she had ever stayed in that always made her feel that she didn't want to be anywhere else. Now she never would be.

Shortly before the wave struck, sitting under the shade of an umbrella, one of the PM's closest advisors, Marcus James, was sipping his glass of chilled white wine, hugely relieved to be back with the in-crowd once more, the PM hoping that a relaxed weekend would help him get over the little scrape his friend had just had, with that meddling prat, Gilmore. Marcus was back at the centre of things, where he felt he belonged, and for the moment, at least, all he wanted to do was forget about Greenland, and concentrate on getting the PM another term in office. Caroline was laughing at his jokes, and he was relaxing into his glass of excellent pinot noir.

"What the hell's that siren?" someone said but got no reply.

One of the security men sat up and became alert at the sound of clamouring voices. But it was Caroline's frozen face that alerted Marcus to the fact that something was wrong. He heard the tsunami before he could see it, and thought at first it was another tremor. The siren seemed to get louder. Then the pouring tide of terrified people were running towards him, like extras in a film, he thought, followed by the rush of hot wind pushed on by the approaching wave. Marcus James didn't even have time to run. Before he got to the cottage door the wave broke over him, with a force that defied comprehension, overwhelming his attempt to escape and mercifully knocking him unconscious before, like so many others, he drowned in the raging deluge.

* * *

Ron Bowman, the Deputy Prime Minister, got the first trickle of news that something was amiss minutes after initial reports began coming in that exceptional tides were hitting the coasts all down the West of Britain and Ireland. He swung the usual emergency plans into action and told his advisors to keep him posted. He saw himself going to Scotland to meet and offer sympathy to flood victims. He saw his holiday being cancelled.

But then the trickle of news reports became a deluge in its own right, as the Coastguards said that they'd been hit by a freak tsunami wave and needed help urgently. Each thought that maybe their area was the only one to suffer, but, one by one, the phone lines jammed as every resort, every town, every beach along the hundreds of miles of coastline, was saying the same thing. The TV interrupted all programmes with a rolling headline that said a freak wave had hit the shorelines of the west of Britain. Then a serious voice announced that they were going over to the Newsroom to cover the story immediately, recognising at once that this was a national emergency of huge magnitude. Within minutes the shaky phone videos, started to tell their own vernacular stories, as eloquently as any professional media could have done.

The DPM felt himself rising to the challenge left to him by the holidaying Premier; he immediately ordered Cobra to convene, and he put the Army on standby. He instructed that the Queen should be kept informed of any developments. He watched with his staff, in growing horror and disbelief the story unfold on his TV set, as the rolling headlines were now starting to get the extent of the catastrophe, and estimate the mounting death toll. People to'd and fro'd through his office with the latest developments, as information began to pour in. The heatwave had caused record numbers of people to be on the beaches when the tsunami struck, causing massive casualties, the numbers of which could only be guessed at for the moment. All eyes were on the screen of the large muttering TV set which virtually had the sound off so everyone could talk uninterrupted, when the door of the DPM's office burst open, shaking everyone, followed by the urgent sound of heels clicking on the wooden floor.

"Turn it up! For God's sake! Get the sound on, quickly! There's a terrible flap on." It was his PPS, at his most officious, only this time he had good reason to be. "We can't get hold of the PM, even on the emergency line. Listen to this!"

The set boomed out its message that sent a shock wave through the whole room.

"...and it seems that the Prime Minister himself has been reported missing – there is as yet no sign of either him or his family who it seems were staying in their holiday home in Devon when the tsunami struck, and their home has been destroyed. So far only one member of his party has been found, one of the security guards, who, himself is quite badly injured, but is trying to help police with their enquiries..."

The DPM went pale with the shock that was reflected in the faces of everyone around him.

"Get the Army onto this, rightaway!" He snapped as his secretary. "Get a special unit down there, with specific instructions to find David and Caroline at all costs....and inform Her Majesty that he is missing and that we are doing everything we can to find out where he is .....and that I will be assuming the position of PM, at least until the crisis is over....I need a draft speech prepared...I'll have to do an interview as soon as I can get enough information to sound as though we are on top of things... where's Marc James, when you need him? Anyone know?"

"He was at the cottage, sir...a guest of the PM...."

The enormity of what was unfolding around them was starting to sink in, with every moment that passed.

In another office in Whitehall, sat Peter Gilmore, watching the story grow before his eyes, as he watched his TV alone and in silence. He could have kicked himself for not acting sooner. He knew with total certainty that the tsunami had something to do with the tremors and the melting ice caps. In his mind's eye he had a passing vision of Dorothy's jabbing finger. He, too, been warning people for years that something like this could happen, and now it had. He rang his opposite number in the Air Force. They'd need to get airborne to monitor any more tidal waves heading our way. Hopefully info would soon be coming in as to whether this was a break off, or a landslip, and whether this was the end of it.

He sent for Dorothy Redmires. Then he picked up his phone and called Amy James.

Amy had been sitting at her computer when Gilmore called, finalising some calculations so that she could get a good 3-D image of the caldera, so Coulson could plan where to lay his explosive for the maximum effect. The others were loading the Cessna ready to go first thing the next morning. She found them all standing around the plane taking a breather. They all looked at her wondering what she was about to say when she joined them looking so solemn. They assumed they would be under pressure to abort their mission, now that the authorities had got Dorothy. Hewitt hoped not. He knew they should have gone a day earlier and not delayed.

"Gilmore's just been on the phone..." Amy said, breathlessly. "He said that we need to get going as soon as is possible. He said if we needed any supplies or equipment, he would help us out…" Everyone looked dumfounded. Why the sudden change of heart?

"Well, gee, would you believe that?" said Becaud, cheering up at the news. But his cheer was short lived.

"That quake we felt this morning….." she continued

"It's actually caused a tsunami. Four metres. Thousands, maybe hundreds of thousands, feared dead. And you won't believe this, but they think the Prime Minister might be dead too. He was on holiday….."

"What?" said Oliver.

"Where?" said Zoe.

"In Devon."

"In England?" said Oliver. "You mean our Prime Minister?"

"Yes. And Marcus is missing. He was with the Prime Minister's party. They think he might be… dead, too." There was a long, sympathetic silence.

"My God, I'm so sorry Ames. I can't believe it. We have to leave as soon as we can," said Zoe. "This is only the start. The ice is so fragile now at the coasts, any of these tremors could cause another break off or a landslip. And they are getting stronger and more frequent with every day that passes. If this continues I believe a collapse into the caldera, or a mega land-slip is almost inevitable. We have to avert that at all costs, or it will make today's tsunami look like a ripple. Let's hope we're not too late."

Amy nodded her agreement, but couldn't find it in herself to say anything just yet. Hewitt slipped his arm gently round her shoulder, and walked her back to the house.

CHAPTER TWENTY-TWO

After a week of searching, the emergency services had no choice but to announce that the Prime Minister and his wife must now be presumed dead. They had to keep looking for David and Caroline, as they had become universally known, and hoping that they would be found, even after the realisation had set in that there could be no chance now of a happy outcome to their efforts. The search went on for a week after the tsunami hit the west coast of Britain on that Tuesday afternoon, but really everyone knew what to expect after the first twenty-four hours had gone by without any positive sighting. People of that profile don't go missing and turn up safe and well at a friend's house, or a nearby hospital. But it was still hard to hear the news that the Prime Minister and his family were gone. It was almost as though they had taken with them everyone's hopes that their own precious relatives could still be found alive.

The death toll had reached one hundred and fifteen thousand. That was the positive identifications. There were so many more missing or unidentifiable bodies that it was bound to double at least when the dental records had told their grim story. It seemed that everyone had lost someone that day. The anxious waiting, felt by so many families, hung palpably in the air, dissipating slowly as bit by bit each person took in the news they never wanted to hear. Hopes gone, they shouldered their piece of the collective grief, and cried it away.

The Deputy Prime Minister, who nobody had much heard of before, had now been officially made Prime Minister, and the name Ron Bowman was suddenly on everyone's lips and in every headline. Having seen himself as tarnished with the same brush as the rest of his party during the chaos of the solar storm, and despite all his previous manoeuvrings, he had expected to go crashing out of office in an electoral defeat that would end his career and all his hopes for ever of getting the ultimate political prize. But now, no-one was in the mood for an election any more, and he had a job to do.

He appointed the Mayor of London as the Minister in charge of the Emergency, due to her experience in running London during the solar storm. Rosa Paine's expertise in marshalling the recovery and the clean up was invaluable, leaving him free to lobby Europe for the funds they would need to rebuild the devastated infrastructure. He'd have his work cut out, he knew, as Spain and Portugal had also been hit by the tsunami, as had Holland, parts of Belgium and the southern regions of Norway - not in the EU, but still forced to ask for help from other countries as they had been overwhelmed by the scale of the damage inflicted on their coastline. He'd been warned that we could expect only limited help from the Disaster Fund, faced as it was with multiple demands on its resources. So Ron Bowman was flying out there today, to see what he could do by being there in person. Never one much inspired by the European ideal, he decided to do as the French do. Push the national interest and ignore seeing things from another's point of view. He admired that about the French. In fact, he saw them as a natural ally in a crumbling world.

And it was almost as though the country itself had started to crumble away. Its battered and inundated edges, broken and derelict, barren as a moonscape in places, piled with the bricks and mortar of destruction in others. When seen from the air many of Britain's coastal towns were now unrecognisable. There was not a trace of Caroline and David's seaside home. Well-loved landmarks had been washed over, the powerful wall of sea water reducing to debris the built environment that had become known in all its minute detail to generations of visitors and local people alike. Like the Devon tea shop, just a short walk away from where Marcus James and the VIP party enjoyed their last few hours, with its stone porch and wedged open door, every bit of its fabric smelling of new baked cakes and freshly cut sandwiches. The worn steps leading down from the promenade to the soft sand, where every week a new hoard of eager children would enter into their beach world, of rock pools and sandy endeavour, busily creating their warm summer memories, of escape and adventure, ready to take back to their Midland fastnesses. The stout, seasoned wooden breakwaters, draped in feathered seaweed, the wooden boardwalks that felt soft and warm on scrambling bare feet. It was all utterly familiar.

And it was all gone.

The Coast, the concept of the coast, was never just a physical place, it is also a state of mind, redolent of, if not exactly escape, then of pushing the boundaries, of living a little beyond yourself; of relaxation. Not only in the sense of resting, but a relaxation of the rules, a place of indulgence or perhaps adventure. And the destruction of those physical places where memories and expectations had taken shape, disturbed the blank faces of the nightly news watchers, clustered round their TV sets every evening, soaking in the alien images and slowly getting used to what they saw.

On the beaches, opportunistic gulls pecked and pulled at the garbage that lay around, never now to be collected, while around them the teams of searchers looked for the missing, catalogued the found, and zipped their sadness and despair into the black bags provided. When they had done all they could, then the teams would withdraw quietly away. The revving engines of the convoys of heavy diggers would then start to bulldoze their way through the rubble and tip the whole lot back into the sea. Other places were so buried in a thick layer of sand and shingle that there was nothing left to see but the odd broken tree stump sticking up out of the newly laid surface. One day it would become a thin sandy line in a cross-section of rock layers. A geological record, the physical evidence of what had occurred there, lay waiting for one of Zoe's descendants to scrape away at sometime in the future. One hoped.

In his office back in Whitehall, Harrington was preparing documents for Ron Bowman's trip to Brussels. He carefully put them in order and highlighted the important points so that he could read them during the flight and be up to speed with the relevant facts by the time he got to the crucial meetings. Bowman knew this trip was vital for getting his Premiership off to a good start. It wasn't just the money. Getting a good deal out of Europe always went down well with the voters, and if he could consolidate his position quickly he could see no reason why there should be any pressure for an early election. He should be able to see out the full term, and that would give him at least two more years in office. The recovery would inevitably take much longer. The main thing now, he thought was to be seen to be getting things done. He needed some quick wins. Something that he could use to make a strong, positive announcement when he got back. Perhaps the rebuilding of Clevedon Pier, or the sea wall and tower in Blackpool. He was mulling over which was the most marginal seat, when Harrington interrupted his thoughts with a last minute suggestion.

"There is one thing, Prime Minister that I think you should be aware of – er just in case you get any awkward questions from people who've been tuning into the website – you know – the Greenland business."

"What should I be aware of Harrington? I thought that had been put away as some student conspiracy theory shite."

"Well not exactly, sir." Harrington didn't like the way this conversation was going already. He could sense that he was going to be blamed for something, but had no choice now but to press on. "Well you know that Gilmore has backed the latest fact-finding expedition out there." Harrington waited for the reply, already wincing inwardly.

"No, I bloody well didn't. And I'm sick of hearing the name Gilmore. What's going on there? Whenever I hear his name my instinct tells me that he's up to something that he's got no business getting involved in without seeing me first! And what fact-finding expedition are we talking about exactly...?"

Harrington took a deep breath. Bowman had stopped blustering and was looking stonily at his Secretary for an explanation.

"He's personally backed a group of scientists to go out there to Greenland. They think they know what's been causing the tremors...."

"I think you could have told me this before, Harrington."

Harrington paused a moment. He heard the word scapegoat enter his head. He could see his career in the balance. Bowman had something of a reputation for never letting go of a grudge, and he didn't want to get on the wrong side of him.

"Marcus James was the link. He is – was - a relative of one of the scientists. And he would have got David's backing for this I'm sure. I don't believe that Gilmore has acted alone even if it is highly unorthodox, what he's doing. But now Marc James is dead, and we have to accept that the PM, sorry, the former PM, David, is too. I couldn't really tell you before, sir. Not till it was official." Bowman grunted his impatience.

"So what's this so-called fact-finding mission all about? It usually means some sort of junket, and a huge waste of tax-payer's money. Or somebody justifying their existence by telling us what we bloody well knew already," said Bowman.

He was deeply angry, and Harrington knew he hadn't heard the last of this. He sat for a few moments trying to think of what to say. Then an idea came to him. There would just be time before Bowman had to leave for the airport.

"There's someone I think you should see," said the PPS with a flash of inspiration. She's almost certainly with Gilmore at the moment, and can explain far better than I ever could, why this expedition was so vital. I'll send for her straightaway if you like, Prime Minister. She's called Dorothy Redmires."

* * *

Ron Bowman climbed up the steps to his waiting plane about two hours later than he'd expected to. Stunned by what Dorothy had told him, he was still trying to take it all in. A continent-wide crack in the ice? This was science fiction, not the political world that he inhabited. He'd told Harrington to set up a working party at once of scientific advisors, to advise him on a course of action on his return. He'd planned to tell Red-mires that the expedition should be aborted immediately rather than risk a diplomatic incident, but mainly because he wanted to wrest back control of the situation from the hands of Gilmore, and show him firmly who was in charge. But the meeting hadn't gone as he'd planned at all. He'd expected a worthy academic trying to bang on about global warming, when he had a crisis of national proportions to sort out. And he suspected Gilmore of having political ambitions of his own, and therefore was distrustful of why he was getting involved with this Greenland thing.

Bowman had become something of a bully, and was used to getting his own way, but when Dorothy strode into his office, wearing a face that was totally unimpressed by his rank, looking him up and down, he felt himself become, at once, the small-town politician, with low-brow culture and narrow suburban values, that she saw standing there in front of her. She took him in in one gulp. She quite clearly thought that he'd be more at home in a Council chamber, debating car park charges, than a man of destiny capable of rising to the occasion now demanded of him. He saw that in her face, and the hint of truth in it made him feel strangely insecure.

"You used to be on Chesterfield Town Council, didn't you?" Dorothy said, going for his weak spot, and not waiting for a reply. "Prime Minister, this mission is going ahead, whether you or anyone else likes it or not." He rankled at her tone. She didn't attempt to be conciliatory or deferential, and he thought her very aggressive. Silly cow. "The truth is that we're running out of time." She explained the situation as briefly as she could, and in layman's terms, whilst making it quite clear that she didn't expect any interruptions. Pressure of time meant that he demurred and listened to her assessment of the situation, at first grudgingly but with increasing alarm and incredulity as she concluded her report. By the end of it he was rapt. Had to admit the old bat was a good speaker. She told it as it was.

"Seismic activity is building dangerously, Mr Bowman, which means possibly that the volcano is going to blow and the Rift will split apart causing a massive tidal wave to head our way. If that happens you probably won't have a country to run. Chesterfield will probably survive though. You could always head back there."

At that his temper rose again, and he'd tried to threaten her not to push too far or she'd have to take the consequences. She was angry, too, as she didn't think he was listening, and she was frustrated at being held for so long against her will, when she wanted to be out there and doing something. The meeting had ended acrimoniously.

He'd tried to take it all in. But it wasn't like anything else anyone had had any experience of. He was now on the plane to Brussels, sitting in his seat in first class, mulling over what he had just learnt. He didn't even acknowledge the scotch and soda that the steward just put in front of him, or respond when politely asked if everything was alright. He didn't even hear it. Automatically he reached for the drink and poured it over the large clear ice cubes sitting at angles in his squat tumbler. He took a good drink and felt the hot liquid glow as it went down. It mellowed his anger enough to allow him a sense of perspective on the meeting he'd just had with Dorothy Redmires. If its aim had been to re-establish control over what was happening back there, then he'd totally failed in that. He had tried to intimidate her by threatening her career, which he knew she valued above all else, or so he thought. She had told him to stuff it.

"Don't you see, Mr Bowman, that this isn't about you, or me, or any context that we've ever had before. This is simply about doing what needs to be done. No academic jealousies, no political posturings. We are trying to survive."

Her words rang around his head, and as they kept reverberating around his thoughts, he knew that she was speaking the truth however bizarre or unpalatable that might be. He wanted to pull the country round, to be in charge of the recovery, not preside over a new age of darkness and savagery. He took another long drink and sat back into his seat, the hum of the engines lessening slightly as they levelled out at their ceiling height.

Harrington was sitting at the PM's side, biding his time, waiting for the scotch to do its work before he ventured to say anything.

"If this scheme works, Prime Minister, you'll get the credit, you know. Good news works its magic, and will reflect back onto you indirectly." He paused to let his words sink in. Then said as a throwaway thought. "Imagine having her on your side." He underlined something of no significance on the paper in front of him. "If you get any flack from the international community on this –er matter, you might need a science spokesperson. Just a thought."

Bowman smiled. The situation might not be too bad after all. He knocked back the rest of his whisky and soda and turned to Harrington.

"You know I think you could be right. She might be just what we need. Now what are you having for dinner?"

He poured over the menu, and made his choice. Harrington said he'd have the same.

Buoyed up, Bowman was determined now to get the best deal out of Europe for the tsunami damage. He had to believe that it was worthwhile to do that.

He just hoped that in the meantime the Greenland expedition would get there in time to avoid a cataclysm beyond imagination; and that their idiotic plan would work.

CHAPTER TWENTY-THREE

"You OK?" said Hewitt, when they got back inside Becaud's house.

"Yes, I will be in a minute." Amy was still trembling. "It's just such a shock."

"I know," he said, and patted her hand rather self-consciously.

Lawrence Hewitt's body language appeared awkward, and Amy was sure that he didn't know how she felt. That is, until she looked up and saw him staring at her hand. He looked distracted and his eyes, though far away, seemed to be full of sadness. For a moment she had wondered if he had been using this opportunity just to touch her hand, but clearly not. There was no subterfuge there, however innocent. He seemed to have forgotten that she was there. Hewitt glanced up to find Amy's eyes looking straight at him. He didn't dart away as she had expected, and his cold defensive manner had gone. He smiled, gently, tentatively. The blackness that had closed around him for so long and held him in its claw was beginning, slowly, to release its grip. It felt like the dawn breaking after the longest night. No longer did it feel like a betrayal to admit that the pain was easing. He felt ready to move on. Ironic that just as he realised that even so great a loss as his could be lived with, that death and tragedy on an epic scale could be waiting to strike them at any time. He didn't even want to think of that right now. The breakthrough had come, and that meant he'd been able to think of Marcus James' death with sympathy and genuine sadness, without the memories of Ben's death slamming into him and sending him reeling back to the bottom of the pit again.

"Are *you* OK, Lawrence?" said Amy, turning the tables on him.

"Oh, yes. I always am when I'm with you." His eyes twinkled at her, and she took the compliment graciously.

Amy remembered that smile for a long time. He actually seemed not bad-looking when he stopped being rude to everyone, she thought, his new demeanour taking her somewhat by surprise. But right now she only wanted to think of poor Marcus and the terrible news from back home.

Later, in her quiet moments, she remembered the way Lawrence had looked at her that day, and the way it had changed the way she had thought about him for ever.

She stood up and, taking a deep breath, she said, "I need to get back on to Gilmore." Amy was desperately trying to recover herself and keep focussed. "He's offered to help, and I've thought of a way he can."

Hewitt pulled himself together and tried to concentrate, "Yes? In what way?"

"We need a more accurate position for the caldera. Zoe's sketch gives us the general idea, but we need a much more detailed picture than that, or we could be wasting days trying to find the best place to blast into. I remember when they thought that there might be a super volcano in Yellowstone Park – the scientists worked out that they thought there was a huge volcano there, but it was too big for them to see it from the ground – then someone taking infra-red pictures from the air got a beautiful image of the caldera, and proved them right. That's what we need – an infra-red picture to give us an exact position. If he could do that, then our plan has a far better chance of success."

"Well, he should have the resources to do that. Why don't you get on to him?"

"Do you think that you could, Lawrence? I still feel a bit shaky. Hard to concentrate." That was only partly due to the tsunami. She was still thinking of the compliment he had paid her.

"Yes, of course, love," he said, at once concerned for her, and glad of the chance to help, but as he wasn't the type for endearments, the word went through her like a shock wave. He'd never called her anything but Amy before; in fact he'd never really called her anything before, come to think of it. He flushed slightly now not sure if he'd said the right thing. As her own emotions rose to the surface, as a result of his concern, she felt herself crumple. She let go and started to cry, the tears triggered by his word of kindness as much as the thought of her poor cousin. He gave her a tissue, as she couldn't find any, and then took her phone as she offered it to him, his hand squeezing hers deliberately in the process. She liked his touch. A diffident man, he could be cool and disdainful at times, but his touch was warm and genuine, with not a trace of furtiveness about it. Before, Amy had always thought of Lawrence, as quite an irritating, rather negative man, whereas now she was beginning to think of him as a man capable of very deep and sincere feelings, but who wasn't very good as expressing them to others, which was why he did not seem to be good at relationships.

And although one needs to be capable of deep and true feelings if a relationship is to last, sometimes one needs a light touch, a little less intensity, or everything becomes a big deal. He needed to lighten up a bit. Lawrence was, thought Amy, a very closed-down person; but he was trying to reach out to her, she knew. She blew her nose on his hanky, and wiped her eyes, still aware of the impression of his hand on hers, even though it was now busy pressing the buttons on her phone.

Hewitt called Gilmore, glad of something to do to distract him, while she again quietly dabbed her nose. He spoke calmly and knowledgeably to him as he explained what it was they needed. Gilmore was onto the case immediately.

"I'll make sure you get what you need, Mr Hewitt – but it's bound to take a few hours. We'll have to get a flight out there. Still no satellite unfortunately. But infra-red imaging shouldn't be too much of a problem. Have you got your co-ordinates to narrow down the search – good – excellent! We'll do our best. The situation here? I couldn't begin to tell you – utter catastrophe. No-one knows yet how many dead. Reports are only just starting to come in from some areas – there's no good news, and not likely to be. Everything's complete chaos here."

Hewitt handed the phone back to Amy. He looked grave.

"He's on to it," he said, simply. "Better let the others know."

* * *

Gilmore proved to be as good as his word when he'd promised to help them out in any way that he could. Within twenty-four hours he'd got them the information that enabled Amy to reconstruct the misshapen pink doughnut on her computer screen which had several bites out of the outer rim. It was the infra-red image of the caldera that they had all been waiting for. Zoe was pouring over it anxiously, while Oliver, Hewitt and Becaud looked on from behind. Coulson stood reticently at the back of the group until Zoe pulled him to the front and pointed to the part of the volcano nearest the Rift. The image was indistinct, quite ragged on that side, and although that made accurate measurements of the co-ordinates a bit more difficult, in other ways it was exactly what Zoe wanted to see.

"Here," she pointed to the thinnest section of the caldera, "is where we need to breech the side. It should be weak enough here – in fact – I would guess by looking at it that it could erupt here naturally in time, that is if the whole lot didn't collapse in on itself first."

Coulson nodded. He didn't say anything, but was quietly working on a plan of action. Zoe left him to it.

"Phil, are you OK with that?"

"Yes, I'm OK." He pointed to a map on the table. "I reckon we can land about here. We've a little way to walk to the actual site with all our equipment, but with the sleds, we should be OK. One problem though."

"What's that?" she said.

"The weather. It's been set fair for so long, but now would you believe, just when we need it to be clear and calm, it could be closing in."

"What do you mean?" said Oliver. "That we might have to delay the mission? We're all packed and ready to go."

"No, quite the opposite. It means we have to set off as soon as we can. We shouldn't really chance it, but we have no choice but to go later today. The low pressure could be set in for a week once it arrives, maybe two; we can't risk delaying for that long."

"That going to make life tough when we get there too, then," Zoe said. "As if we need any further problems."

Hewitt was staring at the screen, taking in every detail of the caldera's shape and studying the co-ordinates closely, then he went over to the map and did the same thing, committing all the details to memory.

He'd spent hours looking at Ray Coulson's video diary, doing the self same thing, learning all the details of the area, till he felt he knew it like his own back yard. Zoe watched him. She knew what he was doing, but said nothing. She didn't know why, but it felt comforting to have him on board.

It was time to go.

"We need to make a move, hon," said Oliver gently, standing behind her and resting his hands on her shoulders.

"Yes, we do," she said, patting his hands before breaking away from him, then pulling on her outdoor clothes, as a cue for others to do the same. Amy closed up her laptop and slipped it into her bag, while Becaud wound his scarf warmly round his neck. He picked up his flying jacket and slipped it on. In silence and in single file they all trudged out to the waiting Cessna and set off for the Atlantis Rift.

* * *

It was with utter relief that Zoe felt the skids of Phil Becaud's plane touch the tiny patch of snow that was level enough for the Cessna to land. How he got it down with the gusting cross winds starting to build, flinging around some light flurries of snow, Zoe couldn't imagine. Her relief was more as a result of her starting to feel queasy, rather than her usual flying nerves, but, whatever. They'd made it. And that was all that mattered at the moment. Becaud cut the engines, and radioed his flight-follower to let him know where and when they had landed. The pilot seemed in good form, unlike everyone else. Buoyed by the challenge of some difficult flying, he'd been in the place where he most wanted to be; at one with his plane, at ease and in control.

"Good run, Phil!" said Oliver Carter, generously.

"All part of the service," said Becaud in his soft drawl, diffidently, but he appreciated the compliment, nonetheless.

Zoe pushed at the door ready to climb out of the plane, but found it hard work opening it against the wind which was growing outside by the minute. She jumped through the smallest of gaps, then stood upright on the white floor spreading out in all directions, breathing in the sharp air, and nestling into her hood at the same time. Oliver jumped down after her, pushing the door open wider as he did so. He and Becaud went straight round to start unloading the cargo, knowing that they had no time to lose if they were set up camp before the weather got any worse. A few metres from where the plane was resting was a bank of snow which provided some vital shelter from the driving wind. So the two tents were set up between the Cessna and the steep bank, firmly tethered and hammered into the ground, with a thoroughness that Oliver always insisted upon. Sleeping bags and other essentials were unloaded into the tents, but everything else was left in the plane, until it was needed. The snow flurries stopped, but they sky remained an unforgiving leaden grey, low and heavy with more to come, they thought. Only now did the group stop for a breather, now their shelter was secure. Oliver brewed up some tea and handed it round to them all, hungry and tired as they were.

Amy noticed that Terry Coulson looked cold, so she made him wrap a rug round him that she got from the plane.

"If you get cold, deal with it straightaway," she advised him, sounding very motherly all of a sudden. "It's not going to get any better, if you leave it, believe me. The colder you get, the harder it then becomes to warm up again – sounds obvious – I know, but it's easy to get caught out."

"Stop clucking over him, Ames, he's a soldier for God's sake," said Oliver. Amy flushed slightly at the inappropriateness of her interference, and Coulson couldn't help a grin, but he nodded anyway, grateful for her concern. And for the rug. He noted that it was the first time she'd spoken to him unless she had to. As a commando he'd done plenty of survival training, but he wasn't experienced in Arctic conditions, and he was surprised how quickly the cold set in, as soon as you stopped any activity.

"I'll fix some food for us all," said Becaud. "We'll all feel better for something to eat."

"Great idea!" said Oliver.

"What'll it be folks?" he said, "burger, fries... Krispy Kreme Donuts?"

"Double cheeseburger, fries, ketchup, and hold the onions, for me," said Zoe, her mouth watering just at the thought.

"Sorry, honey, I'm right out of all that...will a bag of re-hydrated bird seed in a foil bag do instead?" The pilot seemed to be relishing his new role of camp cook.

"Sounds good to me," said Zoe, laughing, and almost hungry enough to mean it.

Phil Becaud set about getting a meal ready for everyone, while Coulson and Oliver built a snow wall a little way from the tents about four feet high, and closed in on three sides. Cutting with large knives, they soon had firm blocks of snow piled up and neatly finished in a 'u' formation.

"This is the bathroom," said Oliver. Coulson laughed amiably. "Don't venture out here without your gun."

"Polar bears?"

"You've got it."

They were all six sitting in the larger of the two tents, as Becaud handed round their evening meal, now smelling surprisingly good, as the deepening cold was draining them of all their energy. Zoe had been carefully sorting out and loading her climbing equipment into the sled ready for an early start the next day, leaving her tired to the point where she felt tremulous, and nervous anyway at the thought of having to attempt the cliff face tomorrow.

"Zo, are you OK?" Amy said looking at her closely.

"Yes, of course," she answered quickly, not wanting to admit how she really felt. "I'm just running on fumes at the moment – need to re-fuel – I'll be alright in a minute when I've had something to eat."

Becaud looked concerned, too. Amy was right, Zoe didn't look good. She so often is right, he thought, and he handed Zoe her food first. She took it gratefully, and started to feel better as soon as the first warm, savoury mouthfuls sat on her tongue, then were swallowed down quickly. She hadn't been in Greenland for very long this time and already she felt that she was losing too much weight.

"You're cold aren't you?" Amy said, persisting.

"Well, I suppose I am a bit. Think I stayed out there too long, that's all."

Oliver without a word untied her boots, and took them off. Holding her feet in his hands, he felt the cold coming through her socks.

"These are bloody freezing – you silly bitch! Really Zo, you must be more careful! We've been lecturing Terry and not looking after you."

He held her feet next to his body to warm them up, while he got his meal and started in on it. Terry sat still, waiting for his own dinner to come round. He noted with satisfaction how they all looked out for each other out here. They were good guys to be with, like the ones in his old unit, and he liked being part of their set-up. The rations were good too, and big enough helpings. That was Becaud's doing. When he could get his hands on Canadian supplies they were always worth waiting for.

Oliver suddenly remembered something, and putting Zoe's feet to one side, while he stretched and reached over to his rucksack, pulled out a large bottle of wine from amongst his rolled up clothes. There was a murmur of approval from the ranks.

"A last little drop of civilisation, before the hard work begins tomorrow, I think," said Oliver, clearly delighted that everyone perked up expectantly at the thought of a nice glass of red. He unscrewed the top and carefully poured everyone a fair measure in their tin cups before the last bit went into his own.

"You haven't got enough yourself there," said Hewitt, offering some of his own to make up the shortfall.

"No, no problem – there's another one where this came from, don't worry."

Everyone laughed. Of course there would be. For a few minutes the only sound was that of the scraping of the last pieces of reconstituted moussaka from their mess tins with plastic spoons. Then, even as they sat, the wind began to rise again. The snow bank was doing its job protecting them from the brunt of the Arctic weather, but even where they were camped in the lee of the snow wall, the tent walls began to billow and sink in turn as the winds strained at its structure. Terry Coulson collected up the mess tins that each one of them had wiped clean, and Becaud refilled them all with a square of cider apple cake. He'd managed to re-heat a pouch of custard over the tiny stove, and then poured a little over each slice of the sticky cake. Now everyone ate more slowly, making the meal last pleasantly long enough to pass the evening. The sun was low on the horizon, and the leaden skies made it feel dark and heavy inside the tent, cramped as it was with them all huddled inside the one.

It was time to get some sleep, and Zoe and Amy had just squeezed inside the smaller of the two tents, reluctantly leaving the warmth of the other one behind them. Zoe and Amy were sharing so that Amy didn't have to with the guys. It was snowing heavily, and they could see the outline of the Cessna already softened by the covering of accumulating snow, making it look rounder and softer in the dull grey light. The fat flakes were gathering fast on the windward side of the tent, banking up against the orange nylon walls, usefully insulating that side from the draining cold. The large zips on first the outer, then the inner nylon door, slid shut with a clumsy gloved hand, at once creating a cosy internal space and a refuge from the buffeting blizzard outside. The two women pulled off their outer clothes and hunkered down as quickly as they could into their sleeping bags. They lay there for some minutes in silence, warming through and listening to the lulling sound of the wind howling and moaning through the metal structures of the plane just metres away, and through the taut guy ropes just the other side of their flimsy shelter.

"Zo."

"Yes?"

"What do you really think of Lawrence?" Zoe took a deep breath, knowing that she would be asked this question sooner or later.

"Can I really answer that truthfully, knowing that you're falling for him?"

"Is it that obvious?"

"It's more obvious that he's falling for you."

"You don't like him, do you?"

"No, I wouldn't say that – I know I didn't much at first, I admit – but then, neither did you. He sought of grows on you, I suppose you could say…"

"Zo! That sounds terrible." Amy laughed.

"A bit of an acquired taste then?"

"No! That's even worse."

"Oliver always liked him – which is why I was prepared to give him a chance. He's a good judge of people, you know, Oliver. But if you're asking me, you don't sound too sure of your own feelings. In the end it's about your feelings, and what you want. Relationships are about what clicks – what sparks between two people. It's not about ticking boxes – it's not a job interview."

"Yes I know. But some people are just harder to get to know than others. I wonder if he could be a bit moody – difficult, you know. Look at you and Oliver. The way you talk to each other – and yet you never take offence or seem to argue."

"But that's just a bit of fun. We respect each other as equals, both at home and at work. At work we both are professionals, and in the home we always shared the responsibilities. There are two adults in our house, not one-and-a half. Oliver, thankfully has never seen women as being some sort of halfway house between childhood and adulthood as some men do. With regard to the children, we saw ourselves as joint carers of the family, none of this head-of the-household crap. I don't believe that women see themselves always as assistants – that's the way they've been defined by men who find that useful to them, and I think that men getting more involved in the family is better for them, too – it means they don't feel pushed out of their children's lives. Oliver is a great dad, whereas he hardly knew his own father."

"Absolutely," Amy said. "Never trusted the little woman type anyway – they're always the ones who secretly like to rule the roost." They both laughed.

"What are you afraid of Ames? Of Lawrence turning out to be the domineering type?"

"I suppose so. I've had enough of bullies and control freaks – been there, done that - I just want someone who's nice to be with."

"He's no bully, I'm sure. And I don't think he's controlling either. If anything he can be a little too self-contained, perhaps. He told Oliver something you ought to know." Zoe paused not knowing how Amy would take it, then said simply,

"He lost his son."

"I didn't know that." Amy was struck. She'd never imagined him having children, or maybe being married. He'd always seemed so alone. She even felt a twinge of jealousy. She didn't know what to say. Then Amy bit the bullet. "Is Lawrence married?"

"No. Not any more." Zoe continued, "He had a really bad time, apparently. He just needs to come out of himself a bit more. A good relationship might enable him to do that. But it needs to be good for you too, Ames. You are a very giving person, but don't be afraid of your own needs. You mustn't be afraid to assert yourself if others are to respect you."

"Yes, but I like caring for others."

"And that's lovely, but you mustn't let people use you."

"Do you think Lawrence would do that?"

"No, actually, I don't. He might be rather reticent, but he's not needy. In fact I think he might be quite good for you. I feel that he needs someone to look after to give him a role in life once more. And don't feel sorry for him either. He wouldn't like that. In the end, I don't think you can pre-judge a relationship. You have to spend time getting to know each other and then make your mind up."

"Mm."

"What about Phil," said Zoe gently. "He's very hurt you know."

"He's no right to be. He was the one who didn't want to get involved." She sighed heavily. "I fancied him so much," said Amy.

She paused as if to add something else, but didn't. Really, there was nothing more to say. The two of them then snuggled further into their sleeping bags as the warmth of their bodies deepened around them both, but their faces could feel cold air hanging just above their heads. A low growl reverberated beneath them and the ground rippled slightly as though something were moving deep below them.

"It's happening all the time now, isn't it Zo, the tremors? I hardly notice it anymore."

"It's building," said Zoe. "Slowly, inexorably. We are getting used to it, you're right. But the pressure's building. There were very slight tremors all last night, it seemed to me. And then yesterday – I thought someone was drilling something when I heard that jarring sound. Like it was coming through the walls."

"All those people," said Amy her thoughts wandering back to the news reports of the tsunami. "I can't believe that Marcus was one of them."

"I keep thinking of that, too. So sorry Ames. He was such a nice guy. Such a waste."

"There could be so many more."

"Let's hope not."

Zoe's eyes closed out any more tired thoughts, and with the ice creaking and groaning beneath them like ships' timbers in a stirring sea, she slipped into a rich warm sleep, unbroken throughout the grey, darkless night.

CHAPTER TWENTY-FOUR

Zoe woke up the next morning knowing that she had to confront one of the most challenging tasks of her life. She had to abseil down into the Atlantis Rift, with Terry Coulson and Amy James so that Terry could lay the charges. Zoe and Amy were the only ones with enough climbing experience to take him down there, and they were going to have to do it, like it or not.

Today.

She'd tried not to think about it too much before, but there was no getting away from it now, and certainly no getting out of it. Difficult memories of her climb on Stanage Edge in the Peak District all those years ago were nudging at her peace of mind, but they had to be kept firmly in their place if this mission were to have any chance of success. Stuart Lightman. She wondered if Stuart ever thought about that day when, due to her mistake he ended up slithering down the rock face, shaken, but thankfully unharmed. She wondered if her name haunted his memories the way his did hers. She hoped not. This time there was no room for a screw-up, nor did she have the luxury of the chance to opt out. This was the time when she must come face to face with both her potential and her past, and learn what she was made of. She had no choice, she knew that, and that insight at least made her at one with her task, as she thought it through. Now that she knew what she had to do she could relax into her decision and go with it.

The earthquakes had got worse throughout the night. No longer were they rumbling gently, creating ripples in the coffee. The short, pokey bursts of seismic energy now seemed angry and insistent, as though the volcano was tired of sending out warning shots and had decided that it was time to blow. The pressure had a latency about it that was almost tangible in the air. She so desperately hoped that their plan would work. She so desperately hoped that they would be in time.

With a resignation that now made her calm, Zoe unzipped her sleeping bag and shook the still sleeping figure of Amy till she stirred and grunted her displeasure at being woken up before she was ready to face the day. Trying to ignore the cold, Zoe got the tiny stove lit and boiled some water on it to make the first brew of the day. They sat up, still with their legs inside their sleeping bags, hugging the hot mugs of sweet tea, like two girls on a sleep over, not speaking till both cups had been drained to the bottom.

It had snowed heavily all night, and the tent sagged slightly along its domed roof under the weight of it. The two women wriggled into their outdoor clothes, rolled up their sleeping bags tightly and unzipped the tents. The fresh air smelt good after the plastic smell of the confined tent and its contents, and Zoe took a deep breath as she stepped out and went towards the other one. She opened the outer door, pressed close behind by Amy, and called out,

"Everybody decent?"

She waited for a reply. There seemed to be a universal yes to her question, then an unknown hand opened the flap and told her it was OK to come in. They crawled in and sat awkwardly with all the others hoping somebody would have got some breakfast organised. All the boys looked pretty dishevelled and Hewitt was desperately trying to comb his hair with his fingers before Amy could get a proper look at him.

"At least it's quietened down a bit this morning," said Terry.

"Yeah, there's hardly any wind at the moment, though I don't expect that to last. The forecast isn't good," said Zoe.

"I meant the tremors, really," said Terry. "I didn't get much sleep, I can tell you."

"I don't like it," said Zoe. "It's too quiet, all of a sudden. Like we're waiting for something to happen."

"Yes, the atmosphere feels tense – I know just what you mean – it's a bit like the feeling you get immediately before a thunder storm – like it's charged, somehow," said Hewitt. The others agreed.

"You OK about going down into the Rift, Terry?" said Zoe, trying to cover her own concern by putting it onto Coulson.

"Yep. I'm good. Can't wait to get started now. Just want to stop thinking about it and get down there."

Zoe wished she could be as positive. She didn't know how much of what he said was a front, but it made the job seem doable, and she was glad of his confident manner.

They breakfasted hurriedly on some chunks of salami and some mugs of piping hot soup to set them up for the day ahead, carefully chewing the savoury, fatty meat as if to extract every last calorie out of it. The soup was filling and warmed them all through, with an energy that was both comforting and motivating at the same time. Then in silence, they cleared their things away, knowing only too well that this was the last they would see of the relative comfort of the camp until the job was done.

They were standing in a group next to the Cessna checking and re-checking the supplies and equipment, knowing that there was no room to take anything else even if they remembered it. It wasn't far to the Rift, if their calculations were correct, but pulling a laden sled over rough terrain in bad weather was not going to be easy and they wanted as little burden as possible to slow them down. Phil Becaud slammed the door shut on the plane, now looking soft and rounded, like a child's toy aeroplane, due to last night's covering of snow. They were ready to leave the relative comfort of the camp. Each one of them was attached by a line to the sled, and after a last look around, somebody said "OK!" and they all set off more or less together.

They had only been walking about five minutes when it began to snow once more. The only compensation was that the wind was behind them, but visibility was still very poor, and the swirling flakes were disorienting. Zoe walked on, head down, just hoping that the others were keeping her headed in the right direction. At the back of the group nearest the sled, all she could see through the tunnel of her hood was the back of Hewitt's boots, rising and falling in a mesmerising fashion, ticking off the moments, till the journey was done. The sled was pulling at her waist as she trudged on, but with all of them sharing the weight it didn't seem too bad. The exercise began to warm her through and the hypnotic effects of the rhythmic walk soon allowed her to mentally relax and her thoughts began to drift. She hoped Dorothy was OK, as they hadn't heard from her in a few days. Then Terry came up beside her, disturbing her thoughts by wanting to talk.

"I couldn't help wondering, Zoe, why you hate the name Atlantis Rift, so much? Becaud thinks it's perfect." He sounded somewhat breathless. He obviously wasn't as fit as he used to be, thought Zoe with some concern. The task ahead would need a lot of stamina.

Zoe thought for a minute how to answer. She didn't want to sound priggish.

"I want to be taken seriously in the academic world, that's all. It sounds too, well, comic book, I suppose." It did sound priggish, but Terry persisted.

"I like comic books," he said.

Zoe smiled, not that Terry could see her anyway, buried in her fur-trimmed hood.

"People seem to like weird or supernatural explanations for things when a perfectly ordinary one will do. It's easy to get carried away. In serious study one can't be seen as joining the ranks of the gullible." Now she sounded harsh, but was in no mood to compromise.

"I don't think I'm gullible, but I do think there's some weird stuff out there – things we can't explain."

"Like what?" said Zoe.

"Like ghosts, for example. Or clairvoyance. How do you account for that?" Zoe snorted.

"It's so easy to get so sucked in to the *idea* of mystery, that it becomes almost an explanation in itself," said Zoe. "First of all, with what you've just said, I would need more convincing that there actually is anything to explain. After all there are thousands of people who claim to be clairvoyants, yet where were they when something really big happened – like the twin towers – they didn't see that one coming, did they? Or you hear about their amazing predictions afterwards."

"Cynic!" said Terry, still wanting to push her for answers. "Don't you think it's a bit arrogant thinking that you've got all the answers? I don't think you can dismiss all the supernatural as fraud, or imagination."

"No. But I don't think that there *is* such a thing as the supernatural, that's all."

"How can you say that? There are loads of things people can't explain."

Zoe trudged on for a few moments before answering.

"Look at it logically, Terry. Either stuff happens or it doesn't happen. One or the other. If it does, then it's a part of the real, natural world, however odd it might seem to us now. It might seem weird or mysterious to us at the moment – we may not have an explanation for it, but that doesn't mean that there isn't one. We scientists are not the arrogant ones. We know we have a lot to learn. It just means we don't understand it *yet*. There could be things we will never understand because of the limits of our human brains, I guess, too. An ant doesn't understand electricity, but that doesn't make it supernatural, although it might seem so in Antworld. And if stuff doesn't happen then you don't need to make a mystery out of it anyway. I sometimes think that today's magic is tomorrow's science. Imagine an Elizabethan's reaction to a remote control or satellite communication, or, or quantum physics. I suppose I just think that if you believe something, then that belief should be based on evidence. Empirical evidence in the case of the sciences; rational argument and good scholarship in the case of the liberal arts. Otherwise you just have unsubstantiated opinion. No – you have to have something to go on; it helps to keep you grounded."

"So does science have an answer to everything?"

"No of course not. And it doesn't try to, so that isn't a valid criticism of science. Take questions like, for example, is free speech worth fighting for? Or is a dead sheep in a tank art? Why is a poem by Wilfred Owen better than the verse I get in my greetings card? They are for the philosophers and artists to chew over. What about you, Terry? Do you think freedom is worth fighting for? You used to be a soldier after all. Is that what you thought you were doing?"

"That was for the politicians, all that crap – it was my job to kick ass." Zoe laughed.

"You're with us now, though."

"I'm doing this for Ray."

"That's a pretty good reason."

"And I like Wilfred Owen."

"So do I," said Zoe, looking down again at the ground in front of her, resuming the steady pace she was into before.

Her feet were warm with the exercise, her hands, too. She wondered how much further there was to go when Oliver, reading her thoughts, called out "We're nearly there." He turned to Zoe so that she could hear him. I'm sure another half hour will do it."

"Great," said Zoe. "This thing's getting heavy."

They pressed on. Then sure enough, after about ten minutes walk, they could see the Rift in the distance. The snow stopped, but the wind was still blowing hard behind them. Zoe's stomach lurched at the sight of the huge crack in the ice lying before them. She looked levelly at Terry Coulson. He was pale but his eyes were steady.

"We'll be OK," he said, and attempted a smile.

I ought to be reassuring him, thought Zoe, and gave an equally unconvincing one back.

They reached the Rift in just under the half hour that Oliver had predicted. When they got there Oliver slipped off his harness and walked straight over to the edge of the massive canyon and looked down into it. In a second he was marching over towards Zoe and Amy who were sitting on the packed sled taking a breather.

"It's absolutely bloody massive!" he said, Zoe thought somewhat needlessly, but she bit her tongue. "It's wider at the top by hundreds of metres, I would say, but it appears to be stretching out into more of a valley shape – which means the sides are no longer a sheer drop – at least here."

This was great news, and Zoe immediately got up and walked with Oliver to the cliff edge to take a look for herself. The view was breathtaking. The Rift stretched out to infinity in both directions, and the bottom looked to be a very, very long way away, but Oliver was right. The top had widened more than the base, leaving the walls sloped and in places ledged. This would certainly make the descent easier, although the walls looked fragile and crumbly in places and that would make problems of its own. Near the base of the Rift and on one of the ledges there were piles of slipped snow that could only have been the result of massive avalanches, presumably caused by the quakes. In the distance a thick pall of steam rose from near the base of the wall indicating a possible lava flow. Zoe pointed towards it.

"I think that's where we need to be headed," she said. "That could be the visible edge of the caldera, and the lava flow is eating away at the ice sheet at a phenomenal rate. Normally this landscape is so static, but look – there's movement everywhere."

Amy craned over her shoulder to see for herself, and immediately could see what Zoe meant. Smoke was leaching out of the orifice where the lava seemed to be oozing, and along the path of its flow steam hung and drifted around, dancing in the wind; hanging in denser clouds where it was sheltered in pockets of ice. Some places glistened as ribbons of thin meltwater dripped down into pools and bored into the ice. And every few minutes somewhere, a fragment of ice would splinter off the main wall and cascade into the abyss, landing with a small explosion of white powder all around it as it hit the bedrock below.

"I see what you mean," said Amy.

Then, even as she spoke there was a deep rumble in the distance, and the ground vibrated beneath their feet, terrifying them with its suddenness as they were so near to the edge of the precipice. Oliver grabbed Zoe's hand and they stumbled backwards together in their haste to get away from the drop. They scrambled back a good twenty metres away in case the edge crumbled under the strain of the vibrations, just to be on the safe side. Zoe could feel her heart pounding, and the adrenaline pricked under her skin like pins for a few minutes till the shuddering stopped and she felt safe again. Amy, amazingly agile, was already well away from the edge when Zoe and Oliver looked around for her. The vibrating stopped as suddenly as it had begun but the quiet that followed lasted only for about a minute before another rumbling sound took its place. This time the sound came clearly through the air and not the ground. Hewitt was the first to realise what was causing it; he grabbed his camera and made towards the Rift tentatively at first but quicker as the sound grew louder.

"Lawrence, be careful!" said Amy, frightened that the ground might not be stable enough to hold his weight.

"It's OK!" he said, "I just need to get this."

He pointed his camera over the drop just in time to capture the sight of the walls of the canyon opposite where he was standing, turn to liquid and slide down into the valley bottom. First a line would appear in the snowy wall, then as it broke away in thick slab-like portions huge hollows would be left behind. As it rolled down the precipitous slopes, the avalanche gathered pace and volume that beggared belief as it crashed down in a mountainous heap at the bottom, throwing up broken snow as though hit by a bomb. It took a long time for the avalanche to reach the ground even at that terrifying speed. It felt as though a mountain the size of the Alps had just broken free and crashed to the Earth. It must have left a drift of broken snow three hundred metres high, dumped on the bottom of the Rift, looking every bit like the spoil heaps left when you dig out the car from a snow drift, only on an epic scale. It was like being miniaturised and seeing everything with new eyes. Then a gust of wind hit them, driven by the racing snow. It took their breath away for a few seconds, then died away into the distance.

Hewitt couldn't hide his excitement at getting the shot. He took off his gloves, and clumsy with impatience he played back the image on his screen. He was totally impervious to the five pairs of eyes stuck to the camera but unable to see the video for themselves.

"Hey! Let someone else get a look in, why don't ya?" said Becaud. "We're itching to see what you got!"

None of the others had dared to go close enough to the edge to actually see the avalanche and couldn't wait to get at the footage. Reluctantly Hewitt relinquished the camera to the cluster of snatching hands, and let them see for themselves what had just happened.

"Awesome!" said Becaud.

"Oh my God!" Zoe said. "And we thought the erosion might make the descent easier – it's very unstable – very volatile. This is turning into a nightmare."

"You don't have to go, sweetheart. Not if you don't want to. We'll think of something else," said Oliver.

"Like what?" Hewitt said, interrupting. "We can't abandon this now."

"Fuck off, Lawrence! I'm not having my wife risking her life needlessly. It's not you going down there, is it?"

Hewitt looked shocked. Oliver had never turned on him before. He was only saying what he thought was obvious. Amy winced. She found herself trying to excuse Lawrence in her mind, but so wished she didn't have to. She was upset that Oliver had been the one to say that, as before he'd always been the one tolerant of Hewitt.

Becaud tried hard not to look pleased. Too hard, so it didn't quite work.

"I...I'm sorry. Didn't mean it to sound like that," said Hewitt. "You must be so worried about Zoe."

Amy listened. He wouldn't have said that before, she thought, trying to be more positive, he would have just turned in on himself.

"And it *is* me going down there," he added. Amy jumped, totally taken unawares by what he had just said. "I have to film it and send a daily video back to Dorothy. That's why I came along. Can't get much from up here."

"But you can't climb, Lawrence!" said Amy. "It was meant to be Zoe, Terry and me going there with you three as back up."

"Had it been a sheer descent there was no way I could have gone down, I'd have been a liability for the rest of you – but I think it's feasible now for us all to go – and I think we should."

"Except Phil. He can't go. We might need him to stay with the plane, and ferry supplies," Terry said.

Zoe thought about what was being said. It made sense, she had to admit that. And there was a huge amount of stuff to transport down there. With her experience she could descend first with Terry, then guide the others down the easiest route. Some of it was even walkable on the lower slopes. Even so it seemed a bit impulsive to change their plan of action so radically at this stage. Zoe wondered if it was a wise move, as she'd been through the scenario dozens of times in her mind and felt that she was prepared for what to do. On the other hand, she was secretly elated and relieved at the thought of Oliver being able to come along.

"It'll mean Phil staying here by himself," said Zoe, feeling obliged to show some concern for their long-suffering pilot, but desperately hoping that he'd be OK about it.

"No problem," said Becaud, taciturnly. "I'd be going back to camp, anyway. There's no way I'm going down there."

It was settled. And the next hour was spent carefully packing as many rations as they could carry into their rucksacks from the supplies on the sled. The boxes of explosives were roped together ready to be lowered down to the group once they had descended the first steep section of the Rift. After that everything would have to be carried, or hauled, but at least the going would be easier further down. Terry and Oliver secured the ropes into the ice at the top of the Rift ready for himself and Zoe to go first. There was quite a drop to the first ledge, so they planned to abseil that section for speed, then continue, roped together for the rest of the descent. Once down there she would have to look for an easier way up – it looked good some miles to the west, so she would be planning to head that way out. Her earlier elation though was turning to unease. The benefits of having extra help on the expedition, at first made Zoe feel less responsible for the success of the whole enterprise, but now she was thinking it through she realised that having two inexperienced people on board might be more of a burden than a help, and only added to her responsibilities. Too late to change again at this late stage; Oliver and Hewitt would insist on going now anyway. Better just get on with it, she thought, as she attended to her last minute preparations. She looked at the others doing the same thing. Oliver and Lawrence were speaking to each other about the minutiae of packing the explosives correctly. They looked absorbed in their task and businesslike in manner, but their body language seemed a little strained, she thought. She might have to have a word with Oliver and try to patch things up before they got going. Under no circumstances did she want any rancour amongst the team before they'd even set off. But she needn't have worried. Oliver patted Lawrence's arm when they'd finished the job, in a matey fashion, a gesture which Lawrence returned, albeit a little self-consciously. Terry, on the other hand suddenly appeared nervous. He prepared efficiently, no doubt his training had taken over, but this was all new territory for him, and he was bound to feel some trepidation.

"Don't think of Ray too much," said Oliver noticing it too, and going over to him. "I know you can't help it. But it will make your judgement sentimental and gesture-driven. What you need now is a bit of detachment in order to let your skills come through. You're our best asset – remember that!"

Terry smiled slightly, and warmed to the praise Oliver had given to him. The trouble was he was by rights a professional amongst amateurs, but they had the edge over him in being familiar with the conditions, far more so than he was, and so his role was slightly confused. He'd just have to learn fast.

It was Phil Becaud's job to make sure the ropes were secure on the top of the cliff face, and feed them down as the first two, Zoe and Terry, abseiled down onto the ledge about three hundred metres below, then prepare for the others to go down after them. Technically, this wasn't too difficult once the technique had been mastered, but it would take a lot of nerve for the beginners to go over the edge. Once comfortable in the harness, Zoe reassured them, and they had begun to feel the rope feeding through their hands, it would feel more like walking than climbing – they'd be fine. Zoe showed them the procedure while they all stood around her taking in every detail, then she let them all try for themselves, to make sure they all knew basically what to do.

Zoe then buckled on her harness and checked it thoroughly, tugging at it firmly partly to put the others at ease, as well as herself.

"Watch carefully as we go down. The key is to relax and let your body weight take you down. Concentrate on simple co-ordinated movements, and remember every step is one more nearer to the safety of the ledge. You'll be there before you know it... OK, Phil?"

He nodded and watched her nimbly drop down into the void as though she were hopping over a fence. Rather you than me, he thought. He needed the thought of the Cessna wrapped around him before he went out over a two mile drop. Terry looked white, and his pulse was racing, but went over the top to keep abreast of Zoe, without a murmur of complaint. Zoe started to feed the rope through her hands with ease, her feet bouncing her off the white snowy wall as she went down. Terry fumbled around and found it harder to get going. He strained at the rope and found his legs slithering about on the slippery surface, which made him bump along uncomfortably. She didn't think he'd respond well to sympathy, so she snapped at him to brace his legs against the cliff face and press himself into the harness to get some grip. She stopped at his side so he felt the comfort of not dangling there alone, and then told him to begin feeding the rope as she was doing and stop arsing about. At that, he mentally got himself together, then had a go at the rope once more. This time he got the technique much better, and made a few steps down in a more controlled movement. Once he'd done that he felt OK as he was a quick learner and could adapt to new situations. They pressed on, this time Zoe staying close to him as she thought that any time she lost by doing that, she could make up for by sorting out his problems promptly. He did OK, and when his feet touched the ground on the ledge he grinned with a deserved sense of achievement, that she fully endorsed. Then his legs, not used to the backwards walking where he was using muscles he didn't normally use, turned to jelly and he sat down harder than he intended on the snow, looking and feeling something of a prat. Zoe, her own relief now showing through, cracked out laughing, regardless of his discomfiture.

"Mine, too," she said, rubbing her legs where they ached.

They slipped off their ropes, and signalled to the others to pull them back up, ready for the other two to make the descent. This time it was to be Oliver and Hewitt, the least experienced of the group. Amy made sure they were roped up correctly and then very, very slowly they inched their way over the edge, and began their own descent. Amy gave instruction from the top till they too had mastered the skill of abseiling, and bit by bit they tiny figures made their way down the sheer cliff. Zoe found it hard to watch, knowing that it was Oliver up there, looking so fragile and vulnerable, and so high up. Somehow it looked worse from down on the ledge, and it was with a huge sigh of relief that Oliver's foot eventually touched the snowy ground, and the rope went slack above him. Hewitt was only a few seconds behind, then he too had made it to the ledge.

"Well done, Darling!" she said, kissing her husband on the cheek. Hewitt looked away a little awkwardly.

"You never gave me a kiss," said Terry hoping to ease Lawrence's embarrassment with a little levity. He then looked at Oliver, "She just told me to stop arsing around."

"She would," said Oliver.

Now it was Amy's turn.

Having some climbing experience, it should have been fairly easy for Amy, but it all started to go wrong very quickly. For some reason Amy just couldn't get over the top. As she backed towards the edge on all fours ready to slip over and begin her descent, she could feel herself ceasing up. She had an uncontrollable urge to grasp at the snow in front of her, and when she felt the void under her feet and the Rift's edge pressing into her stomach a wave of panic swept over her, making her want to scramble and run to safety. She stopped a minute and tried to get a grip, but she just couldn't do it. The others were all waiting, and she knew it, but there was nothing she could do.

"I'll be alright in a minute," she said to Becaud who was leaning over her and asking her what was wrong.

But she couldn't get over the feelings that were rising inside her, and her breath was catching in her throat. After several long minutes the others down below began to shout up their inevitable questions. Becaud used his phone and was about to explain to Zoe that they had a problem, when there was another almost imperceptible vibration starting to come from the ground, and the ice that Amy was hanging on to began to crack with thin menacing lines all over its surface. Instinctively she grabbed at the ropes holding her, a look of sheer terror written all over her face. She froze not knowing what to do.

They all felt the tremor and realised the danger that it posed. Terry Coulson took the phone and shouted down it to tell Amy to get down quickly or they might all be caught in a new wave of avalanches, but Zoe grabbed it back and shouted to Becaud, "No! Pull her up. Now! Get her out of there, Phil! The ropes might not hold if the tremors shake the tethers lose, and you'll never be able to hold her if she falls – she'll pull you off, too! Do it!"

Becaud deferred to Zoe's greater expertise. He slipped his leg behind a rope to give him some kind of anchorage then grabbed Amy who could feel the ice crumbling under her body and her legs no longer having a purchase on the cliff face. As she pulled on the ropes to get herself back over the top of the ice shelf she could feel them give.

"Phil! I'm going to fall!" she screamed.

Hewitt hearing her cry out, said "For God's sake help her, man!" to Becaud, although there wasn't a hope in hell of him hearing it.

Phil clenched his hands around Amy's harness and pulled with all his strength enough for her to get one knee onto the cliff top. She could then lever herself up enough, with Phil's help, and scramble her way back to safety. As she lay trembling on the ice she heard it crack beneath her, and realising that it was going to give, she wriggled, snake-like while Becaud tried to keep up with her by running even before he had time to get upright. When they were both on firmer ice, they lay there panting, shaking with the shock of what might have been.

"If I'd begun abseiling, the ropes could have come lose when I was halfway down," said Amy.

"I'd have made sure they didn't," said Becaud.

And for some reason, Amy believed him.

CHAPTER TWENTY-FIVE

Hewitt's stunned silence lasted only as long as it took him to realise that although Amy was safe, there was no way that she'd now be coming along. The truth was that ninety percent of the reason that he decided to come on this section of the journey was to be with her. Not that there was anything between them, not really even an understanding.

It was just that whenever there was a group that included her he found himself always standing by her, wanting to talk to her. And she didn't seem to mind. Sometimes he thought that she might like him a little, but he hadn't had the courage to ask her out, or tell her how he felt. He knew if he tried he would make a mess of it. He'd tried to say something after she'd got the news about Marcus James, but he couldn't gauge her reaction to what he'd said as she was too upset about her cousin. He was still reeling from the shock of seeing her in danger. And felt totally useless that he hadn't been the one who could have helped her out.

Everyone else seemed to assume that she fancied Phil Becaud – couldn't blame her for that. Phil was good looking, with a mixture of Canadian friendliness and French style, that in Hewitt's eyes must be attractive to women – they were different leagues, he knew that. *And, he thought sullenly, now she would be with Becaud alone for the next few days while I'm trying to blow up some bloody volcano.* How unlucky was that? He would have given anything to have been in Becaud's shoes right now. The sting of jealousy smarted with an intensity that left him in no doubt about how he felt about Amy – and now he felt that he'd left it too late to do anything about it.

"So, what do we do now?" said Hewitt, trying hard to focus on the present.

"We get going. What do you think?" said Terry. "She froze, you could see that, so there's no way she's ever going to make it down that cliff face, even if we wait for her to try again - and we need to get moving."

Terry was unsympathetic, and Hewitt, always quite astute, thought he was covering for the fact that he'd just made a wrong call. If Amy hadn't panicked, and had pressed on as Terry told her to, she would have been killed, no two ways about it. He was obviously emphasising the fact that she could never have attempted the descent to deflect criticism away from himself. She'd been worried that Terry had poor judgement – and now she'd been proved right – almost to her cost.

"You OK, Lawrence?" said Zoe.

"I suppose so," he said, flatly. Inwardly he was still reeling from the shock of what might have been. Better not to dwell on it.

"Come on, then! Let's get cracking," said Oliver.

The next stage of the descent was quite easy, as it was more a case of clambering over piles of broken snow which had built up on the ledge below them. The soft snow at least making secure footholds for them to sink into as Zoe led the way, the others roped to her and following as best they could. Progress was slow, and the going was very tiring, but at least they were going downhill. It went through several of their minds that it was going to be a lot tougher getting back up.

They paused for 'ten' at Terry's insistence, after about an hour. Zoe was keen to keep up the momentum as they were making good progress, but Terry said no. If they only stopped when they were really tired, he said then they'd never be able to get going again. Zoe deferred to his greater experience of survival techniques, seeing the sense of what he said when it was spelled out to her, but she felt that the slow pace was sapping her strength more than if they'd gone flat out. They all ate some chocolate and had a drink. Terry insisted that everyone drank their full ration. Dehydration is just as dangerous in a cold climate, he warned, as a hot one. It creeps up on you making you tired. Then you make mistakes. Zoe and Amy smiled. He was learning fast, and now he was telling them what to do.

Zoe was impatient to re-start but could see that the others were glad of the rest. She looked to where they would be headed, and planned out in her head the route for the next stage of the descent. The direct route was too steep for the inexperienced ones in her party, but she figured out an easier one down a broken section of cliff that had left a series of giant steps. There would be steep climbs down of about twenty-five to thirty metres at a stretch. It didn't look too technically demanding, and there were no sheer drops, which the non-climbers in the party couldn't have been expected to attempt. She went through a couple of times in her imagination working out the time scale in advance so they could plan the next rest break accordingly.

"I reckon an hour, an hour and fifteen will do the next stage, Terry. What do you think?"

"Yeah, maybe. If the others can keep the pace up. We need to rest every hour. And for no more than ten minutes or we'll get cold. So we'll try to complete the next bit in that time. Good?"

"Sounds good to me."

"OK, then, let's get moving. Come on you lot!" Terry glanced at his watch. "Shift your sorry asses, and follow on."

He was sounding more military every second, thought Zoe. He was getting into his stride. She hoped he'd be as good with the explosives.

When they got to the first step, Zoe took stock of her next move, and hammered some metal pitons into the ice to tie the rope in. The cliff face was steep but not vertical with good footholds and she dropped down to the lower ledge in quick time. The others seemed clumsy and hesitant in comparison, and Hewitt slipped the last two metres, landing heavily on his feet at the bottom. Oliver, seeing how easy it was to lose footing was slow on his turn, then Terry joined the group last of all.

"We're holding you up," said Oliver, aware that his wife had been waiting at the bottom of the first step for a good fifteen minutes, while they all got down. "You and Terry would have been faster without us."

"You'll get quicker," she said. "And we couldn't have carried all this stuff on our own. We'd have been exhausted." Oliver nodded his appreciation, and made ready to drop down the next step. Metre by metre they edged their way down the Rift, and Zoe was right, they did get quicker with practice.

When they stopped for their next rest, they'd made it to the base of the steps as Zoe had hoped. Now they seemed a very long way down into the Rift, looking up was almost as vertiginous as glancing down. Through the field glasses Hewitt could make out the rock face rising out of the valley floor, where they were going to lay the charges. Seeing it getting closer hit Hewitt with a wave of depression. It seemed to be getting more massive with every passing step, which only made their attempts at diverting the lava flow seem puny to the point of hopeless. He became engrossed in a 'what the fuck am I doing here?' moment, not helped by the fact that he now seemed a very long way away from Amy. The thought grated on his mind that she was up there with him – Becaud; maybe their isolation bringing them together.

"Hey, Lawrence! Can I take a look, sometime?" Terry butted in on his thoughts. "You've been staring at that point over there for ages."

"Yes, I'm sorry. Didn't realise," said Hewitt. "Here." He handed Coulson the glasses, and he took in the view, thinking exactly the same thought that Hewitt had just had.

"Are we off our fucking heads?" said Terry Coulson.

"Of course we are," said Zoe, interrupting. "But remember, we are not trying to destroy this volcano, we are only trying to divert the lava away from destabilising the ice sheet, using the Rift as a conduit, and relieving the pressure. We have to believe it can work." Hewitt tried, but was finding it hard to do.

They finished their drinks, and chewed the sweet, high calorie energy bars that would keep them going for the next hour. Zoe always felt that the energy was draining away from her in these cold conditions. Oliver was heartily sick of eating sweet things. He so longed for a pork pie, but chewed up his fruit, nut and grain bar diligently.

The next section of the descent was more or less walkable as long as they zig-zagged down, hairpin bend fashion, rather than go straight down. But the ledges in places were stomach churningly narrow – not too bad when the drop below was sloping, but when it got sheer it was terrifying. Zoe stopped at one point, suddenly seeing a path ahead about a body's width wide at its narrowest part. The wall to the left was shiny with running water, making the ice underfoot treacherous, the drop to the right was an empty void, where the snow had broken away and left the path as an overhang. She stopped and looked at the path, trying desperately to think of an alternative to going over it. Searching for a different route was useless, unless they back tracked for about twenty-five minutes and took another way down – but even then she couldn't guarantee that there'd be a route through without a feature such as this one. Really, it was asking too much for the others to attempt it, but they were going to have to. When she turned to face the group she could tell straight away that they'd seen what was ahead. She studied their body language, and could tell that they were shrinking inside themselves. *I need time to think.* She mouthed to herself, and was about to discuss the options with Terry. Then, in a moment of clarity, she realised that she was wasting time going round about a problem that had to solved head on. Realistically, there was no alternative to crossing the narrow path, it was just a matter of getting the others across safely. So she gave them no option.

"Ok, guys. Well you've all seen what's ahead. It's tricky but not that difficult, if you see what I mean. It's scary – no doubt about it. But if it were a foot above the ground we could dance across it. It's a matter of keeping our nerve, and not letting our worst case scenario imaginations get the better of us. I'll go first – I'll be roped of course, then I can guide the rest of you over, and you'll have something to hold on to. So you'll be quite safe. OK? The ledge looks firm enough to me."

Zoe, without waiting for a reaction started to hammer pitons into the cliff then fed the rope through, before clipping onto her harness with a carabena. She then got down on her hands and knees and began the short crawl onto the ledge. The first bit was easy. But once the ground fell away on her right hand side the ledge became so narrow that her gloved hand was almost touching the edge of it. She pressed her body against the icy wall to her right, but the whole surface was glistening and slippery. With great difficulty she knocked in some more pitons and fed the rope through so the ones following would have something to hang on to – they'd need it. The view was magnificent, but the drop below was hundreds of metres. She was scared for them, but actually felt quite calm herself. She forgotten how much she had loved the thrill and the challenge of climbing, held down for so many years by the tethers of negativity, 'what if?' fears, and pointless self-punish-ment. There was no feeling of elation or letting go; in these circumstances that would have been too danger-ous, she just felt at one with her task, absorbed in the moment, which took the clumsiness out of her hands, and the fear out of her stomach.

The water that was dripping down one part of the cliff was causing the ice just ahead of her to glisten warn-ingly. The liquid water was lubricating the snow's surface making it very slippery indeed, but instead of overcom-pensating for that she carried on crawling in the most relaxed and natural way she could, without even slowing down. At least the ledge felt firm. A few more metres, and she was across. She hammered in another piton and secured the rope her side of the ledge, pulling it tight. She looked up to see the others staring enviously across at her. Oliver was full of admiration for her. And not wanting to show his desperate relief that she'd got across safely, he winked at her, and made ready to go next.

"Don't wait for him to cross! Follow on behind!" she yelled. And the other two eagerly got ready to go, not wanting to prolong the misery of anxious waiting any longer than they had to. Oliver found it harder than he thought it would be, his nerve nearly failing when he reached the narrowest bit. Being bigger than Zoe, he felt that he was overhanging the drop, in the most sickening way. There was no room to turn around, which actually made him feel a bit claustrophobic one moment, then agoraphobic the next when he looked over the drop.

"Keep going! You're doing OK," said Zoe. And he sped up a bit, aware that he was stalling.

"Yes. Keep going!" said Hewitt. "I want to get off this fucking shelf in one piece." There was a note of panic in his voice that went through Oliver, aware that they were all roped together. Suddenly he became afraid that Hewitt might lose it and push him onwards, faster than he could safely go, so he upped his speed a little. He felt he couldn't go too fast or he might slip. He kept his eyes firmly on the wall at his side. After a few more agonisingly slow shuffles, Oliver felt his wife's hands on his arms helping him off the ledge, and he was over. His relief was total. He then helped Hewitt and Terry Coulson off in turn.

"Didn't like that much," said Oliver to Zoe. "*You* were bloody amazing."

"No, you three were bloody amazing. Me? I've just decided to move on," she said. Oliver didn't know what the hell she was talking about and was in no mood to ask. Not now at any rate.

"Everyone OK?" she said.

Terry nodded. Then Oliver noticed Hewitt, who had gone a whiter shade of pale. "Hey! You look as though you need to sit down, Lawrence."

"No, I'll be alright in a minute."

He took a deep breath, and as time was slipping by, no-one pressed him. Zoe said they needed to push on for another twenty minutes at least to try to make the next decent sized stopping point down below them. So picking up their packs and dragging the burdensome boxes of explosives, they fell into single file and clambered down the next stage of their descent. They made good time, but as the day wore on the difficult terrain had begun to take its toll. The hours seemed longer and the ten minute breaks got shorter. The food and drinks did less and less to replenish the energy levels that were dwindling fast. Zoe felt that she was running on empty, and felt a lightness in her head that made her detached from the strain she was putting on her body. For a while it had become exhilarating, making her feel that she could go on forever, but when she sat down for the rest break, an overwhelming weariness started to creep over her.

"After the next stage we make camp," said Terry, in a voice that would take no opposition.

Zoe's first reaction was to disagree, to see if she could work through the tiredness, until she felt the will to complete even the next leg ebb away.

"Ten more minutes?" she said tentatively. Not knowing how she was going to stand up.

"No way," said Terry Coulson. "We're getting cold already, and at this rate, if we push too far, we'll have no reserves left to make camp. And we've done OK. We're nearly at the rocky face of the volcano. Tomorrow will be an easier walk. Then we can lay the charges."

Terry and Oliver then pulled Zoe to her feet and told her to get going. Once she began again she worked through her moves like an automaton, feeling her way down the cliff wall, and trying not to think at all about how tired she was. She wasn't even hungry anymore, she just wanted to sleep. She led them down a steep slope, climbing down, not walking, aware that every metre she dropped was one more nearer to the camping spot and rest. It took longer than the hour, but they made it in the end to a flat shelf of ice surrounded by a hollow white cave that would keep them sheltered from any wind or snow that might fall during the night.

"This looks like a good place to set up camp," said Terry. "Absolutely perfect. Everybody agree?"

They could hardly do anything else as the site looked ideal.

"What shall we call it? We've got to have a name to distinguish us from Base Camp when we call in."

"Plato Camp," said Zoe.

"Fair enough," said Coulson. "Sounds pretty stupid to me – but I'm in no mood to argue."

Oliver smiled. He'd not read Plato's 'Republic' but he'd heard of the allegory of the cave, and had got the connection.

They set up their tents, while Terry lit the stove to melt some snow and brew up some tea. They sat round drinking their pint mugs of strong sweet tea while Oliver began to fix them something to eat. The wind flapped around their camp site, buffeting around the walls of the deep canyon, making them feel glad to be in the shelter of the tents at last. The sky was now becoming a narrow strip of blue above them, instead of the hollow sphere that normally stretched from one horizon to the other like a cup resting over the dome of the Earth. In the north, a patch of grey cloud had started to gather and drift over, threatening rising winds and perhaps more snow. The site that they had chosen for their camp was good, and well worth the effort of pressing on to. There was a level area of ice big enough for them to pitch the tents at right angles to one another with the stove in between the two doorways. They were also slightly inside the hollow ice cave that at least gave them the illusion of security from the drop below them.

Zoe sat in one of the tents staring at her cup vacantly. After the first few sips it was almost as though she had forgotten it was in her hands. Hewitt who had been in the other tent, came in and flopped down, his exhaustion made worse by a sulky mood which had only got worse as the day wore on. Terry noticed Zoe first.

"Hey! Come on, girl. You need to get that drink down you." She sat there as though she hadn't heard him. She was just too far gone with fatigue to be bothered to answer. "Hey! Oliver! I think she needs a bit of help here." Oliver looked round and saw the comatose figure of his wife nursing the rapidly cooling mug of tea.

"Hey! Sweetheart, come on, Terry's tea might taste bloody awful, but you've got to drink it."

He sat down beside her, and took the cup from her passive hands. She looked at him a flicker of her eyes appreciating his attempt to cheer her up, but she hadn't the energy to smile, and she didn't move. For a moment she thought she was going to pass out.

"It's not the gas cloud returning is it?" said Terry. "Lawrence are you feeling ill, or just bloody miserable? What about you, Oliver? Any headaches, nausea, or difficulty breathing?"

They all seemed OK. Just tired. Oliver said to his wife, "Come on, Darling. You'll feel better when you've had a drink believe me. You've had it tough, today leading all the way. It's been harder for you than any of us. And you still carried your fair share. Look, tomorrow you get a lighter pack as you have the harder job. Come on Zo…"

Oliver held the cup to her lips and gratefully she took a swallow of the tea, then she drank it down, and handed back the cup to her husband. He looked relieved and said, "Guess what we've got for dinner."

"Don't know. It all smells the same to me."

"Curry! We've got curry! Always does the trick, remember. When you need a morale booster, there's nothing better than a beef Madras. What do you say, Lawrence?"

"Oh yes. I suppose so."

"Fuck me, you lot are hard work! What do you think Terry?"

"Chips. They were always what we had in the army to pull the men round."

"Chips," said Zoe, as though awakening from a coma. "I could murder a plate of chips."

"Well hard luck – you've got curry," said Oliver not seeming the slightest bit offended, by their lack of enthusiasm. They'd come round.

And he was proved right. As the mess tins were scraped empty of every last bit of re-hydrated rations, a general sense of well-being descended on the group, gradually restoring them to a new level of sociability.

"Rice pudding, next. Get your tins ready," said Terry lifting the bubbling pan off the tiny stove, which had been heating while they were eating their first course.

They held out their tins in turn while Terry slopped a measure in each one making sure they all had about the same amount. He knew from experience how important food became on expeditions where it was scarce or limited in variety, and he wanted to make sure that everyone was treated fairly. Silly quarrels could get out of hand when people were tired and hungry, so it was important that no-one was allowed to develop a sense of grievance needlessly. Oliver produced some sachets of jam out of his pack and handed them round to each of the group, who took the treat eagerly, even Hewitt, who hated jam, but didn't want to miss out.

Up above them, the grey sky gradually slid over the opening of the Rift, like the roof of a stadium closing against the weather.

"It's going to get stormy. Don't you think?" said Zoe looking up.

"We'll be alright, down here," said Oliver. At that Hewitt frowned and looked away hurriedly. He was annoyed at the thought of Amy up there at Base Camp with Phil Becaud. He'd tried to forget it but hard as he tried the thought had just stuck in his mind and wouldn't go away. His jealousy was gnawing at him.

"We need to call back to Base," said Zoe, noticing and feeling for Hewitt's frustration. "Why don't you do that Lawrence?"

She dug her spoon into the creamy pudding, enjoying it more than any fancy restaurant meal she'd ever eaten. She shared that thought with Oliver.

"Should save me a bob or two, then, in the future," he said, dryly. "Next anniversary it's rice pudding."

But he was secretly relieved that she was rallying. Hewitt then replied to her original question, now that he'd had a moment to think.

"OK. I'll give base a call. Yes. As soon as we've finished."

And he appeared animated at the thought. Soon he might be talking to Amy, and maybe find out why she had been unable to make the journey. It was not like her to bottle anything, she was always so calm and together normally. This was completely out of character, and he'd been worried about her. Then a dark thought crossed his mind. Maybe she'd set the whole thing up – that freezing business – to be alone with Becaud for a few days, and a wave of depression swept over him. Convincing himself that this was the case, he tried to manoeuvre his way out of making the call when the meal was over, but Zoe was having none of it.

"Lawrence, I'm too bloody tired to argue with you, just do it for God's sake will you?"

Sensing that it would be unwise to make too much of it, he acquiesced and made the call. Amy gave him a weather report and an update on seismic activity. He gave their position as best he could and said they were all fine. Amy confirmed that they were OK, but went into no more detail. He shouldn't have expected her to, the signal was poor and it made conversation difficult.

But the brief and businesslike tone of the exchange only made room for his worst fears to propagate, and he wished that he'd never made the call at all. He glumly handed the phone back to Zoe.

"She's alright. I guess," he said.

Out of range of the others, Zoe leaned over quite close to Hewitt, and said to him. "Ask her out, when we get back. She's been hoping you would for a while now."

At that Hewitt flushed, but didn't look away.

"I should have done."

"Well do it."

"I, I wasn't sure what she would say."

"She might have said 'yes.'"

"Or 'no.' I just didn't want to hear it."

"For goodness sake, Lawrence. You can be so irritating at times."

"I know. That's why I assume that she would have said 'no.'" Zoe wanted to hit him.

"She won't wait around for ever."

"That's what I'm afraid of. She's always liked that French Canadian poser better than me. And now I've blown it. I just know. They'll talk things over and they'll be an item when we get back. You'll see. He might not have wanted her before, but he does now – now he thinks someone else is on the scene."

"I don't think so, Lawrence." But Zoe secretly had been thinking the same thing, and hoped for his sake that he was wrong. ·

Zoe and Oliver retired to their own tent leaving Terry Coulson and Hewitt in the other one. They fitted

438

themselves into their sleeping bags, but sat up propped on their packs for a few moments, glad of some time to be together before they tried to get some sleep. They each clutched a tin cup of high calorie mud that was supposed to taste of chocolate. Zoe could hardly stay awake to drink it. Her legs and back didn't just ache they hurt with the effort that she had put into the climb, and her feet felt tender with the strain of kicking foot-holds in the ice wall as they descended into the Rift.

"What are you thinking?" said Oliver, tentatively sipping the scolding hot chocolate.

"That I'm really enjoying this, whatever it is – it tastes like Maltesers. And I'm thinking about tomorrow. I feel sort of strange about the whole plan."

"How do you mean?" said Oliver. He knew that she had wanted to talk.

"The funny thing is, I think what we're doing will work – I really do. But I am so utterly depressed that our efforts long-term will not amount to a hill of beans. Look at the data that is coming in every year – the Jacob-shavn Isbrae in the South West of Greenland is the larg-est outflow glacier on the continent. It has thinned by fifteen metres per year since 1997, and its flow rate has more than doubled. The Helheim Glacier has thinned by forty metres. As they speed up and dump more ice into the sea the whole melting process is being speeded up and could halve the time we estimated it would take the ice sheet to melt."

"Well all we can do is to try to negate the one fac-tor that could be the amplifier of change that pushes the whole process past its tipping point. If you look at

the whole matrix of events, the volcano is the rogue element that no-one has taken into account. It might not
make any difference long-term what we do tomorrow.
We just don't know. But if the ice sheet south of the
Atlantis Rift slips into the sea on a bed of molten lava,
shaken free by an eruption of Krakatoa-like proportions, it would be as bad for us humans as a meteorite
strike. Simple as that," said Oliver

"I know."

"Our whole field of study, Abrupt Climate Change
teaches us that rapid change in the Earth's climate is
normal, and that what we have experienced in the last
10,000 years is a benign period of human-friendly conditions that have allowed us to progress. We all know
these conditions can't be permanent whatever our input
into the system, but what people are doing now is accelerating change when we need to mitigate it as much
as possible. After all, another 10,000 years of stable
climate is only a blink in the geological timescale, but
think of the effect it could have on human culture and
achievement – where we could be in 10,000 years time."

"We live in a Golden Age – if only people would
realise it," Zoe said. "Climate over the last century has
been very stable compared to any other age we have
records for. And particularly the last fifty years – it's no
co-incidence that as a species our rate of progress has
accelerated at this time. It's mind-boggling to think that
we went from the invention of the first basic motor cars
at the turn of the twentieth century and sixty-nine years
later someone landed on the moon. You know, I've
often thought that if we studied the history of another,

imaginary, way-distant culture that had developed horse and cart technology, and claimed to have gone on to space travel in a single century, we would never have believed it. You and I wouldn't have, hon, for a start. It would be in the realms of fantasy, like stories of alien abductions or something."

Oliver laughed his agreement.

"Yes absolutely," he said. "We do live in a Golden Age. Our generation – post war – have lived here in the West at time of peace, prosperity and opportunity like there's has never been before. The flowering of Ancient Greek culture with its Philosophy, Drama, Geometry and primitive science was never available to any but an elite, unlike now where education and culture has spread further across society than it's ever done before, and where a culture of tolerance and liberal values has made our society a kinder place to live, for most people, despite what the Daily Mail says."

"Sometimes it all seems so fragile – I dread the thought of a troubled and chaotic future giving back hard-won freedoms to fanatical and elitist groups, who are only interested in their own perpetration and are obsessed with the idea of control and punishment. You still see it, of course, with racist groups, and in people who want to keep women in their place, and who hate gays. Why can't they leave people alone who just want to live their lives and who aren't harming anyone else?"

"Oh, it's that shabby Nazi trick – as Captain Main-waring of *Dad's Army* would say – of forming cohesion within your group by focussing hatred on something outside," said Oliver. "It gives a sense of purpose to people whose beliefs are essentially hollow."

He drained his cup while waiting for Zoe to answer him, but the long silence that followed eventually made him turn his head and see that she had dropped into a depth of sleep that wouldn't have been disturbed even if the volcano had erupted then and there. He tucked her hands into the warmth of the sleeping bag, and kissed her goodnight before turning over and sinking into an abyss of his own.

In the other tent, tired as he was, Terry couldn't drop off as he had something on his mind.

"Hey, Lawrence, man – you still awake," said Terry. He was, and he grunted back irritably. He'd just settled down into a comfortable pre-sleep state where he could think his thoughts in peace and he didn't appreciate them being interrupted.

"What do you want?"

"I've been going over wiring up the explosives in my head, ready for tomorrow. I wanted to be prepared – but I keep getting confused. I've done it dozens of times before – can't understand it. It's been a few years but I didn't think I'd forget a thing like that."

"What! You can't be serious! Just don't tell me we've come all the way out here for nothing. Well if it doesn't go off we have to rewire it, then. I guess. Anyway, you've got a manual, I remember looking through it back at Phil's house..." At the mention of Becaud's name Hewitt became sullen again and lost his thread.

"I didn't bring it," said Terry, owning up to what was on his mind.

"You didn't bring it?" said Hewitt. "Why the hell not! Shit! How could you forget a thing like that?"

"I didn't forget it. I didn't think I'd need it. I had too much stuff in my pack as it was." Expletives raced through Hewitt's mind, but all he could do was groan.

"I don't believe I'm hearing this. You stupid bloody idiot!" he said at last.

"Will you tell Zoe for me in the morning. I can't face her."

"No I bloody well won't!" said Hewitt, while already framing in his mind how he was going to break it to her.

He turned his back on Coulson and angrily burrowed his head into the hood of his sleeping bag not wanting to talk any more, and for the first time seriously contemplating that their expedition was about to end in total failure.

It was too much to bear. That all this planning and sheer hard graft could be scuppered by the omission of a trivial detail like a missing manual. Maybe Gilmore could help them - if they could get through to him. It was like being back in the 1920's as far as communications was concerned, they were still so unreliable. Too tired to hold on to his anger any longer, his peace of mind and therefore his chance to rest easy had gone. Hewitt decided there was nothing he could do about the problem till the morning anyway, so he put it out of his mind, resigning himself to a much needed but restless night's sleep.

CHAPTER TWENTY-SIX

It was a lousy morning in Plato Camp, bitingly cold, and full of wind and snow which now lay in a thick layer on the side of the tents sticking out from the cave. With the forethought of experience, their packs and equipment had been tucked under the icy overhang, keeping them dry and free from the mounting drifts, now collecting in corners, and against the sides of the shelter. The wind was roaring through the narrow valley walls, sometimes in big billowy waves of air that seemed to fill the whole Rift with noise, sometimes with mean snatchy gusts that tugged at the flimsy tents till the thin ropes strained at their anchor points. The depression which had brought with it the downturn in the weather looked set to be around for a few days, too, just at the time when they least needed another problem to deal with.

It was imperative that they lay the charges today. Then start to head out as quickly as possible. The journey back was bound to take longer than the descent, and already, supplies were starting to look a bit thin.

Hewitt, first up, made ready to tell Zoe that Terry Coulson had forgotten how to wire up the charges and had then decided not to bring the manual. At the moment he was still thinking that there must be a way out of the problem, and that Coulson would be fine once he started the process. Sleeping on the dilemma had indeed given him a new perspective on the problem. He woke up feeling that there had to be a solution; it was just a matter of finding it. It would all come back to him. Or he'd work it out by trial and error.

His first task was to set up the stove in the shelter of the ice-cave mouth and put some packed snow in the pan ready for the first brew of the day. The white fat flakes swirled past the shallow cave entrance, blowing in all directions at once. He was out of the brunt of the storm but the wind blew into where he was squatting down, buffeting around him uncomfortably. It took him two or three goes to light the burner, as the wind played tricks on his attempt to shelter it. Once it was going it stayed alight, although the flame dipped and leaned precariously in the draught, and looked, more than once, as if it was going to go out. The little gas flame soon worked its alchemy on the packed ice, and in no time at all the steaming pan indicated that the water was ready. Hewitt dropped in a couple of tea bags, and bang on cue he heard the sound of zips ripping open and the figures of Zoe and Oliver appearing, ready to join him.

"Zoe, I need to speak to you," said Hewitt, his serious tone engaging both their attentions almost as much as the unfamiliar sound of her name coming from his lips.

"Why, whatever's the matter, Lawrence? By the look on your face I don't think I'm going to like the sound of this."

"No. I don't think you are."

"Well get on with it man," said Oliver.

Hewitt explained the situation as matter-of-factly as he could whilst seeing the look of growing disbelief reflected back at him from Zoe and Oliver's faces. They kept looking over at the tent where Terry was still skulking as though that might give them some clue as to how this could have happened. For a while no-one spoke as thoughts raced around, from one to the other, trying to work out a solution.

"At least he could come out and bloody well face us," said Oliver.

And Terry must have heard him because a few minutes later a shamefaced figure could be seen emerging from his tent, bracing himself for the condemnation that he knew was coming his way.

"Terry, we've risked our lives coming here to get this job done. The whole point of you coming here with us is that you had the skills that we lacked. What the hell do we do now?" said Zoe.

She was thinking back to the incident in the car park, and knew that everyone else was doing the same. With a cutting insight Zoe suddenly thought that it was they themselves, after all, who had the poor judgement in inviting him along knowing what he was like. They had to shoulder some of the responsibility for this mess.

She said as much to her husband. Hewitt, though, had no time for going over old ground, and blaming each other instead of the real culprit.

"Oh give it a rest, Zoe!" He must be even more tetchy than usual she thought. That was the second time he'd addressed her directly. "Stop blaming yourself for someone else's cock-up. He's loused up. Let him take it on the chin, and let's find a solution, or we'll be here all day."

Chastened, but swallowing her irritation, she turned to her husband with a suggestion.

"Oliver – you are pretty good with electronics. Do you think that you and Terry between you can make this work?"

Oliver shrugged.

"I could in time, I dare say. Trouble is time is what we're short of. And if we get it wrong we can't climb down for another go. It's too risky."

"Well what then? What do we do?"

They stood there wordless for a few more minutes, the wind rising all the time, only adding to their sense of haste.

"Lawrence?" He jumped at the directness of the address, wondering what was going to be asked of him.

"Lawrence. You said that you had flicked through the manual yourself, before we set out, didn't you?"

"Yes, I did. Briefly."

"Well can you remember the wiring diagrams?" Hewitt suddenly knew what was being expected of him.

"I can. Some of them. But there were so many pages. How do I know which one is the relevant one? I've a good visual memory. I'm not superman."

"Can you help him to recall the relevant details, Terry? Come on Lawrence. At least give it a go. You can do it – I know you can. You've got to – otherwise this whole thing is going to end in failure...."

"Look, steady on. Don't now lay this thing on me. It's not my bloody fault this is all going wrong....I'll do what I can."

"I know. I'm sorry Lawrence," Zoe bit her lip, but she could see that she'd offended him by seeming to pick on him, unjustly. Served him right for being so stroppy a moment ago. He turned abruptly away from her and headed back to his tent, where he dipped down and disappeared inside it.

"This is all my fault," said Coulson.

"We know," said Zoe, heavily, emphasising the obviousness of what he had just said. If he was playing the victim to get some sympathy, she was having none of it. "Why don't you just piss off while we get some breakfast ready? Go and help Lawrence or something. Whatever your excuses are, I don't want to hear them." Oliver was impressed. She rarely got angry, but when she did, she really meant it.

Terry followed Hewitt to the tent, crawled inside it and sat down beside him ready to help in whatever way he could.

"I'm pretty sure the page we need is a bit dog-eared – you know there is a crease in the top corner, where I used to constantly refer to it. The only thing is I don't know is if that's the only one with a down turn. Is that any help?"

"Yes it might be...let me think." Hewitt closed his eyes, and tried hard to concentrate on the booklet as

449

he flicked through it that day back at Becaud's house. He could remember the blue cover, and the coffee ring on the front of it. He relived the process of turning the pages, seeing each one in front of his mind's eye as he did so. It was hard work, and every few seconds he felt his concentration go, whereupon, he had to gather his thoughts and reapply his attention to each page. Trouble was, he was tired, cold and hungry, and it was affecting his ability to focus properly.

The door of the tent suddenly opened up from the outside, and a fur-edged hood poked its way through the gap, as Zoe crawled in and rolled on to a sitting position, next to Hewitt. She had brought in the breakfasts which were steaming temptingly, filling the tent with the warm smell of hot oats. She gave him a mess tin full of porridge and kept one for herself. Terry wondered unhappily if he was going to have to get his own food, as some sort of punishment, but when Oliver came in a second or two later, he'd got two more breakfasts in his hands and he gave one of them to Coulson. They were all identical in size. Oliver Carter was not one to be petty. Terry took a mouthful of the hot cereal gratefully, thinking that there was a littleness about some people that was wholly absent from Oliver's make up; it was probably the thing that Zoe loved best about him.

"How's it going?" said Oliver to Hewitt.

"Don't know. It's not easy," said Hewitt.

Breakfast was eaten in a respectful silence, everyone aware that he was trying to concentrate as best he could.

"We'll leave you alone then. Come on Zo. We'll pack up and get ready to leave while these two try to sort something out."

Oliver gathered up the empties and gestured with a tilt of his head to his wife that they should get going. She nodded back and followed him on all fours out of the tent and into the rising wind. They stood up straight, once they were outside, and were alarmed at how much the weather had deteriorated. Visibility was down to twenty-five metres and the snow was accumulating thickly on the route they were going to be taking down to the rock face of the volcano. Oliver shouted to make himself heard above the driving gale.

"There's no way we can go if this doesn't ease off!"

"There's no way we can stay here! This isn't like an expedition where you can turn back if things go wrong – we have to go through with this now we are here – no matter what," Zoe said.

"But there's no point in us getting ourselves killed – that won't get any charges laid and divert any lava flows – we'd be better waiting a few hours, or even a day or two, and get it done properly."

"I don't think we have the time to wait a day or two."

"You don't?"

"No." Zoe shook her head.

"What do you mean, hon?" Oliver waited for her answer.

"The tremors are definitely getting worse. It goes completely still for a while, then when the quakes return they are stronger all the time I don't know which is worse – when things go quiet or when they start up again. There's low level noise coming from deep inside the earth all the time. And slight feelings of disorientation or giddiness two or three times an hour now. Last night I woke up repeatedly as really quite strong vibrations passed through at least four or five times. A couple of times I woke up, my heart racing, remembering we were sleeping on a ledge. And I was so tired last night it would have taken a lot to get through to me. I don't think we've got much time before there is a major eruption."

Oliver mulled over what she had just said. The trouble was they had absolutely no way of knowing when an eruption would happen, if it did at all. It could be now. It could be in six weeks. But she was right about the tremors; they were definitely getting worse. So they packed up the equipment they needed for the last leg of their journey, and hoped that in the meantime Hewitt could remember the vital information, they so desperately needed.

* * *

Amy, meanwhile had been pouring out her heart to Phil Becaud, back at base camp. Phil was trying to hide behind his book as she talked to its cover, as she was trying to explain why she felt the way she did, and he so desperately didn't want to hear it.

"You might find this strange, Phil, but we do have a lot in common, me and Lawrence. When we talk about – stuff – we agree on most things, and I, like him, need to talk about interesting things – my work, issues the arts, the news, politics, anything. I've never been one for idle gossip, and neither has he. He hates small talk and just can't be bothered with the trivial."

"What's politics if it's not gossip on a big scale?" said Becaud, dismissively.

"Well, OK, maybe not politics," she said. She was impressed. She'd never heard Phil be so insightful before. "The trouble is, he is really a very closed down person. He seems very lonely, both physically and emotionally, and he finds it hard to break out. But that's with good reason, believe me. I feel that I'm trying to give something into this relationship, such as it is at the moment – but I get nothing back. I think that to thrive, relationships need to be nurtured, tended, a bit like a garden, and he seems either unable or unwilling to do that."

"Has he asked you out yet?"

"No."

"Then in what sense of the word is this a relationship?"

Amy couldn't answer. She realised that she was jumping the gun, and she didn't know why this was spilling out to Becaud of all people. Did she just need to talk? Or was she justifying her actions to Becaud so that he'd understand.

"You're flogging a dead horse, honey." Becaud didn't look up.

"But I definitely think there is something between us. And I think he wants us to get together. I just don't know if I could be happy with him. He can be totally intransigent at times, even if it means hurting other people. He's very principled, I think, which means he finds it hard to compromise, but isn't that a good thing?

"No, not really. He just seems to make up his mind about things then expect everyone else to lump it."

"But isn't it good to stick to what you think is right?"

"Sure.... sometimes. It depends. It can also be a form of self-indulgence. It's certainly very self-centred. The whole basis of a relationship is that you have to think as a couple and not as an individual, which means that sometimes you have to take into account how other people are affected by what you do. Sometimes you have to be pragmatic and compromise. My dad was the self-righteous type. Sometimes it's better to be kind."

"And what if you can't be pragmatic?"

"Then either you surround yourself by people who agree with you, so you are never challenged, or you turn into a lonely old loser like him."

"Phil! That's enough! You're very hard on him."

"No. Just realistic. You would be wasted on him."

"I agree he can be hard work."

"Then marry me instead, honey. We could have a great time. We could fly into the sunset and never look back."

His tone was jokey, but Amy knew that he meant what he said. She felt her heart quicken. She still found him very attractive.

"I think you're married to that plane of yours, Phil – I can't see you settling down. You like your freedom too much," she said. Her tone was bright, but she was totally sincere in what she said.

"Yeah. I guess you're right there. Can't you see yourself sharing that with me?"

"It wouldn't be sharing that with you, Phil. It would just be fitting in around you. I think I would lose myself....I want to marry a man, not his lifestyle."

"It's a great lifestyle, though, baby. More fun than spending your life trying to cheer up that miserable, no-hoper...."

"Phil!"

"OK! OK! But if he doesn't get around to asking you for a date, you know where I'll be, and the offer still stands."

Amy was touched by what he said, and she looked at him for several long seconds as he continued to read his book. For so long she had flirted with him, desperately hoping that he would notice her. Now he wanted to marry her. Was she mad not to accept him? But she was old enough to know that having a crush on someone wasn't enough to make a relationship work. He looked up and caught her eye. She leaned over and kissed him on the mouth. He responded and kissed her back, not with passion, but with sadness, as though he knew it was for the last time.

* * *

Hewitt knew at once when he had found the right page. It was there in his mind's eye, right in front of him. All he had to do right now was to try to download the information to Terry Coulson who was sitting patiently beside him. Trouble was it was not as easy for him as everyone else seemed to think it was. His memory was phenomenal in the short term – he could see a whole page in front of him just after he had read it. But this was some days after, and the image just didn't stay around for that long. He could recall a diagram, which he drew for Terry to interpret. But the writing didn't mean anything anymore. It was a complicated diagram, using a mobile phone to detonate the charges. Hewitt got out his own mobile and showed it to Terry.

"This isn't going to work," said Hewitt.

"Why not?" said Terry. I think I've got enough here to go on."

"No signal," said Hewitt, who always seemed to be the bringer of bad news. "We're too deep. You will have to do it the more conventional way by an electrical current. I think I remember seeing that. I'll just go through it again."

He concentrated for a few more minutes, then said that he thought that he'd got the relevant diagrams. Quickly he sketched them down while he still could and gave the paper to Terry.

"It's the best I can do. The more I focus on it the more it's fading out now. I'm shot."

"That's OK. This is the easier method, anyway. I should be able to make this work from what you've given me."

"You'd bloody well better do," said Hewitt.

"You guys ready?" said Zoe, shouting from outside the thin tent wall. "We need to get going. It's stopped snowing for the moment, and the wind at least isn't getting any worse."

"OK, we're as ready as we'll ever be."

They both emerged from the tent, Terry stuffing the dog-eared scraps of paper with the pencil sketches on them into his pocket, as he got to his feet and pulled up his hood against the wind. Zoe came up close to them so that she could make herself heard and got to the point at once.

"It's going to be a tough day – much worse than yesterday even though the distance that we need to cover is less. The wind and snow are going to be very tiring, and by the looks of it there is more actual climbing for the first leg, until we get to the exposed section of the volcano wall which looks walkable. But I suggest we stick to the hour on, ten off routine as far as conditions will allow, and just hope that this slight easing off of the weather lasts a while. OK with that everybody?"

They all nodded, now keen to begin. They pulled on their outer gloves and zipped up their parkas as far as they would go. They hauled their packs onto their backs, each one also dragging some boxes of explosives to add to their burden. Zoe's pack was lighter than the others but she still had to carry her share, which she was happy to do. They adjusted each other's packs and did a last minute check of equipment and supplies, then with no other reason for delay Zoe took the first step towards the edge of their little plateau, and began the slow descent towards the Rift's base. She clambered down for about thirty to forty metres until it became too steep to continue and she began to hammer in the pitons and thread the rope through. She lowered herself down carefully choosing her movements so that each one could be reversed if she had to. That way she could always go back and start again if she reached an impasse. The thing was never to do a series of moves where you found you could no longer move either forward or back. She was used to the series of patterns in her head that enabled her to do that, but it took a lot of concentration, and she was constantly aware that she was going to have to think for the others too. She reached a point where she could reasonably stop, then beckoned for the others to begin their stint. They did their best but they were clumsy and hesitant, and it seemed to take them forever. She called out instructions as tentatively they made their way down the snowy wall of the Rift. It was slow, but as each one made their way down she could see a learning process taking shape, and gradually their confidence grew, as they relaxed into their task and became absorbed by it. They were lucky it was fairly basic stuff. Zoe was constantly aware that if they'd had any really challenging climbs, she knew that the others would never have been able to deal with them.

She pressed on relentlessly, only resting for the required breaks, and not stopping for long enough to allow lethargy to creep in and destroy everyone's motivation. She became very focussed on the present, not enlarging the task she had to do by seeing too much of it at once. That way time faded into the background and the pressures it brought with it faded too. Then after about five hours steady progress, her boot felt something unfamiliar as it reached out for the next step, and crunched on a rocky gritty surface instead of the ice it had become used to. She looked down and saw the unusual sight of warm brown rock below her instead of the packed snow that she had felt before. At last there was a surface that she could stand on, and with huge relief she called out to the struggling novices behind her that had reached the easy stage and could now at least proceed on foot.

When one by one they stepped off the ice wall and onto the rocky slope. The relief was visible in everyone's eyes.

They dropped down onto the ground, slipping off their burdensome packs as they did so, and revelled in their opportunity to rest and enjoy their sense of achievement.

Someone brewed up some tea, and rations were handed round. They ate in silence, as people who are really hungry often do, and in a few moments it was all gone. Terry nudged Oliver who looked over to where his wife was propped up against her pack. She was fast asleep. The others left her to it. She deserved it the way she had got them all this far.

Now that they were down on the rocky slopes near the base of the Rift, they could see pretty well exactly where they needed to be headed. A flow of lava was leaching out of a fissure in the volcano wall and trickling along the valley bottom, beneath a snake of steam rising up from it, till it ground to a halt as it cooled, they guessed about a kilometre away. This was forming a damn of solidified lava which was causing a build up of molten rock behind it. The lava was then being forced to spread outwards, which was presumably why it was

leeching under the ice sheet and causing it to destabilise. And this was only the fissure that they could see.
There could be hundreds more doing the same thing,
deep below the surface.

The sight was spectacular, and Hewitt busied
himself by taking photographs and a video of their
progress to send back to Dorothy Redmires' website.
He got some general panoramic views for reference,
and also managed to get some interesting shots that he
thought would make good pictures in their own right.
Including Zoe slumped over her rucksack, dead to the
world.

But after ten solid minutes of oblivion, Zoe surfaced, instantly awake and talking as though she had
never been away. She was now keen to get going, and
didn't appreciate being told that they had all been waiting for her. Which was blatantly untrue anyway. She
was alert, and felt totally refreshed by the short sleep.
She got to her feet and looked around her.

"There's something wrong," she said, flatly. The
other three looked at her. They'd been in jovial mood
to know that they were on the last leg, and so close
to completing their task. Now they'd come this far the
whole thing seemed more doable and they couldn't wait
to press ahead. What now?

She looked around again as though for inspiration,
but couldn't articulate what had been nagging at her.
It was as though something had occurred to her during her nap, and like a dream that slips away, she just
couldn't bring it back.

"I don't know."

"Oh come on," said Oliver testily. "We were all feeling really positive. Talk about dampening the mood."

He clearly had no time for anyone imagining potential problems, so Zoe bit her lip and said nothing else. They hitched up their packs and once more made ready to move on, Hewitt pointing to the sky, as it changed from mid to dark grey and was thickening fast.

"This section looks pretty easy after what we've just done," he said. "But it might not seem so if it snows heavily again. We could easily take the wrong direction if visibility goes right down."

They set off in single file. This time Oliver at the front, followed by Terry and Hewitt at the rear. The slope was about thirty-five degrees on average, in places, much steeper, and going downhill they made good progress, especially at first, until their shin muscles started to complain. The weather continued to close in, creating a light that seemed more like dusk, than the endless summer light that they had become used to. Zoe walked with her head down, eyes focussed on the rock in front of her feet. It felt good to walk with some speed and fall into a natural rhythm, but then gradually she became aware of something strange on the grey-brown slopes either side and in front of her boots. There were dark spots multiplying all around her, and a new smell that she hadn't experienced since they arrived in Greenland.

It was raining.

A blue white light flickered around the whole of the inside of the Rift, followed in a second by a deafening high pitched crack of thunder, which tumbled and rolled around the enclosed space of the deep valley. Terry Coulson hit the ground instantly and lay there with his hands over his head. He'd not been struck, but he'd been near enough to the grounding to feel the pressure wave knock him off balance and he'd instinctively taken cover. The others looked on at him thinking they should have been alert enough to have done the same, but now it seemed too late to do anything but stand there and help him up.

"You OK?" said Zoe.

"Yeah. Sorry. Thought it was the volcano going. Thought we'd had it there for a minute."

He dusted himself off, and as he did so the clouds let go their burden and the rain came down in torrents, the dark spots of a minute ago now all joined up, the whole of the rock surface shiny and wet, and already channelling tiny rivulets of water down into the valley bottom. Underfoot it became slippery and treacherous, the driving rain beat into their faces and ran off their clothes. And they had begun to experience another sensation. As they retreated into their anorak hoods to keep dry, they felt too warm. Dressed against snow and sudden Arctic gales, they were now in a pocket of warm air, heated by the lava and rising in upward currents, which hit the cold, snow-bearing clouds above. The warmer air could absorb more moisture than cold air, and so the heavy-laden clouds had begun to rain.

Zoe looked through the driving rods of water as it splashed and hissed around her, now gathering into larger streams and cascading down the rock forming cataracts on the jutting ledges and pools wherever there were depressions in the smooth surface. She recalled the geological timeline in her head. The first ice sheet would have been formed here about three million years ago, ushering in the beginning of the cycle of regular ice ages and inter-glacials, where early species of man like Australopithecus were trying to survive, by hunting and scavenging. Here, where the ice sheet was two kilometres thick, in the interior of the Greenland continent, it had not disappeared, entirely, even in the warm periods of prehistory, so now was the first time in three million years that this rock had felt rain on its face. It felt like being witness to an awakening. It was hard not to feel instinctively optimistic. The image of a sleeping desert brought to fecundity by the kiss of rain causing it to bloom was utterly compelling, and Zoe had to remind herself that this was a beauty that was best left to slumber undisturbed.

They reached the bottom of the Rift late in the day, their dripping clothes now steaming in the warm air as they were next to the lava flow leaching steadily out of the wall of the straining caldera. The rain had stopped but the liquid water hung around in pools in the valley bottom and a tiny river had begun to form and make its way along the length of the Rift, eventually pouring out to the sea. Mist was gathering in slow, white swirls above the water, filling the deep chasm with an other-worldly atmosphere, quiet and eerie, with nothing but their scraping footfalls to be heard, anywhere. The reduced visibility created a disturbing feeling of claustrophobia, as the only vista they now had was up above them. The walls towered against the sky, now blue against the white sides of the Rift. Inadvertently, Hewitt looked up and staggered as he felt a slight wave of panic hit him at the realisation of how far they had travelled down. He remembered the first time they had spotted it from the Cessna, when they'd thought of it as a mere curiosity, only weeks ago. And now he was standing at its depth, feeling as though the Earth had engulfed him, and was about to close up around him at any time.

"It's OK," said Zoe. "Looking up can be as bad as looking down."

"I can't see how we're going to get back," said Hewitt.

"We'll be OK," Zoe said, but actually she agreed with him.

She was feeling deeply uneasy too, and not just about the return journey. The feeling that they were at the base of an active and erupting volcano, and could be swallowed up in a lava flow or blown away in an explosion, at times terrified her, and at other times seemed so unreal as to disappear from her thoughts altogether. Right now she was terrified, and all she wanted to do was to get the job done and get out as quickly as possible. She'd tried to comfort Hewitt, but really she needed that reassurance herself. Better put on a brave face. Didn't want anyone losing their nerve now.

They reached a point where they felt they could stop, and immediately they slung their packs on the ground, pleased to be without their constant burden for a little while. The next thing they all did was to undo their anoraks and peel them off as quickly as they could. This was followed by their outer fleeces. Oliver was about to take off his thin, shell fleece when Terry Coulson stepped in and advised him not to. They had all been sweating under their heavy Arctic gear, and there was the risk that they could cool off too rapidly. He suggested that they all rest and reacclimatise, dry out their heavy outer garments and then see how they go from there. It was sound advice, but very frustrating, as the unaccustomed warmth was making them tired.

"Time for some refreshment," said Zoe brightly, looking at Oliver and hoping that he would get up and fix them something. But he didn't move, and when she looked again more closely, she could see that he was absolutely done in. With the insight and experience of someone who had lived with another person for a long time, she got up and left him to rest a little longer.

This was the balance in their relationship that had made it work so well. Recognising a need, and responding to it, or knowing when you've reached your personal limit and taking something back when you need to. This was the hub that they orbited around, the quiet centre that kept them grounded. Dependence, dominance, neediness and caring were all be present in their relationship, yet none of those things were owned by one person all of the time, but shared according to time and circumstance. That way it remained a relationship, and not just a role to play.

Zoe fished the stove out from the pack of supplies, and began to fill the kettle – with water, not snow. Terry lit the stove and Hewitt chose some packs of food and tipped them into the mess tins in preparation for the boiling water when it was ready. Zoe made some tea first and put an extra sugar in Oliver's, which she handed to him. He accepted it gratefully and took a drink straightaway. She then refilled the kettle and set it back on the stove. The pasta when it was reconstituted looked so disappointing that Zoe decided that now was the time to share out a piece of the salami. It was chewy and deeply savoury after so much sweet food, and with lots of fat to make it succulent and to give them some energy.

"Any chance of a beer!" said Oliver, rallying. "I could just drink a pint, right now."

"So could I mate," said Terry. He now felt he was back in the fold enough to join in with the banter, and hoped to redeem himself fully by getting the job in hand done as soon as possible. "If we pull this off it's drinks all round when we get back."

"I'll hold you to that," said Hewitt, also joining in. Terry stood up.

"I'm going down to do a reccy," he said, casually. "I'll be back in a while – half an hour or so I guess. Then we'll get cracking."

He had taken them all a bit by surprise. They'd been thinking about this task for so long the reality of it still seemed some way in the future. They were finding it hard to adjust to the here and now. Daunted by the enormity of what they were taking on, they'd all hoped to put it off for another day, and were shocked that Terry was intending to work through instead of sleeping first and carrying out the blast in the morning.

"I know we're all tired. But we have to press on."

"I thought we'd try to get about four hours sleep and then begin," said Oliver.

"Why waste time? We need to keep going. We don't know how long we've got before this thing erupts," said Terry.

None of them wanted to agree with him, but they all had to admit he had a point. And instinctively they all looked towards the rocky wall of the caldera, as if to reassure themselves that it was still OK for the moment. Zoe then had a thought occur to her, in a flash of recognition that made her wonder why she hadn't twigged it before.

"I know what's wrong," said Zoe. "You know I said before that I thought that something was seemed strange, but I didn't know what. Well I now realise what it was that was bugging me."

"I thought you meant the rain," said Oliver

"I did too," said Hewitt."

"No, that was just co-incidence," said Zoe. "It wasn't the rain. I'd got used to the noises, the creaks and groans in the ice sheet. And while I was asleep I must have been aware that it had gone completely quiet again. It's like that now. Totally quiet. It has been like that for about some hours now. Not a rumble."

"She's right," said Hewitt.

They sat in silence for a full minute. There was not a sound anywhere. The cries and moans from deep inside the Earth that had been so frightening when they first occurred were now causing more concern by their absence.

"Shit, you know what this means," said Hewitt. "It's the calm before the storm. The tectonic plates are straining, and could flip at any time. Or the pressure is building inside the volcano, ready to go when it can't hold it any longer..."

"OK, Lawrence. We get the picture," said Oliver.

"So I am going to get started on my reccy. We get wired up and we get the fuck out of here as soon as possible. OK?" Terry got up.

It was OK. Nobody was prepared to argue with him now.

CHAPTER TWENTY-SEVEN

Terry Coulson's forehead glistened with droplets of sweat as he hammered away at the rock face. He was as close as he could get to the long, thin sliver of an opening in the caldera. Lava was leaching out and solidifying as it hit the cooler air, like a wound seeping and scabbing over, but never properly healing. It was now Terry's job to lance the boil. He was doing well. He'd always worked well in the heat. His training in Belize and his stint in the bandit country of the Stans had prepared him perfectly for this. He was stripped down to his thin sleeveless under vest and trousers, as were all the others, their thick four season outer garments all stored carefully in a sheltered spot near to where they were working. It felt great to be out of all of the layers of clothes that they'd needed up till now, and to feel some warmth on their skin again.

The Rift bottom was a trap for the warm air heated by the lava, creating a microclimate of dripping meltwater that turned to mist as it drifted too close the molten rock.

Terry had marked out the positions on the rock face where he thought the charges should go, and Zoe, Oliver and Lawrence Hewitt were all clanging away at the stone in an effort to get the job done as quickly as possible. The rock itself was quite sandy and therefore not too hard to knock a hole in, but Terry was working perilously close to the lava flow, making the conditions for him very difficult. He was leaning over at an angle to reach the spot where his charge was to go which was hard work in itself. He could hardly get a purchase on the rock, or get enough power behind the hammer blows to get his task done quickly. Hot with the effort he scrunched up the front of his vest to wipe his face, then immediately got back to what he was doing.

"I'm done here!" said Oliver slipping his tube of explosive in the hole he had just made, and finding that it was deep enough.

"Well done, that man!" said Terry. "Go and help the others. We need to crack on." Oliver went over straightaway to help Zoe with her charge, but she was already done and was just sliding the explosive into the waiting sleeve. Oliver helped her to pack it, then they too were ready.

"Can someone fetch me some water?" said Terry, stopping again for a moment's respite.

Zoe got him some straightaway, while Oliver went over to help Hewitt finish off setting his explosive in its allotted place.

When Zoe got over to Terry she was taken aback as he turned towards her and she could see his face properly. He was bright red and running with sweat. At first she assumed it was with the effort, but on closer inspection she realised that his face looked burnt. His lips were slightly blistered, and she could smell an unpleasant whiff of singed hair. He took her offer of water without further comment and downed it in one go, not pausing again until the job was done and the last of the charges was in place.

He then started on the wiring. The others left him to it, as they could see he did not want to be disturbed. Constantly referring to Hewitt's sketchy diagram his deft, patient fingers screwed the detonators into place. Concentrating hard and ignoring the beads of sweat that were gathering on the tip of his nose, he didn't look up until he was satisfied that the job was done, and done properly. The wires coiled and bounced without tangling as he fed them through his fingers with a delicacy that seemed impossible for his big hands. He made the last connection to the main fuse, without fuss or comment, simply announcing to the waiting group that his task was done by standing up and wiping his hands on his trousers. They stood for a moment waiting for him to say something, but when he didn't Zoe decided to be practical by handing him a screwed up tee-shirt for him to wipe his face and body on, which he did gratefully. They don't know how he did it – keeping going in that heat. They hadn't done half as much, and they were utterly exhausted. Oliver handed him some more water, which he drank more slowly this time, now aware of his sore and cracked lips.

"We'll make a brew," said Zoe, "I think we all need to rest."

"No time for resting I'm afraid," said Terry. "We can have a drink, but then we head out."

"You can't go like that," said Oliver. "As soon as we get away from this molten rock we are in Arctic temperatures once more. You could get hypothermic in no time. You have to dry off and cool down a little first."

Oliver got up and picked up the tee-shirt, and began rubbing down Terry's back to help him to dry off, like a second fussing over a boxer between rounds. Hewitt, trying to be helpful found a dry top in the pack and brought it over for him to change into. Oliver had worked his way round to Terry's chest and tried to dry him there too, but Terry winced as the cloth touched his red, burnt skin, and just said gently, "Leave it, mate. I'll be OK." Oliver deferred to his instruction, but was concerned by the state of him. How he was going to cope with carrying a pack, Oliver just didn't know.

They handed him his tea, and then Oliver brought one of the rucksacks over, got some something for burns out of the first aid kit, which he then diligently applied to all the affected skin on Terry's arms chest and face. They gave him a couple of painkillers, and Hewitt helped him on with his dry clothes.

Ten minutes later the rucksack was repacked. Tiredness didn't matter any more. They were all ready to go. The bottom of the Rift was now filled with a silence that was getting unbearable, having the signs of danger written all over it. Even Zoe, who could have spent the next year at the bottom of the ice sheet taking samples of rock and ice cores, knowing that there would be enough information lying here to fuel a lifetime of study, couldn't wait to get out. The oppressiveness of being surrounded by so much raw, explosive power, made her feel one moment panicked, and the next blasé, as the danger seemed so great as to be unreal. A tightrope walk of overconfidence where one part of her mind was accommodating the situation, and sheer terror at the thought of being engulfed by a wall of molten rock, was getting too much to bear. The adrenaline was building, and she needed to take flight.

And then like a dam bursting, as though the silence couldn't take the strain any longer, a deep grating moan welled up from deep underground filling the valley with menace, and sending a shock wave like electricity through the four anxious figures. It was a terrible sound, coming from a place so deep it was beyond their experience. It was impossible to say what it sounded like, because it didn't sound like anything they had ever heard before, and so loud it filled the Rift with its presence. It seemed as though their flimsy human world was being greyed out, to be replaced by forces that played out on a planetary scale. The dumb Earth, indifferent to our presence moved and groaned as it would.

Zoe, alert with fear, thoughts racing, understood in one moment and with total clarity the futility of human pleading.

Like ants in a rainstorm one could be swept away by the blind indifference of the forces of nature, together with one's fragile hopes, needs and aspirations. Zoe felt humbled. But with humility came a glimmer of pride. Pride in human achievement that gave one the chance to make a difference. To use the knowledge that had been accumulated to help ourselves and protect civilisation from the harsh disinterest of the natural world. Zoe thought that if one wants life to be better then we have to accept responsibility for it and do it for ourselves. And what we have no control over, we just have to learn to live with.

"We've got to go!" said Zoe, her eyes wide with fear. She strode out to where their other packs and clothing were being kept. They were tucked into a shallow cave up on the path out of the Rift, to keep safe and dry in case it had rained again. The others didn't need to be told twice, and were already following her to the place where everything was stashed, a short distance away. But as they neared the cave the tremors began, first hardly perceptible, then they became angry and meant business. The hideous noise if anything got even louder. Rocks started falling like hail all around them, and a large crack opened up on the rift floor, swallowing up some of the lava flow, down into the ultimate darkness. Instinctively they crouched down and just had to hope that none of the falling rocks would make a direct hit.

The quake subsided.

They were all OK, but Zoe couldn't see the cave. She darted a glance all around her, then looked to the others for help. They appeared to be just as disoriented as she was. The landscape had changed slightly all around them.

In the distance, a powdery white cloud on the side of the Rift had appeared. No-one could make out what it was until they eventually realised that it was an avalanche of immense proportions. The steep sides of the ice cliff made the gathering speed of the avalanche awesome to watch, followed a couple of seconds later by the dull roar as it grazed and thumped its way down the slopes almost in free fall, until coming to rest at the bottom. They were then hit by a shockingly cold blast of air, sent down the valley bottom by the force of the avalanche. Zoe winced as it struck her, the cold, thin air full of ice dust which was pricking her skin and snatching at her hair. They were still wearing light clothes, and were instantly shivering, in its wake. They needed to find their supplies fast and get out of there. It felt as though the whole world were about to close in on them. If they didn't detonate soon, the volcano would blow first and mitigate all their attempts to avoid disaster. Her heart thumped, partly with the sudden chill that had swept over her, and partly at the thought of lying, trapped underneath two kilometres of broken ice.

Zoe couldn't believe how quickly things had gone wrong. Loosened boulders were still scraping down the exposed rocks where they had worked away from their moorings, bouncing as they fell to the base. It was like being under siege. Dark clouds were gathering high above them getting ready either to snow or rain, no-one could tell which. If they got rained on while they were still lightly dressed, in this cold air it could finish them off, she thought desperately. After all this, and we could be thwarted by a shower of rain. They couldn't let that happen. Not now. They had to find their stuff. Hewitt was the first to spot something.

"Over here!" he said. "Oh my God! Look at this! No!"

Zoe and Oliver followed his gaze, and realised instantly what he had seen, and what it meant. There was a pile of rubble where the shallow cave had once been; and their stuff was all behind it.

"Shit!" said Oliver. "This is all we bloody well need."

"I don't believe this," said Hewitt.

Zoe took a deep breath in as if to say something, but only a sob shuddered out, as she looked helplessly on at the blocked entrance to the cave.

"Oh, stop being such a girl!" said Oliver, not feeling in the mood to hand out sympathy. He needn't have worried. Zoe didn't want any.

"Oh, just fuck off can't you!" she said back at him, needing to hit out at something. Oliver took it on the chin and said nothing. Zoe then went up to the rubble and started pulling at it with her bare hands, to see if she could find a way through to get at any of their supplies.

The others all joined her, grabbing at rocks to loosen some and throw them down the path to roll and gather at random below. They managed to dislodge a few, but the larger ones were too heavy to be shifted even with all of them pulling at once. It was sapping too much of their energy to go on trying, but Zoe had a plan.

She could see a small gap at floor level that if they cleared it of lightweight dust and rubble, she might just be small enough to wriggle through and reach some of their stuff. Worth a go. It was highly perilous for her, but no-one argued, even for form's sake. They scraped at the aperture till it looked big enough for her to try to get inside it, and without any hesitation she fell on hands and knees, then flat on the ground and started to wriggle inside. There was no room to move so she put her hands out ahead of her while the others pushed her along. She was in further than her waist when she thought she could hear a rumble like thunder. Being in an enclosed space, and with her head next to the ground she could now clearly hear the squeaks and cracks coming from the Earth's crust.

No time for panic. Just find the stuff and get out.

Her hands searched around touching only rock and grit, quickly going numb against the stone which had been frozen by an everlasting coldness. Zoe tried to think of her warm garden back home, but she could only smell the cold rock. She so much wanted to be back there. This was a miserable place to die.

Her hand felt something soft. She felt around and got hold of a strap. She pulled as hard as she could, but it wouldn't move. Her deft fingers walked around till the strap became an opening, then they felt inside a bag, clung on to as much as she could get hold of, and gripped it for all she was worth while she shouted at the others to get her out. They pulled her back together with her trophies, which turned out to be some thick fleeces, gloves, and two hats. She went back again and got some slabs of chocolate, a tube of mints and another fleece. The pack itself was trapped under a rock and stood no chance of coming out.

"I'll give it one more go," Zoe said. "The bags were stowed close together. I might be able to find another one."

A rock the size of a football hit the ground not twenty metres from where they were standing, sending shards of shattered stone in their direction.

"OK. But this is one last go. It's too dangerous to stand around here any longer," said Oliver.

Zoe wriggled back into the hole. The others pushing her in as far as they could. She strained and stretched as the empty space around her groping hand, but she couldn't locate the other bags. She moved to the left, rotating her wrist around in one last attempt to find something of value. She touched something. Hooking her little finger into a fold of material, she let the others drag her back out. She didn't dare move her hand in case she lost her precious catch. When the daylight hit her once more, she examined what she had just been so desperate to hold on to. It was a roll containing some thin base layers and some socks. Zoe looked at Oliver, Terry and Hewitt all standing there in silence. What they had now was what they must make do with.

It wasn't enough.

They shared out the clothing so everyone had about the same. The fleeces were thick, heavy gauge ones, but no-one had an outer coat. They layered up with all the garments they had as best they could. Everyone had gloves and the socks would make good glove liners, but they had only two hats between them.

Terry Coulson tied a spare base-layer long sleeved tee around his head, Afghan style. Zoe tied a micro fleece towel around hers, tucking in her shoulder length fair hair for extra protection. They might be OK if the weather stayed good, but if they had wind chill, or particularly rain or snow to wet them though, they wouldn't make it, not once they were out of the warm zone of the Rift.

"So what do we do now?" said Hewitt.

"We head for Plato Camp," said Terry, with the composure of someone who was used to improvising. "We'll be bloody cold by the time we get there. But we'll have shelter, and more supplies."

"Not got any more anoraks though – we had one each and they're stuck behind that rock," said Zoe.

"Well we can't stay here, that's for sure. We have to blow the charges as soon as we get to Plato – we should be far enough away by then – and then we'll have to take it from there."

"We can't do that till we're actually clear of the Rift," said Oliver. "We might be stuck on a ledge which could disintegrate in the blast."

"Well if that happens, it happens. Without a mobile phone signal we have to detonate while we're still in range to do it manually. We're here to defuse the power of that volcano, not to save our own sorry asses."

They were shocked into silence. Terry was used to operations where you had to put the job first, and where the possibility of one's own demise was always a danger. It was a tough call, when you had to face up to it yourself.

They walked the first bit of the journey that had seemed so easy on the way down, but now seemed cripplingly steep on the way back. At least the effort warmed them up. It didn't take long for the warm air to give way to cold, and by the time they reached the icy section they really needed the exercise to keep them going. Terry decided that they must stop now every half hour as they were so fatigued, but then only for five minutes to avoid getting cold.

Zoe went first once they had reached the part of the climb where the pitons and the ropes were still in place. Her head felt tight with the effort now required to keep going, but the constant presence of danger snapping at her heels kept her going one step at a time. It was hard to concentrate, even so, and she kept lapsing into daydreams about her work, where she was slicing up ice cores and labelling them, over and over while her body, now on automatic pilot, pressed on. Hewitt and Oliver were doing pretty well, but they were growing concerned about Terry Coulson, who had gone too quiet. He was in a lot of pain, and was struggling to keep up.

They stopped for another five, and the deliciousness of taking a rest engulfed Zoe, making her treasure every second. The hard part was getting moving again. Taking the first step after a break took an act of will that she didn't know she had. They had to stay disciplined. If they'd delayed moving out they would never have got the energy to try again. As they started up for another half hour of climbing, Zoe had reached a point where she had ceased to think about their destination, now not really believing that their labour would ever end. She was shivering with the cold. Her hands and feet now so numb that she was miserably sure that she was getting frostbite. She rubbed her hands vigorously and flexed her toes as she walked to try to keep them moving, but as each half hour went passed it seemed to do less and less good. Zoe paused to look into the distance to see if they were still on the right path. It seemed like hours had passed. She could make out the churned up snow where they had walked down here. Then she saw something in the distance. It was there, closer than she could have hoped; maybe only about five hundred metres away. It was Plato Camp. The bright tents billowed in the wind, beckoning them onwards for the last leg of this part of their journey. There was a long pause while she got her breath back and waited for them all to catch up. She pointed the camp out to the others. She'd waited as long as possible to tell them, as once the end was in sight, those last few metres could have been overwhelming; when impatience takes over from resignation and every step seems to go on forever. Now clumsy with the numbing cold, the last leg of the journey was incredibly hard going and took longer than any of them thought it would.

When thy arrived at Plato they were nearly spent.

Zoe hoisted her body up onto the ledge very slowly. It was like dragging a dead weight along that didn't belong to her any more. Every limb was heavy, and stiff with cold, and the short-lived ease that had seemed so good – climbing without the encumbrance of outer coats – had soon became a burden in itself as her arms and legs became dull and unresponsive.

Crawling over to the first tent, its bright coloured walls swelling and sagging alternately in the wind, Zoe fumbled with the zip, trying to make fat, useless fingers work on the metal tag. There was the familiar ripping sound as the flap opened, and the closed-in rubbery smell filled her nostrils with the promise of rest and shelter. She almost switched off too soon, sagging down halfway into the tent instead of pushing her way right inside. She wanted to go to sleep more than anything in the world. Two pairs of hands bundled her further inside the tent, where she lay, unmoving, literally too tired to move a muscle.

Oliver and Hewitt more or less fell into the tent when they got there. The cold wrapped around them as soon as the effect of their exertions started to wear off, they felt they were all hypothermic. Oliver ordered everyone to unroll a sleeping bag each and to climb inside, but he realised the futility of telling that to his wife, who was totally out of it. Somehow he and Hewitt rolled her into her bag as best they could, before collapsing themselves from the exertion.

Some time passed. It could have been a minute, or twenty, they couldn't tell, then Zoe said, with her eyes still closed.

"Where's Terry?"

Oliver opened his eyes.

"He was right behind us, he should have been here by now."

But he wasn't.

Zoe sat up. "If he's not here, then he's in trouble. We have to go and get him."

She was still desperately cold and the thought of having to get out of the sleeping bag seemed like pure torture, but they couldn't leave him out there, they had no choice.

They had a drink of water and a few squares of chocolate each. Then Hewitt said, "You're not going anywhere yet, I'll nip outside and take a look."

He made sure that he had his binoculars with him, before shaking off the sleeping bag and going outside. He scanned all around the route they had taken to get up there, but there was no sign of him. Hewitt was consumed with feelings of guilt that they hadn't noticed him not keeping up. Then he saw the distinct figure of Terry Coulson on a step some distance away. He raised the powerful binoculars to his eyes and focussed in him to see what he was doing. He was bent over something in his hands, studying it intently.

Terry had deliberately let the others go on ahead, knowing what he had to do. There was no point in everyone killing themselves. He'd got as high as he could to give himself a fighting chance. He wasn't into being any sort of a martyr. No time for crap like that. Just knew what the job required. He thought of his brother, Ray, trying to get away from that gas cloud. Now it was his turn to go over the top, and face himself. He felt that all the arrows that marked the direction of his life were now converging on this focal point in time, like the lines of perspective joining at the point of infinity. Not destiny, but the matrix of opportunity. He had no sense of vanity, no heroics, no precious self-importance. He just wanted to be of some use. Like all true heroes, he was an ordinary man at heart, with all his many flaws and imperfections, but a man, who, when his time came, was able to rise to the occasion and not flinch. He was scared, yes. But he'd been scared before. Think about that later.

"Te-rry!" said Hewitt, cupping his hands round his mouth and shouting for all he was worth. Hewitt saw him look around.

"Are-you-OK?" he said.

The other man waved his acknowledgement. Hewitt didn't really know what to do. Nobody was up to doubling back. They'd just have to wait for him to catch up, he supposed. He looked again through the glasses. Terry was trying to tell him something. He pointed at the device in his hand then up to where Hewitt was standing and made a cut throat gesture. He then made the OK sign and pointed to the bottom of the Rift, where they had just come from. Hewitt didn't get it. He shouted again.

"Terry! You have to get to the Camp. Come on!" His voice echoed hollowly around the Rift. He didn't know if the other man could make out what he was saying, or whether he could just hear the shout.

He put the glasses to his eyes once more to see Terry held up his outstretched hand and then count down, five-four-three-two-one.....

Now Hewitt twigged straightaway. Terry was going ahead with the detonation. Right now. He was doing it now because if he'd gone up to Plato Camp he would have been out of range. He stayed behind to do that on his own as he didn't want to hold the others up, and risk their lives. He wouldn't make it. He was just too close. Terry knew that, so he'd dropped behind and said nothing. And none of them had noticed till it was too late. Hewitt shouted to his colleagues,

"Oliver! Zoe!"

A series of muffled retorts reached them from deep within the Rift. One after the other the explosives blew, shaking the ground beneath their feet and filling the air with dull, aching booms that just kept on coming.

Terry Coulson counted the blasts out loud as he tried desperately to make his way upwards and to the shelter of Plato before the shockwave hit him. But he only managed a few frantic, scrambled steps before his world dissolved into a whiteout that filled his lungs and his brain, and he wondered why he was floating, when in fact he was falling in an avalanche to the Rift bottom.

Zoe and Oliver, hearing Hewitt's call, were half way out of the tent, when the sound of the blasts drowned out the rest of what Hewitt was trying to say. The noise echoed menacingly round the Rift, creating an awful pause, a void between cause and effect, when for a moment time seemed to be suspended; when the deed was done and there was no going back, but no-one yet knew what the result was going to be. Zoe looked on, suddenly engulfed by a dead fear that they had done the wrong thing, and could be causing more damage than ever by interfering in the natural process. What if their explosion caused the ice sheet to fracture and cascade into the sea? She felt at one with the flawed heroes of the ancient world, guilty of hubris, and waiting to be dashed down, to see all her efforts reduced to vain shards all around her. They drew level with Hewitt who was still looking intently through the binoculars. The booming blasts didn't die away as they has expected the sound to do. Instead the gathering roar became louder, rising from the valley floor like an unstoppable tide of pure energy.

The pressure wave hit them and knocked them down like they were nothing. A cloud of white billowed up from deep beneath them as the sides of the Rift metamorphosed into one giant avalanche of pelting ice and rocks. They didn't bother getting up, expecting at any moment to be dragged down into the broiling abyss. Steam forged its way through the ice clouds and the smell of sulphur permeated the pristine air like something fetid had been disturbed and was contaminating all around it. The ground shook with a force that made them claw at the ground to keep from falling. The quake lasted for four minutes and twenty-eight seconds of vicious turbulence. Zoe, in her terror thought that they had caused the eruption that they had gone to Greenland to avoid, and that their world was caving in around them. This was nemesis. The fate of retributive justice.

There was a huge crack of thunder over their heads, and higher up, part of the Rift wall exploded apart and rained down a cascade of ice and rock where the lightning had struck it. They squeezed under the shelter of the cave while the debris thudded down outside, collapsing one of the tents as it did so. When they could venture out again, Hewitt was desperate to see if he could see any sign of Terry. He strained at the binoculars, trying to work out the spot where he had last seen him, but there were clouds of blowing snow, water vapour, smoke and ash everywhere. It was a scene of utter chaos. Reluctantly Hewitt had to admit that if

Terry had been able to climb to safety after the detonation, he should have been with them by now, or at least in sight. He so hoped that he was wrong, and that any minute he would come crawling into the camp. There was time yet. But Hewitt realised even as he thought it, that he was trying to delay thinking the inevitable.

Part of the ledge that they had all been clinging to had broken away, leaving the collapsed tent perilously close to the edge of the drop. It was too dangerous to try to remove it. Instead, they decided to move the other tent back as far as it would go under the shelter of the cave. Their few, now precious possessions were now stashed inside.

Then Hewitt said, "We might be back in range for a signal here. I'll try to call Base Camp."

"We have to go back for Terry," said Zoe, shaking with both shock and the cold.

"We can't," Hewitt said.

"Why not?"

"I could see no sign of our ropes or pitons. I think they were swept down into the Rift. I can't even recognise the path we took. It's disintegrated in the quake."

"Then he stands no chance of getting up here," said Zoe. "He could be stranded!"

"There was no sign of him," said Hewitt. "Nothing at all. I took a good look."

"He's not coming back, sweetheart," said Oliver gently. There was a long pause. Zoe didn't argue. Her eyes welled up with pain and sorrow. She already knew that he was right. They stood there, trembling for some time before they could tear themselves away and get back inside the tent. Every instinct was telling them to get off the ledge and head out of the Rift as quickly as possible, but even if they'd had the energy to move they couldn't go anywhere without proper clothing. Phil could be waiting for hours or even days before realising that they were in trouble. They had to try to get through to him.

* * *

When Hewitt's voice crackled over the radio in the grounded Cessna, Both Amy and Phil nearly jumped out of their skins.

"Mike-Delta-Tango, are you receiving me?"

They had heard the muffled explosions from where they were encamped, and had felt them, but without knowing if was more quakes or the blast, that they were waiting for. They had been nearly three days without any word from the gang, and they were itching for news.

"This is Mike-Delta-Tango, receiving you. Hey guys. You OK? What's going on out there?"

Phil wanted to ask so many questions he could hardly wait for their answers.

"Phil, listen. We've detonated."

"Jeez!"

"All hell's let loose down there. There are mega-avalanches, rock falls, the lot, so we can't see yet if we've blown a hole in the side of the volcano. We're stuck on a narrow and crumbling ledge – yes we're back at Plato Camp. And we've got some bad news"

Phil didn't pick up on the last bit of what Hewitt was saying, as the line broke up slightly at that point, and he pressed on with his questions.

"Did you get down to the bottom, then?"

"Yeah. Fill you in later. It's like a lost world down there – shirt-sleeve warm, but Phil…"

"Are you all OK. Is everyone in one piece?" said Phil, anxiously. The line wasn't good and they had to keep communication brief.

"No. We've lost Terry."

The starkness of what Hewitt had just said hit Phil like a hammer blow. He didn't know what to say.

"Say again," said the pilot, eventually. Hewitt repeated that Terry was missing and they must assume the worst. He went on with the rest of his message, now hoping that he would take it in.

"Phil. We're trapped down here. On this ledge. We have a tent, but not enough warm clothing. We've lost nearly all our supplies. We're nearly out of food. You have to organise a rescue."

"What do you mean? Can't you climb back up?"

"We have no outdoor clothing – we have to stay here in our sleeping bags or we'll get hypothermia. We've lost everything else – got some chocolate, and a few mints left, that's all. And no climbing gear. It was all swept away."

Amy was listening intently to the conversation, and at that she took the mic from Phil's hand, unable to contain herself any longer.

"Lawrence, it's Amy." He didn't answer straight-away, the sound of her voice was almost too much to bear. "Look. We'll get you out of there." She spoke firmly and with a total calm that she did not feel. "We're onto it already. I'll get a call out to Frank Gilmore. He's backing us now, and I'll contact Dorothy Redmires. If she gets this on her blog, the story will grip the nation, and she'll make sure Gilmore doesn't drag his feet. Just stay put, and don't get disheartened – we'll get you out of there, I promise."

* * *

Frank Gilmore had been at his desk since six o'clock that morning. Cobra had convened, but at the moment was only telling the public that the emergency measures were exercises. If anyone believed that it was only because they wanted to. It was getting around that the government had left London and the public were getting twitchy. Scientists had got a satellite working that could detect an incoming tidal wave, but even that would give them precious little time to do anything about it. People right on the coasts might have five or ten minutes to get a little further in land, but if there was a mega-tsunami, no-one would stand a chance anyway.

The Prime Minister, Ron Bowman, had decamped to Wiltshire, together with the Cabinet, but Gilmore had preferred to stay on in London. His main worry had been his family. He'd wanted them to be nearby, but when their flat on the Thames waterfront suddenly looked too high risk for them to remain in the City, Dorothy Redmires, of all people, had been an absolute brick. She'd insisted on them staying in the cottage she had rented in the Peak District while her own was being repaired. So Gilmore's wife and children had decamped to Derbyshire, taking a load off his mind.

He'd never forget that.

In front of Gilmore, on his desk, was the print-out that had been faxed to him from the seismology people at Isaac Newton. The black line on the graph had shot upwards to a sharp peak at five thirty-two a.m. Dorothy had arranged that for him, so would know immediately what was going on. She'd called him as soon as she heard that they had detected the detonation, and he'd set off straightaway for his office as soon as he got the news.

He had been expecting the call that Amy put through to him, only to find that when the phone rang his hand reached out a little tentatively towards the receiver. He was desperate for news, but was fearful of what he was about to learn, bringing the phone to his ear with some trepidation.

"Frank. Amy. I've just had contact from Lawrence."

"You've detonated," Gilmore said.

"Yes, they've detonated. You know already?"

"I've got a graph here in front of me."

"You said *they*. Aren't you with them?"

"No. I'm with Phil Becaud and the Cessna at Base Camp."

"So you don't know if they've been successful."

"Not yet. They've stirred things up a bit, from what I can gather...can't yet see what's going on."

"Let me know as soon as you hear anything," said Gilmore."

"Of course I will," said Amy. "But listen, Frank, they have a problem."

"What sort of a problem?"

"They can't get out of the Rift. And....and Terry Coulson is missing."

"Oh my God!"

"Can you mount a rescue?"

"I...I don't know. Getting an expedition together is going to take time, and everyone here is stretched to the limit. We're on a State of Emergency here, in case there are any repercussions. We're holding our breath in case there is another tidal wave. They can hold out for while can't they?"

"No, that's just what they can't do. They've no food, and no proper clothing. They can't leave Plato Camp, as they've called it."

"I can get something together, but I don't know if we can organise anything quick enough. We'd need climbers, and they'd have to get to you."

"You have to do something, Frank. They've risked their lives to make this operation a success. We can't now just leave them there."

"No. I'm not suggesting that."

His mind was racing, but he could see so many problems that could take days to solve when realistically they should be thinking in terms of hours. Without proper clothing Zoe and the gang wouldn't last long. His office door opened and then closed noisily behind the bustling figure of Dorothy Redmires, as she marched in on him, her face full of questions, when she spotted him on the phone. He told Amy that he would get right back to her, now needing to speak to Dorothy. He filled her in on the situation, glad of someone to talk to. No, more than that. Glad of her to talk to. Her presence filled the room with determination.

"OK, as you say, Frank, time is of the essence. Can you get a plane organised?"

"Yes but I don't know if I can get a military plane into the main airport..."

"No, go straight to Angmagssalik with food, clothing and climbing equipment. We don't know the location of the Rift still with any accuracy, and we certainly don't know the exact position of the operation, so get Becaud to meet you at Angmagssalic, and take the stuff back to their Base Camp. Then Amy will have to get down there, and bring them out."

"I can't see this working. We should be sending a team of Special Forces in."

"And how likely is that to happen, Frank?"

He didn't need to answer.

CHAPTER TWENTY-EIGHT

A my felt like the ultimate traitor as the Cessna soared into the Arctic sky in a steep take off. They curled round and left the mighty Atlantis Rift behind, until once more it became a jagged line in the otherwise pristine ice sheet. It made it so much worse that she had a way out of there to a place of safety when she should have been down there with Zoe, Oliver and Lawrence at Plato. They had become the people that meant most to her in her life. They were her best friends, her work colleagues, and in the case of Lawrence, maybe much more than that.

His absence had given her time for reflection; to get to know her feelings for him on her own terms, and not always influenced by the opinions of others, however well-meaning. It gave her time to get to know herself better too and to challenge some of her own preconceptions. Her natural warmth and caring nature had always attracted a kind of neediness from others before in her relationships, which was sapping for her and had always ended in disappointment and frustration.

But in Lawrence, there was a sense of realness about him, which she admired. There was no false cheeriness in him, actually, there wasn't much cheeriness at all, she thought, a flicker appearing at the side of her mouth at the observation, but he was not as dour as many people thought. His sense of humour was dry and incisive, and she'd grown to like it. Cutting, but never cruel or personal, he could be very amusing. The thought kicked into her head that she might never see him again, and her eyes felt heavy with a well of emotion. Get a grip. For now, just keep going.

In real terms the party stranded down there on the ledge at Plato Camp were only about a kilometre away from safety at a guess, but a vertical kilometre is a whole different ball game to a horizontal one, and what they must be going through now, was anyone's call. Amy should have been sharing that with them; instead she was a passenger in a plane going to get supplies, with no real role to play, and a growing sense of survivor's guilt. The worse thing was that she had let Lawrence down. What must he think of her now? She was desperately concerned for his safety, but almost more dreading the thought of facing him when he got back. She was poor company for Phil, who despite his concerns, was pleased to be back in the air again, and to have the feeling that he was doing something constructive at last; she in the meantime just looked out of the window, seeing nothing.

Amy was dozing when Becaud began the descent into Angmagssalik, the change in altitude and the angle of the plane bringing her round in time for the landing.

He taxied to the end of the runway and stopped close to a private jet. He wondered if this was the plane they were supposed to be meeting. Seeing no-one around he jumped down from the cockpit and onto the runway, swinging his scarf over his shoulder as he did so. He took off his sunglasses just in time to see the door of the jet drop open, then two military types walk down the short flight of steps, and walk towards him with outstretched hands. The first one to reach the pilot was a Captain Pountney, who was followed half a pace behind by Quartermaster-Sergeant Baines.

"You're in good time, Becaud," said Captain Pountney, clearly not needing an introduction. They nodded in Amy's direction and briefly shook her hand. She noted that neither of them said who they were. They were a little older than Becaud had expected. Guess they'd been brought out of mothballs for the occasion, he thought.

"Got the scientific instruments you ordered," said Sergeant Baines, with a just perceptible wink.

Becaud wondered aloud how they were ever going to get away with this.

"You're in the air freight business, aren't you? Not that unusual for you to be picking up a delivery," said the Captain, tetchily.

Becaud decided to shut up, and load the plane as quickly as he could, with Amy's help. Clearly these two were having a ball. It was the first time in years that they weren't pen-pushing, and they didn't want to hear any complaining. They got the equipment as quickly as they could into the hold of Becaud's plane. It was bulky and there was a reassuringly large amount of stuff that they'd brought.

"Nice aeroplane, the Cessna. Is she new?" said Captain Pountney.

Becaud confirmed that she was. He was flattered that someone had noticed.

"You should be alright for the weight – most of this isn't heavy – got the figures here for you, anyway."

Becaud nodded and made a mental note of the poundage. Not that it made much difference on this trip. He could hardly leave anything behind.

The boxes were all stowed, and the hold door was slammed shut. It had all happened seamlessly, and now Becaud was keen to get going before his presence at the airstrip attracted any attention and raised too many questions.

"Well, best of luck, you two. This is where we have to leave you," said the Captain. "Got you some first rate tackle there, but rather you than me," he said cheerfully, directly to Amy, which surprised her. *What on earth did he mean?*

Amy felt herself going first hot then cold as the realisation had begun to dawn on her of what his words implied. She had thought that these guys were coming out on a rescue mission. Now she realised that there was only the two of them and that their part in all this was now over. There was only one person who could get this equipment down to Zoe and the others, and that was her. Now she thought about it no-one had actually said that these two were joining them and going to Base Camp – she'd just assumed that. Wrongly as it turned out.

When they were airborne once more, Amy asked Phil if he knew that she was going to have to go down into the Rift. He tried to shrug it off, knowing that she was trying to make something of it. What the hell did it matter if he knew or not?

"It matters that *I* didn't know," said Amy, self-righteously.

"Well you know now."

"You all kept this from me," said Amy.

"Well it would have only meant you worrying for another day – what would be the point of that."

"You didn't want to give me the chance to opt out."

"There was no other option. They couldn't find anyone with experience of climbing in the time available. Sending in equipment has saved us hours trying to source it for ourselves – perhaps even a day. So we had to take what was on offer. We could wait for a team of rescue workers, but they're needed back in the UK where they are all on full alert. By that time we could have been too late."

No pressure there then. Amy's stomach churned. Even the mere thought of the Rift made her feel panicky now.

* * *

Back at Plato Camp, things were not going well. The weather had taken a turn for the worse and there was now a gale raging at their tent, and a total white out as the blizzard conditions settled in for no-one knew how long. Nothing could have been worse for morale at this stage. As the wind banked the driving snow higher up against the tent wall everyone knew that this was going to make any hope of rescue take longer. Zoe was so hungry that all she could think about was food, and she knew the others must feel the same. As she had eaten a square of chocolate about an hour ago, she knew that there wouldn't be another one for about three more hours. Sleep would make the time pass quicker but she was too cold to sleep now. Her hands and feet ached with the cold, and all the time she was nervously checking them for the tell-tale signs of frostbite.

She, Oliver and Lawrence all huddled together unselfconsciously as their common peril obliterated the normal boundaries. They rubbed and checked each others hands and feet in a desperate attempt to keep the seeping cold at bay. They really needed to drink, but no-one wanted to have to take the consequences of that, which meant going outside the tent to relieve themselves. Once the core body temperature fell below a certain point they wouldn't get it back. If only the wind would drop. They talked endlessly about anything and everything. Any subject was allowed – except that of food, which was the only thing anyone could think of.

Zoe suggested that they go back down to the Rift bottom and wait for rescue in the warm. She could feel the delicious sensation of warm rock on her feet. Don't be so bloody stupid. The walls are crumbling and the valley floor should now be a river of molten lava. And we've no ropes or pitons. She'd forgotten that. Wished she'd never spoken.

* * *

The weather had been pretty good when the Cessna left Angmagssalik, but as Phil and Amy neared Base Camp they began to fly into the low pressure that was causing the gales and blizzards down in the Atlantis Rift. As the turbulence grew worse Amy didn't know weather to feel sick or terrified, both vying for her attention at every lurch and drop. The engines sounded as though they were labouring, and even a seat of the pants flier like Becaud, was looking white and strained with the effort of concentration required. Normally he wouldn't have considered flying in these conditions, as he hadn't the instruments to land blind like a commercial airliner. But he had to push his luck, and keep going for as long as he dared. As he neared the place where they set up Base Camp the weather cleared slightly, so he dropped in below the low cloud and searched visually for the Camp and a good level spot to land. It had stopped snowing, but visibility still wasn't good and it took them what seemed to be an age to locate their landing strip. At last they saw the tents, half-covered in snow, with a huge sense of relief. Phil landed the plane almost sideways in the crosswinds, bumping onto the icy runway heavily before coming to a standstill.

"You OK, honey?"

No. Actually, she wanted to die. It would have been preferable to feeling like this. She jumped out of the plane and into the cold reviving air before becoming engulfed in a wave of nausea.

Within the hour, Amy stood outside the tent, fully kitted up, and with her rucksack firmly secured on her back, ticking everything off with Becaud before she set off into the Rift. She felt like a schoolkid again, but for now the nerves were in check, and now she was just desperate to get going. Now Becaud looked more worried than she did, and he obviously was not happy that she had to go down there alone.

"I'll be OK," she said.

She was trying to focus on seeing Lawrence again so as not to get hung up on all the other, very real, dangers. Becaud guessed that, too. Which was why he hated letting her go. He kissed her affectionately on the cheek, and she shuffled off to the edge of the Rift, where she turned around and backed gently over the edge, resting her forearms on the top while her feet found the first grip. This time she didn't pause, or give herself time for fear to disable her. The dread world of the 'what ifs' or the worst case scenarios, was banished in the here and now. Take one step at a time. Deal only with the real. Stay in the moment. She remained focussed, and before she knew it she had descended fifty metres.

For the moment Amy had conquered her panic, but she it was with total dread that she contemplated its return. Funny thing is, that when fear takes root it can be as difficult to eradicate as the most persistent and deep-rooted weed. It grows until the fear itself becomes the problem. The thought of being engulfed in the sensation of panic, with the ensuing feelings of loss of control become disabling, far more so than any outside threat. Amy still didn't know why she froze back on the day of the descent, but felt that it might be because she had been expected to climb down into the void rather than go upwards. And the sheer scale of the thing. She contemplated how long she would be falling if she slipped, then banished the thought and got back to the real. She still didn't like the feeling of going down into the Rift, so, instead, she thought only of her friends, and how much they needed her.

She radioed back to Base Camp, and immediately felt better for talking to another human being. Becaud lowered a pack of equipment to her, which, from now on, she could drag along. She took a drink, then pressed on. She scrambled over rock falls, through piles of broken ice, steadily down till she was at the level that she thought Plato Camp should be, but she couldn't see any trace of it as she scanned the cliff wall for a sign of the coloured tents. There was nothing. She radioed back to Phil Becaud to tell him.

"I guess I'll just have to keep going down till I find them," said Amy, unconvincingly.

"No. Don't descend any further, or you could miss them altogether. This could turn into a total disaster, with you needing rescue, too. You need to work your way further east if you can. Then you should see the camp soon."

"That's been the problem. There been a massive avalanche here which has piled up banks of ice and slow, where I think they took their path."

"Is it passable?"

"Maybe. I can't tell."

So Amy headed east, labouring over piles of soft snow, which she sank into constantly. She was carrying a lot of equipment in her pack, and dragging a lot more behind her. Sometimes she was sinking up to her waist. It was exhausting. She looked again, but could see no sign of Plato Camp. She could be wasting hours and all her energy going in the wrong direction. If the need to get to her friends had driven her on to make the journey down into the Rift, and had given her the urgency and the courage to get on with the task of finding them all while they still had time to get out, then now the sheer hopelessness of being alone and unable to find them was sapping her will to go on. Now she had the doubt in her mind that every step she took could be taking her further away from them instead of leading to their rescue, and the anger at her frustration, rose with every moment that passed. The only thing that kept her going was the thought that she mustn't linger on the soft snow of the avalanche, as it was very insecure. Another large quake, and she could be rolling down to the bottom of the Rift under fifty metres of tumbling snow. She stopped again to scan around the Rift walls, but she could make out nothing that looked like their tents. The thought occurred to her that maybe the camp had been swept away, and that she was already too late. She hated that thought, so she pushed it away.

The light was turning grey, but even so, the normal concepts of day and night seemed like an artificial construct in a land where the sun never went below the horizon during the summer months. So it always made it seem that stopping for the day seemed like an arbitrary choice rather than the necessity that nightfall would bring. But it had been a long day, and she would have to stop to rest sometime. This was a major setback, and with a real sense of defeat she had thought that she would find them relatively quickly, and that the hard part would be getting them out of there. Amy squeezed into a cupped out gap in the cliff face that would make a good snow hole for her to rest in for a few hours. She got out her sleeping bag and wrapped it around herself. It was reasonably warm in there, and she would have slept if it wasn't for the bizarre nature of her situation that kept her alert. But eventually the body defeated the mind and utter exhaustion forced her to doze for a couple of hours. When she did wake it was with a start. Her body still felt tired and heavy, but her mind had reasserted itself and was pressing upon her the job she had yet to complete. It seemed so hopeless.

Only the vision in her mind that her friends might even now be slowly freezing to death stopped her from throwing in the towel and climbing back to safety. No-one would blame her if she turned back now, she thought as the worm of self-interest wriggled into her sense of duty and responsibility. She thought of Phil Becaud waiting to fly her back to the warmth and comfort of Angmagssalic, and to take care of her.

For a while it was almost tempting.

* * *

Zoe had reached the stage where she could lie in the tent no longer, pretending that she didn't need to go. The men had said that they should all stay inside the tent, rather than risk hypothermia, but Zoe couldn't agree. She put on an extra fleece and went out to brave the elements as best she could. She was shivering with the cold as she drew back next to the tent. She looked around to see if there was any sign of rescue, but could see nothing but grey cloud and the blank wall of the ice cliff wherever she looked. She noticed that the blizzard had piled up snow right up on the wall of the tent blanking it out completely. The wind was now dying down, but the snow was providing them with an extra layer of insulation, that had probably got them through the night. She got back in and pulled the sleeping bag tight around her in an effort to get warm again.

"We were lucky to have that blanket of snow on us," said Zoe to Oliver and Lawrence. It's covered us completely. It looks like an igloo from out there."

Hewitt looked aghast. The penny visibly dropped as Zoe's words sank in.

"Then no-one out there can see us," he said.

Zoe and Oliver sat up in alarm, realising the implications of what she had said at once, and already wondering if they'd worked this out too late. For all they knew the now hoped-for rescue could have given up, and gone back home. That appalling thought got them all to their feet, and outside to try to scrape the snow away from the tent. Idiots. What complete idiots. It wasn't as though they were novices out here. But the combined effects of exhaustion, the cold and burning hunger had slowed the mental processes down more than they believed possible. The thought that a rescue party had come and gone, and that they had been missed was too much to bear. Heads dropped, and the group went very quiet. Morale was at rock bottom, and somehow they all felt colder than at any time since they'd arrived at Plato. Hewitt radioed Becaud to tell him what had happened. They tried to put a good spin on it, explaining that they'd only just realised, and that they'd been held down by the blizzard, but Becaud was having none of it. He was merciless.

"Do you want to get out of there of what? You stupid idiots! Don't you realise that Amy could have passed you by, God knows how many times, and putting her own fucking life at risk to get you out of that stupid crack-in-the-ice shit-hole! Haven't one of you had the wit to leave any kind of a marker for her? A bright piece of clothing…"

"We haven't got any spare clothing, that's why we're here," said Hewitt, scoring a point.

"Well OK. But a bag, or even an SOS of rocks in the snow. Or just banging off the walls of the tent. Jeez, guys….."

The worst thing was that Hewitt thought that Becaud was right, and blamed himself as much as Becaud did. If only Terry had still been with them. He would have known what to do. In a situation like this his training would have kicked in, and mistakes like this would have been avoided. What was worse was that Becaud had lost radio contact with Amy, adding to their fears that she had missed them and had now descended further into the Rift than she needed to have done. Hewitt, stung, hit back.

"It's OK for you sitting up there in your precious aeroplane, telling everyone else what they should be doing. You try doing what we've done, without food or supplies, instead of sitting on your arse all day doing sudokus."

Zoe, told him to cool it, but secretly agreed with him. Becaud wished he'd not said so much. He clicked off the mic hoping that wouldn't be the last thing he'd ever say to Lawrence. He had an impulse to prove them all wrong and go down after Amy, but what could he do? He'd got no experience or climbing gear, and he was needed to man the radio. He'd no choice but to stay at his post.

Zoe handed out three squares of chocolate instead of the one they were all expecting. She didn't tell the others, but there was no more left after that. It was a gamble, but she reasoned that they needed something to keep them going now. If Amy didn't reach them by the end of today she didn't think they'd make it anyway.

An hour later they all had a mint taken carefully from the torn down tube, which they sucked for as long as was possible, down to the last molecule. Every last calorie was sponged into their desperate bodies, then it was gone. The urge to sleep was now becoming irresistible.

It felt like everything was slipping away.

* * *

Amy stuffed her sleeping bag into her pack, then took out the field glasses to scan the landscape for any sign of the camp. She ran the glasses to and fro, like reading the lines on a page, then double checked by using the naked eye in case she'd missed any part of the vista due to the narrowing of her field of vision when looking through the binoculars. Nothing. How was she able to decide where to search having nothing to go on? She set off, following a sort of path that led to place with an easier looking ascent in the distance. At least there was some logic to that.

She stopped again and once more took out the glasses. She did the methodical sweep that she had done before, looking at the same cliff wall that she'd done before, now not even expecting to see anything, if she was honest. So it was all the more surprising, when a tiny blurred dot of orange shot passed her eyes, before she was ready to take it in. She gasped. It was above her to her right, awkward to see as it was on the same cliff face as her, and as she re-scanned the area she couldn't find where she thought she'd seen it. She did a visual check, and thought she could see something, then followed it through by lining up the glasses. Up and down. Side to side.

Got it.

Focus in. Plato Camp. This was it. No doubt about it. She could have wept for joy, but there was no time for that now. She planned a route in her head after looking carefully at the terrain, and she set off as quickly as she could.

After two hours of tortuous slog, she neared Plato and called out, "Hello! Hello! Zo? Guys? Are you OK?"

There was no reply. The wind was still quite gusty and it was throwing her voice back at her.

"Hey! Is anyone there? Lawrence, Zoe!"

She was busy constructing every possible reason in her head as to why she wasn't getting any response, apart from the two obvious ones. That they were no longer there – or they hadn't pulled through. The camp looked derelict. Even a temporary camp like this one had a look about it if was inhabited, of being kempt, an oasis set apart from its surroundings that Plato Camp lacked. The tents sagged and swayed in the wind, one of which had collapsed completely into the snow. Nature looked as though it was gaining the upper hand. It was too quiet. Amy felt her knees give way as the shock of what she might find forced its way into her consciousness. She was trembling, as she approached the nearest tent – the one almost overhanging the ledge. It was empty. She blew a deep breath outwards. Not knowing if this was a good sign or not. She couldn't help but feel relieved, as hope was able to persist a little longer.

Crunch time.

She took a deep breath in and made the first step towards the second tent. She crouched down, desperately afraid that she was about to see three frozen bodies inside.

There was a sudden and totally unexpected noise as the tent zipper buzzed open, and the fabric fell away to reveal the doorway. Amy nearly jumped out of her skin. All she could see was a fleece hat, and then two dull, sunken eyes, so changed that she hardly recognised them. It was Lawrence Hewitt. His skin looked papery and too pale. Her shocked look embarrassed him. He couldn't speak. And neither could she.

She squeezed Lawrence's arm, only to get a feeble response back. An attempt at a smile foundered upon his cracked lips. Then she gave him a hug. He felt so cold. My God! She'd not been prepared for the reality of seeing them in so distressed a state. She crawled into the tent, and gave Zoe and Oliver a hug, too. She pulled in the packs of equipment after her whilst mentally deciding what to do first to help them. She tried to keep them talking while she undid the first pack and sorted out some supplies.

"So you blew the charges," said Amy.

"And now we're waiting to see if it's worked," said Zoe, weakly. "After the weather closed in we couldn't even see if the hole was big enough to release the pressure on the caldera. We are just holding our breath and hoping that it's worked, and that we've managed to avoid a cataclysmic eruption."

"I just hope you were in time," said Amy. "Been getting updates from Isaac Newton. Seismology says the tremors have been getting angrier and more frequent, as though something's been building up. And rumours have been getting out and into the tabloids about a hundred foot tidal wave, headed for the UK. The detonation was picked up, but I don't know anything after that."

"Think the tabloids are being a bit conservative for once," said Zoe.

Amy's eyes widened, and she looked long and hard at Zoe, astonished as what she had just said. But now was not the time to go into all that. Her friends needed help of a more immediate nature.

"You've had a bad time," said Amy, with her usual sympathy and practicality. Ignoring her own exhaustion, she looked at them all, one at a time. "You all look badly dehydrated to me. Have you been taking in plenty of fluids?"

They admitted that they hadn't. Nobody had wanted to take in too much icy water as they were so cold already, and they'd all been trying to avoid going outside too often. The result was worse than the hunger that was gnawing at them. They had deteriorated fast.

Amy dipped straight into her pack and handed them round an energy drink each, which they took with relish. She next gave them a high calorie type of biscuit, with strict instructions that they were to eat it slowly. They tried but failed dismally. Every crumb was gone in seconds.

While they were busy eating, Amy rummaged through her rucksack once more and brought out the thick over trousers, thermal layers and anoraks that she had brought with her. Shaking them out as they had been really tightly packed, she handed them in turn the clothes that they so desperately needed. Cramped and crowded as it was inside the tent, Amy had to help them with their things. She then went outside and set up the stove in the lee of the cave, lighting it and turning the flame up high to boil some water. When eventually the water's surface began to roll she removed the kettle and dropped a couple of tea bags in there. Nothing would be better for morale, than a mug of tea, and the quicker she got them all hydrated and warm, the quicker they could get going and get out of there.

She shared out the hot liquid equally into the four waiting mugs, spooning in the regulation sugar and dried milk into each one before returning to the tent, with the steaming vessels.

"Brew's ready guys!" said Amy. Zoe had never tasted anything so perfect in her life before. She felt that if she died right now she could go happily, knowing that nothing could ever top this moment. She could want for nothing more. She shared that thought with her husband.

"Silly cow," said Oliver. He was obviously rallying, Zoe thought with some relief. Amy got them all a meal ready which they wolfed down in record time. The moment the hot food touched their sore and cracked lips, it began its restorative effect, coursing energy and heat back into their empty bodies. And for the next few hours it was Amy's job to nursemaid the dilapidated crew, her friends, back to some kind of condition where they could begin to think about their escape.

CHAPTER TWENTY-NINE

Terry Coulson had chosen the positions well for explosives he'd set in the rock face. The thin fissure that had allowed the molten lava to seep through very slowly, had in a matter of seconds become a gaping hole in the caldera's wall large enough to drive a truck through. Immediately after the detonation, the rock all around the seepage had turned to rubble and collapsed, allowing a hot river of glowing red viscous fire to haemorrhage out of the newly inflicted wound on the Earth's surface. It sped along the base of the Atlantis Rift, the huge crack in the ice creating a natural channel for the lava flow to forge its way along and out towards the sea. The heat that the flow generated was so intense that the driving blizzard above it, first melted then evaporated, turning to steam that hung in a layer below the dark low cloud, making visibility almost nil in places.

The force of the surging river of lava shook the whole of the Rift to its foundations. The deafening roar and the constant vibrations, threatened to break the Rift apart. The sides of the ice cliff walls were melting at the base causing the undermined walls to collapse in places. Zoe and the rest could see none of this, from their tiny, precarious perch high above the racing torrent below. It was a grand battle between ice and fire, with each element vying for supremacy, until ultimately they would cancel each other out and reach their equilibrium.

Or at least that was the plan. As the lava was now carving out a path for itself through the bottom of the Rift and headed out to sea, it should no longer be seeping inexorably under the ice sheet and destabilising it over a country-wide area. The cooling magma would begin to solidify and re-anchor the ice sheet to its bedrock base. And hopefully the ultimate nightmare scenario would have been avoided, that of ice cover collapse into the boiling caldera, and causing a cataclysmic eruption of epic proportion, sending a continent sized ice sheet slipping into the sea.

Phil Becaud paced around at Base Camp, waiting for Amy to return. Isolated and feeling impotent, unable to either help with the rescue of his friends or to know what was even going on down there, time dragged by painfully slowly. One thing he did know was that the periodic tremors had given way to a continuous deep vibration, so intense that he could no longer say whether it was in his head or coming from the Earth's crust. And he didn't know whether that was a good thing, or maybe something very bad indeed was going on beneath his feet. He couldn't sleep, being constantly tormented by an image that the whole ice sheet under him was about to shatter into fragments and swallow him up.

He wanted more than anything to see Amy safe once more, and to get himself airborne. He wanted to feel the controls in his hands, and the pressure of the seat in his back as he opened up the throttle and powered into the sky; he wanted to hear the crackle of the radio in his ears, as he exchanged some banter with his flight-follower back in Angmagssalic; he wanted to see his house again. He needed so much to keep hold of the world he knew; and then it hit him like a ton of bricks: that that was why they were here in the first place. If they'd sat back and just hoped the tremors would go away, and the fracturing icebergs had caused a massive tidal wave, then none of them would have had a world to *go* back to. It's one thing to be away from all that is familiar to you but to know that it's still there; it's quite another to have to come to terms with its total destruction.

Becaud got himself together and made a decision to spend the day working on the Cessna. Diligently he cleared off the ice and snow that had collected on her during the blizzard. He did all the safety checks, and started her up to warm the engine through. It felt so satisfying to hear the familiar sound of her engine again; it was like she had come to life once more. And it drowned out the awful noise of the vibrations coming from the Rift. Without making a conscious decision, he started to pack everything up from the camp that wasn't absolutely necessary for his immediate needs. He had assumed previously that when the gang returned to Base Camp they would need to rest for a while before heading out. Now, suddenly, he knew with certainty that all they would want to do was get out of there as quickly as possible. He stowed what he could in the hold, then cleaned every last bit of her. He was sick of making do. Of being the one left hanging around.

It was going to be his job to get everyone out of there, and he was going to do it in style.

* * *

Back in Whitehall, Frank Gilmore had practically taken root at his desk, now covered in printouts from the updates sent straight to him from Isaac Newton. Dorothy Redmires rarely left his side. She interpreted the line graphs for him, on his laptop, after they had zig-zagged their way over endless rolls of paper telling the story of what was happening in Greenland even before the people on the ground knew. When the needle in the seismology department suddenly swung from side to side drawing a set of peaks and troughs, Dorothy studied the information as it came through on her computer screen, and, looking triumphant, declared it definitely to be the detonation.

"Look, if you compare it to these other peaks of activity you can see how this one differs in character," she patiently explained to Gilmore, pointing at the printout that he had been looking at earlier. It all looked the same to him, but he thought it best not to say so. Instead he just took her word for it, and made up his mind to act.

"Then we have to get airborne," was all he said, and gave orders for the reconnaissance planes to head out towards the Greenland coast to detect any signs of tidal waves.

* * *

For two days the country held its breath.

Ron Bowman spent long hours in the cabinet room with his ministers planning strategy and wondering what to say to a seismically angry Ambassador from Greenland. Bowman, with his usual belligerence, had insisted when they met that Britain had acted in the national interest and was therefore entitled to do what had to be done. The Ambassador had stormed out of the meeting outraged at the total disregard for her country. She had threatened to break off diplomatic relations. As if he had time for all this at the moment. Meetings went on long into the night to discuss the strategies needed if a tsunami were to hit. Different plans were mooted depending on the size on any possible wave.

"And what if a one hundred foot wave hits us, like the bloody papers are saying? said Bowman. "What then?"

"Then we head for France," said one of the military advisors. A nervous ripple of laughter went around the room. But stopped at the military guy who remained stony-faced. "No. I'm not joking. We head for France."

Bowman stared at him as silence gripped the room, which suddenly seemed stuffy in the stale, nervous air. White-faced and tired, the meeting lost its focus as thoughts wandered to more personal concerns; their families, homes – everything that made up the structure and the fabric of their lives.

"I think we need to take a break," one of the scientific advisors suggested, noticing that the common purpose of the group was crumbling away.

"Fifteen minutes," Ron Bowman barked. "And get some coffee sent up here."

With that he stood up. On cue everyone else followed suit, and with scraping chairs the session adjourned.

Harrington was sitting in his office reading the Daily Telegraph. He looked haggard and drawn and was clearly finding it difficult to keep up his normal composure. He looked up as the PM walked into the room tentatively, as though he had forgotten what he had come in for.

"Has the meeting finished, sir?" Harrington ventured.

"What are they saying?" the PM snapped, looking at the newspaper and ignoring Harrington's enquiry.

"It depends which one you read, Prime Minister. *Scientists warn of more coastal flooding – evacuations likely.* Or, if you read the Sun – he unfolded the tabloid as he spoke – then it's *Killer Wave Set to Smash UK.*" Harrington went on, "The Greenland Ambassador is waiting to see you, sir. Shall I tell her to come in?"

"No. Not yet. I don't know what the hell to say to her. What *can* I say to her?"

"Well, she needs to go back with something..."

"An apology you mean?"

"Our chaps have just blown a big hole in their country. She'll need more than that." Harrington paused for a second or two to let his words sink in.

"Go on."

"Been talking to my son who's at uni. It's all on YouTube – been following it like a soap, they all have. They see it as a very much a joint enterprise, this expedition. After all, three local people lost their lives out there, and have become national heroes as a result. The young people don't see it as being in any way political: for them, a team of scientists were just doing what had to be done. You could identify with that instead of apologising for it. Both governments could."

"And jointly soak up the credit, you mean." Bowman almost smiled. "And what if it all goes wrong?" he added, "and the killer wave gets us?"

"Then you can forget political niceties altogether. We'll be back in the Stone Age."

Bowman didn't smile at that; instead he told Harrington to send the ambassador into his office, and with that he turned on his heel and marched out of the room.

Harrington felt utterly dejected. For the first time in his career he felt that he really didn't want to be here – at the centre of things. He folded up his newspapers and put them neatly at the top corner of his desk. He then called his son to make sure he was somewhere safe. *I'm fine, dad, I'm home with mum.* Really? In term-time? Then people were already reading the newspapers and making their own arrangements. Families were gathering. He sent a message to the Greenland Ambassador to say that the Prime Minister was ready to see her.

Harrington didn't really make a decision to leave. He just found himself walking out of the old country house which was being used as the temporary government HQ, and got into his car.

His mother, Celia Harrington lived in a cottage on the Somerset coast. There was no point in phoning her and telling her to leave, as she didn't drive anymore, and wouldn't know where to go.

He couldn't believe that he was leaving his post. He felt reckless. It might put him beyond the pale. But he was already turning out of the tree-lined drive without any doubt in his mind about where he was heading. It was as though his subconscious had taken over, done all the decision-making for him and was now guiding him along till his conscious mind caught up and had learnt to assimilate the situation. He didn't remember doing it, but his foot went down on the accelerator as he took the sliproad and joined the M4 at Chippenham. He sped towards the Almondsbury interchange at Bristol.

He made good time as the motorway was quiet. Too quiet. Pity the poor sods on the other carriageway, he thought; they were nose to tail. Must have been an accident or something. He neared the M32 turn-off to Bristol, which was usually a bottleneck as everyone was getting off the motorway there and blocking the nearside lane. There were only another one or two vehicles in sight. And about the same in the rear-view mirror.

It was then he realised. People were leaving the low lying coasts already. They were heading out. Stuck in isolation in the government HQ, he'd known nothing of what was happening out here. He still felt bad about leaving his post after all those years of built-up loyalty, even though it now seemed totally irrelevant. Ignoring the spiteful flash of the speed cameras above him, he took advantage of the open road and headed flat out for the M5.

Despite the fact that Harrington had the luxury of having an empty road in front of him, there was something deeply disconcerting about going the opposite way to everyone else, which exacerbated the feeling in him that he was very much in the wrong for being where he was at all. He toyed for a moment with the idea of putting the radio on, but didn't. Whatever they had to say, illogically, he didn't want to hear it right now.

Twenty minutes later Harrington stopped the car outside the familiar Victorian cottage where his mother lived, and pulled on the handbrake with a series of smooth clicks. He could see the sea through the tangle of shrubs and windswept trees. Grey and relatively calm, the sea looked so ordinary lying there under a blue sky with a few innocuous looking nimbus clouds hovering above the glinting surface. He actually felt a bit foolish for a moment. It seemed ludicrous to imagine that this landscape could ever change and become malignant; that the lapping seashore could become a terrifying mountain of water that could engulf them all. This was England after all.

He found himself wondering what on earth he was going to say to his mother. She was probably outside in the garden weeding the perennial border. He hoped she wouldn't be difficult; or even worse, derisive.

He walked up the worn stone path to the front door which was set in the middle of the house in between two bay windows. The unruly potentillas and creeping cranesbill brushed past his smart city shoes as he made his way towards the house. The swaying sea-side grasses did the same against his clothes. Unconsciously he stroked the taller ones with his hand, crushing some of the riper seed heads as he did so then scattering them on the dry soil before he got to the door. He noticed that the sitting room window was open on the bay to his left, which wasn't unusual, and that he could hear the television on from inside, which was. Celia never had the TV on during the day.

He had his own key and therefore could let himself in, calling out as he did so, so as not to startle her by his sudden appearance. As it happened it was she who startled him by darting out of the sitting room, practically bumping into him in her haste.

"Adrian!" Celia said, looking pleased to see him, but without smiling. "You're here, at last!" Harrington looked at her. It was an odd thing to say. As though she had been expecting him.

The house was very tidy. It was normally only like this when she was going on holiday and liked to leave everything just so. Then he noticed, through the open doorway there was a suitcase next to the sofa.

"I'm just being prepared," she said, following his eyeline. "I knew you'd come."

The fact that his mother, normally so brisk and confident, was taking these tremors seriously, altered everything. Suddenly he knew the risks were real.

For two days Celia had had the TV on night and day and had hardly left its side, not even to go out into her beloved garden. The tedious game shows and endless rolling news bored her to death, but resolutely she kept an eye on the screen for any hint that a tsunami might be on the way. Occasionally she crept to the kitchen window at the back of the house and watched the sea for signs of change, and she watched the people strolling down there, walking their dogs or running along the wet, firm sand right next to the water line. And she noted with mounting unease that many of her neighbours were quietly getting into their cars and leaving. Some had left during the hours of darkness so as not to arouse suspicion or to look obvious, but Celia heard them as she lay on the sofa unable to sleep. Hurt that not one had told her what they were doing, or asking if she was alright, she felt increasingly alone. She had begun to make her own preparations to leave. Adrian must come for me, she told herself, and she packed her bag in readiness. She had made up her mind to give him until nightfall; then she would call the number of the taxi firm left on the pad on the hall table.

"You should have called me, mother. I'd have come before."

"You're here now," she said, turning to look in the direction of her packed case.

"You'd better put that in the car."

Harrington stepped over to the case and picked it up. It was very heavy. He pulled out the telescopic handle then rolled it down the hall, over the step and down the path to his car where he hauled it into the boot, then slammed the lid shut. Once more he trudged his way up the garden path to the now open door. He thought it was time for coffee. And maybe a bite to eat. Then he'd think what to do. In a few easy steps he was through the hall and into the sitting room. Celia was watching out of the front window. She turned towards him as he sank down on the comfortable sofa. She was about to say something, her face animated, her mouth poised to speak, when an alarm sounded. Automatically she spun round to the open window, thinking for a second it must be a car or burglar alarm. But it wasn't that. It was the mournful sound of a siren. The sound of an air-raid. The sound of a generation; her generation, now haunting her again. Then Harrington saw the red band appear on the TV screen in front of him. It was actually happening. A thump of adrenaline hit him in the stomach as the read the impossible words: *TSUNAMI WARNING....18 MINUTES...TSUNAMI WARNING...WEST AND SOUTH WEST COASTS...* He sprang out of the chair and stupidly was about to go and turn off the set, wailing in the corner.

"Leave it!" Celia said making for the door. Harrington followed then dashed past her. She was surprisingly nimble for a woman her age. He was amazed at her presence of mind, but she'd been there before and knew exactly what one had to do to survive. You act; you don't dither. She was no longer a woman in her late eighties, but a teenager again, running from a London bus as fast as she could go to the nearest air-raid shelter. She had made it only seconds before the street blew apart behind her. So long ago.

The car door slammed shut and they jolted forward as they sped off up the road. People were on the pavements running, and some stayed at their upstairs windows, hoping they'd be safe; scornful of those who ran.

The deceitful sea didn't look any different.

Harrington's heart was racing. Where to go. What to do. Even if one had time it would be difficult to know what to do. He could head for any higher ground, but that would mean staying near the coast and maybe getting cut off. Or he could head inland and just hope to get far enough away from the coast to be away from any flooding. At the moment the road ran parallel to the coast and wasn't taking them anywhere nearer to safety. His frustration mounted. A car sped past him recklessly. Oddly it made him slow down slightly. His two worst nightmares were that they might crash, or they might get stranded in a traffic jam. As Celia couldn't run they must stay with the car as all costs. It was their only hope.

"Adrian, look!" Celia pointed out of the car window at the sea on her left, now clearly visible, where the row of houses had petered out.

The beach was now exposed where the tide had been lapping only minutes before. Soon it would be leaving rocks and shingle uncovered that had not seen a dry day in the last ten thousand years. Its brief nakedness unaware of the deluge about to wash over it.

"Which way?" Harrington said, his voice strained and high-pitched with anxiety, after glancing at the sea for the briefest of moments. There was some rising ground straight ahead with a small cluster of houses at the top.

"No!" said Celia. "Go right, and head inland." She had obviously been giving this some thought. "There's nothing up there. There'll be no food or water after a day. Even if we can only get a couple of miles inland we should be able to avoid the flooding. And we'll be able to get away afterwards."

"OK, OK."

He put his foot down hard now, unable to resist the temptation to flee. They lurched round a tight corner which made Celia hold tight onto the door handle. They drove for four or five minutes at breakneck speed along the bumpy B-roads, which were maddeningly flat. He wondered how many of the eighteen minutes had already gone by. Celia read her son's thoughts and punched on the car radio. Every station had the sound of the siren on and the commentators voice was interrupted every twenty seconds with a woman's pre-recorded voice like that of a satnav saying *nine minutes.* Then *eight minutes.*

"We can get a long way in eight minutes," said Celia.

"We can if the road stays clear," said Harrington. He was aware of every passing metre and ticking second. He could see brake lights ahead.

"Shit! Shit!" he said. The road was blocked by slow moving cars occupying both lanes of the road. They pulled up to a crawl, unable to see what the hold-up was, but knowing that it was almost certainly the amount of traffic building up all with the same idea as themselves.

"We might be alright here. We are quite a way from the beach now." Celia didn't sound convincing.

"We just need to get moving. What's the matter with the fucking idiots at the front?"...*seven minutes...*

There was a farm gate at the side of them. Harrington got out of the car and opened it, then jumped back into the driver's seat revving hard and setting off the wheels scuffing the road surface as he turned into the field. It was a risk. The field dipped down before rising up towards a clump of trees in the distance. There could be a farm track up there by the looks of things, but he couldn't see if he could get access to it.

They bumped along, jolting over the hard ground. Celia couldn't hold on properly but didn't dare complain. They got to the foot of the rise. It wasn't very high but it was much steeper than it had looked for a car not built for off-roading and they struggled to keep going over rocks which were poking out of the turf. It wasn't really a hill but it would give them a few precious metres. Harrington swung the wheel this way and that trying to avoid any deep hollows or hummocks that could leave them stranded. Celia kept an eye on the wing mirror.

"They're following. Loads of them," she said.

There were cars jolting along the field behind them. It would have looked like a really fun day's off-roading at any other time. But these vehicles were being driven by people white-faced with terror. They were being joined by people spilling out of their cars still stuck on the road who were now pushing through the hedges, scrambling over the ditches and running across the meadow. They were stumbling, pulling each other on, in a desperate agony of frustration that they could go no quicker.

Harrington didn't reply to his mother's observation. He was nearly at the trees and he still couldn't see any way of joining the track. He drove into the copse on the brow of the hill, then stopped, unable to get any further because of the tangle of undergrowth.

"This will have to do. I can't risk damaging the car by driving through."

They got out of the vehicle and scanned the horizon. The radio was on very loud so they could hear it clearly as they looked around. ...*two minutes*...The commentator babbled on breathlessly. Already Scotland and the north of England had been hit. Harrington strained to hear how big the wave was. He caught the words *up to three metres*. Shit. Now they were on the slight rise they could see the sea from their vantage point. They were only about a mile, maybe two from the coast. It might not be enough.

* * *

For two days the country had held its breath.

Then, just as they thought they had got away with it, there was the huge break off that everyone had been dreading. A piece of the ice sheet, already hanging by a thread, slid into the sea, causing millions of tons of ice hit the water and fragment in the impact. The ensuing swell rippled out, hardly detectable in the open sea, except with special instruments. Even the shipping wasn't aware of the wave rising and dipping under them, too big to be seen, but racing at 300 miles an hour to the coasts of Britain and Northern Europe. Most people got between fifteen and twenty minutes warning by the time the wave was confirmed and the red stripe was flashed onto TV screens all over Britain, accompanied by the wailing sound of a siren. The wave was six to ten feet high, when it hit, depending on the geography of the coastline. Damage was extensive, but many lives had been saved by the warnings, as people in vulnerable areas only had to get inland a short distance, or to higher ground to escape the worst of it. It was the aftermath that was worse, with many people made homeless, and more infrastructure ruined.

* * *

Harrington squinted at the horizon. They were now being joined by others, breathless and exhausted by the run. Most of the other vehicles pulled up to where his car was parked and the passengers spilled out. One or two four-tracks smashed though a fence and forced their way through the shrubs and out onto the track that Harrington had seen from the road. Celia asked if they should do the same.

"I don't think so. We can't risk it. If we damage the car fatally we are stuck here for God knows how long."

But it was tempting. And many people kept going on foot whose cars couldn't get any further.

"I wouldn't leave your cars if I were you!" shouted Harrington to the straggles of people going past him. But no-one listened...*one minute*...

The shouting and screaming got louder.

A thin white line appeared on the horizon.

Underneath it was a grey cliff of racing water. The characteristic lightning danced on the top of the wave, leaving no-one in any doubt that this was the real thing. Still, people pushed past the Harrington's car shouting and jostling.

"Oh my God!" Someone screamed. "It's here! It's hit the beach."

There was no doubt about it. The wave moved in like a juggernaut, turning the quiet bay into a maelstrom of white water and floating debris. Trees moved around in the mayhem, stately, at first, then crashing down into the tumult. Dipping and spinning, carrying everything with them while keeping the steady forward momentum of the forging sea. Buildings dissolved like sandcastles before an oncoming tide. The fields and coastal settlements were being swallowed up by an unstoppable surge of an ocean that had remembered its power but forgotten its place. And it just kept on coming.

"Oh, Adrian! I think we should get out of here," said Celia. The water now seemed frighteningly close.

"We'll be OK up here, mother," said Harrington. "It can't get this far."

But Celia's mind was racing. The water was now rising inexorably, and showed no signs of stopping as the land was flat. It was almost at the line of cars on the road below them. The road disappeared and the fields became salt-water lakes in front of their eyes. Those taking refuge on the hill could see their last few possessions floating away. And their means of escape. The atmosphere was turning from panic to menace and Celia could feel it in her bones. There was screaming from the cars as people were overtaken by the wave and had left it too late to get away. Harrington felt the colour drain away from his face, and he turned away. Celia said to him quietly.

"Let's walk back to the car. I need a sit down."

Her son agreed readily. At first, no-one noticed them. But then as soon as they got inside the car a bald-headed man, stockily-built, looked their way, then looked away quickly when he saw he'd been clocked. He had just watched his car float away on the road beneath them, and sink into a ditch, only one corner of its roof still visible above the swirling water. Adrian sank back into the driver's seat and was about to close his eyes when Celia said in a firm, quiet voice,

"Adrian, lock the doors."

"What?"

"Just do as I say. Lock the doors."

"As if that's going to keep the water out..." he said, not getting what she was saying, and not seeing the man who'd been watching them starting to approach the car, followed by one or two others.

"Start the car. Start the car now. We need to get out of here."

Harrington was about to tell his mother to stop fussing when he saw, too late, a hand on the door handle. He tried to activate the lock but the door opened, and the man confronted him. Harrington started the car, suddenly aware that he looked every inch the government official, in a government car, and was therefore a target for everyone's wrath and frustration. He tried to set off, but the man grabbed him by the lapels and started to pull him bodily from the car. Celia shrieked. The car stalled.

Harrington was dragged from the car.

A scuffle followed with both men ending up on the floor. Harrington took a punch on the ribs but got one back in before his opponent could get the advantage. He might have looked every inch the civil servant but he could handle himself pretty well. A couple of women walked up to the side of the car where Celia was sitting, trembling. She could hardly breathe as her heart was racing so fast. Frantically she pushed and pulled all the levers and switches on the door until she heard a click, and the door locked. Angry fists pummelled her window, and horrible, twisted mouths shouted obscenities at her. Harrington, fired up by concern for his mother, managed to land a punch on the guy's chin stunning him slightly. It was enough for him to get away. In one movement he was back in the car and was moving forward before he even had time to shut the door. They crashed and jolted over the undergrowth, scraping the underside of the vehicle. They hoped the damage was only superficial. They had to keep going now. They skidded and swerved round the broken down fence, through a hedge and at last made it onto the white, dusty track. They picked up speed and lurched around some farm buildings, then down the long drive till they met up once more with the road.

The road was quiet. Celia sat in the passenger seat, tears rolling softly down her cheeks. Harrington patted her hand with his, which was bruised and swollen from the fight.

"Your father would have been proud of you."

It was the nicest thing anyone had ever said to him.

* * *

After the detonation, the graph flattened out, the tremors had stopped, and now the only thing was to wait. Either the plan had worked and the pressure had been released from the volcano, or it could be the quiet before the storm. It was agonising, not knowing. And Gilmore had had no word back from Zoe Carter or Amy James. Didn't even know if they'd made it. After hearing about Terry Coulson, he had become more pessimistic about the rest of them getting out of there, if he was honest. Dorothy was more overtly optimistic.

"We'll soon hear from them, don't you worry – it's bound to take time for them to get back."

But deep down, she wasn't as confident as she sounded, and she, too, was desperate for news.

"There's nothing much more we can do here, is there really?" said Gilmore, lightly. "The Government's co-ordinating everything from its new temporary HQ in Wiltshire from now on, till this flap's over. The PM was talking about me going out there to join them, apparently. Until we get word back from the expedition as to how it went, there's no real point in us being here in London, is there."

Dorothy got his drift straightaway.

"No, you're quite right. Frank. No point at all. Zoe can contact us just as well, if we up sticks. Corsham's up and running now. Not that Ron Bowman needs you there, in my opinion. He just doesn't like you staying in London now that he isn't here – makes him look like a deserter – he doesn't want anyone stealing his limelight now."

Dorothy tapped the desk annoyed by the thought of Bowman soaking up the praise for everyone else's hard work and sacrifice. Her face showed in no uncertain terms that she had come to a decision on Frank's behalf, knowing that he didn't feel comfortable about leaving London when so many others couldn't. They had worked together closely over the last few days and Dorothy had found a growing respect for Gilmore, the better she got to know him. He now wondered what she had planned.

There was no point in arguing when she looked like that.

"I'll get my car – we're leaving," she said.

And with that she marched out of his office. Stunned by what he had just set in motion, by a tentative remark, he watched her disappear out of the doorway and heard her clicking down the deserted corridor on the way to fetch her car. He put away his papers in his briefcase and folded up his laptop, ready for their departure. He made a couple of phone calls, then picked up his jacket, slipping his bunch of keys into the inner pocket as he did so. There was a blast on the horn outside, signalling that Dorothy was ready with the car. He couldn't understand why Dorothy had wanted to go to Wiltshire with him, though. Suppose she just wanted to see this thing through to the end. He closed his office door, and walked quickly along the corridor and down a short flight of steps to the pavement outside where Dorothy was waiting impatiently for him to put his stuff on the back seat and then climb in beside her.

She set off with a lurch, even before he'd had time to do up his seat belt, and headed north through the city streets.

"You're going the wrong way," he said, anxiously watching the road signs. He pointed left. "Wiltshire's that way."

"Wiltshire be fucked," she said briskly. "We're heading for the Peak District. I think it's time I checked out the progress they are making on my cottage." And out of the corner of her eye she could see Gilmore trying not to grin at the thought of soon being with his family again.

CHAPTER THIRTY

Somehow, Amy James got the crew on their feet and ready to leave Plato Camp. It took a lot of harsh words and determination, even to get them to understand. At first she was able to be sympathetic to their plight and put their lack of resolution down to lack of food and the disorienting effects of creeping hypothermia, but after two good meals, both within a short space of time, she could only put it down to their stupidity, and told them so.

"We have to begin the ascent – not tomorrow, not even sometime today – but right now – we have to go. Can't you understand?"

"But I don't think we're ready," said Hewitt.

"You're as ready as you'll ever be," said Amy. "If we stay any longer we run out of food, then we're back to square one. How much do you think I could get into my one pack, you idiots?"

"I thought someone was going to mount a rescue," said Oliver.

"Yes, they did – it's me. This is it. Yes I know it's a big disappointment. I thought Gilmore was going to send in a crack team of Special Forces to abseil in and pull you all to safety, but no. I'm all there is. Zo - you will have to go first, as you are a much more experienced climber than me. And we need to get off this ledge before it gives way and we all end up down at the bottom in a pit of molten lava. Staying at Plato Camp is not an option. I need to see some resolution. Come on guys!"

Hewitt, who'd been very sullen up till now, trying to work out whether or not Amy was still interested in him, said nothing, but at least began to get his stuff together.

"Amy's right. We could get caught in an avalanche, if we stay here," said Zoe.

"We could get caught in an avalanche if we don't stay here," said Hewitt, reasonably, but it was not the most tactful thing to say just before a hazardous climb.

Oliver glared at him.

"Oh, Lawrence! I've missed you!" said Amy, grinning

Hewitt flushed slightly, not knowing whether she was taking the piss out of him. His heart thumped for one heavy beat inside his chest. And in that one second he saw himself in stark contrast to her warm and giving nature. He'd become such a closed-down person; wrapped up in negativity. He had become oblivious to the effect it had had on those around him. In relation to other people he came across as someone who gave nothing back. He gave the impression that, when it came to feelings of warmth, generosity or kindness, he just couldn't spare it, and whose role had become to point out the downside of everything.

It's normal to think of a person as having a particular character. They are either this or that. Warm or cold. Honest or deceitful. Shy or outgoing. Angry or calm. But in fact character is in part a shorthand or snapshot view of a whole bundle of attributes and failings that bloom or fade according to the context one is in. Hewitt had let his pessimism prosper in a field of bitterness and loss, till he had forgotten how to react in any other way. In the light of all that, how could he blame Amy if she'd been attracted to Becaud, the adventurer?

"I've missed you too," he said, dragging the uncharacteristic phrase out of somewhere inside himself. For a while he didn't know where to look, but he could feel Amy's eyes bearing down on him.

"Bloody Hell, Lawrence," said Oliver. But stopped short of any further remark when Zoe kicked him on the leg, firmly, but with a thickly padded foot.

"We need to get moving," said Amy, always practical but nevertheless, shining inside. "Come on, guys. Get these ropes on – carry what you can. Come on everybody – we're out of here!"

And with that they left Plato Camp, and headed upwards and out of the Rift.

CHAPTER THIRTY-ONE

It was with a feeling of utter joy that Phil Becaud heard the faint, rather muffled voice of Zoe Carter trying to remember his call sign, and let him know that they were nearing the summit and would soon be with him at Base Camp. Amongst the static and the wind noise he could hardly make out the words she was shouting at him, but it didn't matter one jot. He could tell it was her, and by the tone of her delivery he guessed that they were all OK. He dashed over to the edge of the Rift unable to wait until they came into view from the camp. Tentatively he peered over the edge, and, yes, he could make out a line of tiny figures like soldier ants, crawling the last few hundred metres out of the Rift. He called out to them, and they were close enough to acknowledge his shout and yell back. He thought they'd be about five minutes, but half an hour later they were still agonisingly far away. The soft crumbling snow of the Rift walls was a nightmare to climb, and utterly strength-sapping for the already exhausted crew. Sometimes they were only making ten metres before they had to stop for a rest.

As they neared the summit, they appeared to be climbing in slow motion, each deliberate hand and foot movement seeming like an effort of supreme will, which indeed it was. Becaud, at last, could touch Zoe's hand, and he prepared to use all his strength to haul her over the top. But it was like lifting a child, she was so light and he set her down on the ice next to him with ease. One by one he helped the others over the lip, and hugged each one in turn, even Hewitt, who patted him feebly on the arm by way of return.

"So sorry about Terry," said Becaud, aware of the empty space his absence had created. They all nodded and Zoe wiped away a tear with the back of her glove. Unable to deal with his loss before now, the enormity of what he had done and what he had had to face hit them full on.

"Guess we all owe him, big time," said Becaud. And they had to agree that they did.

There was a silent pause, which was broken by Zoe, eventually.

"We don't know yet if it's worked – down there."

"There have been no more tremors – since the detonation it's been quiet – I think that's a positive sign," said Becaud.

"What do we tell Dorothy, and Gilmore? They'll be waiting for news."

"We tell them it's too soon to tell," said Hewitt.

"They'll also be hanging on for news of your return," said Becaud, "You'd better call them."

Zoe did that straightaway. It was great to hear Dorothy's voice once more.

"There's been a second tsunami here," she said.

"How bad?"

"Bad enough."

"What's the latest from seismology?"

"There's been a cessation of the quakes. It's looking good, but we need to know from your end – what's the state of play?"

"We don't know yet."

"How come? You must know what you did!"

"We were too far away, and visibility was virtually nil. The heat at the bottom of the Rift triggered an inversion."

"We really need to know. They're waiting for your data at Isaac's so they can factor it into their model of the blast. If the pressure's still building up inside the caldera, they are talking about a mega-eruption openly now – to each other at least. Not to the public, of course. I heard the word tsunami and sky-scraper high in the same sentence. I've seen some white faces on people who are normally very hard to impress."

"We've done our best," said Zoe. It sounded rather pathetic after the phrase had left her lips, and not one to bring out the best in Dorothy.

"Your job's not done yet," she said, flatly.

Silly bitch. Has she no idea what we've just been through?

"You have to try to get a visual on the caldera, Zoe – and we need pictures, stills and video so we can estimate the lava flow. Without that data we are still guessing."

"OK," said Zoe. "We'll get onto it."

She really had thought that they would be back in Phil's house by tonight, in a hot bath, and eating a proper dinner. Now, normality seemed like an impossible dream once more. She had to tell the others.

"Am I getting this right?" said Phil, with heavy emphasis on the first syllable. "You want me to fly over the Rift so you can get some pictures? Haven't we done enough, already? And there's still a lot of cloud, fog whatever lying around – we won't see much anyway from that height!"

Zoe looked at him, in that way that meant that the seeds of his questions already contained the germ of his own answers. He realised what he had just said, and saw the look on her face.

"Oh no! You want me to go down into the Rift, don't you? I get it now. No way, honey! Not in a million years with that visibility. Do you think I'm crazy or something? You didn't speak to Gilmore, did you? This is that mad old bat, the sudoku-playing witch-queen of New Orleans, to quote the lyrics of a Golden Oldie, setting you up for this, while she sits there in London, dry and safe and not a bit hungry, telling everybody else what they should be doing!"

"She's not in London, she gone back to Derbyshire with Gilmore."

"Oh! Brilliant. Even better. So while she asks us to risk our asses, she's sitting pretty on some peak or something!"

"We have to do it, Phil. Whatever it takes. Terry knew that. And now so must we. It's a big ask, but we have to finish the job. You do see, don't you?"

Of course he saw. He'd had his say. There was never any way he wouldn't have done what he had to. He just needed his moment of protest.

When Becaud fired up the engine of the Cessna, the familiar, powerful roar sent a frisson of excitement through the camp that lifted everyone's spirits and engendered a new sense of purpose into the jaded crew. Everyone got their stuff into the plane as quickly as they could, but the tents were left where they stood, no-one having the time or the energy to dismantle the camp completely and re-pack all their bulky equipment. Becaud didn't want the extra weight anyway. The next bit of flying would be tricky enough without any excess baggage to lug around. Lucky you've all lost a bit of weight, he thought insensitively.

Zoe climbed into the Super Caravan and sat in the seat that had become hers through habit, Oliver automatically dropping down on the seat beside her. The seat moulded luxuriously to her body, tired and thin as it was, and she felt truly comfortable for the first time in many days. Funny the things you miss when they are not there. During the camp there was never anywhere to sit properly. She wriggled about to settle deep into the leather, then clicked on the seat belt before reaching for the cans. Becaud checked that everyone was ready for take off. He flicked his scarf over his shoulder, then he radioed the details back to his flight-follower. He slowly let out the throttle and as the engine noise rose to a new level the Cessna eased forward. Zoe thrilled to the new sense of effortless movement. Let the plane do the work. It seemed little short of miraculous to be making such progress while just sitting there in that soft, springy seat, after only hours ago every single step had been a labour of Herculean proportions.

She so loved modernity. Let's hope we've done enough to keep it, she thought.

Becaud pulled back the joystick, and with a backward tilt, she was being lifted smoothly into the air.

Hewitt was busy getting his camera and video equipment ready for when they were over the Rift. He knew he wouldn't have much time to get the shots he needed, so he had to be well-prepared. Amy had gone to sit in the seat next to Becaud so as to give Lawrence access to both windows. They flew back beyond the place where the caldera was situated so that they could fly along the length of the Rift to where the lava flow should have started. When Becaud was confident that they'd gone far enough along, he banked round and got in as low as he could. It was hopeless. There was still swirling mist everywhere, not always dense, but getting progressively thicker as they neared the area where they thought the caldera was sited. Sometimes they couldn't even see the Rift where the white fog blended in with the top of the cliffs.

Becaud got in very low and used his radio altimeter to gauge where the Rift would be. It being so deep, and now so wide, he got a good clear reading when he was over the drop, but try as they might they could see nothing, especially from that height. Zoe couldn't see how they could get into the Rift when they couldn't make out where it was. It looked just too perilous.

"Well, there's only one thing for it, guys," said Becaud, cheerily, his cloud of angry cynicism having been dispersed by him being in his beloved plane once more.

Reluctantly, they agreed. They would have to turn back and go home. And simply tell everyone that nothing could be seen from the air. It seemed like a cop-out, but they'd tried their best, and could do no more.

"Hang on then, guys! Oky-doky. We're going in now!"

Zoe sat up bolt upright, eyes wide, unable to speak.

"What the fuck are you doing?" shouted Oliver, straining forward against his seat belt.

Hewitt just retreated to the virtual world behind his camera and resigned himself to getting what he could on record, and leaving the flying to Becaud.

They were in the Rift, below ground level and were dropping down through the mist, into the abyss. The cloud was not dense, or they wouldn't have stood a chance, but it swirled around disconcertingly, making the judgement of distances very difficult. They dropped lower, Becaud following the cliff on his right for guidance till, out of nowhere a white wall appeared in front of him, and he had to bank like he was in a dog-fight to avoid it. It was like being on a roller-coaster ride.

"That was where a zig must have zagged," he said, but his voice was shaky with adrenalin, and his crew were not happy.

They flew on, Becaud in total concentration, slipped the plane lower and lower into the valley until, at last they could see something. They'd managed to dip down under the fog, and they could see clearly all around and below them to the bedrock at the bottom of the Rift. But it was pretty narrow now, and keeping the little plane away from the valley sides was the most difficult flying that Becaud had ever done. Zoe spotted the caldera, and straightaway Hewitt began to film so as not to miss a single frame of information when the detonation sight came into view.

It took their breath away when they saw it. This was the first time they knew for sure that they had actually holed the caldera, and boy, had they holed it. The gap, at first big enough to drive a truck through, was now large enough to hold an entire eight-lane freeway. Lava was storming out of the mountainside, red hot and glowing at a torrential speed, filling the Rift bottom with an eerie orange glow as it made the cliff faces glisten with meltwater, and steam in the wet, moist air. They followed it as it made its progress snaking along the base, gradually slowing and cooling the further it got away from the rupture.

"Looks like you guys did it!" said Becaud. And with that he spotted a thinning of the mist ceiling hanging above them, and without a second's doubt or hesitation, he powered the Cessna in a steep climb, and punched his way through the hole, and back up out of the Atlantis Rift. They looked down at the slit in the ground that they had left behind. The walls had just started to squeeze closer together from that point on, narrowing down to a thin chicane that no plane could have got through. Becaud hoped that no-one else had seen how close he'd brought them to total disaster, but the look on their frozen faces left him in no doubt that they knew. He loosened his scarf from around his neck to get some much needed air, and without even an attempt at conversation, he set the course back to Angmagssalik.

CHAPTER THIRTY-TWO

Zoe and the team got Lawrence Hewitt's pictures of the punctured volcano back to Isaac Newton College as soon as they landed safely at Angmagssalik, so that the climate scientists back home could work the data into their computer models as soon as it was possible for them to do so. The information that the pictures gave them was invaluable to their predictions, and the country was stood down from tsunami alert after three more weeks of helpless uncertainty.

The tremors subsided; the country held its breath until they were sure that the volcano had become dormant once more, which was more or less confirmed by the autumn. The bloggers had decided that the volcano needed an Inuit name, and had called it Ningakpok, or Angry, even although its anger now was spent, and it had become peaceful once more. Ningakpok had, on Dorothy's website, become a symbol for the climate's revenge on its ungrateful guests. A beast woken to anger by persistent abuse, until it turned and threatened the very people it had once nurtured.

Not that that was the end of the story. Zoe Carter, her husband Oliver, Phil Becaud, Amy James and Lawrence Hewitt had between them discovered and thwarted the threat of an unimaginable catastrophe hitting the shores of Britain and the rest of Northern Europe, and by doing so had bought the people of those regions some time.

But, they were only too aware that the climate change clock was still ticking; the melting of the continental ice sheet was still happening and the melting of the polar ice was still stoking up trouble. The situation was getting dangerously close to the tipping point, beyond which, there could be no going back. The volcano, Ningakpok, would not be erupting again just yet, hopefully, but Ningakpok was not the real problem, it was only an amplifier of the many factors which might have caused the climate to lurch from one state to another, as has happened many times in pre-history. Now, the under-lying factors would have to be faced up to and dealt with. The study of the science of Abrupt Climate Change tells us, frighteningly, that wild fluctuations in our climate is the norm for our planet, and might be inevitable. But, we should be looking for ways to care for and preserve our existing environment if we are to prolong our ability to stay within our comfort zone, which we have in this golden age here in the West. Environmentalism shouldn't be about self-denial and a pinched, limited view of the world. It also shouldn't be about collective self-loathing, where humanity berates itself for its greed, laziness and wastefulness, in a sort of secular punishment fantasy. Environmentalism could be about responsible abundance, comfort and progress if we want it to be. And about sharing that prosperity amongst the poor, the hungry, and the oppressed people in other parts of the world who reasonably aspire to a better standard of living.

* * *

Zoe and Oliver Carter, after a few months break, went back to Greenland to continue their research in the field of Abrupt Climate Change. Only this time they had a helicopter to take them down into the accessible parts of the Atlantis Rift to collect their precious samples. Zoe was right when she thought that there was enough material down there to last her a lifetime. The gash in the ice sheet was like an opened book to her, where she could go in and wonder at how much there was still to learn.

Lawrence Hewitt had just published a successful new book of photographs as a tie-in to a TV programme made about the expedition, while Amy Hewitt had given up field work for the time being and had taken up a teaching post at Isaac Newton College, so that she could spend more time with her husband. Later, they planned to travel together. Dorothy Redmires had moved back into her cottage in Castleton, quite close to where her friends, the Gilmores, had now bought a place and had taken early retirement. Phil Becaud was taking helicopter lessons, and had begun to expand his business into the Eco-Tourist trade as well as delivering freight. There was no shortage of travellers now wanting to see the Atlantis Rift, and Ningakpok, for themselves.

Zoe and Oliver booked him for a flight very early one morning, just after they returned from the UK.

"We just want you to fly out into the emptiness," said Zoe. "Where there is nothing but a flat, white sheet of ice, and a huge blue dome above it."

"OK," said Becaud.

And he found a place that was exactly what they wanted. He didn't ask why. Didn't need to. He swooped in low, as per instructions, then Zoe opened the large box that she had with her on the seat, squeezed between her and Oliver. After getting the go-ahead from their pilot, they opened the window of the plane as far as it would go, then Oliver threw out a simple tied bunch of flowers, for Ray Coulson, another for Coulson's brother Terry, one for Marcus James, for the two Inuit guides Kuvageegai, and Iqniq, and lastly one for Joe Kristenssen. Becaud choked at that one.

He took one last look out of his window, and saw the tributes flutter down onto the pristine snow, and scatter there as they hit the ground. He circled around one last time to fly past, low and fast, and as he reached the point where he could make out that Joe's tribute had landed, he tipped his wing in a gesture of salute, before rising once more, lifting the Cessna as high as he could take her, until he could see nothing but the beautiful curve of the horizon arcing under widest of skies.

BIBLIOGRAPHY

<u>BOOKS</u>

Mark Lynas	**Six Degrees**	Harper Perennial
Fred Pearce	**The Last Generation**	Eden Project Books
Malcolm Gladwell	**Blink**	Penguin
Malcolm Gladwell	**The Tipping Point**	Penguin
Hewitt	**From Earthquake Fire & Flood**	Allen & Unwin
Robert Matthews	**A Storm is Coming**	BBC Focus Magazine
The Times Atlas of the World		Times Books
Anil Ananthaswamy	**Does rainfall vary with sunspot activity**	New Scientist 08/11/08

INTERNET

Spaceweather.com

www.cessna.com

www.natis/greenlandeng/angmagssalikeng.htm

en.wikipedia.org/wiki/Greenland

http://www.wunderground.com/education/abrupt-climate.asp **The Science of Abrupt Climate Change: Weather Underground,** by Dr Jeffrey M Masters, The Weather Underground, Inc

http://environment.independent.co.uk/climate_change/article2941866.ece

Shockwaves from melting ice caps are triggering earthquakes, say scientists. By Daniel Howden, in Ilulissat, Greenland. 08/09/07.

http://environment.independent.co.uk/climate_change/article3087271.ece

Carbon sinks lose ability to soak up emissions. By Steve Connor, Science Editor 23/10/07

http://environment.independentco.uk/climate_change/article2675747.ece

The Earth today stands in imminent peril. By Science Editor Steve Connor 19/06/07

www.peakdistrictinformation.com/visits/stanage.php

9085884R0

Made in the USA
Charleston, SC
09 August 2011